THE
SILVER
CURSE

THE SILVER CURSE

ANNA ORR

Podium

To my best friend, Jessica. Thank you for being my first, biggest, and most rant-fueled supporter. I could not have done this without you. Could have done with less rants though, just saying.

This is a work of fiction. Names, characters, places, and incidents are either products of the author's imagination or used fictitiously. Any resemblance to actual events, locales, or persons, living, dead, or undead, is entirely coincidental.

Cover design by Edward Bettison

ISBN: 978-1-0394-5768-3

Published in 2024 by Podium Publishing
www.podiumaudio.com

THE
SILVER
CURSE

CHAPTER ONE

You're a Horrible Pacifist

I won't be fighting in the match today," Rasp said. "I'm a pacifist now. In case you haven't heard."

"You stabbed me with a fork at breakfast."

Rasp placed his hand on Faris's shoulder in the same manner others did to him when trying to convey a sense of reassurance. Faris's taut muscles flinched beneath the unwelcome touch. That was only fair, Rasp supposed. He *had* stabbed Faris at breakfast. But honestly, what did he expect after serving him a bowl of oversalted oat mush? If there was any real crime, it was Faris's idea of a hearty breakfast. "That was a long time ago. I've since realized the error of my ways."

Faris's voice was flat with disbelief. "If I searched your pockets, I bet I'd find another fork to stab me with the moment my back's turned."

"Not true." It was a butter knife, actually. And Rasp wouldn't wait for Faris's back to be turned. There was hardly a challenge in that.

Faris, one of the many faun folk that resided in the village, produced a loud, breathy snort, accompanied by an irritated flap of his ears. It sounded like a leathery butterfly trying to take flight. One that gave up after a single snap of its useless wings, forced to concede that perhaps walking was the more practical option, after all.

Rasp was human. In the isolated mountains where he had been raised, other than the occasional missing eye or amputated leg, his people lacked severely in the diversity department. Here, in the quaint little village known as Lonebrook, the citizens were a good mix of species, though the majority were fauns. After having spent every waking moment in the company of his keeper, Faris Belfast, Rasp had cultivated a rather detailed understanding of faun mannerisms. This particular sound meant the time to turn and run had been precisely thirty seconds ago.

"Bye!" Rasp spun sharply on his heel and hightailed it in the direction of the front door.

"Oh, come on. I just finished spot-cleaning the blood off my jacket from your last getaway. Why do you insist on doing this the hard way?" The faun's hooves clacked against the hardwood as he took chase. Reluctantly, from the sound of his slow, dragging steps. His voice reverberated along the narrow walls of the dim hallway, nipping at Rasp's heels. "You can't see, idiot! This never works out for you!"

The worn floorboards creaked underfoot as Rasp doubled his speed. Burnt incense, intermingled with the earthy undertones of faun musk, hung heavy in the air like stale clouds. He breathed the familiar scents in through his nose and out his mouth as the blurry green and brown tinted walls passed at a dizzying rate. Without warning, the heavy oak door swung open ahead of him with a raspy groan. A channel of harsh light poured in from the outside and illuminated the surrounding gloom.

"Gangway!" Rasp called to the fuzzy shape that took up most of the doorway.

"Mister Snow, you blind fool!" the washerwoman squawked as she scuttled backward in fright, hooves scraping the stone porch in her haste to escape the oncoming collision. "You're going to be the death of me one of these days, I swear it!"

Her squat frame, backlit by the gray light of the outdoors, had a peculiar lump protruding from her hip area that suggested she was carrying something. A basket, Rasp realized as he drew nearer. A maniacal smile formed across his face. "Why, Miss Beechum, is that the freshly dried laundry?"

"You know it is, boy. And don't you even *think* about rolling in my clean sheets again."

"Here, let Faris help you with that!" Rasp grabbed the reed basket from her and heaved it behind him. There was a curse, followed immediately by a dry crunch and heavy thump as Faris failed to dodge the basket on his way out the door. Not slowing his breakneck pace, Rasp cleared the stone steps in a single leap and landed ankle-deep in an icy puddle. Cold mud squelched between his bare toes as he forced his legs to move even faster across the slippery courtyard.

Thlop, thlop, thlop. The sound of Faris's fast footsteps grew louder behind him. "You're dead when I catch you!"

As far as escapes went, this one was poorly thought out. The courtyard of Belfast Manor was open and kept clear of obstacles. Navigating it would be a breeze. It was the woodlot beyond that presented a complication. Rasp didn't normally give problems much thought. For the most part, this tactic worked remarkably well for him. Right up until it came time to face said problem, which, alas, was now. The terrain underfoot shifted from mud to loose piles of slippery, wet leaves. Around him, the crisp air turned sharp with the lingering scent of decayed vegetation and damp soil.

Faris's voice rang out from behind him with sudden urgency. "Tree! To your left!"

Rasp dodged right, narrowly missing the towering object that came into blurred focus far too late to be helpful. More trees cropped up along the edge of his murky vision, forcing him to slow his pace in order to avoid running face-first into them. "I thought you wanted me dead," he puffed, already beginning to feel the invisible fire that burned within his lungs. It tightened like a hot vise over his throat and clogged his airways.

"By my hand, obviously. There's no satisfaction in watching you get taken out by a tree."

Faris sounded nearer than before. Another cruel reminder that any moment now Rasp's keeper would be upon him and his sudden rendezvous through the woods would be cut regrettably short. There would be consequences for inciting a chase, of course. But it rarely amounted to anything serious. Despite Faris's threats, his people did things differently than the mountain folk. They were light-handed and used words in lieu of fists.

Rasp didn't understand their peculiar ways any more than he had six months ago, when he first arrived in Lonebrook. There was something deeply unsettling about walking away with a simple telling off when he rightfully deserved a thrashing. At first, he mistook their gentleness for pity. It seemed plausible, given how helpless he was after the whole left-for-dead thing. But their treatment of him never changed, not even after he was strong enough to defend himself. Rasp had begun to wonder if they were taunting him. Treating him like an invalid as a reminder that he would never again be what he once was.

Gods, Rasp thought. Is this who he was now? The mighty Rasp Stoneclaw reduced to being chased by a physically inferior opponent? And for what, a stolen butter knife? This was degrading. Downright humiliating, in fact. A year ago it was *he* who'd held the power. In Rasp's prime, before the exile, the good folk of Lonebrook would have cowered in his presence. Now? Now they laughed. He, a formidable Stoneclaw warrior, the Iron Devil himself, was but a shadow of his former glorious might. And they knew it.

A hand grabbed the base of his neck and yanked him backward. "Caught you, you little—"

"I'm still a Stoneclaw!"

A properly executed back throw was a beautiful thing. The one Rasp attempted could only be classified as a *thing*. He seized Faris's hand and tucked it into position, then stopped, bent at the waist, and allowed the faun's momentum to send him hurtling the rest of the way over. Faris rolled over the top of him and struck the ground. As did Rasp, too, unfortunately, since their arms were still intertwined. The pair tumbled downhill in a flailing tangle of limbs and muffled curses through the slimy, leaf-littered muck, until at last they rolled to a stop with the aid of a very sturdy tree trunk.

Despite the ache in his lungs and the sudden, excruciating pain that flared across the hinge of his elbow, Rasp recovered first. He clambered over Faris, clawing, punching, grabbing at whatever he could find. "And stop calling me little! I'm bigger than you!"

"Not where it counts." Faris's knee shot upward and slammed into the delicate spot between Rasp's legs. The impact stole the last of the air from Rasp's battered lungs.

Rasp wheezed, unable to speak as he slowly listed to the side. He struck the cold forest floor in a splatter of wet leaves and mud. No matter how vehemently he willed his legs to get up and take flight once more, the fight was gone. The festering rage that boiled deep within his gut settled to a gentle simmer as pain took up its place. Rasp drew his knees to his chest and desperately tried to recall the steps necessary to breathe. Something about in and out?

"First of all, you're a horrible pacifist," Faris panted. There was a noticeable pause as he sucked in enough breath to continue his rant. "Secondly, you do not announce to the world who you are! Only my family knows. And for good reason. The townsfolk would hang you from the nearest tree if they knew who you were. Understand?"

Rasp's agreement came in the form of a low-pitched moan.

This was not good enough for Faris, who clamped his hand over Rasp's shoulder in a manner that was neither friendly nor reassuring. Painful was the foremost word that came to mind. "So when people ask, you tell them your name is?"

"Snow."

Faris's grip tightened. "I'm sorry, what was that?"

"Snow! My name is Snow." Rasp batted him away with his hand and slumped back into the mud with a whimpered groan. At times like these, a little voice emerged in the back of his head. Not to offer comfort, of course, but to add a layer of insult to the steady stream of agony coursing through his already tormented body. Without hesitation, it slunk from the dark, unvisited corner of Rasp's mind and bared its ugly teeth.

Oh, how the mighty have fallen.

CHAPTER TWO

Winds of Change

The breeze rattled the barren tops of the birch and poplar trees like a symphony of hollow bones. Leaves leftover from the autumn past, curled and slick with slime, tumbled lazily across the swampy ground, stirring the air with the growing stench of forest rot. The harsh call of a blue jay rang in the distance. Rasp, however, noticed none of this over his own pained wheezing. Save for one sound, which dragged him kicking and screaming from his internal wallowing.

"You're lucky I don't tell Father about this," Faris snapped.

The bolts of lightning slamming between his sore legs had lessened to a deep, throbbing ache. Hot tears stung Rasp's eyes as he managed to speak around shaky gasps. "You're lucky I don't tell him you whore me out for fights!"

Faris's father, the esteemed Judge Trant Belfast, served as the elected official for the sleepy village of Lonebrook. A former soldier turned peacekeeper, Trant had been attempting to teach Rasp the joys of reformation and what it meant to embrace a future without violence. The judge's efforts, albeit noble, had fallen largely on deaf ears. Rasp could strive to be a better person, sure. But violence was a basic tenet of being a mountain man. And as much as Rasp enjoyed protesting Faris's arranged fights, he enjoyed the actual fighting even more.

"Go ahead, tell him," Faris said. "He'll have no choice but to appoint you a new keeper. And let's be honest here, you're a handful. The whole village knows it. No one would accept. Father would be forced to take up the position himself. Do you really want to spend your days listening to him drone on about the philosophies of the enlightened mind? Or would you rather stir up shit with me?"

Rasp decided no answer was better than confirming what Faris obviously already knew.

"That's what I thought."

The sensible thing would have been to let it go. Sensible, however, was not how Rasp had ended up as a long-term guest of the Belfast household. A guest who couldn't leave or go outside to take a piss without someone hovering over him, for that matter. Rasp raised his head from the cradle of his arms and hawked a glob of phlegm in the vicinity of what he hoped was Faris's smug face.

"Gods dammit!" There was a rustle of damp foliage as the faun scrambled backward out of spitting range. "What is with you today? You claim you don't want to fight, but you've been trying to pick a scrap with me since breakfast. The whole reason for the matches is to vent your rage in a controlled environment. Which you love, by the way. Why are you acting like an ungrateful brat all of a sudden?"

Why indeed?

An uneasy feeling had been gnawing at his insides all morning, hanging heavy in his soul like a black cloud on the horizon. Rasp could feel the winds of change stirring. What exactly it would bring, he didn't know. His life in Lonebrook wasn't anything spectacular. But it was a life, at the very least—a living, breathing one that allowed him to exist outside the confines of a prison cell. Something worth celebrating, really, considering his people wanted him dead and his enemies wanted him deader. A quiet existence in Lonebrook was the absolute best his outcast ass could hope for.

Rasp couldn't say any of this, of course. Faris wasn't born the cursed offspring of a mighty Stoneclaw leader. He wouldn't understand. And there were some things that just couldn't be explained to outsiders. "I don't know what you're yammering on about. The only thing troubling me is my stomach. Must be those oats you tried to poison me with earlier."

"Fine, don't tell me," Faris said. "If you want to avoid the subject so badly, we'll get right down to business. You're still fighting in today's match. And we're headed there next. But first, you're gonna hand over whatever it is you stole."

Or I'm going to kick you in the gems again was the part Faris didn't need to say. Stifling a groan, Rasp eased upright and searched his pockets. He produced a spoon, a butter knife, and what he suspected was a little tidbit of jewelry, and deposited them into Faris's outstretched hand.

"This is Mum's earring. She's been looking for this one," Faris said with a remarkable lack of accusation in his voice.

Rasp was a thief, yes, but not of jewelry. And certainly not anything belonging to Faris's saint of a mother, Novera Belfast. Rasp only pocketed things of the sharp, stabby variety. The earring was something he'd simply picked up during one of his restless nights wandering the halls while the rest of the household slept, pleasantly unaware of his nocturnal activities.

"Where'd you find it?" Faris asked.

"In my foot." That was the trouble with wandering without shoes. You found a lot of interesting things with the bottoms of your feet. The earring hadn't been nearly as bad as the time he found the lost embroidery needle.

Faris pried Rasp's fingers back and placed the earring in the center of his palm. "You'd make her day if you returned it to her. She might even bake those sweet buns you like so much."

"I was waiting for the right moment." Rasp had hoped to give it to her in private, away from the watchful eye of her son. While he normally enjoyed Faris's relentless taunting, sometimes it reminded him too much of home. Faris was like the unofficial seventh brother that Rasp neither wanted nor asked for, but got all the same. "She seemed sad the last few days. Did you notice?"

Faris produced a hoarse laugh from the back of his throat as he reached under Rasp's arm and heaved him upright. "The Iron Devil's got a soft spot for my mum. Who would have thought?"

"Maybe I've just got a soft spot for her buns." Rasp ducked to the side to avoid Faris's upcoming slap. He was semi-successful; Faris's hand glanced harmlessly off Rasp's shoulder. He spun out of range, throwing his arms out at his sides in a playful manner. "What? I can't help it. They're so warm and buttery. Don't get me started on the sticky sweetness. It's no wonder your father hoards them all to himself."

The faun's stocky shape bridged the distance between them in a single lunge. "If I hear another word out of your mouth about my mum, I'm going to jump into that ring and kick your ass myself."

Rasp linked his elbow with Faris's and started off at a clumsy skip, not entirely sure what direction he was supposed to be going. He picked one nevertheless, certain Faris would correct their trajectory along the way. "Don't make promises you can't keep, Dingle. It's cruel to keep stringing me along with that same empty threat, you know."

"Stop prancing and save your energy for the match. I don't want another repeat of the woodcutter incident."

Rasp slowed his pace to match Faris's. He did so not out of obedience, but for the fact that he'd tweaked his knee in the tumble and skipping sent jolts of white hot agony up his thigh with every unnecessary bounce. A point in the favor of his opponent, he supposed. Rasp rarely lost a match. Maybe today would be some lucky sap's day. Maybe Rasp would lose on purpose, just to stick it to Faris.

"The woodcutter? I won that one."

"You bit the man's ear off! I had to pay him half the pot to keep his mouth shut. You revert to dirty tricks when you're tired. Which is great for the crowds, don't get me wrong. Half the people are there just to see what stunt you're going to pull. But you've got to rein it in a little. We're starting to draw attention."

It was only the tip of the ear, technically. Not the whole thing. And Rasp had been generous enough to spit it out and give it back afterward. "Fine," he said. "Who's on the chopping block today?"

"The blacksmith."

"Again?" He would have thought the smith had learned his lesson by now. There were only so many times you could have your nose broken before you realized that fighting wasn't your forte. The blacksmith outmatched him in both size and strength, but Rasp hailed from the Iron Ridge. Combat was his people's favorite pastime and as such, mountain folk warriors were downright vicious. As were their healers and foragers and schoolteachers. Gods above, even the babies could bite off an unsuspecting finger when they wanted.

Faris's gruff voice cut back in. "I suspect the blacksmith is out for revenge."

"It was just a nose break!"

"Not for that. It was the hickey you planted on his neck afterward. His missus wasn't very pleased. Seamus had to spend the next week sleeping in the forge, from what I heard."

A snaggletoothed grin spread across Rasp's thin mouth. "So you're saying I should rub some lip color on his collar this time? Dingle, you devious little cuss. You really shouldn't encourage me this way."

Faris hooked his arm tighter and pulled Rasp along the slippery trail with a grunt. "Just focus on winning the match, alright? Seamus is not as twisted as you are, but he is bigger. And he's going to come at you with everything he's got."

CHAPTER THREE

Fight Like a Man

Seamus gave the fight his all. It was a pity that his all amounted to all of nothing. Bigger wasn't always better, not when your opponent could simply sidestep you at every turn. Which, given Rasp's inability to see most of what was going on, succeeded only in making the blacksmith angrier. Rasp, standing with his thumbs hooked into his pockets, allowed Seamus to do the majority of the work. Each time the faun charged, Rasp waited until the last possible second to duck safely out of the way. It was a continual dance. Left, right, back and forth, Rasp strung him along, purposefully stoking his opponent's mounting frustration.

"Stop moving and fight me like a man!" Seamus bellowed.

"I *am* fighting you like a man." Rasp rocked back on his heels and cracked a grin. "We like to dance around the issue until the other party gives up. Did no one tell you?"

This quip earned several drunken guffaws from the surrounding crowd. Faris had been right. There were more villagers present than usual. Rasp wasn't sure how many exactly, as their shapes all melded into a continuous gray blur around him. But he could pick out individual voices he hadn't heard before. The smell, too, was worse. Someone near the orchard end had already vomited on their neighbor's shoes.

Seamus emitted a frustrated snort and charged. While Rasp couldn't pick out the finer features of his opponent's face or clothes, it was hard to miss the imposing brown shape growing noticeably larger in his limited field of vision. With the blacksmith all but blinded by rage, Rasp made his move at last. He faked right and then ducked, taking the faun down with a sweep of his leg.

Rasp dropped into the mud and caught Seamus from behind. Seamus flipped onto his back, but it didn't matter. Rasp's legs were already wrapped over the faun's chest. He locked his ankles and secured Seamus's head with one arm while clamping down over his throat with the other. This was no longer a fight, but a test of endurance. Specifically, if Rasp's strength would outlast Seamus's need to breathe.

The heavyset faun's muscles twitched beneath Rasp. Already, he could feel Seamus's strength begin to sap. Only a few seconds more, and it would all be over. The smell of sweat and faun musk permeated Rasp's nostrils and trickled into his mouth, coating his tongue in a salty, gag-inducing film. The edges of his mouth began to water as that morning's oat mush threatened to make a reappearance.

Gods, not now, Rasp pleaded. His antics were only entertaining if they were at someone else's expense. Vomiting now would only ensure the majority of the splatter ended up on himself. He wanted the crowd to laugh with him, not at him.

"Mister Snow." A stern voice cut through the ruckus with the weight of a sledgehammer. The crowd went eerily quiet until the only sound Rasp could hear was the snap of brittle twigs underfoot as the speaker drew nearer. "Kindly release Seamus. The doctor has already made three house calls this week. Let's not waste her time with another."

Shit.

Rasp was all smiles. Like a puppy eager to show off its newest trick, he rolled away and left his opponent facedown in the mud, gasping for breath. He shot upright and attempted to dust the grime from his trousers, succeeding only in smearing it further into the grain of the thick wool. "Nice day for a stroll, sir?"

Judge Trant Belfast's voice was flat with irritation. "Where is your keeper?"

Rasp gripped the wet soil between his toes as he considered which direction to run. The surrounding landscape was uneven and riddled with white spruce and poplars. While inconvenient, the trees were the least of his worries. It was the inconspicuous hazards like upturned roots, ground squirrel burrows, and the occasional steep cliffside that presented the true peril. As much as it pained him to admit, Rasp stood a better chance of talking his way out of trouble. A feat he was well practiced in, except the part where anyone believed him. Particularly Judge Belfast.

"Who, Faris?" Rasp said. "I think he fell down a well somewhere. These nice people offered to help pull him out. But then Seamus and I got into a bit of a disagreement over who got to carry the rope. That's what you walked in on, in case you were wondering."

"Are you finished?" Trant asked.

"I don't know. Is it working?"

There was that damn snort again. Followed closely by an ear flap. And then a hoof stomp. Oh dear gods, the holy trifecta. Trant wasn't just mad, he was positively fuming. Rasp wondered if this would be enough to make the judge reconsider his stance on pacifism.

Faris was going to owe him big for this. Rasp didn't take responsibility for his own actions, let alone someone else's. "Oh, alright. You caught me. He didn't fall down the well. I pushed him."

If Faris had any sense at all, he'd be halfway back to the house by now. He was a survivor who, above all else, valued self-preservation and knowing the precise moment to slip out the back unnoticed. Which failed to explain why the idiot chose that moment to step forward from the crowd and accept his fate. "You can stop now," he said, placing his hand on Rasp's shoulder. "I'm here, Father."

Trant's calm voice sent a chill up Rasp's spine. "Out of the well so soon?"

"It was more of a trough, really."

"I came to check on this so-called training regimen of yours. Imagine my surprise when I found not an exercise yard, but an unauthorized gambling operation. I suppose it explains why half the village is sporting mysterious bruises." Before Faris could interrupt, Trant continued, "At least tell me you split the earnings. Your ward is doing most of the work."

"I—uh," Faris stammered.

"Snow, has Faris been giving you a fair share?"

Rasp paused to consider his answer. Judge Belfast had most definitely laid a verbal trap for him to stumble into. Alas, the only way for Rasp to find it was to fall in headfirst. A nervous grin spread across his muddied face. "He pays me in buttons, actually. He doesn't think I know the difference."

"You never complained before!"

With a wearisome sigh, Trant turned and addressed the crowd. "Go home, all of you. If you have time to stand around then you're not busy enough. Anyone caught out here again will be assigned extra work duties."

The blurred shapes around them shifted, moving as one back through the sparse orchard toward the main path. The clearing grew eerily quiet once more. Rasp rolled his weight from one foot to the other, feeling suddenly exposed. Trant and Faris spoke softly beside him, but he didn't catch a word they said. The skin on the back of his arms prickled as he tilted his head this way and that, listening for a sound that was not there. Something was wrong.

The croak of a raven echoed between the trees. Alas, there wasn't time to decipher its warning call. Trant's gruff voice snapped Rasp back to the present. "Hold out your hand, Snow."

Rasp curled his fingers in hesitation. Why? Was he going to slap it? Cut it off, perhaps? That didn't seem very pacifistic. Maybe he'd finally succeeded in pushing the judge over the moralistic cliffside. After a few agonizing seconds of deliberation, Rasp raised his hand in front of him.

"Palm up, boy."

Rasp twisted his hand into the correct position and was taken aback when the judge deposited something cold and clinking into it. A fistful of coins, he realized. Collected from Faris's money purse, no doubt. What in the realm was this?

"In the future," Trant said, "if you let my son take advantage of you, at least make sure you're getting a share."

Rasp sucked his bottom lip between his teeth. "I'm very confused right now."

"Did you just pocket my half?" Faris said to his father.

A sharp snort from Trant silenced his son's protests. "Take Snow back to the house and get him presentable. We have guests," he added, with a tone Rasp couldn't quite pin down. "And for the gods' sakes, take him the back way. I can't afford for the two of you to be seen like this."

With a meek acknowledgment to his father, Faris hooked his arm through Rasp's and escorted him from the clearing. The journey was as awkward as it was quiet. For a long while, the only sound between them was the occasional splash of a puddle underfoot. They were already halfway, having cut through the back apple orchard and nearing the garden that was presently little more than an empty stretch of frozen dirt, before Rasp found the courage to speak. "How dead are we?"

"I don't know," Faris murmured. "That didn't go anything like I expected."

"I can't believe he didn't hit you."

"Father's never hit me."

"Ah," Rasp concluded, "explains why you turned out so rotten."

This earned a lackluster shove from Faris. His heart wasn't in it though, as made evident by the fact that Rasp was still standing. "What's your excuse then? Hit too many times?"

Not hard enough, Rasp's father would have said. That was probably the most confounding piece to this puzzle of a situation. Like Trant, Rasp's father had also been the leader of his people. But the two men's approaches to discipline were as different as night from day. Paler Stoneclaw had ruled with an iron first. Honor and duty came before all else, including his sons. Judge Belfast may not have understood Faris, but he didn't spend his every waking moment tearing him down one fault at a time. Beneath all the bickering, Rasp swore the two actually liked each other. A fact he still couldn't seem to wrap his mind around.

"Faris!" a gentle voice hissed, tearing Rasp from his thoughts.

Faris jerked to a stop. "Mum?"

Novera Belfast's voice came from within the blurry tangle of shoulder-height shrubbery located to their right. "In the thicket, dear. You'll have to come to me, I'm afraid. It's best if I'm not seen near the house."

Faris released his grip on Rasp's arm and grabbed his hand instead, pulling him into the very heart of the twisted nest of interwoven branches and brittle twigs. Rasp considered making a snide comment about the unexpected hand holding, but the thorns that tore at his bare arms and face sufficiently distracted him from doing so.

Faris didn't appear to mind. With his fist locked around Rasp's hand, tightening each time his ward pulled in the opposite direction, Faris plowed a path through the thicket and delivered them safely onto the other side. Rasp's only consolation was that the ground here was less thick with stabby vegetation. He felt Faris's grip lessen and ripped free, muttering as he picked the thorns from his abraded skin.

"You're wearing your travel clothes," Faris whispered, his hoarse voice marked with sudden urgency. "Mum, what's going on? Why are you leaving? It's not seekers, is it? It's too early in the season for them to be here."

"They're not from the division, no," Novera said. Her scruffy shape was roughly the same height as Faris's. For some reason, Rasp always envisioned her taller. It was the demeanor, he decided. Novera had the temperament of a housecat. Warm, affectionate, and capable of sending the entire household scurrying like a nest of plague rats with a single hiss. "Your father asked me to take my students into the hills as a precaution. I don't know how long I'll be away. I'm sorry, I wish I had more time. I only wanted to say goodbye."

Faris staggered forward and enveloped his mother in what Rasp assumed was a heartfelt embrace. That, or they were trying to strangle each other in the most inefficient way possible. Rasp shuffled his aching feet and tilted his head in the other direction, silently wishing Faris had left him on the path. He didn't like this sort of thing. The way their voices cracked with unabashed emotion, the crying, all that disgusting snuffling—it left him uneasy. Like a turtle without its shell.

Faris's and Novera's hushed conversation shifted to goodbyes as Rasp's thoughts turned inward. He had overheard Novera and Trant arguing a few nights before. They weren't yelling, merely talking loud enough for a person creeping the halls to overhear. Rasp didn't catch most of what was said. He'd heard Novera sobbing afterward, though. And the judge had been in something of a mood ever since. Was it somehow related to this?

Rasp nearly jumped out of his skin when Novera clasped his hand with her own. Despite the lines that creased her calloused palm, her grip was as strong as his. "I know you're not what everyone thinks you are," Novera said softly. "And there will always be those who won't accept you. Just know it gets easier once you're able to accept it yourself. No one wants to be the first break in the family chain."

Rasp stared up at the shifting gray light that filtered in through the hazy branches overhead. Novera often knew what she was talking about. He just wished, for the life of him, that he knew what she was talking about, too. His banishment from the Iron Ridge, maybe? It'd hurt, sure, but Rasp was over it now. There was no sense in wallowing over a situation you couldn't change.

Something about Novera's goodbye felt strangely permanent. "Am I going to see you again?"

"I don't know, love. I wish I could take you and Faris with me, but I'm afraid it's not in the cards."

What an odd thing to say. Faris, he could understand. He was her blasted son, after all. Rasp was just an overstayed houseguest that may or may not have been a prisoner. Despite this, Novera was nice to him. Possibly the nicest anyone had *ever* been to him. But that didn't explain why she'd take him with her, or why she was leaving in the first place.

Maybe it was the same reason Rasp had been picking fights all morning. The apprehension in the air, the feeling that something was coming. Rasp could feel it stewing in his lower gut, twisting his intestines into knots as the dread slowly ate away at him from the inside out. Did Novera feel it, too?

The scent of lemongrass and tears enveloped Rasp as Novera threw her arms around him with a sudden shaking shudder, whispering so only he would hear, "Promise me you'll take care of my son."

CHAPTER FOUR

The Protector Comes to Collect

That's who we came all this way for?" Rali said, peering through the tangle of naked branches. They were positioned ten yards back from the action, close enough to see without being seen. Except for Rali, of course, whose height and refusal to climb anything taller than a bar stool meant the dwarf caught only glimpses of the fight through the legs of the shifting crowd. "Iron Devil, my ass. That boy's a half-drowned rat."

The barren treetops rustled above them. Snag edged further out along the arm of a black and white birch to gain a better vantage point. The willowy branch barely bent beneath his lithe frame. "Rat or not," Snag said, wrinkling his upturned nose at what he saw, "he's definitely a Stoneclaw."

"Chip in two silver each and he can be a dead Stoneclaw," Ellisar offered flatly, lounging against a nearby tree trunk. With her mottled green hood pulled over her eyes, she was nearly indiscernible from their bleak surroundings. A glare from Oralia elicited a contemptuous shrug from the elf huntress. "What?" Ellisar said. "You don't want to be here any more than the rest of us.

Curly, the final member of Protector Oralia Dawnsight's personal company, was already loading a bolt into his crossbow. While the cool weather encouraged the others to stay bundled, the orc alone braved the elements in little more than a cotton shirt riddled with moth holes. He glanced over his shoulder at Ellisar, black eyes gleaming. "Why would I pay you when I could just do the job myself?"

"They understand they're not to harm him, yes?" Judge Belfast stood beside Oralia. He was wrapped so tightly beneath a wool cloak, she could barely see the tips of his horns peeking out from his hood each time he stole a worried glance her way.

Oralia and her company had ridden two weeks to get to Lonebrook, the small village nestled at the foot of the Iron Ridge Mountains. Judge Belfast had harbored a fugitive all winter, waiting for the moment the pass cleared and the protector could come collect. After sitting on their hands for four months, her warriors were hungry for action. Starved, in fact. So much so, they seemed to have forgotten all of the manners Oralia had hammered into them over the years.

"No one is killing the Stoneclaw." Oralia's voice made all four collectively flinch. Five, if she counted Judge Belfast.

A sudden cheer from the crowd drew Oralia's attention back to the match. The fight, which thus far consisted solely of a childish game of cat-and-mouse, had finally turned serious. The Stoneclaw had his opponent on the ground now, with the crook of his elbow locked so tightly around the faun's throat that there was a chance only one of them would be getting up again. At least for a little while.

With a solemn shake of his horns, Trant picked his way through the dense overgrowth with little mind for the stickers that tore at his cloak. "If you'll excuse me, Protector Dawnsight. I will have to intervene before our blacksmith loses consciousness."

"Since you won't let us take out the Stoneclaw," Curly said, stealing a glance at Oralia, "can I at least pick off the white faun?"

The judge whipped around, his brown cloak swirling dramatically behind him, and struck his hoof against the soft ground with an infuriated snort. From beneath his hood, Trant's amber eyes burned bright. "That is my son!"

"Apologies, Judge Belfast." Oralia swiveled her head at Curly and forced the words through gritted teeth. "It was a poor jest. I will ensure it does not happen again. See to your people. I will rejoin you afterward." She waited until he'd cleared the thicket and disappeared among the throng of onlookers before lifting her weary stare skyward. "I specifically said to be on your best behavior." Oralia massaged her aching temples as she spoke. "*Best.* If this is your idea of exemplary conduct, then perhaps it is time to take a closer look at what I am paying you."

The faithful four, that's what the realm had dubbed her company of misfit warriors. Four deadly, overgrown children would be a more apt description. Although, admittedly, not as catchy. They were loyal, Oralia gave them that. Mostly because they were too feral to find gainful employment elsewhere. Nevertheless, her faithful four would follow her to the seven realms of chaos and back. Not without question, of course . . . and complaining. There would always be lots of complaining.

"Aye-aye, boss. Message received loud and clear. No more fuck-uppery from here on—" Rali faltered, midspeech, realizing Curly was still pointing his weapon in the direction of the crowd. She dutifully tipped the nose of his crossbow skyward. "Bucko, you are not doing me any favors here. What idiot let you have this death contraption, anyway?"

A look of hurt crossed his broad, tusked face. "You did! Got it off that traveling salesman two towns back? You said somethin' about the price being a real steal."

Rali's pale nose and cheeks were stung pink by the frosty air. She squinted one dark eye at him, suspiciously. "How far into my cups was I?"

"Practically licking the bottom of the mug by the time the barkeep kicked us out." Incapable of remaining still for any length of time, Ellisar had turned her attention from murder to breakfast. She rooted among the dead foliage for the first mushrooms of the season, regaling the event in question over her shoulder to Rali, "We got stopped by the salesman on the way back. You were eight silver short and pulled the 'look, a dragon' bit. When I finally found you again, you were passed out under a wagon."

"Oi!" A gritty voice shouted from above. "Can you all shut it already? Some of us are trying to work here." The tarnished hoops and piercings dangling from Snag's ears jangled softly as he glared down at them. The goblin's yellow eyes grew wide as he noticed the crossbow pointed in his direction. "For fuck's sake, that damn thing's loaded! Point it elsewhere."

"Lieutenant Ralizak," Oralia said sharply.

Rali plucked the crossbow from Curly and disabled the firing mechanism with a simple twist of her deft hand. She slung the weapon over her shoulder and started toward Oralia with a fresh spring in her step. "Alright, I know what I said before, but it's true this time. The fuck-uppery has officially stopped."

"Take Curly and see to the horses. You may set up camp when you are finished. And for the gods' sakes, get rid of that contraption before he maims someone." Oralia's eyes darted in Ellisar's direction. She wanted to tell Ellisar not to burn down the village in her absence, but opted for a more specific set of instructions, not wanting to give the elf any bright ideas. "Patrol the area, Ellisar. Make a note of any potential escape routes. And if you come across any locals, do play nice."

"Wait, she doesn't have to help with camp? Not fair!" Curly protested.

Rali punched him in the arm, muttering, "Shut it before you get us more work."

Oralia caught Curly as he passed, grunting through her tusks at him, "The next time you see Judge Belfast, you will apologize."

"For what?"

If there was a brain somewhere in Curly's thick skull, it was abnormally small. "You threatened our host's son."

"Oh . . ." Curly was smaller than her, with deep, smoky blue-gray skin, a shaved head, and a curved left tusk. The young orc offered her his most pained expression. It looked more constipated than remorseful, but Oralia supposed there wasn't any fixing that. "Because I threatened to shoot him, right. Sorry about that."

When Oralia made no reply, Curly wriggled free of her grasp and turned tail, hurrying after the others. "Hey, Ellisar! You gonna share those mushrooms first, right? I'm starving."

Ellisar threw a rock at him with impeccable aim, inciting a chase which inevitably she would win. Curly tore after her, shouting a barrage of foul language. Black and brown leaves stirred into the air behind them. The breeze caught the dead foliage, buffeting it across the barren ground. Oralia watched them go, sighing. She kept the faithful four for their lethal skills, not because they were house trained. Unfortunately, it was moments like this that she wished she'd taken the time to domesticate them.

Snag slid from the tree and landed on both feet beside her with the grace of a lame housecat. His trousers, patched in so many places they now had more in common with a decorative quilt than a uniform, had surpassed the worn stage and were bordering dangerously on threadbare. He dusted his palms against his tattered clothes. "The boy's a Stoneclaw, that's for sure. His old man sired a handful of offspring, though. I won't be able to confirm if we've got the right one without a closer inspection."

"Let us hope we did not come all this way for nothing," Oralia said. Her gaze moved back over the small clearing. Under Judge Belfast's order, the crowd had begun to disperse. Three figures hung back: the judge, the white faun whom he'd identified as his son, and a very sickly looking human. Rali's assessment of the boy had been correct. This wasn't a mighty Stoneclaw warrior; this was, indeed, a half-drowned rat. But Oralia had no use for a warrior. She needed a prince. And it seemed fate had finally delivered.

Movement broke Oralia from her thoughts. Trant was plodding back through the thicket toward her. His cloven feet scoured deep imprints into the soft earth with each burdensome step. The young Belfast and the Stoneclaw, Oralia noted, were moving in the opposite direction, back toward the main house. "There was no need to send him away, Judge," Oralia said. "My best work is done in the field."

Usually with a blade involved. And, depending on the situation, with Oralia covered in the blood of her enemies. Minor details.

Trant wrinkled his nose at her as he stalked past. "The decision wasn't for your benefit. If I'm expected to help you draft an alliance with the future ruler of the Iron Ridge, I may as well do it by a nice fire."

Oralia slogged through the mud beside him, feeling the wet soil suck her boots deeper with each squelchy step. She was sick of the rain and the cold, and the heavy ache in her bones. She pressed forward, secretly relieved there was a warm hearth awaiting them inside. Behind them, Snag trailed as silent and inconspicuous as a shadow.

"Why the matches?" Oralia said. "I thought you renounced the path of violence."

"My son, Faris, is the one who arranges the matches." Trant's breath crystalized into the air over his whiskered nose. "I don't condone the fighting, don't get me wrong. But if I banned it, they'd simply take it elsewhere. By turning a blind eye, I can ensure things don't get out of hand."

Her breath, warm and heavy, puffed in front of her face as she clambered to the top of the hill overlooking the main courtyard. The air was crisp and Oralia could smell the tantalizing smoke of a wood-burning fire from the main house ahead of them. She sensed rain, too. Judging by the dark clouds rolling in from the north, the storm would break by supper. "Do you ever watch the matches?"

"Sometimes." With a shiver, Trant gathered his scarf around his shoulders and started downhill without her.

He had served under her as a captain many years ago. Since then, time had taken its toll on the old faun. His black beard had grayed and worry lines now wrinkled the brown skin around his eyes and mouth. Oralia wondered if she looked as old as he did. Her face, long and grizzled and riddled with battle scars, had yet to lose its deep, slate-colored glow. But she was an orc, a being with a life expectancy three times his. Time was unfair that way. It was shorter for those who deserved it most.

It took three of her long strides to fall back into step alongside him. "And?"

"And what?" Trant snorted.

"You claim he is the Iron Devil. Surely you would have noticed by now whether or not the boy is good at the one thing the Iron Devil is acclaimed for."

"Oh, yes. The boy's a natural. It's all he does, morning, noon, and night. We got into it again only this morning because I had the audacity to suggest he wear pants at the breakfast table." Trant glanced across at her, grinning. The expression looked entirely out of place on his normally stoic features. "Were we not talking about complaining? Because that's where he truly shines."

"Fighting, Trant."

"He's decent at that too, I suppose. Had the realm given me more time, I think I could have changed him. From Iron Devil to reformed pacifist, a true success story." Trant reached the base of the hill and started out across the slippery lot toward the front stoop. Oralia detected an edge of sadness to his words. "But that didn't fit into your grand scheme, did it?"

CHAPTER FIVE

The Silver Curse

Trant led Oralia and Snag up the steps of the stone cottage and into the house. Polished black oak floorboards clacked under his hooves as he took them through the interior of the home and into the back study. The few sparse patches of wall space not covered in maps, diagrams, or book-laden shelves were painted a soft dandelion yellow. There was a scattering of mismatched furniture, the largest of which was Trant's heavy writing desk. It occupied the corner closest to the entrance, barely visible under a pile of scrolls and loose parchment. From the looks of it, the room had been picked up in a hurry.

Snag padded in behind Oralia and took up his position by the door. The goblin stared straight ahead with a glazed look in his eyes. He was listening, no doubt, but maintained the expression that no matter what he heard, it would be forgotten the moment he left the room.

"I heard a rumor, Protector, that you intend to retire after this," Trant said, easing into the overstuffed chair by the stone hearth. His thick cloak and scarf hung on the hook behind him. "Is it true?"

Word certainly had a way of getting around. Lonebrook was located in Mossborn, the second farthest territory from the capital. Oralia's retirement hadn't been made public yet. So far only her fellow figureheads had been made aware. Oralia glanced over her shoulder at Snag, who was maintaining his best *I'm not here* expression. He knew already, of course. As did the other three. It was only fair. Goblins in particular found employment difficult within the United Territories of the Realm. Oralia imagined the prospects of soon being out of a job were already flittering through his mazework of a mind.

"There is talk of retirement, yes," she admitted.

"It's not like you to go out with a big show. Why not just retire and be done with it?" Trant studied her for a breath, as his amber eyes pried away at her secrets. "And don't tell me you're doing this in the name of peace, either. I'd like to think we're both smarter than that."

Trant certainly hadn't lost his knack for seeing through political bullshit. Age, at the very least, had made him more diplomatic. The young Trant Belfast would have told her she was out of her blasted mind.

"An alliance with Rasp verges on suicidal, I am aware," Oralia replied. It was probably the reason she'd been handpicked for the task. "But I vowed to leave the realm in a better state than when I started, and this mission will ensure that."

Trant said nothing. He only kept looking at her with a purposely blank expression. One she was all too familiar with. Oralia sighed. "If there is something you wish to say, Trant, then do so. I have always valued your opinion."

"You and the Speaker of the People rarely agree on anything. The fact that the two of you set aside your differences and banded together on this speaks volumes. What it says to me, specifically, is that whatever *actual* motives you have for this undertaking are indispensable to you. Possibly lucrative. However," Trant said with an irritated flick of his ear, "if there is an alternative way, I urge you to take it. The realm has no place in the Iron Ridge. Silver-haired or not, Rasp Stoneclaw is not your answer."

In mountain folk tradition, only a silver-haired was fit to rule. When one leader died, fate chose another. Paler Stoneclaw was rumored to have passed around the end of summer. Of his four surviving sons, it was Rasp, the youngest, who took on the change. By autumn, the boy's hair had turned silver—the irrefutable sign that he would be the next ruler of the Iron Ridge. Be it jealousy, fear, or perhaps suspicion that Rasp had taken their father's life himself, the young Stoneclaw was driven from the mountainside by his brothers. They caught him at the base of the cliffs, near the Lonebrook forest, and left the young man for dead.

Rasp had crawled as far as the main road before succumbing to his injuries. Drawn by the circling ravens overhead, it was the lady of the house, Novera Belfast, who found Rasp hours from death. Realizing what fortune had delivered onto their doorstep, she and Trant took the boy into their care and spent the last six months nursing him back to health.

Oralia watched the judge's face as she spoke, curious to see if his carefully guarded expression would reveal anything his mouth didn't. "No place in the Iron Ridge?" she repeated. "Do not tell me you believe in the old superstitions."

"The sixth son, born of a mighty Stoneclaw leader, shall inherit the silver-hair and bring destruction and darkness to the world" was of course one of the more

notorious prophecies to come from the Iron Ridge. Oralia personally preferred the tall tales of the ridge's cursed magical bears, but to each their own.

"Do I think Rasp's going to bring on the end of the world? No," Trant said, as if he were resisting the urge to roll his eyes. "But even in superstition there is some granule of truth. I have lived in the shadow of the mountains my whole life. Something rotten resides there. It seeps into the trees, and the rock, and the people especially. If you trespass into the Iron Ridge, the darkness will consume you, too."

The sounds of approaching footsteps kept Oralia from responding. It was just as well, she supposed. The Iron Ridge was a deadly place. There was no denying it. But the legends of the Stoneclaws and their supposed curse was just that: stories. Old wives' tales told around the fire to frighten little children to bed. There were no supernatural forces at work here. This was simply a matter of convincing people—a very particularly stubborn clan of people—to get with the times.

Faris appeared from the hallway with Rasp in tow. He ushered the human forward and nearly bolted back out again when he noticed Snag standing guard alongside the door. "Madam Protector, welcome," Faris greeted, marking Snag's position from the corner of his eye in the event the goblin suddenly stopped pretending to be a wall fixture. "Should I wait outside the door, Father?"

Trant excused him with a tilt of his horns. "Keep to the kitchen. Make sure we are left undisturbed."

Faris drew the door shut behind him. Rasp lingered near the doorway alone, awaiting further instruction. He was small for a full-grown human, hovering barely an inch or two over his faun captors at his tallest. After months of rich food and easy living, Oralia had expected him to be fatter. Rasp's body was the opposite; thin, gangly, and oddly reminiscent of a plucked chicken. His hair was cut to the scalp. Even then, from a distance, Oralia swore she saw a shimmer of silver reflecting the firelight.

"Madam Protector?" The man's pink, freshly scrubbed face changed. Oralia had expected fear, or anger, maybe even smug indifference, but not awe. Rasp stepped cautiously into the room, running his hand along the wall. He was dressed in plain brown trousers and a thin linen shirt that Oralia suspected was supposed to be worn as an undergarment. Considering the man was barefoot, it was probably the closest to presentable his willful nature would allow. "Oralia Dawnsight? The Protector of the Realm? She's here?"

Rasp's odd movements from the match now made sense. Oralia's cold gaze shifted from him to Trant. "You failed to mention he was blind."

"You know what he's not? Deaf," Rasp said, starting toward her voice. "Don't speak like I'm not here, Protector."

"Forgive me." She hadn't factored this in. An outcast Stoneclaw she could use. But a blind one? Oralia wasn't sure. She would make a decision later, after having collected the necessary information. For now, it was business as usual. "Thank you for meeting with me on such short notice, Rasp. Due to the sensitive nature of my visit, I asked Judge Belfast to keep the details of my arrival discreet."

In other words, she couldn't afford to have him run away. In Oralia's experience, the enemy often took drastic measures to avoid being in the same room as her. Not that they ever got far. Her elf huntress, Ellisar, specialized in tracking runaways. It was the state in which the runaways returned that caused problems. So far, interrogating a corpse had yet to prove insightful.

"Gods, you're polite. You always hear about the size and the ferocity and that time you ripped that ogre's arm right from his socket, but never the nice things." Rasp stepped further into the room, moving with more confidence than before. "It's flattering that you came for me yourself, Protector. Had I known to expect you, I might have cleaned the blood out from under my fingernails."

A silent command from Oralia prompted Snag to begin his inspection. The goblin stepped from the wall and intercepted Rasp's path. "Arms up," he instructed, tugging the man's shirt from his trousers. "There's supposed to be a—ahh!"

Rasp grasped Snag around the ribs and flipped him onto his back with a slam. The goblin recovered with remarkable speed. He rolled into a crouch and drew the dagger from his belt, snarling, "You're dead, maggot!"

"Snaglebrag, stand down," Oralia ordered, placing her weight onto her front foot in the event she was forced to intervene. She would attempt to defuse the situation verbally first. Hot-blooded warriors were like fire, and an aggressive response would only stoke their violence. "Easy, Stoneclaw. Back off him."

"Sorry, Madam Protector." Rasp, with his hands held in the air, inched away. "For future note, please don't sic your pet on me without warning. As the judge often reminds me, I react too quickly and think too slow."

"Pet?" The ring strung through Snag's lower lip trembled as he sheathed his blade. His nose and cheeks flushed crimson as the blood boiled beneath the surface of his leathery, moss-colored skin. "I ain't no fuckin' pet! You're just saying that because I'm a goblin, aren't you? What, don't think we belong in houses, is that it?"

"It's the little tinkling sound when you walk, actually. I assumed the protector had clipped a name tag to your collar."

From the corner of her eye, Oralia saw Judge Belfast plant his face into his hands with a soft groan. Contrary to the judge's reaction, she felt it was a step in the right direction. Hurling insults at one another was preferable to fists, anyway. "That was my fault, Rasp. Snaglebrag was tasked with verifying your identity. I should have warned you," she said. "Take a moment to collect yourself and then we will try again. I cannot proceed until I know for certain to whom I am speaking."

Rasp bristled at the idea. His shoulders held high and rigid. "Identify how?"

"Snaglebrag, if you would."

Muttering under his breath, the goblin retrieved a rolled parchment from the pouch slung across his hip. He unraveled the scroll with a flourish of his wrist and imparted its contents without actually looking at the page. His long-range vision was troublesome when it came to fine print. As such, Snag would rather commit an entire document to memory than be seen wearing his reading spectacles. "Six years ago, Rasp Stoneclaw and his older brother Mul were taken prisoner by slave traders while traveling through the swamplands. According to realm sources, both Stoneclaws were branded on the shoulder with the slaver's mark."

"They paid for it with blood, too. I didn't leave a single one of those bastards alive." Rasp's jaw unclenched. "Which begs the question, how does the realm know about it?"

Snag looked up over the edge of the parchment at him, delighted to provide the answer. "Your relationship with the farmer's daughter was not as secretive as you had hoped. She received a hundred pieces of silver for every mark the realm could use to identify you. Sweet of her, innit?"

Oralia expected a slew of curses. Rasp broke into a smile instead, shaking his head. "Priss, you clever girl. Found a way to escape the farm life after all. Good for you." He paused, tilting his head in Snag's direction. "I suppose she told you about the tattoo then?"

"You mean the winged worm on your back?"

"I told her it was a dragon. In hindsight, I should have waited for the needler to sober up first. Is that all? Don't need to peek at my"—here Rasp spoke something in a language Oralia did not understand.

It had been for Snag's benefit, evidently. The goblin furrowed his brow in disgust. "The brand and tattoo will be sufficient."

Rasp lifted his shirt over his head, cackling. "Clearly Priss didn't tell the realm everything. Now I feel guilty for not marrying her like I promised."

Snag edged closer. His hand hovered over the hilt of his dagger as he examined Rasp's scarred shoulders. "The brand is present." He spoke his findings out loud. "There's a tattoo, too. But it's difficult to decipher. The mountain folk numeral for six has been carved into the flesh over it."

"A message to the undertaker." Rasp explained from within the confines of the shirt with what might have been a shrug. "Courtesy of my brothers."

Snag stepped away from the Stoneclaw, appearing equal parts exhausted and unnerved. "I can confirm he's Rasp Stoneclaw, Madam Protector."

"Thank you, Snaglebrag. You may go."

Without Snag to hinder him, Rasp was across the study with alarming speed. His eyes, green and glimmering, roved upward. Had he been capable of sight, he would have gotten a good glimpse of Oralia's nose hairs. "My father claimed you were an eleven-foot swamp monster with two heads who could blow fire out your ass. But I'm not getting that." He cracked a smile, as though he could sense her confusion even without the ability to see it. "Everyone assumes being blind is like closing your eyes, you know. The truth is I can see light and dark. Shapes, too, if they're up close. I don't know about the fire, but I definitely don't see two heads. May I touch your face, Madam Protector?"

"You may," Oralia said. What a strange individual. No enemy ever drew this close to her, not unless they were armed. And even then, it never worked out the way they intended. "If that hand strays anywhere near my ass, you will lose it."

Her words produced an unexpected laugh from Rasp. "And all this time I was told you had no sense of humor."

Along with his sight, Rasp's brothers had taken the tip of his right ear, several teeth, and what might have been a handsome face. His nose had healed crooked. Raised pink and silver scars snaked from the crown of his pale head, over the brow, and down his neck, disappearing beneath the man's loose-fitted clothes. He smelled like sweat and soil disguised beneath several layers of floral soap. It was pleasant in comparison to the stench of horse that had not yet been scrubbed from Oralia's own underarms. Despite the odor, Rasp pressed closer, lifting his hands to her face. His fingertips traced the outline of her jaw first and edged steadily upward toward her protruding tusks.

He brushed against her left tusk and a look of surprise flooded his gaunt face. "I didn't realize the realm employed elephants in their service. I suppose that explains your size."

Oralia resisted the urge to stomp his foot. She slapped his hands away instead, snarling, "Introductions are over. Find a seat, Stoneclaw. We have business to discuss."

CHAPTER SIX

The Sixth Son

If nothing else, Rasp demonstrated a healthy respect for authority. He turned sharply on his heel and sought the wall, following it until his foot bumped into an object large enough to use as a chair. It was a footstool, but he didn't seem to care and Oralia wasn't in the mood to help him find something more accommodating.

She took the wooden chair across from him. Oralia grimaced the moment she sat, suddenly wishing she hadn't. The tufted cushion felt like sandpaper against her saddle sores. Rasp wasn't capable of seeing her pained expression, fortunately. And if Trant noticed, he kept his observations to himself. "Before we delve any further, I must make something abundantly clear. Judge Belfast, at the risk of his own welfare, has gone to great lengths to hide your identity. For his sake, and yours, what is discussed will not be mentioned outside of this room. Is that understood?"

Rasp made a gesture with his fingertips, drawing them silently over his lips.

"I fail to grasp your meaning."

"You're an elephant, right. I forgot." Rasp sighed, resting his head against the wall. "I understand, Protector. My lips are sealed."

That was obviously not the case as his confounded lips were still moving. Oralia turned to Trant with her mouth curled in annoyance. "Does he always speak in riddles?"

Trant's weary gaze drifted upward, studying the planked ceiling as if it were the only thing in the room worth his attention. "The military opened its ranks to humans two centuries ago. Surely you have a better understanding of them by now."

She didn't. Humans tended to avoid her. She was an orc, after all. Not to mention the highest ranking military officer in the realm. Everyone avoided her, even the other figureheads. "You have a growing human population, Judge Belfast, yes? You may translate for me."

The faun's left ear twitched with irritation. "As you wish, Madam Protector."

Great. Now they were both throwing titles around like insults. Negotiations hadn't even started yet. Still, with Trant's assistance, Oralia would muddle through. She would send for Rali if she had to. Her dwarf lieutenant was fluent in a number of obscure languages, including sarcasm.

Drawing a breath, Oralia addressed Rasp once more. "This conversation is between you, me, and the judge. Clear?"

"Yes."

"Good." Oralia realized she'd lost her place. She thought for a moment, trying to recall where she had left off. This was the problem with dealing with civilians. They spoke indirectly. She was barely past introductions and already the conversation had gone sideways. "The realm is aware you were driven from your homeland some months ago. Is it true you bear the silver curse, and are therefore the rightful leader of the Stoneclaw clan?"

"Silver-hair," he corrected. "Only outsiders call it a curse."

"Is it true?"

"Yes," Rasp said bitterly, as if the very word tasted of poison.

She watched him carefully for her next question. It was the only one so far to which she didn't already know the answer. "It is also my understanding that in order for the silver-hair to pass on, the previous leader has to have died. That person would have been your father. Did you kill him, Rasp?"

"I'm flattered, but no. He got struck by lightning, actually. Nature robbed me of the chance."

There was nothing suspicious about his demeanor. Rasp didn't shift or fidget. He sat reclined, legs wide, toes pointed in her direction. His eyes gave away nothing. Either he was telling the truth, or had perfected the art of feigned innocence.

"From your response, I assume you did not mourn his passing then?"

"Nah," he said with a shrug. "The man was an asshole."

"Language," Trant muttered from the corner.

"Oh, please. You didn't like him any better."

Once more, Oralia was forced to steer the conversation back on track. "So if you did not kill your father, and are the rightful leader of the Stoneclaw clan, what caused your brothers to banish you?"

Finally, Rasp's face changed. A dark line formed over his brow and his thin lips pulled into a scowl. After an uncomfortable pause, he cleared his throat and said so low Oralia strained to catch it, "I was accused of being a witch."

Rasp whipped his head in Trant's direction, mouth flared back in a snarl. "Oh, come on! Don't laugh. I know how it sounds."

Oralia watched him with mild indifference. "A witch?"

"You heard right." The man's fingertips worked at the fabric of his trousers near the knee, as if unconsciously attempting to bore a hole into the thick wool. "A witch. Can you believe that? Most ridiculous thing I've ever heard."

"Under what circumstances?"

"Jealousy, mostly. I'm one of seven siblings, you know. The three brothers still kicking all thought they were destined to be the next silver-haired. You can imagine everyone's surprise when it was me, the family fuckup, that woke up one morning with a head full of silvers." Despite his calm words, Rasp's fingers clawed at the wool of his trousers with twice the intensity as before. "The coup didn't take much, to be honest. My people have a real hard-on for omens and signs and shit. With the whole birth order thing, I never stood a chance."

Oralia knew the legend. Six was a cursed number among the mountain folk. Seven, by contrast, was considered lucky. Rasp's mother, Tal Stoneclaw, bore twins in her sixth pregnancy. Only one of the infants survived the night. Paler declared it a good omen. By eliminating the other hungry mouth, baby number seven would grow into the strongest warrior the clan had seen. But as the years progressed and blight and drought poisoned the land, rumors began to circulate. What first started as mere whispers grew stronger with each retelling until the entire mountainside wondered the same:

What if it was the sixth child, not the seventh, that survived? Was Rasp the curse that would bring the Stoneclaw dynasty to ruin?

"And which version do you see yourself as?" Oralia asked. "Are you the cursed offspring of Paler Stoneclaw? Or the one destined to bring the mountain folk to glory?"

"Doesn't seem to matter, at this point. My family chose for me."

"What if I could change that?" Oralia said. "Accept the help of the realm and you will be restored to power within the year. With a single word, you get revenge on the brothers that betrayed you, all while ensuring a better future for your people." The advisors had designed the pitch, not her. After weeks of back and forth, they finally agreed on the one they felt would best appeal to Rasp. Had it been left to Oralia, she would have kept it short and sweet, with the point of her blade held to the man's throat. Evidently that method was frowned upon.

Alas, Rasp's face slipped strangely unreadable. "Unless tides have shifted dramatically in my absence, I'm pretty sure my people are still at odds with yours."

"That is the beauty of it. Once reinstated, you will sign a truce with the realm. No more war. Our lands will finally be at peace."

"Let me guess, you're willing to do all of this from the kindness of your heart, right?"

"As Protector of the Realm, it is my duty to achieve harmony with our neighbors. However," Oralia added, "as a token of your appreciation, you will allow our supply trains to cut through your mountains unaccosted."

"You're doing this over *trade routes*?" Rasp asked, incredulous. "Is it really that much of an inconvenience to go around?"

It was, actually. The mountain folk defended their territory relentlessly, and the safest detour added an extra three weeks each way. Safe passage through the Iron Ridge would increase the realm's exports threefold.

"We help you. You help us." She didn't bother to explain it to him. A mountain man wasn't privy to the business of the realm. "What say you, Rasp Stoneclaw? Join forces with me and together, we fulfill your destiny."

Rasp picked at a loose thread on his shirt absentmindedly. "Nah, I'm good."

Oralia doubted her ears at first. But then, after glancing at Trant and confirming he wore the same befuddled expression as her, she realized she'd heard correctly. ". . .You are good?"

"Sorry, more human riddles." He tilted his head at her and smiled. Even with all of his teeth it would not have been a comforting expression. "It means no thank you. Offer rejected. Stoneclaws don't make deals with the realm. Not then, not now, not ever."

"You cannot be serious. I am offering you a kingdom and all you have to do in exchange is get us up the blasted mountain!" Months of planning and not once did the damn advisors think Rasp would turn them down. He was the rightful heir. His brothers tried to murder him. It had all the makings of an easy alliance.

"Yeah, after the whole assassination attempt, I'm not all that keen to return. The mountains aren't all they're cracked up to be. The food's bad. The weather sucks. Most of the women are related to me. I'll take my chances elsewhere." Rasp leaned forward, as if imparting a grave secret. "Between you and me, you're better off doing nothing. Sit back. Watch my brothers tear the clan apart from the inside. They couldn't even agree on how to kill me—while they were standing over my body, nonetheless. Give it three years, five tops, and the mountains will be free for the taking."

"You are a prisoner, Rasp. A sworn enemy, no less. It is within my power to kill you." Oralia ignored the glare from Judge Belfast. It was true, technically. After she received permission from the other heads of power. But the little shit didn't know that.

"Oh, good. Death threats. We're finally getting somewhere." Rasp drummed his feet against the ground eagerly. "Is this the part where I beg for mercy? Should I drop to my knees and grovel? Does crying make you uncomfortable, Protector? Wouldn't want that."

This was the reason humans confused her. They often said what they meant. The trouble was they said things they didn't mean almost as often. Sometimes with conviction. And sometimes with . . . whatever in the seven realms of chaos this was. Surely the Stoneclaw didn't intend to grovel, but Rasp had already proved unpredictable when turning down the realm's offer. Perhaps he needed to feel pressure in order to acquiesce? Oralia looked to Trant for clarification. "Is this another riddle?"

"No," the judge said, stroking the scruff below his chin. "I believe he's mocking you."

"Even though I have the power to kill him?"

"All part of the appeal, I suspect. He is a Stoneclaw, if you remember. It is considered an honor to die by your hand."

"Bonus points if you get her to do it with a smile," Rasp contributed helpfully.

Oralia felt her confidence falter. The time, energy, and resources the realm had poured into this venture were slowly slipping through her fingers. There had to be a way for her to salvage it. Rasp *was* a prisoner. He didn't have to go willingly. Could a blind man find his way up the Iron Ridge? Even if all went according to plan and she overthrew the residing rule, what then? Rasp didn't want to lead. The mountain folk wouldn't honor a peace treaty signed by someone who had no intention of sticking around afterward.

"Fine," Oralia said coolly. Her thoughts slowed, forming together into a cohesive strategy. She hadn't lasted this long as Protector of the Realm to be thwarted by a disrespectful man-child. "I will barter a deal with your brothers instead. After all, a new leader will not emerge until the old one dies, correct? Your brothers can finish you properly this time, thus bringing an end to your rule and allowing the silver curse to select another. I get my trade routes regardless."

Rasp's face lost some of its color. "Shit."

Oralia's eyes darted back to Trant. He nodded, making a gesture with his hand that would go undetected by Rasp. Oralia understood its meaning. *Proceed respectfully. Don't gloat.* She had him where she wanted. If she pushed too hard, Rasp would double down just to spite her.

"Rasp," Oralia spoke firmly, but kindly. She wasn't sure it mattered, as the Stoneclaw appeared unresponsive with fear. "Take the night to think on it. Perhaps you will feel differently in the morning. The offer stands until noon tomorrow."

CHAPTER SEVEN

A Good Dose of Introspection

*S*hit. *Shit. Shit.*

Rasp's panicked thoughts raced as quickly as his heartbeat. Escape. That's what he would do. He knew the layout of the house well enough. He could steal the key from Faris, slip out the back door, and then sneak away into the night. Alas, even if Rasp managed to do all of that without breaking his neck, he didn't know his way through the surrounding forest. With his luck, he'd stumble right into the protector's encampment. And then what would he do? Slip into Oralia's tent and pretend it was on purpose? It wouldn't be the first time he'd shared a bedroll with the enemy, he supposed.

Shit. Shit. Shit.

"Will you give it a rest already?" Faris's exasperated voice came from the left side of the room. "I can't sleep with your blasted pacing. Go to bed."

Rasp had roomed with Faris since his arrival. Originally, the faun had been helpful. Assisting him in and out of the bunk, getting him dressed, emptying the bedpan. It wasn't until Rasp's strength returned that his roommate's true purpose surfaced. Faris wasn't an aide. He was the damn jailkeeper. What's worse, he was surprisingly decent at it, too.

"Stuff shit in your ears. Maybe that'll help," Rasp said.

The straw mattress shifted under the faun's weight with a dry crunch. "Are you looking for another ass kicking? Because if you are, by all means, continue."

Was he? The Belfast household handled conflict by addressing the issue head on—verbally, of course. Not literally, as that would have been far too brutal for their delicate sensibilities. Rasp had been taught to work through his problems with his fists. Fortunately, Faris was happy to oblige whenever Rasp needed a good dose of physical introspection.

Rasp searched the wall for his bearings. His fingers touched cold glass—the window. The sky outside was a moonless one. On clear nights, the moonlight filtered in and highlighted the dark shapes of their shared bedroom. His surroundings presently were an indiscernible blur of darkness. Rasp rubbed the moisture from the window between his thumb and forefinger, calculating the movements necessary to reach Faris's side of the room without tripping. Fortunately, there wasn't any furniture in the room other than the beds. A result of previous fights gone awry.

Something whistled through the air toward him. Rasp attempted to duck, but the object struck him solidly in the chest all the same. He sucked air between his teeth with a hiss, searching the worn floor for the offending projectile. A boot, he concluded. His boot, specifically, as the faun had no need for them.

"I believe these come in a pair." The second shoe quickly followed. Rasp caught it, laughing. "Ha! Now you don't have anything left to throw at me."

Faris screamed, his voice muffled by the pillow. "Stop talking and go the muck to sleep!"

Rasp banged the hard soles of the boots together obnoxiously. "Can't you see I'm in turmoil? Have a heart, Faris!"

Gods, he really was looking for another fight. Protector Dawnsight had him on edge. More than he'd been in a long time. Rasp needed to expend his nervous energy, else it would manifest in more inconvenient ways.

Noise from the other side of the room alerted him that Faris was on the move. The bedframe groaned as the heavy faun rolled from it. Rasp heard his keeper's hoofed feet scrape the slick wood for traction. Rasp counted the approaching footfalls. They were unusually soft. He heard one. Two. Three. Then nothing.

Faris was launching a sneak attack. Without sight or sound to guide him, Rasp focused on his other senses. Fauns produced a musky odor that, while not completely unpleasant, made them easy to detect. Rasp caught the scent of the nearing faun and spun, whipping the boot in front of him. The shoe connected with a soft thud in what Rasp hoped was Faris's face. Faris cursed and grabbed at Rasp's clothes. His strong fingers scraped along Rasp's rib cage but came up empty. Rasp landed a series of punches to his opponent's unprotected torso before dancing out of range.

Faris went eerily quiet once more. Rasp stomped his foot and snorted. If his matches with the local faun population had taught him anything, it was how to use their mannerisms to his advantage.

Faris's hoof instinctively smacked the ground in response before realizing his mistake. ". . . Crap."

Rasp rushed him. He secured Faris's arms, preventing the faun from striking him, and then hooked his foot behind his opponent's heel. Rasp swept his foot forward, simultaneously pushing Faris backward. The faun's body hit the floor with a muffled thump.

"Dammit! You're getting it now. And don't even think about crying. That won't work this time."

Rasp shifted his weight to his back leg eagerly. "That's right, Dingle. Talk dirty to me. Just how I like it."

"You're the dingle, not me!"

"Talk. Talk. Talk. Are you going to finish me with your fists or your mouth?"

That did it. Pushed over the edge, Faris abandoned all sense of stealth and charged. The sounds of his footsteps reverberated against the walls. Rasp dodged left, but the faun anticipated him. Faris rammed his head into Rasp's gut. He struck the hardwood, head reeling, unable to breathe, certain the faun had shattered his ribs. Faris straddled him, using his powerful legs to squeeze the last of the air from Rasp's lungs.

Rasp made a noise. A squeak, like an animal about to die. He was no animal. He was a damned Stoneclaw! He clawed upward, hands grasping for something, anything to sink his fingernails into. Something cold brushed his hand. Metal? The key! The one Faris kept around his neck. Rasp pulled the chain taut, digging the metal links into the faun's flesh. Faris rewarded him with two solid punches to his bruised rib cage. Tears sprang from Rasp's eyes. His arms fell limp, a pained whimper escaping his mouth.

Faris pinned Rasp's wrists over his head. The faun's weight shifted as he leaned closer. The smell of barley ale lingered on his breath. "Are . . . you . . . finished?"

"No," Rasp gasped. His lungs were on fire. If Faris pressed into him any more he would soon lose consciousness. He forced the words through his splintered teeth. "I'm hardly stiff."

Faris slammed his broad forehead into Rasp's unprotected nose.

Hot blood squirted from his nostrils. Rasp rolled his head back, groaning, "Oh, gods, there it is. Sweet release."

Faris pushed away with a disgusted snort.

From the way the floorboards shook, Rasp suspected his keeper had collapsed onto the ground beside him. A tentative search confirmed the faun was within arm's reach. Rasp found what he hoped was Faris's head. He intertwined his fingers between the faun's shaggy hair, fascinated by the texture. "I needed that. Thank you."

"There is something seriously wrong with you."

"Tell me I drew blood this time," he said wistfully.

Rasp rested his head against the cold floor, savoring the throbbing sensation that spread across his aching face. Pain was an old friend. It brought not only euphoria, but clarity, too. With his mind unburdened, Rasp could finally weigh his options. There was only one logical course. Acceptance.

In the morning, he would agree to Protector Dawnsight's terms. It would take weeks, maybe more, for her to assemble a traveling party. They would need supplies, too. And as Rasp was the supposed expert, he would be sure to suggest as many heavy and unnecessary items as possible. Oralia wasn't an idiot, though. He would have to play his hand carefully. Given enough hardships, perhaps she would realize the Iron Ridge was better left untamed.

CHAPTER EIGHT

Wisdom of the Raven

The house was quiet around him. It was early. Even the cook wouldn't be up for another hour. On the other side of the window, the frostbitten land, too, slept. Soon, the forest would come alive. Rasp had reveled in the idea of enjoying his first spring among the good folk of Lonebrook. The thought bordered on fantasy now. There was no place for a Stoneclaw here, not even a reformed one.

Rasp waited for Faris's throaty snores to fill the room. He eased from his cot, wincing. Movement, any movement, be it sitting, standing, or breathing, made his ribs ache. Rasp slung the woven blanket over his shoulders and limped forward, slipping his coat from its hook by the door. He didn't bother with shoes. They'd gotten misplaced during the brawl and he didn't want to wake Faris searching for them. He reached into his trousers, relieved to find the key still tucked along his waistband. After several tries, he wedged it successfully into the lock and turned the knob. The door opened with a creak. Rasp froze, as if staying still would somehow spare him from Faris's impending wrath. To his relief, the faun only snored louder.

Rasp softly closed the door behind him and then staggered toward the front of the house. Cold floorboards creaked underfoot. The hallway stretched endlessly, leading him past the guest quarters, kitchen, and eventually into the foyer. Rasp explored the front door with his hands. The deadbolt was located lower than on a standard human door. To accommodate a faun's height, he supposed. With a simple twist of the polished handle, Rasp was outside.

His toes curled in protest, finding the porch covered in a fine dusting of frost. Should have brought his damn shoes after all. Rasp proceeded cautiously, sliding his soles across the stone, mindful of the oncoming steps. He made it down the first without incident. Content to go no farther, Rasp laid the blanket over the stone and eased onto it, tucking his frozen toes beneath him for warmth.

The air stirred. Rasp listened for other movements, but heard only the creak and groan of the birch trees. He put his fingers to his lips and blew. Rasp repeated the whistle twice more and then waited. A flutter of wings responded. Soft feathers brushed against his left ear as the bird landed, its sharp claws digging into his shoulder.

The raven nuzzled his neck affectionately.

"Hello, Mother." Rasp searched his coat pocket for coins and offered one to the bird. "Silver for your thoughts?"

The raven snapped its bill in agreement.

Rasp tilted his head and listened to the rustling flap of the others. He heard the flock land around him, the *skitter-pat-pat* of their clawed feet as they hopped along the stone. Several of the more impatient members pecked at his clothes.

"Did you have to bring the whole family?" He fished the fistful of coins from his pocket. At this rate there wouldn't be any left for him. A small price, he supposed. He needed all the wisdom he could get. "Mind the fingers," he grumbled, offering the pieces of silver one at a time. He continued until every snapping maw had collected its payment.

His debt settled, Rasp told them his troubles. "It's Protector Dawnsight. She's going to drag me back to the ridge. The realm plans to reinstate me into power. They want a path through for their trouble, too."

The ravens voiced their disapproval.

"I know that. Refusal isn't exactly an option."

Croak!

"Tell her the prophecy? Oh, great suggestion, guys. Really. That won't make me sound crazy at all." Rasp didn't understand much about destiny, but this felt more like the overzealous wantings of the realm. Not fate. "Besides, Oralia doesn't strike me as the believing type."

Fate had driven Rasp from the Iron Ridge. When he first awoke, emaciated and weak from the mountain's justice, Rasp realized the gift he'd been given. Rebirth. His previous life had been an immoral one, even by Stoneclaw standards. Fate had spared him to mend the error of his ways. Why in the realm would it demand he return now?

A raven hopped onto his knee and produced a repetitive click from the back of its throat.

"Speak her language? How would that help?" Rasp knew a few words of the most common orc tongue. He doubted the protector would appreciate being called a corpse sodomizer, though.

The raven croaked harshly at his ignorance.

"Oh, I see. The name-calling wasn't necessary, by the way." Rasp scratched at the dry trickle of blood clogging his left nostril. His nose was swollen and puffy, but the cold predawn air was beginning to lessen the overall sting. "Go on then. Tell me more."

The ravens argued back and forth among themselves. It wasn't until Rasp noticed the soft light growing around him that he realized the hour. Sunrise. *Shit.* He didn't get the chance to sneak back inside. The front door opened and shut with a slam. The ravens skittered around him, giving the approaching hooves a cautious berth.

"Count yourself fortunate." Trant's voice sounded gruffer than usual. "The protector assigned a watch over the house last night. Her soldiers had orders to intercept the moment you left the porch."

"Well then, I'm sorry to disappoint."

"She told them to use arrows, if necessary."

Rasp twisted his head in the judge's direction, scowling. "And they accuse me of being the violent one?"

"Gods, boy! Your face."

There was a swift rustle of clothes and then Trant was kneeling beside him. Rasp could make out the judge's blurred shape as his hands reached out and felt along Rasp's swollen nose. The sudden warmth stung his frostbitten skin. Rasp's instinct was to respond with a snap of his teeth, but he didn't. He stubbornly twisted his head in the other direction instead.

"What happened?"

"Lovers' quarrel."

There was a brief pause. Followed by a long, exasperated sigh. The old faun took Rasp under the arm and yanked him upright. For a person older than time, Trant was surprisingly strong. "Walk," he grunted. "Getting beat senseless will not shirk you of your duties. The protector is expecting an answer by midday. I hope you've thought this through."

CHAPTER NINE

The Viper's Bargain

Rasp was already in the study when Oralia and her officers arrived. He sat poised with his back straight and fingers laced together, expression impossibly blank. Yesterday she'd bargained with a boy. Today, he was a snake. Any fear Oralia had instilled the day before was gone. If it weren't for the Stoneclaw's distinct features, Oralia would have sworn this was a different human entirely.

A table had been brought in from another room. Rasp sat on one end with his back to the stone hearth. The chair intended for Oralia was across from him. Even in the company of allies, she never left her back exposed to the door. Rasp had done this purposely, no doubt. Oralia took a stool from along the yellow wall and placed it to his right. If it was power games the boy wanted, she could play, too.

Ellisar dropped into the seat intended for Oralia and placed her worn boots onto the table, absolutely indifferent to the disapproving look from Judge Belfast. Rali was more selective with her choice of furniture. After carefully considering all possibilities, she opted for the overstuffed chair by the hearth and dragged it all the way around the table behind her. The padded legs scraped softly against the hardwood.

Rali aligned her seat next to Oralia's and set about fluffing the feather pillows. "Oh my gods." She sank deep into the nest of cushions. "Tie the damn chair to my pony, I'm never getting up again."

"Did you bring friends, Protector?" Along with his demeanor, Rasp's voice had changed as well. This difference, however, was explained by the discolored line that bridged his nose and pooled beneath each swollen eye. "I'm told you keep unusual company. Are they going to rough me up if I decline?"

"I don't mean to be insulting here, bucko, but from the state of your face, it looks like someone beat us to it." Rali's muffled voice came from somewhere underneath the colorful mound of pillows. The only visible trace of the dwarf was her stubby legs and boots sticking out near the lip of the chair.

"My officers are here to serve as official witnesses." Oralia formally introduced them. "That is my first officer, Lieutenant Quartz Ralizak, who was just speaking. Sergeant Ellisar Farrow is seated at the table across from you. She will be making notes of today's meeting."

A polite cough from Judge Belfast drew her attention. Trant was situated at his writing desk, wrapped in a garment that may or may not have been a fluffy bathrobe. He had a supply of paper and quill at the ready. "Rasp requested that I record today's negotiations as well."

"Excellent," Oralia replied, silently relieved. Ellisar's notetaking took brevity to the extreme and usually amounted to little more than: *They talked for hours. It was boring.*

Ellisar was in the midst of balancing her notepad on her forehead when she heard this. She was up and halfway out the door before the back of her chair struck the hardwood floor with a resounding clatter. "Thank goddess. Suck it, Rali. I'm out."

"Sergeant Farrow, I have not dismissed you yet." To a stranger, Oralia's tone sounded nothing short of pleasant. To Ellisar, who was versed in all of Oralia's tones, particularly the bad ones, it said, *Return to the table or I will tie you to that blasted chair myself.*

One of the pillows near the top of Rali's pile lifted away, allowing the dwarf's brown, glittering eyes to peek through. "Oof," she said with a cluck of her tongue. "Still in timeout, it seems. It might benefit you to learn how to grovel properly."

Ellisar picked the chair up from the floor and sat, folding her arms across her tight-fitted jerkin. The shirt she was supposed to be wearing underneath was absent, rendering visible the weave of scars and questionable tattoos that decorated her arms. "It was one measly cock. I don't see what the fuss is."

There was a nervous snort from the far corner of the room. Judge Belfast dipped his quill into the inkwell and proceeded to strike his previous line from the record. "For the sake of whomever reads this, I will omit that disturbing detail."

"She means a rooster." With a shake of her shoulders, Lieutenant Ralizak sent her pillow fortress tumbling down around her. She twisted around and placed a single cushion at the small of her back, allowing her to reach the table. "You really should stop phrasing it that way, El."

Ellisar carried on as though she hadn't heard the others. "Wandered right up to me while I was on watch. It was going to give my position away with all its obnoxious crowing. How was I supposed to know it was a pet? If anything, I did them a favor. Damn thing was practically begging to be put out of its misery."

"Offering to cook it for the owners was a nice touch."

Ellisar narrowed her golden eyes at Rali. "They insisted on burying it. Waste of food, if you ask me."

It was only partially true that Ellisar was here as punishment. Though the rooster incident, regretfully, was not a fabrication, the real reason Oralia demanded Sergeant Farrow's presence was for shock value. The elf didn't bother with pretenses. Or basic decorum. Combine that with Rali's sharp mind and even sharper tongue, and the two would provoke one another into obscenity until the entire room was nervously eyeing the exit. Oralia had discovered that if she put the pair at the table during negotiations, her opponent would forget all prior sense of strategy. Negotiations were about having the upper hand, and Oralia intended to tip the scale in her favor any way possible.

As far as roles went, Oralia's was straightforward. She was the voice of reason; the foil to Rali and Ellisar's escalating antics. With the room now uncomfortably silent, Oralia knew it was her move. She folded her hands primly on the table. "Have you reached a decision, Rasp?"

"Are you sure your people don't want to talk about cocks some more first?" he asked. "I don't mind, really. It happens to be a favorite subject of mine."

Rasp seemed strangely immune to Ellisar and Rali's tactics. Such crass behavior normally had the other party squirming in their chairs by now. This was going to be more difficult than Oralia had hoped. Regardless, if there was anyone who could get the boy to crack, it would be these two. "Your answer to yesterday's proposal will suffice, thank you."

He spoke as though he was reciting from memory. "After much consideration, I realize I can't come to a true decision without knowing the master plan first. It would be foolish to agree to something so, shall we say, blindly?"

Having grown bored of arranging her pillows, Rali had turned to re-braiding her hair to pass the time. What had previously been a sensible loose plait was slowly transforming into a crown braid. She looked across at Rasp, her fingers working the thick strands of black hair in and out and over one another with effortless precision. "That's easy. You tell us how to get up the mountain. That's as much of the plan as you need to know."

He leaned in her direction with his chin cupped in his hands and smiled. "Well then, I advise you walk. There, see? I can be needlessly vague, too."

There was a loud, disruptive clatter. Oralia's gaze shifted from the pair of iron pliers that had appeared on the tabletop next to their owner. "You heard him." Ellisar's silvery eyebrows perked in Oralia's direction as the edge of her mouth pulled into an eager snarl. "Sounded like a *no* to me."

"El, you found your pliers," Rali congratulated. "What a relief. Watching you pull fingernails off with your teeth last time really upset my appetite."

"I wasn't finished!" Rasp's voice raised ever so slightly in pitch as he rushed through the rest of his prepared material. "The issue is, I don't think the realm actually has a plan. At least not a well-thought-out one. And that they sent you, Madam Protector, here to strongarm me into agreeing, with the intention of drawing one up later."

Oralia's gaze darted to Trant. He held his palms up innocently. As if the Stoneclaw's sudden clarity was as much of a surprise to him as it was to her.

Her silence gave Rasp the assurance he needed. He took a breath and then continued, more slowly this time. "Before you let your secretary draw and quarter me, at least hear me out. You put me in a very difficult position. If I refuse your offer, I die. If I blindly accept, you march us up the mountain under a half-cocked plan and we all die. Do you see my issue? Unless you are prepared to offer concrete evidence of an actual strategy, my decision is irrelevant. I'm dead. You're dead. Everyone's dead."

Rali leaned closer to Oralia and whispered, "He means poorly prepared. He's not actually talking about his privates this time."

Rasp waited. When Oralia provided no answer, he rapped his knuckles against the table and sighed. "I'm willing to work with you, but I need some sort of assurance that the realm knows what it's asking of me. Saying you'll get a small army up the Iron Ridge is a lot different than actually doing it."

Ellisar squinted across the table at Oralia. "I thought you said he was stupid."

"Nah, that's what the advisors said." Rali spoke around the hairpin in her mouth. There were a handful of others spread out on the table in front of her. Where they'd appeared from, Oralia hadn't noticed. "Boss said she couldn't tell if he was actually stupid or just really convincing at playing the part."

Oralia resisted the urge to kick Rali under the table. It wouldn't do any good, as the damage was already done and Ralizak's feet hung far too high off the ground for Oralia to reach. She focused on keeping her tone amicable instead.

"Admittedly, much of the strategy is still in the preliminary stages, yes. Without insider knowledge of the Iron Ridge, the realm is unsure how to proceed. The advisors insisted that once we reached an agreement, we could devise a sensible approach together."

"Now really, was that so hard?" Rasp's devilish smile was back, taunting her. "In light of your honesty, I shall grant you the same. What you're proposing will be difficult, possibly deadly, but not impossible. I can guarantee one thing. Without my help, you will fail. Therefore, I am issuing a counteroffer. Agree to my terms, and I'll save both you and the realm from looking like complete idiots."

Where was this viper yesterday? Oralia found herself wishing the advisors were here. Not to advise, of course. Rasp had proved them wrong at every turn so far. No, she wanted them to see firsthand the "naïve" boy they had believed the Stoneclaw to be. Had Oralia not been the one they sent to broker the deal, she would have found it humorous.

Ellisar set her notepad aside. The top page consisted of two lines and what looked like several crude drawings. "Plier time?" She reached for the set on the table. The pliers were small. The leather grips on the handles had been worn down from years of use and the once gleaming jaws were now an unsettling reddish-brown color. "I'm not limited to fingernails. They work just as well on teeth."

"I will hear him out first," Oralia said. "Continue, Rasp."

Instead of getting straight to the point, the damn boy felt the need to demonstrate just how fucked they would be without him. Rasp took his time listing the hidden dangers of the Iron Ridge. From the dragons, to the bears and wolves, all the way down to the mosquitoes, he painted each and every one in great detail. Alas, it did not stop there. Evidently the mountain folk were not only great warriors, but inventors, too. The entire range was set with booby traps just waiting for an unwary trespasser to stumble into.

"Let's pretend by some hand of fate, you reach the village with your company intact, Protector," Rasp carried on. "Which would be a miracle on its own, considering you don't know which peak it's on. What happens when you lose the element of surprise? My people don't live in freestanding houses. Our homes are burrowed into the mountain. The clan spends all summer storing food for the winter. All they have to do is seal the caves and wait for the cold season to kill you. If the bears don't see to it first, that is."

The war council was lacking in nearly all of its information. It was a wonder they had managed to even identify the Stoneclaw correctly. "You have made your point," Oralia said reluctantly. "Am I to understand that if the realm agrees to your terms, you will furnish us with the needed information?"

"Precisely." Rasp spread his hands over the table palm-side up. "But if you want the keys to the Iron Ridge, you're going to have to offer me more than a crown."

CHAPTER TEN

Emergency Use Only

This serpent had fangs, it seemed. Oralia didn't know whether to be impressed or annoyed by Rasp's sudden backbone. "Alright, Stoneclaw. Get it over with then."

"I demand a voice in your ear, for one. If I make a suggestion, I expect consideration. It benefits me to reach the summit with as much of your force intact as much as it does you. Secondly, I require a residing presence to remain afterward. Your trade routes only last as long as I do. Silver-haired or not, the mountain folk will kill me if you pull your army too soon. My people will need time to adjust."

Doable so far. They would have difficulty finding volunteers to remain on the ridge afterward, but a lottery would solve that.

"Once your supply routes are established, I will require an annual percentage. Thirty should do nicely. Payment will be accepted in the form of goods. Food, steel, wool, what-have-you."

Oralia raised her eyebrows. A futile expression, she realized, as the Stoneclaw wouldn't notice. "I have limited say in how the realm dictates its resources."

"Which is precisely the reason I asked the judge to take notes," Rasp replied shortly. "A single head of the realm can't barter the takeover of an enemy territory without consulting the other two. Even I know that. You will send my terms to the Leader and the Speaker of the People. If they want passage badly enough, the three of you will agree."

The realm would never agree to thirty percent. They would counter with a lower offer and the two would go back and forth until an agreement was struck. It would take weeks. Months even. And the damn Stoneclaw knew it, too. He was buying time. Though for what, Oralia wasn't sure.

Regrettably, Rasp's demands only grew more ridiculous from there. He wanted a statue made up of him and put on display in the capital, commemorating the peace between their lands. He also requested the realm find him a suitable wife. A woman from a good family and of high standing. One unopposed to living on the mountain, of course. And a chef, too. For his future wife, not him. To ensure that his bride was kept, in Rasp's own words, "fat and happy."

Rali and Ellisar gave it their best, but the Stoneclaw's resolve was unshakable. Rasp welcomed their abhorrent behavior. He played the game just as well as them, escalating the vulgarity until it reached the point even Oralia was repulsed. Was it possible that he was as twisted as them? Oralia had assumed the Iron Devil's reputation had been a heavily falsified one. In hindsight, this had been the wrong move. She should have made the meeting as rigid and formal as possible.

Oralia looked to the ceiling, exhausted. "Is that all?"

"One last item. In addition to my other terms, I would like to make several personnel requests for the expedition. Hunters, gatherers, and such. In the event we're delayed and rations run low, we will need experienced foragers. As Lonebrook is the most similar in terms of terrain, plant, and animal life, I would suggest recruiting them from the local community."

Trant's head jerked upright. "What?"

"Oh, and Faris Belfast." A smirk, so small it was nearly indistinguishable, pulled at the corner of Rasp's thin mouth. "With the loss of my vision, I'll need a personal aid for travel. As Faris and I have a current working relationship, he's my first choice."

"Absolutely not!" Trant slammed his fist onto the top of his desk, causing the stack of loose parchment to jump several inches into the air. "He is a civilian. The realm cannot force him into service."

Ellisar started to rise, but a shake of Oralia's head sat her back down again. "The judge has a point, Rasp. The most I can do is ask."

Rasp stood and pushed in his chair, allowing the wooden legs to scrape against the floor with an unpleasant screech. "Faris has been pining to get out of Lonebrook for years. Silver is all the convincing he'll need."

The old faun leapt to his feet, bellowing, "After everything I've done for you! This is how you repay me? You devise the death of my son?"

"It's not my plan. It's hers. I'm only trying to make it feasible." Rasp walked forward with one hand stretched in front of him and the other wrapped over his ribcage. There was a noticeable limp in his stride. He paused at the door, adding, "I can't help but notice you think it doomed, Judge Belfast. Feel free to add that in the notes if you wish. I'm sure the realm would appreciate your expert opinion."

Oralia hadn't excused Rasp, but she wasn't going to stop him, either. The Stoneclaw had created enough problems for her already. She didn't need to invite more by demanding he stay. "Lieutenant Ralizak, Sergeant Farrow, ensure that he is delivered to his keeper safely. The chair stays here, Ralizak." Rali lifted her hands innocently. "Thank you." Oralia waited for their footsteps to recede before addressing Trant through her teeth. "Who counseled him?"

"No one."

"Impossible." Either the warmth from the hearth had increased significantly, or her anger had leapt to her face. Oralia's slate-colored skin was hot to the touch and had taken on an unbecoming violet glow. "The watch saw him on the front steps before dawn. He must have spoken to someone."

"He was arguing with the ravens. That in itself isn't usual."

"These birds," Oralia said, "could they have been carrying a message? Is he using them to communicate with an outside party?"

"And how would that work? Does he consume the scroll to decipher the message? He is blind, Oralia. Don't turn this into a conspiracy. You underestimated the competency of your opponent. That is all." Trant made a pained face as he glared down at his work. "I am guilty of the same."

Trade was the only reason the realm had taken on this mission. Despite their lofty talks of peace, Oralia knew it was greed, not harmony, that motivated her fellow figureheads. Rasp's terms presented the others with an opportunity to decide whether it was worth keeping him on. If the boy demanded too much, the realm could nix him and claim the entire range for themselves, instead.

Oralia didn't have the will for another pointless war. A deadly coup, maybe, but it would be her last. After this, she was done. The politics, the games, the relentless tit for tat, over with. Some of the weight in her chest lifted just thinking of it.

Oralia looked to Trant, noting the way his fingers wore at the edge of his desk. "It was not my intention to involve your people. But Rasp has a point. I will need individuals who know how to survive off the land."

His amber eyes flicked upward. "Then you had best pay their families upfront."

Damn the Stoneclaw. Damn him. Damn him. Damn him! Judge Belfast had only been reluctant before. Mildly vocal in his disapproval, yes. But now—now he was almost hostile. "Say what you mean to say, Trant."

"I supplied Rasp. That was my only condition in this. My people are not soldiers. My son, despite what he thinks, is no warrior. I have already lost two children to war." The faun's hoof smacked against the hardwood. His eyes were large and his nostrils flared. "I will not allow another to be sacrificed in the name of the realm!"

"If the realm agrees to these terms, then I am bound by oath to ask. That does not mean I have to be persuasive."

The fight left Trant's face and he appeared old once more. He sank back into his chair with a distant look in his eye. "You won't have to be persuasive. He follows Rasp like a scavenger. I paired them hoping it would teach Faris some blasted responsibility. I thought maybe if he saw firsthand what happens when you go down the wrong path, he'd finally do something with his life. I never expected them to *bond*."

"And if you forbid Faris's involvement?"

"He will only run up that mountain all the faster," Trant said. "That's a trait of mankind, you know. They live such short lifespans they form bonds quickly. It's contagious, unfortunately. To be honest, I didn't think Rasp was capable of something so . . . human."

Oralia sensed the conversation coming to a close. Or perhaps it was simply that she wanted it to end. She rose, tucking the stool back alongside the wall as she strode for the exit. "I will keep your son safe, Trant."

The old faun chewed his lip and watched her go. "Don't make promises you can't keep, Madam Protector. I have heard that one too many times before."

The hallway was empty as she walked it. The homely, yeasty smell of rising bread wafted in from the kitchen. Oralia saw no one inside as she passed. Certain she was alone, she reached into the front of her tunic and grasped the pendant that hung below her collar. The opal felt warm in her hand. Oralia tapped it twice and then dropped it back into place. She was crossing the green and brown foyer toward the front door when the pendant pulsed back.

Once . . . twice . . .

By the time the pendant died back down again, Oralia counted three distinct energy pulses. The code was straightforward. One pulse meant "I am unavailable to speak." Two was "Now is good." And three, "Give me time to scurry somewhere dark and abandoned to ensure we are not overheard."

Several strides later, Oralia was out the door and across the damp courtyard. The sun had made its long-overdue appearance and hung high in the sky above her. A gang of rowdy children played on the grassy knoll on the far side of Belfast Manor. Oralia started. A second glance confirmed what her eyes had refused to believe on the first pass. Darting among the happily shrieking children was a familiar shape: Snag, barely a green and tan blur, jumped and tumbled alongside them. The goblin was performing acrobatic feats Oralia had only ever seen in trapeze acts in order to evade their sticky, marmalade clutches. From his ragged laughter, she wasn't sure who was enjoying it more.

Several concerned parents watched along the sidelines. Judging from their stances, they were uneasy allowing their precious offspring to play not only with any member of the faithful four, but this one, specifically. Oralia knew the type. When pressed, they would ramble on about safety, and bad influences, and doing everything in their power to avoid the words "because he's a baby-snatching goblin."

The sight made Oralia grind her tusks against the flat of her upper teeth. She would not have to intervene on his behalf this time, fortunately. Curly was also on scene. He stood shoulder to shoulder with the adults, laughing, swapping stories, silently daring one of them to be the first to say something. Content that Curly could handle at least this, Oralia stepped into the adjoining woods as the sounds of laughter faded in the distance. The smell of spruce and wet moss grew thicker as she plunged deeper into the dark forest.

Once certain she was alone, Oralia unclasped the pendant from around her neck, held it in her hand, and waited. The stone glowed a brilliant shade of sapphire blue, bathing the shaggy trees in its unearthly glow. Magic radiated from the gem, traveled up Oralia's arms, and rippled across her mind in the form of a melodic voice. **This stone is for emergency use only. If you think I'm going to sit through another drunk retelling of your nightly escapades, you've got another thing—**

Oralia placed one hand over her eyes, groaning, "Hello to you, too, Dear Whisper."

Oh, it's you. I thought maybe you were the dwarf. Whisper cleared their throat before offering an official-sounding, **You summoned, old friend?**

"I will keep this brief. I know your time is valuable," Oralia said. "Negotiations for the Iron Ridge pass have begun. I will need your eyes and ears in court. When an arrangement is struck, ride with the convoy that departs for Lonebrook. They will place a spy within the camp. Discover all that you can."

As you wish.

"And, Whisper." Oralia found the words strangely difficult to say. She had waited sixty-eight years for this moment. Somehow, it still felt unreal to her. "This will be my final request."

CHAPTER ELEVEN

A Self-Fulfilling Prophecy

Dirt shifted underfoot with a dry crunch. Twigs snapped and leaves rustled as Rasp trotted along the forest path. He heard songbirds too, barely, over the sound of his own rasping breath. Faris's breathing, by comparison, was light and easy. There were many things that rubbed Rasp the wrong way, but this one, in particular, was especially annoying. He'd spent the last six months thinking he and Faris were close, if not matched, for speed. As it turned out, the faun had been playing him all along. "You're easier to deal with when you think you're winning" was the answer Faris provided.

The exercise was the protector's idea. Oralia had Rasp on what she lovingly referred to as a "health regimen." Three hearty meals a day, endurance training, hiking, running—all while lugging a pack, of course. As if, for some reason, she expected him to need half a house's worth of belongings for the trip. Stoneclaws traveled light: a cloak, a flint, and something sharp to stab with. Considering they still didn't trust him to cut his own dinner, Rasp doubted they'd afford him anything sharper than a spoon.

Despite his attempts to stall progress, the sendoff date loomed. The realm was eager for their trade routes, and negotiations went much quicker than Rasp expected. The heads agreed to most of his conditions—no statue, however, and the thirty percent had been whittled down to a modest eight. The promise of a wife and cook would be fulfilled only after the trade route was established. It took four back and forths before the realm settled. Rasp would have pushed for more but, as the protector already suspected him of purposefully delaying negotiations, he was forced to concede. That was six weeks ago. Since then, the last of the ice had melted and spring was quickly merging into summer. As soon as the realm's additional forces arrived, they would be off.

"Branch on your left. Three paces," Faris said, pulling the tether that connected them.

Rasp found it three steps later, noting it felt less like a branch and more akin to a tree as his foot caught and he stumbled over it face-first into the dirt. The rope lead pulled Faris down with him.

"Gods, Rasp!" The faun's sharp elbows and knees jostled against him as Faris untangled them. "That's the second time! What's the point of giving directions if you're not going to follow?"

"I was in my head, sorry." Rasp eased into a sitting position. His palms were scraped and the rope had dug into his waist, but other than that he was unhurt. A shame. He wondered if there were any reasonably tall cliffs nearby.

"Liar. You're trying to break something, aren't you?"

Rasp, taken aback by the sudden and strangely accurate nature of Faris's accusation, dismissed it with a wave of his hand. "You're reading way too much into this. I didn't hear you and tripped. The end."

"Oh really?" Faris leaned close enough for Rasp to feel the faun's hot breath against his face. Breakfast had been a hearty bowl of oats and dried berries, according to Rasp's sense of smell. His keeper had gone and spoiled himself with the fancy clover honey, too. "Because from here it looks like you don't actually want anything to do with your reinstatement," Faris carried on. "And for the life of me, I can't figure out why. You get to be king of your kingdom and line your pockets with the realm's money. What more could you ask for?"

"Tell you what, Dingle. You take it," Rasp said, patting the faun's cheek affectionately. "Silver hair? White hair? Close enough for my people."

His keeper's voice hardened. "Was that an albino joke?"

"Gods, no. We have a deal, remember? I don't make fun of your skin and you don't tease me for my enormous cock."

Faris didn't talk about his albinism much. It got brought up sometimes by the other villagers often in jest. Depending on the level of offense, the faun either smacked the ignorance out of the offender or ignored it. Rasp suspected Faris's temperament was the reason they'd been paired together. Years of torment had left the faun thick-skinned. No matter what Rasp said, so long as it wasn't about his skin color, Faris was largely unbothered by insults. And, in the event Rasp needed to be reminded of his place, correction was delivered swiftly and without fuss.

"I'm right though, aren't I?" Faris kept at it despite Rasp's attempts to change the subject. "You requested me because you knew it would pit my father against the protector. Everything you've done has been to slow her down. Why?"

This was approaching dangerous territory. Only the ravens knew Rasp's intentions. Everyone else, including Faris, was the enemy. "Even if what you're saying were true—and it's not, by the way, I'm making that perfectly clear," Rasp said. "Why in the realm would I tell you? The judge's son? Would that not seem counterintuitive?"

"Because it's more lucrative to befriend the future king than appease my father. I already have his unconditional love. Power and money sounds more fun."

"Well then, I hate to disappoint." Rasp stood, stretching his legs. "But there won't be any power or money."

Faris pulled him back down with the tether. "Why not?"

Rasp landed on his ass and grimaced. "Because we're not making it to the top of that mountain."

"Then why have you convinced the realm otherwise? Isn't it in your contract to do just that?"

Was he really doing this? Rasp had never confided in anyone before, not even his own people. Maybe that's where he had gone wrong. Perhaps he needed a confidant to guide him. Dare he say it? A friend? The word was like soot in his mouth. Still, if there was anyone in all the realm he trusted, it was Faris. Sort of.

Rasp rolled his head back, sighing. "I only agreed because I thought I could get them to back down. Costs, resources, a damn percentage of their trade. I had hoped it would be enough for them to realize it was a stupid idea. They're too blinded by their own greed to realize they're walking into a death trap. My goal now, as you so brilliantly observed, is to prevent the expedition from moving forward. Or, if I can't manage that, find a way to turn it back before everyone's dead."

"Why?"

Rasp's hands shot into the air with exasperation. "Because I'm trying this whole 'be a good person' thing, Faris! Preventing people from dying a gruesome death is apparently a really big part of that."

"No, Dinglehead," Faris said. "Saving people is obvious. You've been promised everything a sane person could possibly want. Why are you trying to make it fail?"

Shit. Here it was. The part where he sounded crazy. He could lie, he supposed. But that seemed pointless, as Faris had a knack for seeing right through him. "There is a prophecy among my people. It states that the sixth son born of a powerful leader will inherit the silver-hair and bring his people, and possibly the world, to ruin." Rasp hung his head as his stomach tied itself in knots. "I think that might be me. And the only way I can prevent it from happening is to stay away. Which was working perfectly, by the way, until that very persistent orc showed up."

"So by bringing the realm up the mountain, you're basically bringing about the end of your people, yeah?"

"Something like that, yes."

"Talk about self-fulfilling."

"Precisely."

CHAPTER TWELVE

Poison

A breeze drifted between them, stirring the air with the smells of the forest. Rasp breathed in soil, and bark, and the sticky sweet fragrance of fawn lilies. A part of him wanted to stay forever. Meanwhile, a second, much larger part of him, wanted to retch the contents of his churning stomach onto the ground.

"You know my plan now," he said, kicking himself for opening his blasted mouth. Stoneclaws didn't do vulnerable, especially not when the truth had the power to rip the ground out from under them. "You also know I don't have the funds to buy you off, either. Will you tell?"

"Nah." Faris was chewing something. A twig, likely, from the audible crunch. "The protector scares me. I still can't string a cohesive sentence together in front of her. Plus, Father's working on his own sabotage. Throwing you in quicksand, mainly. I wouldn't go anywhere alone with him for a while."

"How pacifistic of him," Rasp murmured. "I didn't have a choice in this. I threw out as many stops as I could and nothing's worked. He could have pushed the realm harder, you know."

Faris stood, tugging the tether for Rasp to follow suit. "I suspect he will push plenty when he gets you near the bog."

This was his life now. Being led along like a pet on a leash. Rasp grasped the lead and yanked back. Not hard, only enough to let his guide know that he wouldn't follow him. "You can prevent this," he said, his mind racing. His heart thumped loudly in his ears. Sweat trickled down his forehead. This was it. Now or never. He had to at least try. "Take me away from here. Just you and me. You know the forest better than the protector's people. Get us out and I will find a way to repay you, I swear."

"I'm going to act like you didn't ask that."

"Please, Faris. There is darkness on that mountain, more than you realize. I can't go back."

"Look"—Faris emphasized his point with a sharp tug of the rope—"try to stall the protector all you like. I don't care. I get paid regardless. But you will not involve me in your schemes. Is that understood?"

Hope sank lower in his chest. So much for a confidant. Rasp realized he had been stupid. It was foolish to expect a good folk like Faris to see him as anything more than an underhanded Stoneclaw. "No."

"Excuse me?"

"I don't understand." Rasp held his arms out from his sides invitingly. "Teach me."

The faun snorted. "You mean beat you? And what, break something in the process? A leg, preferably, I imagine. I'm not daft, Dinglehead. Forget it."

"Pasty, lily-livered little fuck. You're scared, aren't you?" The protector's health regimen had at least one positive effect—Rasp had returned to his former strength. His body was no longer skin stretched taut over bones, but thick with muscle and meat. The villagers had stopped pitting themselves against him in the ring. Rasp had taken to challenging Oralia's soldiers instead.

"That's cute," Faris said. Rasp felt the lead jerk as his keeper started off without him. "Come on, we've got another two miles to go. Try to keep pace this time. You've been lagging."

Reluctantly, Rasp followed. By his own stupid actions he'd become a pet. A trained animal led about by a leash for all the realm to mock. An ugliness filled him, starting in the pit of his stomach and spreading until it was poison, not blood, that pumped through his veins. Rasp's fingers curled into a fist at his side.

Magic buzzed across his skin, gathering in his fingertips until they burned as hot as his rage.

Rasp slowed as much as the lead would allow without pulling. With his blood boiling, he threw his hand into the air, fingers held wide. He heard the soil rip apart ahead of him and the splinter of wood as a tree root tore upward from beneath the ground. A split second later, Faris yelped and the tether lurched, nearly bringing Rasp with it. Rasp braced against the weight and kept his footing.

"What the muck was that?" Faris's voice was more startled than accusatory. "Damn root came out of nowhere! How are you still standing?"

"It came out of nowhere? Really? Methinks the Dingle wasn't paying attention," Rasp replied, shaking the last of the sting from his fingertips. The branches above him rustled and a raven croaked its disapproval. Rasp lifted his head in its direction, scowling. "Don't you start! I'm not in the mood."

"Must you argue with the blasted bird right now?" Faris's pained voice came from somewhere on the ground to his right.

"Don't speak about Mother that way."

"You know what? Forget I asked. I've entertained enough of your craziness today. We're going back. Help me up."

Rasp followed the lead to Faris's position on the ground. He reached out, purposely missing the faun's outstretched hand twice. Faris caught Rasp's wrist on the third pass and heaved his weight upward. Rasp considered falling on top of him, but decided against it. He'd pushed his luck enough for one day. Any more, and Faris might turn him in to the protector.

"You hurt?" Rasp at least tried to sound concerned.

"You would like that, wouldn't you? It was just a tumble. I'll be fine."

Croak!

Rasp whipped his head upward once more. "You can't be serious. They're here? Already?"

The raven snapped its bill twice.

"Shit." Even without the aid of sight, Rasp could feel Faris watching him. "It's impolite to stare."

"You're the crazy person talking to birds. It can't be helped. And now you're involving me, because I want to know what the blasted thing said."

Rasp considered keeping it to himself, but ultimately, it didn't matter. Faris would see for himself the moment they returned to the house. Rasp ran his calloused hand over his face, sighing, "The convoy from the capital has arrived."

"Well then." From the way the tether jostled, there was a sudden spring in the faun's step that had been missing before. "Let's not keep them waiting. Fresh bodies and coin. I hope you're still in the mood for a fight, Dinglehead. We're going to have ourselves a proper sendoff."

CHAPTER THIRTEEN

Death Can't Be Far Now

The carriage rocked along the dirt road. Every bump and jostle reminded Daana how painfully close her bladder was to bursting. She crossed and uncrossed her legs, focusing her attention on the journal in hand. It was no use. She'd read the same passage four times already and retained none of it. The view from the carriage window did not offer much in the way of a distraction. The passing scenery was mostly trees. Tall, scraggly needled trees. Thin, straight trees with white bark that flaked along the edges like chipped paint. Dead trees. Fallen trees. Trees, trees, and more trees. Some days the forest was so dense, she'd go hours without glimpsing sunlight.

Willem sat across from her, watching her from the corner of his eye through heavy lashes. "Are you unwell, Lady Lazuli?"

The left wheel hit a low spot, sparing him from her wrathful glare. With her hand braced against the ceiling, Daana managed to mimic his formality between small breaths. "Perfectly fine, sir. Thank you."

"This is what happens when you have a third tea with breakfast."

It took effort not to call him the first nasty name that sprang to mind. Not in the mood to be the recipient of another of Willem's tiresome lectures, Daana returned to her reading instead. "Just indigestion."

She hoped it would be enough to shut the old killjoy up, but alas, it was not so. With a dreary sigh, Willem reached for the door. "I'll tell the driver to stop."

"No!" Daana sat higher on the bench, grasping her skirts. The musty smell that hung thick in the carriage had permeated her clothes and hair. Even in the sparse moments she was allowed fresh air, free of her wooden cage, she could not escape the scent of confinement. Liberation, fortunately, was not far. According to the soldiers she'd overheard at breakfast, the traveling party would reach their destination by noon. Daana would ditch the carriage after that. The prissy skirts, too. It was a pity she could not do the same with Willem. "We're almost there. I can hold it."

"Lady Lazuli, please. Don't be ridiculous."

"I'm being ridiculous? Me? No, *he* is the one being ridiculous. I should be allowed to pee without some pervert watching!"

In the wilderness, safety trumped privacy. According to Captain Monk, anyway—the officer charged with leading the realm's supplementary forces to Lonebrook, where the protector awaited them with their guide. Since leaving Sunstorn, Daana had not been allowed out of sight for any reason, not even to relieve herself. She had never traveled under such harsh restrictions before and found it not only hindersome, but rage-inducing. This was precisely the reason she never used her real name in the field.

Captain Monk's coddling hadn't stopped her from slipping her detail, of course. After the third offense, the captain arranged for her to ride the rest of the way by carriage. Clearly unaware of what duties befell an etiquette instructor, Captain Monk assumed Willem functioned as Daana's escort and ordered him not to let her stray again. Daana didn't know which she found more infuriating, that she was being treated as a child, or the fact that Willem hadn't bothered to correct the misconception. He insisted it was a matter of practicality. It would be easier to relay information if they stayed together. Daana was beginning to sense the real reason was so he could claim her discoveries as his own.

The model of perfect posture, Willem sat impossibly straight, with shoulders back and boots pressed together. "Did you learn nothing from your recent clash with authority? You cannot afford another poor impression. Not after what you said to the captain."

"I called the man a driveling dunce, Willem. He's been referred to as worse in his lifetime, I'm sure." Daana peeked over the edge of her book, intrigued by her partner's ability to do a near perfect impression of a housecat caught in the rain. "Don't look at me like that. I see the way your eyes glaze over when he talks. You know it just as well as I do."

"I only think it. You said it to his face."

"That's generally how communication works. You would know that if you ever bothered to set foot outside that dingy library of yours."

"You got a pass because of your family name. The captain could have done far worse than lock you in a carriage. I caution you not to make that mistake with the protector. Oralia despises your uncle, and by proxy, you too. If you have any sort of charm, now would be the time to start using it." Willem's thin pink lips pressed together in an impossibly tight frown. "On that note, I implore you one final time, stop the carriage. Meeting the Protector of the Realm wet and reeking of urine is not the sort of impression you should be striving for, either."

"I told you, I'm fine. And it doesn't matter, anyway. Oralia Dawnsight is going to take one look at my clothes, offer a curt hello, and then ignore me for the remainder of the journey." Daana shifted, attempting to alleviate the worsening pains in her belly. The dress was tight around her midsection, making an already unpleasant situation substantially worse. "I still don't know why you insisted on me wearing this ridiculous thing. We're on a field mission, for the gods' sakes! Not at court."

"Appearances, my dear. You are Lady Lazuli, future emissary of the Iron Ridge, remember? You have an image to live up to."

"Oh, you mean the image that I'm a starry-eyed idiot? Who earned this position through nepotism and not merit?" It was decided. Daana was burning the dress the moment she reached Lonebrook. She didn't care if she had to make the rest of the journey in stockings. Anything was better than the rigid boning channels currently digging trenches into the tender flesh along her ribcage. "Thank you for reminding me."

"An optimist, not an idiot. One set on embettering the realm by setting aside old family feuds, uniting the figureheads under one vision, and," Willem fluttered his hand impatiently, "well, you read the dossier, you know the rest."

"Doing the impossible and winning over Oralia," Daana finished with a groan, rolling her head against the cushioned backrest. "It's as if they expect it to be so easy. If Uncle hasn't managed to do it in court, what makes them think I can manage it out here in the wild? This is her element, for the gods' sakes!"

"It's that sort of attitude that gets you nowhere."

From the concentrated look on his face, Daana could feel the start of a lecture blossoming. Left to his own devices, Willem could go on for ages. In these instances, she found the best recourse was to remain silent and remember to nod her head on occasion.

Ironically, if she'd been given this assignment a year ago, Daana would have been thrilled. Not because of Oralia, of course, but at the opportunity to meet the notorious inner circle. The faithful four stayed well out of the public eye. They were the shadow force of the realm and their work was renowned. And, just like every other starry-eyed citizen, Daana had once clung to every two-bit piece of gossip as if it were legend. But not anymore. Not after reading the personal files her uncle kept on each member.

Oralia's faithful were not the heroes their adoring audience believed. They were cutthroat killers whose sole function was to wreak unimaginable destruction upon the realm's enemies. In the right hands, Uncle Geralt believed they could be wielded safely. But he suspected their handler had begun to lose faith in the system. Left unchecked, Oralia and her faithful four could bring the current governing body to its knees. In order to assess whether or not Protector Dawnsight's ideals still aligned with the realm, Daana would first have to infiltrate her inner circle. A task that was as dangerous as it was impossible.

Willem's sour voice broke Daana from her thoughts. "You're fixating again, aren't you?"

"Excuse me?" Daana snapped her head up in surprise and immediately regretted it. Willem was watching her with the full force of his thumbscrew stare. She had seen division members more powerful than her crumble beneath its unflinching scrutiny.

His words all but bit with every crisp syllable. "Your uncle has an unhealthy obsession with Protector Dawnsight. I am concerned that his conspiracies are beginning to cloud your judgment. You and I are here on behalf of the Division of Divination, first and foremost. Do not lose sight of the assignment. Your main concern is the ghost. Anything else your uncle may have tasked you with falls second, understood?"

"Yes," she groaned, tilting her head back.

The traveling party hadn't even reached Lonebrook and already Daana was on what was quickly becoming her thousandth lecture since leaving Sunstorn. That was the trouble with having a partner who could read your thoughts with a single glance. You got away with absolutely nothing. Willem wasn't actually a clairvoyant—not according to the few pages of information the intelligence officer had provided, anyway. Just very, very good at peeling away at a person's layers and exposing their inner secrets.

A former seeker, Willem Foss was the lowest-ranking member of the Division of Divination council. He came equipped with a hypervigilant eye for details and a nasty habit of pointing out other people's shortcomings, particularly Daana's. As the only person to have encountered the ghost and lived, Willem was the voice of authority on the matter and would be integral to her success. He would be an asset, the Director of Magical Affairs had assured her.

Daana was only now beginning to realize that "asset" was synonymous with "pain in the ass."

"And you're fixating again."

Daana slammed the journal into her lap, ignoring the twinge of pain that erupted across her abdomen. "It's your own fault you're here, you know. You told the director I couldn't carry out the mission by myself!"

"And I stand by that statement," Willem sighed, tugging the hem of his dark gloves back over his wrist as he watched the drab scenery rattle past. "What I didn't mean was for them to send me."

Prior to being saddled as partners, she'd only ever known Willem as the crotchety division librarian who, admittedly, gave her excellent reading recommendations. While they had never diverted from the subjects of books, he'd at least been friendly. That was more courtesy than anyone else had extended to her. Daana had spent many of her early years curled up under his main window with her nose in a book. If not friends, they were at least on friendly terms. Until he turned on her. In front of the entire council, no less.

Alas, the council sided with Willem and decided he would accompany her on the mission. Despite protests from both sides, the decision was final. Everything moved quickly into place after that. With Uncle Geralt's help, the Division of Divination supplied the pair with false backgrounds and a secured position among Protector Dawnsight's traveling party. To the others, Daana and Willem would appear as another lowly cog in the wheel of Uncle Geralt's plan to incorporate the Iron Ridge into the realm. Uncle handled the most difficult part of preparations—convincing his fellow figureheads that an emissary and an etiquette instructor were integral to the mission. The motion was passed two to one, with Protector Dawnsight being a miserable stick in the mud as usual.

Willem slid to one side as the carriage lurched suddenly. "We're off the main road," he announced drearily. "Death can't be far now."

CHAPTER FOURTEEN

Wielder of Secrets

Daana pressed her knees together as the bench beneath her jostled with twice the intensity as before. She didn't bother to collect the books and loose papers that scattered around her feet. Her entire concentration was focused on holding her bladder. After what felt like an eternity, the carriage rolled to a halt in front of the main house. Belfast Manor, according to Daana's itinerary.

From the name, Daana had pictured a multi-storied mansion with pillars, steps, and a vast, cobbled courtyard with flowers and a fountain. The manor was nothing more than an overgrown stone cottage. There was an abundance of flowers, at least, and a courtyard, though it was paved in dirt, not stone. Her disappointment was not so much in the aesthetics but the realization that, based on the home's ancient appearance, there would not be a privy inside. No matter. Stupid dress or not, she would make do.

"Ladies first!" She barreled past Willem out the carriage door, nearly tripping over her own blasted clothes. Hiking her skirts above the knee, she raced through the mud and a throng of soldiers who watched her with mild confusion. Daana wasn't sure where exactly she was going, just away. Before Captain Monk realized she'd slipped her detail and sent Willem after her.

She rounded the back of the property. A pair of soldiers, wearing mismatched uniforms Daana did not recognize, were standing alongside the woodshed. Daana called to the closer of the two, desperately, "You, sir! Is there a—"

The orc swiveled his blue-gray head at her and pressed a thick finger to his lips. "Shh!"

"Excuse me?" The words blurted from Daana's mouth before she could consider a more diplomatic approach.

"Do you not understand what 'shh' means?" The orc returned her heated stare with a snarl, "Shut your yap, elfling. You're going to scare it off."

"Let her," his companion muttered, not bothering to give Daana so much as a courtesy glance. "She'll spare you from losing your silver." From the voice, Daana guessed the second soldier was female, though the elf's long hair and androgynous features made it difficult to tell.

Momentarily forgetting her bladder pains, Daana turned to see what they were watching with such fixed interest. A freshly planted garden stretched between them and the tree line. Tiny sprouts popped out of the soil in neat rows, their leaves stretching toward the sun. Had she been closer, Daana might have been able to identify the different varieties of vegetables. From her position, however, the only plant she could make out with any certainty was the apple tree shading the far corner of the plot.

Daana doubted the pair were bored enough to watch seedlings grow. "I'm clearly missing something."

"Under the tree," the orc grunted.

After some searching, Daana noticed a squirrel hidden in the grass along the tree's gnarled trunk. It nibbled a leaf between its paws, pausing every so often to listen. ". . . You're watching a squirrel?"

"Come on, Rasp. Make your move already," the orc said.

The elf kicked her companion in the shin, eyes darting in Daana's direction.

"Shit. Uh, I called him the wrong name again, didn't I?"

The elf's long, straw-colored hair swayed back and forth as she shook her head at him. "And you wonder why you're never sent to gather intelligence."

A whistle pierced the air. The pair whipped their heads back in the direction of the squirrel. Daana looked in time to see a raven swoop beneath the tree, cawing as it passed over the squirrel. The rodent dropped flat against the ground as it assessed the danger. There was a flash of silver and in the next moment, the squirrel was dead. Fixed to the ground with a knife struck through it.

"Dear gods!" Daana cried, covering her mouth.

The orc did not share her horror. He punched the air excitedly. "Right through the head!"

The elf maintained her bored expression. "Pure luck."

The branches of the apple tree stirred as the hunter swung from his hiding spot. He was human and, for some reason, half naked. The little man descended, gripping the rough bark with his bare hands and toes until he touched the ground. The raven chattered excitedly as it hopped at his feet, leading him to the squirrel. The man crouched, waving the raven away, before tugging the blade from his kill.

Croak! The raven pecked angrily at the human's foot.

"I didn't forget. You're just impatient," he snapped. The man pulled something from the pocket of his trousers and offered it to the bird. The raven snatched the prize in its bill and fluttered into the tree.

"Told you he could do it." The orc rocked back on his heels, grinning up at his taller companion. "Pay up, Ellisar."

Speechless, Daana pivoted in their direction. Dread bubbled in her chest and her knees felt like they had turned to liquid. Ellisar Farrow, the infamous cutthroat herself. Ellisar was older than Daana had pictured. She was tall and narrow, like a reed, with waist-length hair and a ghostly complexion. The eyes were right, though. Piercing gold-colored irises that caught the light in the most breathtaking manner.

With great effort, Daana averted her gaze to the orc, noting his bent tusk. This had to be Curly. Built like a bull, broad and thick, with short legs and arms that were disproportionately long, the very top of his freshly shaved head barely reached Ellisar's shoulder. Despite the violet scars that crisscrossed his blue-gray skin, the orc was young. It showed in the taunting smile that hovered over his curled lips.

Still wearing an expression of complete disinterest, Ellisar slapped a coin into Curly's outstretched hand.

"The bet was two silver," he reminded her.

"The other half is to keep my mouth shut," Ellisar said, shouldering past him. She glanced back, her golden eyes shimmering in a manner that was more unsettling than beautiful. "Wouldn't want Oralia to know you called Snow by the wrong name again, would you?"

"Oh, come on! That's not fair."

"The elfling heard you. You have the hour to come up with something convincing before I deal with her." Ellisar's eyes narrowed as she vanished around the backside of the shed.

Daana's dread sank lower, lower, lower, until it settled into her stomach. She felt sick. And it wasn't just the fullness of her bladder.

Curly scratched the back of his head, avoiding direct eye contact. "So, uh, funny story. I'm terrible with names and . . ."

"Save your breath. I already know who the human is." From the man's ghastly appearance, it was not a stretch to assume he was Rasp Stoneclaw, the infamous silver-haired warrior. Or would be, if he had any hair to speak of.

Curly's shoulders relaxed. "Oh, good. Guess we don't have to kill you, then."

"No, you most certainly cannot!" Daana stomped her foot and immediately regretted it as a shockwave of pain reverberated up her leg and spread across her swollen midsection.

"Who are we killing?" Rasp picked his way through the garden toward them. He grasped a reed cane in one hand and carried the squirrel by the tail with the other. He was shorter than her, trimmer, too.

"Not sure yet," Curly said. He was quiet for a moment, silently taking stock of Daana's formal clothing. She did not like how his eyes paused over her decorative armlets. Her seeker's robes normally covered them. The cloak given to her for the mission was open in the front and, coupled with the low cut dress, left less to the imagination. "Does the elfling have a name?"

Daana bristled at the term. She and the orc were the same age. By definition, she was as much an elfling as he was a youngling. "Lady Daana Lazuli." She didn't bother with her official titles. Her name spoke for itself. She squared her shoulders and waited for him to apologize.

"Lady, huh?" Rasp said, prodding her with his cane. "I assumed from the smell you were a musty old man."

The triumphant smirk vanished from Daana's lips.

The orc burst into laughter, clasping his monstrous hand over the human's shoulder. "And to think your keeper paid me to babysit. This is the most entertainment I've had in weeks!" Curly took a breath, wiping the moisture from under his eyes, and added, "Speaking of the white demon, how's about you give my knife back before Faris filets me with it, eh? I was told specifically not to let you have weapons."

"How do you expect me to skin a squirrel without a blade?"

Curly snatched the knife from Rasp's belt, shrugging. "You got teeth, don't you?"

Muttering beneath his breath, Rasp found the woodshed with his cane and followed the splintered wall until he came across a suitable seating arrangement. It was an upturned barrel, but the Stoneclaw didn't appear to mind. Once seated, Rasp slipped a folding knife from his trousers and tested its sharpness against his thumb.

"Another one?" Curly glared at him. "For fuck's sake, Snow. Oralia's going to be on her way over any moment now. Put that away before she sees!"

The introductions, naturally, had slipped Daana's mind. It wouldn't just be Protector Dawnsight either, but Captain Monk, too. And Willem. Daana shuddered, deciding she couldn't ignore the pain in her bladder any longer. She turned to Curly. "I need the privy. Can you point me in the right direction, please?"

"The what?"

Good gods. Daana peered past the woodshed to the bustling courtyard, confirming the trio was nowhere near. "The, uh, latrine?" Judging from the orc's mixed expression, he had no idea to what she was referring. "For the gods' sakes, you are from a noble family, Benton Cortair! You cannot possibly be this daft."

"What's this?" Rasp whipped his head in their direction.

"Curly is just a nickname," Daana said.

"No! *Benton*, really?"

"Shut it, Snow."

"Gods, I feel so underdressed. Might I borrow one of your petticoats, m'lord?"

Daana wondered if Rasp knew what a petticoat was. Perhaps it was part of the insult. "You may have mine."

"Do not encourage this," Curly snarled.

Emboldened by the orc's flaring temper, the Stoneclaw stood and performed a mocking bow, nearly falling from his barrel. "Doth thou desire tea, m'lord? Scones, perchance? How goeth the yearly peasant uprising?"

Curly clicked his tusks at Daana. His dark eyes gleamed murderously. "I'm never going to hear the end of this."

Daana fought the urge to squirm beneath his steely gaze. "Tell me where the latrine is and I'll get him to stop."

"You think you can control that?" Curly gestured to Rasp, who had since fallen from his barrel and was lying on the ground, still managing to crack jokes between fits of uncontrolled laughter. "Alright, princess. You've got a deal."

Daana moved to the Stoneclaw's side, wincing with each step. She knelt beside his ear and whispered, "Keep it up and I will tell him your real name."

Rasp smiled at her with all of his teeth. Well, the ones not already knocked out of his mouth, at least. "And how doth the lady knoweth such information?"

"The same way I know his," she replied sweetly. "Want to try me?"

"Normally I bed anyone who offers, but I find your tone highly concerning. I think I'll pass." Rasp tilted his head at her, his unfocused eyes staring somewhere above her head. "What kind of soldier are you again?"

She was Emissary Daana Lazuli. Wielder of secrets. Champion bladder holder. The best fucking seeker the Division of Divination had to offer. Daana stood swiftly and looked at Curly. "Satisfied?"

"Impressive, princess." Curly gestured over his shoulder with the knife, grinning. "You may piss under any tree you like."

CHAPTER FIFTEEN

One Dead, Two Dead, Three Dead More

The narrow road to the judge's house twisted like a tan and brown serpent. Dust kicked into the air as the capital procession rode toward Belfast Manor, snaking in and out of sight between the trees. Forty additional soldiers, officers plus horses, twelve pack mules, two foragers, a hunter, a herbalist, and—Oralia wrinkled her nose at the carriage parked at the corner of the lot—a useless emissary and an etiquette instructor. The latter two courtesy of the Speaker of the People. At least when the damn Stoneclaw suggested bodies, they were fundamentally useful. What in the seven realms of chaos would they need two members of court for?

Oralia looked to the soft blue sky that stretched above, unobstructed by clouds. She breathed the warm breeze slowly in through her nostrils and out the gap between her tusks. The air was thick with the smell of animals. They were here, at last. That was all that mattered. The other figureheads could play their silly games whatever way they pleased. Soon, the realm would find a new enforcer to carry out its tireless bidding.

The packed courtyard was the epicenter of the chaos. Soldiers and house servants raced back and forth across the square, herding mules, unloading supplies, and trying their very best to do so without getting trampled by each other. Judge Belfast had cleared one of his storage barns to temporarily house the animals. The traveling party would be afforded two days to rest before the real journey began.

Rali stood beside Oralia, reviewing the manifest. The dwarf's larger-than-life personality often made her forget their differences in size. Oralia was tall and hovered in that undefined area above brawny but several steps short of hulking. Rali, by contrast, was short, stout, and built like a boulder. She could throw down as easily as the larger members of the company, of course, and had gained a rather infamous reputation for shattering kneecaps.

The dwarf's thick eyebrows were currently scrunched together, reminding Oralia of some sort of large, black caterpillar. "I don't like this."

Oralia was hardly surprised. With the exception of strong ale and gambling, Rali rarely liked anything. "Is there a problem, Lieutenant?"

"I don't recognize a damn name on this list so far. It's bad enough we're going to be in unfamiliar territory, but with a bunch of greenhorns, too? This is unacceptable."

"They are Captain Monk's soldiers," Oralia reminded her.

A clump of hair had escaped Rali's thick braid and clung to her fair forehead. She blew the offending flyaways from her vision. "So we're in agreement then."

They were, actually. With so many unfamiliar ears nearby, Oralia dared not state her mounting suspicions out loud. Her fellow figureheads always found ways to upset her. Oralia hoped this was simply a minor annoyance, and not evidence of something more sinister. "The realm is depending on these trade routes. It would be counterproductive to send anyone but the best."

"Four hundred years later and you still haven't lost your sense of humor," Rali said. "I admire that about you."

Oralia appreciated Lieutenant Ralizak not only for her ability to hear what Oralia said, but also what she *didn't* say. Currently, Oralia *wasn't* saying "Drop the subject and we will discuss it in depth somewhere private." What Oralia said instead was, "I am four hundred and thirteen, actually."

"Good gods, catching up to Ellisar. That's not a contest you want to win, you know." Something on the third page of the manifest caught Rali's attention. Her mouth tumbled open, aghast. "Unbelievable! Every one of my personnel requests was ignored and you somehow got your fuckmate?"

Oralia flinched. This particular offense was a result of her own damn doing. As she had forbidden Rali from using the word "lover," the dwarf naturally had taken it upon herself to come up with something substantially worse. "Do you have a more productive task you should be doing?" Oralia fixed her lieutenant with her most severe glare. "Or shall I devise one for you?"

"I suppose I could fetch an extra bedroll for your tent." Rali waggled her eyebrows.

Oralia, torn between reprimanding the dwarf and giving in to curiosity, succumbed to the latter. She pinched the bridge of her nose and sighed. "Which one?"

"You mean you didn't have a hand in this? Gods, the fool must have requested the posting himself. Can't say I blame him. I'd be taken with you too if I were an orc."

"Ralizak!"

Rali relented. "Sascha Yukah, madam."

Sweet, merciful gods. There was an upside to this mission, after all. Oralia would locate Sascha later. First, duty called. Watching a sensibly dressed officer approach, she muttered to Rali, "You are dismissed, Lieutenant. Make yourself useful and go count something."

"As you wish, Protector." Rali departed quickly, with a song on her lips:

"One dead, two dead, three dead more,
Six dead, seven dead, on the floor.
He's dead, she's dead, this one too,
Faces frozen and lips a'blue.
No ax, no arrow, nary a knife,
Grim sir, what ended your waste of a life?"

Rali bowed to the approaching officer with more flourish than was necessary and boomed, "Good afternoon, Captain Monk, sir! Good to see you again, sir!"

". . . Lieutenant Ralizak," the confused captain replied. His gaze followed her progress across the chaotic yard until she disappeared among the bustle of moving bodies. His voice was uncharacteristically soft. "She's more cheerful than I remember."

"Excited to be underway is all."

"Ah, of course!" This appeared to snap him out of his daze. Captain Monk offered a short bow at the waist. "A pleasure to be of assistance, Madam Protector. As always!"

"Captain," she greeted, less enthusiastically.

Like the others, Captain Monk wore a simple uniform of tan and brown. The traditional royal blue and yellow gold colors of the realm had been ditched in favor of something that would look less like a target against the bleak landscape of the Iron Ridge. Gazing across the sea of shifting browns, Oralia realized she preferred the change. She needed soldiers, after all, not blasted peacocks.

A loud, over-enunciated series of sounds made her painfully aware that Captain Monk was doing what he did best and most often—talking. It wouldn't have been nearly so unbearable, Oralia theorized, if he had any sense of volume control. Alas, every other word came out one decibel shy of a scream. "The journey was an uneventful one. The best kind of journey, if I do say so myself! Didn't lose so much as a single horse! Nary a bandit in sight, either. The scoundrels flock to the roads this time of year, you know. Didn't want to take their chances, I suppose. What with a mighty realm caravan . . ."

Oralia soon lost interest and the captain's voice faded into the background at a loud hum. He was human, with tawny brown skin and facial hair that twisted and curled in such an intricate manner it looked more like an ornamental nest than a beard. Captain Alin Monk was good-natured, possessed a keen sense of style that bordered on flamboyant, and exuded enough enthusiasm to make up for his overall lack of competency. The realm advisors claimed they'd chosen based on merit. That, and species of course, as the mountain folk would be more inclined to listen to a fellow human.

Oralia knew the truth, however. Captain Monk was expendable. As was she.

"Captain," Oralia cut in before he unwittingly destroyed the hearing in both her ears. She gestured to the cart beside them with more flair than she would normally allow. Good gods, he was already rubbing off on her. "The emissary realizes one cannot take a carriage up the mountain, correct?"

"The carriage was at my insistence, actually! Our dear emissary has a terrible sense of direction, I'm afraid. Tragic, really. Every time I turned my back, the poor thing was gone again!" Captain Monk paused, watching as a harsh figure stalked from the front of the cottage. From the way the stranger's hardened gaze moved across the courtyard, he appeared to be looking for something. Captain Monk cupped his hands over the curl of his mustache and called, "Have you gone and lost her again already, Willem?"

The man flinched. It was subtle enough that it would likely go unnoticed by the human eye, but Oralia noticed. Reluctantly, the gray-haired man approached. "A momentary setback, sir. Lady Lazuli could not have gotten far."

Not a man, Oralia realized, as he drew nearer. Willem's pointed ears and fine bone structure were that of an elf. The wrinkles around his hard eyes and mouth, however, indicated the accelerated aging of a human—a half elf, half human, most likely. His salt-and-pepper hair was pulled back in a tight tie near the nape of his neck, highlighting a forehead marred with worry lines. Willem was dressed in a simple black frock coat and equally black trousers. Clean cut. No nonsense. Not what Oralia had expected from a member of the court. She half wondered if he knew how to handle the decorative knife strapped to his side.

"Madam Protector." He spoke politely without breaking the perpetual frown stretched across his pallid face. With the ghost of Captain Monk's voice still ringing in her ears, Oralia found herself leaning in Willem's direction, straining to catch the words that flowed as effortlessly as water from his still lips. "It was to be my honor to present Lady Daana Lazuli, but her ladyship has slipped my care."

Captain Monk stroked his beard. "You're getting slow, Willem."

Willem's tone lacked the fire that shone in his eyes. "Be that as it may, sir, I am supposed to be bringing sophistication to the outer realm, not supervising the unruly offspring of the court."

"Cheer up, Will. You should be honored! The speaker handpicked you himself." The captain turned to Oralia and formally introduced him. "Willem Foss. Finishing instructor and etiquette expert extraordinaire!"

Oralia's gaze shifted from Captain Monk to Willem. "As I told my fellow figureheads, there is no place for a member of the court in my ranks. If you have any sense at all, you will pack yourself back into that carriage and return to Sunstorn. You will lose more than just the emissary if you continue up the mountain."

Willem's pale cheeks flushed with color. "Madam Protector, I—"

"Nonsense, Protector! Mister Foss is perfectly capable of the task. Someone has to teach our mountain man basic manners, you know. As to avoid embarrassment in the event he's summoned to court," Captain Monk said. He shielded his eyes with the flat of his hand and peered across the crowded yard. "Ah! There's your pupil now, Willem. Currently field dressing a squirrel by the woodshed. And what luck! It appears Lady Lazuli is in that very same direction."

"Unbelievable," Willem muttered under his breath.

Oralia strode ahead of him, wondering if his disgust was meant for the squirrel or the unescorted lady. She'd offered the fool a chance to turn around. As she had been outvoted on the matter of his presence, that was the most she could do without going against direct orders. Whatever happened to Willem now was his own damn fault.

CHAPTER SIXTEEN

Lucky Sap

The bustling mix of house servants and soldiers scattered around Oralia like leaves in the wind. "Snow," the protector called, noting with secret pleasure how the rest of the yard flinched at her thunderous voice. "Where is your keeper?"

Rasp was propped on top of a barrel against the woodshed, tugging the hide from his kill. He was shirtless, as usual, though nudity aside, Oralia was pleased with his appearance. After weeks of regular feedings, the boy had finally ceased to resemble an emaciated plague victim. She could no longer count his individual ribs. "Who, Faris? Off building a roster, last I heard. Why?" Rasp's smile was all teeth and no lip. "You finally want to have a chance at me in the ring?"

Rasp had not been left entirely unattended, she realized. Curly was stationed nearby, maintaining a semi-watchful eye over him. He scoffed at Rasp. "She'd break your neck like a twig."

Rasp snapped the squirrel's tail away with a sharp twist and threw it at the young orc. "Oh, just like you were going to do? Because I remember our match ending much differently."

"I see now why I'm needed," Willem said drearily. He stepped forward, mindful of the growing mess that collected at the Stoneclaw's bare feet. "Where is Lady Lazuli? She was seen coming this way."

"Little Miss Secrets?" Rasp ran his fingers along the skinned underside of the squirrel and made a face. "Pudgy little fucker."

"Excuse me?"

"The squirrel, not the lady." Rasp slid his blade along the flesh from the underside of its neck to between its legs. He hooked his finger inside, pulling the entrails free, unbothered by the smell.

Curly answered for him. "She's around back taking a piss."

Oralia winced at his candidness. Perhaps an etiquette instructor wasn't such a terrible idea, after all. Willem could make himself truly useful and teach her four how to conduct themselves as civilized members of society. It was wishful thinking, of course, as her warriors would learn nothing. Still, finishing lessons would make a fitting punishment the next time one of them stepped out of line.

"If you will excuse me." Willem disappeared around the back of the shed, shielding his eyes against the sun. "Your Ladyship, I really must insist you stay within sight! This is wilderness territory."

Rasp turned his head in Oralia's direction and addressed her. "No mice today, Protector. But I got a nice squirrel if you want half. Might be your last decent meal for a while."

"Our host is preparing a feast for tomorrow," Oralia said coolly. "I will abstain until then."

Judge Belfast and his household were vegetarians. Mealtimes consisted of various vegetable dishes, seasonal fruits, grains, and bread. It was divine compared to the military rations Oralia was used to. Rasp, however, insisted on hunting to fill the gap in his diet. His prey was mostly mice and rats caught by means she didn't care to know. Oralia had discovered him roasting a hare on a spit at the edge of the garden two evenings before. He offered to split it with her so long as she didn't tell. They shared the meat in silence and afterward, pretended it never happened. Rasp had become more amicable since. Or perhaps he'd finally run out of stupid things to say.

"I look forward to never eating another clover salad again." Rasp wiped the blade against his trouser leg and then tucked it into his pocket. "Squirrel, though? Now that's a treat. Arguably, mice heads have a more satisfying crunch, but squirrels are more filling."

"Dear gods!" Captain Monk said, in what he probably thought passed for a whisper.

Rasp's eyes pinched around the edges as he peered hard at the captain. "The vermin are nice and fat here. Not like on the mountain. If you're one of the lucky saps that gets stuck up there, you'll learn to appreciate the difference."

As the officer chosen to stay after Rasp's reinstatement, Captain Monk unfortunately was that lucky sap. Oralia supposed it was only fair to acquaint them, seeing as they were destined to spend their miserable futures together. "Snow," she gestured to the captain beside her, realizing only after the fact it was to no one's benefit, "Captain Monk."

Rasp held his palm upward. "Face here, please. You sound important enough to remember."

Captain Monk moved to step forward but Oralia stopped him, shaking her head. "Do not indulge him. He will know you by your voice. This is a ploy to get rodent innards on your face."

"I'm gonna help find the elf." Curly, his broad face contorted in a poor attempt to hide his mirth, hurried around the corner. He had the sense to constrain his laughter until he was out of sight.

"Spoilsport." Rasp produced a thin branch from somewhere behind him and threaded the kill onto his makeshift skewer. "Indifferent to meet you, Captain. Hopefully you will be more fun than the protector."

"I run a tight ship, sir!"

"For fuck's sake!" Rasp's body spasmed in response to the captain's sheer volume, nearly dropping his squirrel-on-a-stick. His next words, accentuated with a flared upper lip, were directed at Oralia. "He knows I'm blind, not hard of hearing, right?"

Oralia offered a tight smile that was entirely wasted upon him. "I foresee an eventful future together."

"Loud and boring. Got it," Rasp grumbled, working the tip of his pinky finger into his ear, as if to free the inner canal of the words Captain Monk had unknowingly lodged there. "What about the pissing elf? She didn't sound the soldiering type. Is she the medic? Cook? Concubine?"

Rasp had been integral to the planning process. And, as Oralia regretfully discovered, highly meticulous in his suggestions. No horses beyond the foothills. No hounds. No instruments. Fires only when necessary and when the wind favored them. He had been especially particular about the traveling party. They would need a good mix of scouts, archers, and brute force. There was no place for bystanders on the mountain. Anyone traveling with them had to serve an irrefutable purpose. This, naturally, was the reason Oralia hadn't told him about the emissary. She would never have heard the end of it.

Captain Monk dutifully obliged the Stoneclaw. He twisted his mustache while he spoke. "That is Lady Daana Lazuli. The future liaison between the realm and your people. Fresh from her studies, but you know what they say, experience is the best teacher!"

Rasp's jaw tightened. He said nothing, only glared in Oralia's direction with a fixed expression.

It was surprisingly effective. Oralia sighed, massaging her aching temples. "It was not my idea."

Rasp tested the tip of his skewer with his finger. "Nothing ever is, is it?"

"Mind your tongue, sir! You are speaking to the Protector of the Realm. I will gladly remind you, if need be!" Captain Monk instinctively reached for the hilt of his sword.

Oh dear gods, no. Monk was too inexperienced to know this was the absolute worst way to handle the Stoneclaw. Rasp thrived on conflict. Oralia held back from interfering. She would give Rasp the benefit of the doubt, in the unlikely event he opted to bow out gracefully.

He did not.

"Are you threatening to raise steel against a blind man? One you can clearly see isn't armed?" Rasp, the pinnacle of human pettiness, matched the captain's volume. "Tells a lot about the measure of a man, doesn't it?"

"I would never! I only meant to—"

A wolf-like smile curled over Rasp's sharp mouth. Still speaking as though he were attempting to be heard over a thunderstorm, he said, "What? Bark worse than your bite, Captain?"

"Enough, boy." Oralia caught Rasp by the wrist and lifted him from the barrel. Shoving his cane into his free hand, she directed him away from the woodshed with an ungentle push. "They've lit the cooking pit behind the kitchen. Go eat. Save your taunting for the ring."

"Oh, come on, Protector. How often do you get to see a man slapped with a squirrel?" Rasp adjusted his grip on the cane and sauntered away, sweeping it across the ground ahead of him as he hollered over his shoulder. "If you really want to have a go at me, Captain, come to the match tonight. I'm curious to know if your blood tastes as sweet as it smells!"

"Not another word," Oralia warned in a tone that demonstrated the power of inflection without having to rely solely on volume.

Whether Captain Monk took note or not was unclear. His proud shoulders deflated with a forlorn sigh. "That went poorly, didn't it? I was advised to put him in his place at my first opportunity."

"Whoever told you that is an idiot."

"I suppose it would have been prudent to have consulted you first. Nevertheless, I will have to prove to him that I am not to be trifled with! The sooner the better, I'm afraid." Captain Monk tilted his head, peering at her through heavy lidded eyes. "What is this match he speaks of?"

Damn the Stoneclaw and his infernal baiting. "It is more of a spectacle than anything. Some of the villagers get together once a week and place bets on amateur fights."

In her earlier years, Oralia would have forbidden the matches. Now, older, possibly wiser, definitely more tired, she realized the fighting would happen regardless. At her insistence, there were set rules. No weapons, no eye gouging, no biting—the latter two a direct result of the Stoneclaw's unrivaled savagery. There was a set timer and if both opponents were still standing after three rounds, it was an automatic draw. Each winner advanced until the final two faced off. The point of the ring was to vent frustrations while earning some extra coin, not to disembowel one another. She'd made that last point perfectly clear.

"The organizer tries to keep an even playing field. Most contestants are paired based on size and skill. Snow is the house wild card." Oralia hadn't understood what that meant when she first heard it. Fortunately, Rali had been generous enough to explain it to her. "The more outrageous the fight, the better the crowds. Just last week they pitted him against my orc soldier."

Curly had been blindfolded, of course. A detail Oralia intentionally omitted. Rasp hadn't won, either. At least not by skill. The match was declared a forfeit after Curly stormed away, unwilling to continue as the Stoneclaw insisted on landing open-mouthed kisses in lieu of punches.

Captain Monk stroked his beard as if deep in thought. Which could not have possibly been the case, as the next words out of his mouth were woefully idiotic. "Would I earn his respect if I challenged him?"

"Only if you win," she said shortly. "You will forever be known as the officer bested by a blind drunk if he beats you. That sort of reputation will follow you for life. Unless you are fully confident in your abilities, Alin, I would strongly advise against it."

"I am no stranger to combat, madam," Captain Monk said. "The art to any battle is finding your opponent's weakness and exploiting it. I have the advantage already!"

There was no saving Captain Monk. Oralia could see that now. The foolishness of human pride knew no bounds. "His keeper, Faris, runs the events out of a barn on the edge of the orchard. Go and watch the first matches. See for yourself before you throw your good name away."

"I appreciate the advice, Madam Protector. Good day!" The captain departed with a foolish smile, the echo of his deafening words still ringing in Oralia's eardrums.

CHAPTER SEVENTEEN

Adapt or Get Left Behind

Oralia moved to the far side of the woodshed and waited. It didn't take long. Several minutes later, a curious-looking figure stole past, picking her way across the muddied ground with silent care. The elf had a round, fleshy face with brown skin and large, bright eyes. Oralia noticed the soft curves of someone who'd spent a lifetime indoors with her nose buried in a book, not the hardened figure a soldier. By the time Daana noticed her watching, it was too late for the girl to duck back out of view. The elf froze in place, and for a few awkward heartbeats they stared without speaking.

Having sufficiently tortured the young Lazuli with uninterrupted eye contact, Oralia offered a warm greeting. "Emissary Lazuli."

Remembering herself, Daana managed a quick curtsy without losing her white-knuckled grip on what appeared to be a saddle blanket. Somewhere along the way, the elf had ditched her heavy skirts and was attempting, unsuccessfully, to conceal the fact that she was wearing nothing but a pair of white, tufted bloomers and a thin undershirt. "Protector Dawnsight! I, uh, did not intend to meet you this way," she said, pulling at the stubborn wool in order to keep her chest and nether regions simultaneously covered. It was unfortunate that it was not working. "There was a very untimely incident with my dress involving mud and possibly a pitchfork. One of the stable hands lent me this. I had hoped I could slip to the house without running into you, but, well . . ."

Oralia seemed to recall a human phrase detailing this exact circumstance. Something about downed trousers? Oh well. It was no matter. She would undoubtedly say it wrong, and Daana looked sufficiently embarrassed already. Oralia stepped forward, unclasping the cape from her shoulders. "I understand the predicament. Lieutenant Ralizak rescued my ceremonial cape from a similar incident with the hearth only this morning." She extended the cloth in Daana's direction. "Perhaps it will be of better use to you."

Daana's dark, hickory eyes moved from Oralia to the cape, like a mouse that had found a hole to dart into. "Are you sure?"

"I insist."

The cape had been a gift from the court to earmark an anniversary of some sort. Truth be told, Oralia couldn't remember which. It was a lovely piece, though. Crafted from the finest silks, the inner side was a brilliant sapphire blue, paired with a rich black backing. Like everything associated with the court, the cape had not come without issue. It was a tripping hazard, for one, and had a nasty habit of getting stuck in closed doors. On the upside, it did allow for a certain dramatic flair whenever Oralia stormed the hallways of the capital palace. At just the right speed, the fabric produced a satisfying, billowy snap.

Daana draped the cape across her shoulders like an oversized cloak before wrapping each corner across the front and tucking it in under the arms. For a makeshift garment, it at least covered the necessary areas. "Much better." She gave an experimental twirl, then stopped halfway, suddenly remembering who her audience was. Daana coughed into her hand, managing a dignified "Thank you."

"We are pleased to have you, Lady Lazuli. Judge Belfast has reserved a room for you in the main house. There is a small library, too, if that interests you." Oralia saw the relief that flooded Daana's face and took secret pleasure in crushing it. "But that can wait. You and I need to have a conversation first. Walk with me."

"Now?" Daana scurried after her, nearly tripping over the ends of the cape. "If this is about the issue between Captain Monk and I, I can assure you it was a momentary lapse in judgment. It won't happen again."

Oralia did not bother to adjust her natural stride to account for the elf's shorter legs. Adapt or get left behind, such was life. "Excellent. Consider it forgotten." Oralia had no idea what Daana was blathering on about. She also didn't care. Monk was an idiot and probably deserved whatever trouble the emissary had thrown his way.

"Does that mean I don't have to ride in the carriage anymore?"

Dear gods, Geralt Lazuli had sent her a child. The speaker was normally craftier than this. This effort to annoy her, if Oralia even dared call it that, was half-assed at best. She wondered, briefly, from whom Daana was supposed to be distracting her. With Oralia's attention centered on the decoy, the real spy would be free to sleuth undetected. It was a shame Oralia had come prepared. For Geralt, anyway.

Oralia chose not to answer. If a carriage was all it took to instill dread into the young Lazuli, then it was better to let it remain a possibility. "We must discuss the expectations of your assignment."

"Oh," Daana said, her shoulders drooping.

"But first, I feel I must clear the air. As you are already aware, I argued against having you here. The idea of sending an emissary of peace on a war mission is deeply illogical." Oralia allowed for one of her notoriously long pauses, curious to see whether Lady Lazuli would defend her position. When the girl succeeded in keeping her thoughts to herself, Oralia continued. "After some consideration, I realize I was perhaps too hasty in my decision. It is no secret that the Speaker of the People and I butt heads. I allowed my personal feelings to cloud my judgment and for that, I apologize."

"Really?" Daana's eyebrows shot upward in surprise.

"Your position has value. I was naive to think otherwise."

"Thank you. No apology necessary. I'm just happy to be of service . . ." Oralia let Daana prattle on in the background as the pair rounded the final corner, arriving at the front of the house.

The courtyard was less chaotic than Oralia had left it, thanks largely to the efforts of Lieutenant Ralizak, who was marching between the neat rows of soldiers wielding her manifest as if it were a weapon. Movement along the edge of the house caught Oralia's eye. An unsupervised gaggle of children stood below the overhang of the roof with their heads bent upward. Oralia followed their line of sight, suddenly realizing where her missing goblin had gone. Snaglebrag was perched like a gargoyle among the clay tiles, watching the milling courtyard from a safe distance. Occasionally he would reach into his pocket and drop something below. The morsel would hit the ground and bounce, causing a wild scatter as the children raced to capture whatever goods were on offer. Knowing Snag, it was candied nuts or something equally harmless. Unlike Ellisar, who would have been whipping rocks.

Glancing over her shoulder, Oralia found the emissary still talking, seemingly unaware of the goings on around her. ". . . I must admit, I had concerns that you and I would start off on the wrong foot, but I can see now they were unfounded. It will be my honor working alongside you, Protector."

"As it will be mine," Oralia seized the opportunity to cut in before the girl started up again. "As future emissary of the Iron Ridge, you will be responsible for fostering peace between our nations. That is a task you should not take lightly." Oralia led Daana up the stone steps of the main house and inside, taking care to wipe her feet first. Ruthless, yes. But she wasn't a complete monster, after all. She strolled to the back study, pleased to see the sheets of loose parchment, various writing implements, and ink that awaited them.

"I took the liberty of reviewing the credentials the realm provided on your behalf," Oralia said. "Is it true you speak seven languages?"

"Yes. Mostly elven languages. And some better than others, admittedly. My grutohk—common dwarfish—in particular, needs brushing up on. No matter how I try, I can never seem to roll the right sounds. My instructor told me I sound less like a dwarf and more like a dying seal." Daana tiptoed in behind her, casting a cautious glance up and down the cluttered room. Her gaze settled on the mass collection of supplies. "What is all this?"

"Your first project." Oralia selected the worn journal from the center of the worktable and turned it over in her hands with care. It had arrived two weeks prior with explicit instructions from Whisper. "You are aware who Snow is, yes?"

"Yes, madam."

That was one thing Oralia could count on Geralt for. Lady Lazuli likely had entire manuals of information committed to memory regarding the travel party and its key members. It was a shame there was no way for Oralia to tease out this information—short of leaving the girl in a locked room with Snaglebrag while he performed his rendition of *Lilies of the Pond* on the pipe, of course. As tempting as the thought was, Oralia was certain Snag's musical talents qualified as torture.

"In order to win the hearts of the mountain folk, you must first win over their leader. For this reason, I am tasking you with building a rapport with the future ruler of the Iron Ridge. Educate him on the ways of the realm and, in turn, learn all that you can about his people. This"—she delivered the journal to Daana—"will give you common ground."

Daana accepted it, gingerly. She flipped through the first pages and her expression fell. "I—I can't read this."

"I am told it is stolac," Oralia said. "The language of the mountain folk. Very few in the realm speak it. It is derived from laftak, which, according to your credentials, you are fluent in. Translating it will be difficult, but I am certain there is no one better equipped for the challenge."

"I—"

"I expect your first full report by the week's end."

Daana clutched the journal to her chest. "But—"

"I will leave you to it. Good day, Lady Lazuli." Oralia whipped around and was out the door and down the hallway in a matter of strides. She passed Judge Belfast on her way out, acknowledging his suspicious frown with a smirk as she slipped soundlessly through the back door. Descending the steps in two easy bounds, she fought to stifle the laugh that bubbled in her throat.

One nuisance down. One more to go.

CHAPTER EIGHTEEN

Bribery

It was not often that she gave in to such immaturity. With Daana burdened with busywork and consequently out of the way, Oralia's sense of discipline should have returned. And yet, when she saw a familiar face duck into the far barn, she threw all sense of self control to the wind. Oralia changed course and strode in after him. Unfurling a random strip of parchment from her pocket, she pretended to study it with fixed interest.

"Mister Yukah?" Her thunderous voice cut through the bustle, stopping all in their tracks. She glanced up over the list of officer names she was supposed to have committed to memory by now. Every spine in the room had suddenly gone rigid. Even the animals appeared prepared to bolt the moment she brandished her tusks.

"Is there a Mister Yukah present?" Oralia's gaze moved across the line of bleak-faced soldiers, purposely skimming over the top of the one that stood out like a mountain amongst molehills. She glanced back down at her list for effect. "The cook, if I am not mistaken."

"Here, Madam Protector." Sascha's hulking form waded through the soldiers with deceptive speed.

The orc's intimidating appearance was made a little less so by the flower print apron that hung over the front of his billowy white tunic and breeches. While pitchfork-wielding mobs were few and far between these days, the colorful print operated better than any shield. For one, everyone knew no marauding orc would be caught dead wearing a sunflower smock into battle. Secondly, the apron proclaimed his station to leery villagers and overeager soldiers alike—as, sadly, Sascha's size usually meant his attackers stabbed first and left pesky questions such as "Who are you?" and "What are you doing here?" for afterward.

Oralia knew all of this, not due to impeccable powers of discernment, but because she was the one who had given it to him. Somewhat jokingly, actually. "Ah, good." She kept her voice flat and free of the sudden flutter stirring to life within her rapidly beating chest. "There is an urgent supply discrepancy I wish to discuss with you."

"I can assure you, madam, I checked the lists twice myself. I—"

"In private, Mister Yukah. This way, please." She turned swiftly on her heel and strode free of the musty barn and around the back.

She led him past the barn and toward the abandoned paddock, mindful to keep several paces ahead of him as she crossed though the broken fence line. The drab, half-rotted loafing shed was the outermost building on the lot. Meaning, of course, that no one would have any reason to be out this far. A cautious glance in either direction confirmed the surrounding stretch of freshly tilled field was indeed empty. As was the wooded lot beyond, whose thick trees acted as the artificial fence line for the back of the property.

When Sascha came ambling around the corner after her, Oralia was ready for him. She threw her weight forward and pinned him to the aged siding. From his amused smile, he had expected as much from her and played along, throwing his broad shoulders into the wood with enough force to make it slam without toppling it over. It was all an act, of course. Had this been a real scuffle, Sascha—a head taller and close to double her weight—would have taken a small army to pin.

"Moonflower." The skin creased along the edges of his sable eyes as his smile turned from amused to mischievous. "Did you just fake a supply emergency to get me alone?"

"There was a disturbing lack of wine on the manifest. Ralizak was quite concerned." She threaded her fingers through his soot-colored beard and tugged his chin in her direction. It took standing on damn near tip toe in order for her face to reach his. Sascha's scent engulfed her, an intoxicating combination of fresh mint leaves and ground cloves. There was the sharp, lingering odor of garlic, too. But that served only to remind her of dinner, not passion, and was promptly expelled from her mind. "I had to do my due diligence and investigate the matter."

"Captain Monk's orders," he said matter-of-factly. "No alcohol on the road. He wants his people at their sharpest."

"No wonder they look so miserable."

Oralia drew her arms over his neck and pressed her lips to his. Sascha responded, his strong hands already working down her hips. The kiss was warm, passionate, and entirely too short. A shrill whistle split the air in three rapid blasts, causing Sascha to lift his head. His dark eyes focused on something in the distance. "We have an audience," he grunted. "Your people, I suspect. Given how enthusiastically they're cheering us on."

"Dear gods," Oralia buried her forehead into the center of his bright, grease-stained apron with a groan.

"Your elf is making hand gestures I dare not describe to you."

"Nothing I have not seen before." Of course Ellisar was back here. Likely Curly, too. The pair had enough sense to stay as far from the front of the manor as possible, thus limiting their chance of being assigned actual work. It was not the blatant shirking of duties that bothered her, but the inevitable ribbing she would receive for this later.

Duties. The word disrupted her thoughts like a stone through still water. Something she probably should be seeing about. Whereas most would have settled for a peck on the cheek, Oralia preferred to show her affection in . . . less affectionate ways. She nipped his earlobe between her teeth. Not hard, just enough to let him know she could tear it away if she wanted to. And, with a little tug, let go and untangled her arms from around his thick neck.

Disappointment soured his broad face. "You know, a true display of dominance would be to continue, knowing they are watching."

"I believe you are mistaking dominance with lechery."

Sunlight reflected off of Sascha's thick hide, making his smoky, slate-colored skin appear more blue than gray. His gaze darted back to the tree line, where Ellisar's and Curly's figures stood against the black and green forest, still communicating through fast, lascivious hand signals. "It's been a while since I last rampaged," he said. "Years, in fact. I think I could muster one more, given the circumstances."

As much as it would thrill her to watch him chase the pair through the trees, the ruckus would undoubtedly draw attention. Not just from the soldiers, but possibly the entire countryside. An orc in a full blown rampage was not a subtle affair. The last thing Oralia needed was to advertise her personal relations for the entire realm to see. Besides, when it was all said and done, such a reaction would only encourage Curly and Ellisar.

"Another time, perhaps." Oralia touched his shoulder as she passed, working her way back through the paddock toward the front of the property. With every step, she could feel his hungry eyes watching her.

She did not know how to roll her hips, and dared not try now. Rali had attempted to demonstrate the "come hither" walk one drunken night several summers ago. What had been even more laughable than Oralia's piss-poor attempt was the fact that Snaglebrag proved most competent at it. She would have to leave the seduction to those who could sway their ass without looking like they were trying to scratch an unreachable itch.

Words, fortunately, were still of some use to her. It may not have been the most sultry thing to say, but it communicated her point well enough. "They will be away at the matches tonight. Come find me then."

With Sascha's exasperated huff lingering in her ears, Oralia rounded the corner, fighting the smile that tugged at the edge of her downturned mouth. She resumed her patrol of the grounds, keeping an ever watchful eye for her final mark, Faris Belfast. It took effort to find him. Faris was never in the same place for long. The young Belfast was like a dandelion seed, springing up in plain view one moment and gone on the wind by the next. No matter how many times you plucked him from the garden, however, he would eventually reappear.

Oralia found the faun stationed near the makeshift stables. He was in the midst of a heated quarrel when she arrived. Upon Oralia's approach, the other party quickly departed in the opposite direction.

She recognized the gray overcoat he wore, complete with its shiny brass buttons and the collection of faded ribbons pinned to the chest. Rali, having already spent her silver, had bet it in a high-stakes card game and lost. Faris was cautious by nature and didn't normally boast his winnings, though the jacket seemed to be the exception. He wore it often and blatantly. A reminder perhaps that no one, not even the faithful four, walked away from his tables without settling their bill.

In the absence of trousers, the faun wore a dark green kilt, the hem of which was embroidered with leaves of red and gold. Oralia was unsure whether the kilt paired with the coat was meant to be fashion-forward or ironic. Perhaps he had simply run out of clean garments. Faris oozed such charm he could have strutted around in nothing but his fur and no one would have batted an eye.

He watched her warily from beneath heavy white lashes as she neared. "Protector."

Oralia took him by the elbow, muttering, "Around the corner, Mister Belfast. This will be a private conversation."

Faris's hooves scraped against the dirt in a useless attempt to slow her. "Whatever he did, I had nothing to do with it!"

"Is that the first thing you think to say?" Having learned from her previous mistake, she dragged Faris past the outer barn, across the freshly tilled field, and into the privacy of the trees. Having ensured that Ellisar and Curly had vacated the area and were no longer in earshot, she released him with a grunt. "I have business with you. Nothing more."

"For the record, it's a reflex. You try babysitting a wild animal and see what ticks you develop." Faris massaged the underside of his arm as he took a calculating sweep of their surroundings. He must have come to the same conclusion as Oralia, because his rigid shoulders relaxed slightly. "You have, uh, business, you said?"

He looked prepared to bolt the moment she bared her teeth. "Are you always this nervous?"

Faris shifted from one hoof to the other, refusing to meet her stare. "I think it's safe to assume you aren't my usual clientele."

That much was true. In addition to the organized fighting, the young Belfast was responsible for the steady supply of ale and tobacco that permeated her camp. Oralia did not doubt the cunning faun had other, less obvious lines of profit as well. She retrieved a drawstring bag from her doublet and deposited it into his hand. "Captain Monk is going to challenge your champion. This is twice what you would make if Rasp won."

"So . . . this is your bet then?" Faris raised a single eyebrow questionably.

Oralia glanced around them once more. If she was going to do this, she had to be sure no one overheard. "Rasp is going to throw the fight. Put on a show and make it look good. I want Captain Monk and the audience convinced the match was fair."

Faris drew the bag open and peered inside. His cynical gaze lifted to meet hers. "And you think a handful of silver is going to convince him? Rasp doesn't do it for the money. He gives his earnings to the birds, for muck's sake."

"Then be convincing, Faris. It does not take brilliance to recognize you are the driving force of the operation." The brains, too. And apparently, from the look the faun was giving her, he was already working through several scenarios in his head. "Why?"

"The traveling party needs to have faith in their leaders. Captain Monk, now more than ever, needs to look strong. Tonight sets the tone for the rest of this journey. If the crowd sees Rasp defeat him, we lose everything."

Faris tossed the bag from hand to hand as a calculating smile danced over his lips. "Silver for the fate of the mission? Seems a little light when you put it that way. Throw in that lovely stone you keep around your neck, and I might be more inclined."

She resisted the urge to check that the pendant was still there. The opal, hidden beneath her uniform, never left its chain. The little shit was goading her into showing it to him. Oralia loomed over the faun, her teeth locked in a menacing snarl. "Do not test me, Faris. Either you take the coin or I challenge Rasp myself. A match I will not need to rig to win, mind you."

Faris extended the coin purse in her direction. "Sounds good, then. Let's do that."

Alas, her glare did nothing to ruffle his newfound confidence. Without one of her faithful to explain where she had misstepped, Oralia was forced to admit her confusion. "Explain to me what I am missing in this scenario."

"Getting you in the ring would be the pinnacle of my career." Faris tilted his horns at her, his mouth upturned in an amused expression. "The ticket sales would make up for the loss alone. And Rasp, well, frankly you'd be fulfilling one of his sicker fantasies, so . . . everyone wins? Anyway, I doubt that's what you were going for."

Damn him. Clever faun.

"Alright, easy with the murder eyes." Faris pocketed the drawstring bag with a nervous laugh. "In appreciation for the business you've brought me, Protector, I will do as you ask. But don't hold me accountable for whatever stunt Rasp pulls tonight. He might agree to lose, but he's going to do it in the most memorable way possible."

Oralia recalled Rasp's last fight before being banned from fighting the villagers, in which he had ripped a dwarf's beard from his face and shoved it down his throat. "Can you convince him to be less dramatic?"

"I can barely get him to put pants on in the morning. Let's pray dramatic is the worst he gives us."

CHAPTER NINETEEN

Witch

He missed the stars. It wasn't like the sunshine, which was bright and hot on his skin. Nor the flowers, which he knew by smell. Even the grasses had their sweet, earthy fragrances. Rasp could hear the songbirds and the rain and all the things he used to love. But the stars were silent. He could not smell them any more than he could reach up and touch them. The same constellations that kept him company on those long, lonely mountain nights still stretched endlessly above and yet, he saw only darkness.

Creeping, crawling, endless dark. A forever reminder of what he had been, of the darkness he'd caused.

"Word must have got out." Faris's voice came from behind him. "It's a full house in there. I've got people sitting in the rafters. You ready?"

Rasp smelled smoke. The sweet combination of cherry tobacco and burnt paper. Faris only smoked when he was nervous.

"I don't understand you," Rasp said, still gazing pointlessly upward. He was on the knoll behind the old orchard barn. He could hear crickets chirp and feel the cool grass between his toes. He understood these things. They lived, they died, they came back. It was natural. Friendships were not. "I thought you didn't want to be involved in my schemes."

"What do I tell you in the ring? The one thing I've hammered into that thick skull of yours over and over again?"

Rasp repeated the line from memory, "Don't be predictable."

"Exactly." The faun settled onto the grass beside him, puffing smoke into the air. "Life's no different. You start being predictable and suddenly everyone expects something of you."

"Still doesn't explain why you told me about the protector's bargain." Specifically her fear that if Rasp won, the soldiers would lose heart in the mission.

"In my defense, I made it very clear you're supposed to throw the match. She can't blame me for whatever happens tonight. Everyone knows you're shit at following directions."

"Oralia could take back her silver."

"She could," Faris agreed, talking around the rolled cigarette in his mouth. "And there's a chance Monk beats you and I keep it regardless. It's been a while since I've had a gamble this good."

Was this a test? Not from Faris. Not even from the protector. But fate? Rasp was supposed to be reformed. Was beating the snot out of Captain Monk really the right thing? Or just the thing that felt right? The path of morality was as unclear to him as the stars above.

From inside the barn, the crowd roared a deafening cheer. Faris slapped Rasp's shoulder and stood. "That's your cue, Dinglehead. Whatever you decide, make it good. They paid handsomely to watch."

Rasp lifted his tankard. The unfinished ale, warm like piss and not much better tasting, sloshed against the sides. With a reluctant sigh, he raised his drink and dumped it over his head. Lukewarm liquid ran down his face and chest. "Alright, let's get it over with."

Faris helped him upright. "Going with the drunken fool then?"

"It's what they expect." Predictable wasn't all bad. Captain Monk was expecting to go toe-to-toe with a feral mountain man, after all. Rasp could play his part. At least long enough to rip that arrogant smile from the captain's face and wipe the floor with it.

Gripping Faris's shoulder, Rasp staggered after him through the open barn doors. Inside, the sound was amplified tenfold. He smelled sweat and straw mixed with the faint undertones of blood. It was hot. Already, the ale had begun to dry and stick to his skin. Unfamiliar hands reached out and touched him as he passed. Rasp wasn't allowed to yell at them. It was bad for business, Faris said. It wouldn't have mattered anyway. They wouldn't have heard. The surrounding noise melded into a single, deafening blare.

Rasp shouldered his way into the ring. There were only two things that mattered now—his opponent, and the ten foot circle of dirt that separated them. Here, among the jeering crowd, he felt a small piece of his former life. To fight was to be a Stoneclaw. He rolled back his head and soaked it in. This was his arena. His kingdom. Home.

"Alright you bastards, it's the fight you've all been waiting for!" Faris's voice cut through the clamor. The faun had a talent for inciting a crowd like no other. In another life, he would have sold pitchforks to a mob. "Our challenger hails from the capital of our great and mighty realm. Defender of the people and beholder of our hearts, the prestigious Captain Alin Monk!"

Faris waited for the cheers to die down before raising his voice louder. "Here tonight for one round only, he faces off our titleholder. That's right folks! The spawn of the mountain! Hailing from the great Iron Ridge itself, our champion, Snow!"

"Faris, hol' up," Rasp slurred over the uproar. He staggered a step and then righted himself. "The drink's hittin' me. I gotta take a piss."

Faris sounded incredulous. "You were just outside!"

"Never mind. It's takin' care of itself." Rasp unbuttoned his trousers and relieved himself. He swayed from side to side, rocking on his heels and taking secret delight in the mix of gasped curses and laughs. Finished, he gave it a good shake and tucked himself back in. "Oh gods, that's better. Right then, I'm good."

"I've had house pets more civilized than you." Captain Monk's disgusted voice came from across the ring.

Gotcha. Rasp tilted his head in his direction and smiled. Monk was barely a blur, but it wouldn't matter. As soon as Rasp got him to the ground, it would all be over. The match, the morale, gods above, maybe even the cursed mission itself. "Shit, my bad. Guess you'll 'ave to rub my nose in it."

The bell rang. Rasp swayed, stupidly, and waited. The dirt crunched beneath the captain's advancing feet. Rasp lurched out of range the moment Captain Monk threw his first swing. Miss. The captain pivoted and swung with his left, but Rasp dodged him. Miss again. Rasp stumbled across the ring, faking a fumble each time his opponent neared. He listened to the captain's steps and counted the swings, noting how many were from the left versus the right. Monk was a righty. If he was standard trained, like most of the realm soldiers were, he led with his left leg.

"He's wide open!" someone screamed.

"Hit him!"

Captain Monk, emboldened by the bloodthirsty crowd, charged. One step. Two steps. Three.

Rasp faked with his right and struck with his left. Monk's body doubled over from the impact. Rasp delivered three fast punches: shoulder, head, neck. With his opponent dazed, he took him to the ground. Rasp pinned his quarry with his knees and unleashed his fury. He hit and hit and kept hitting. His knuckles split. He felt the spray of blood and heard the startled cries from the audience.

Captain Monk wouldn't last. Rasp felt his opponent's body quiver beneath him. "Say it!" he roared. "Surrender before I end you!"

The captain tried to wrestle out from under him but another crippling blow to the shoulder stunned him.

Rasp dug the point of his elbow into Captain Monk's neck. "Say it!"

A wave of pain erupted across his back.

Rasp rolled away and grabbed for the interferer. He caught nothing. There was no one in the ring other than him and Captain Monk. He rose, shaking, when the same blistering pain slammed into the back of his knees. Rasp fell to his hands, fingers grasping at the dirt uselessly. His skin buzzed with a familiar vibration. He felt it thrum deep in his bones.

Magic?

Rasp checked to be sure it wasn't his own, choking on the breath that caught in his throat. *What the fuck is going on?*

"He's up, you idiot!" Faris's scream dragged him back to the goings-on outside his head. "Get your ass back into the fight! Finish him!"

He lurched for the captain. A burst of magic struck Rasp across the jaw and he dropped. Captain Monk scrambled over him and landed a decent punch before Rasp flipped him.

One close-fisted slam to the temple. That's all he needed for it to be over. Rasp raised his arm to strike. A searing ripple of magic surged across his arm and his shoulder dislocated with a sickening pop, paralyzing his throw. He fell uselessly over the top of Captain Monk, screaming in pain. His body twitched and convulsed. Bile churned in the pit of his gut. It crawled upward, through his chest, up his throat. Rasp tasted the poison. It wormed through his aching bones and pooled in the tips of his fingers.

No!

He'd already lost control once that day, he vowed he wouldn't do it again. He clambered over Monk, fingers grasping for his opponent's face. A head-butt to the nose would end it. Rasp reared his head back when the final bolt cut across his neck.

His throat clenched. His breath stopped. Blood spurted from his mouth. Captain Monk seized his opportunity and struck back. Rasp hit the ground, already stunned, helpless against the onslaught. The punches landed one after another but he felt nothing. The darkness spread to his hands and then his legs. It swallowed him. Deeper, deeper, deeper, until he disappeared into the black.

His last thoughts were hazy. They danced in the space between consciousness and the quiet lull of the deep.

Witch . . . the realm had sent . . . a . . .

Witch . . .

CHAPTER TWENTY

Fire Starter

Oralia awoke to the rumbling snores of the orc beside her. Sascha's large belly rose and fell with each laborious breath. Overhead, the lantern rocked gently on its hook. Its flickering flame cast a warm glow over the tangle of blankets spread across their intertwined bodies. *Unusual*, Oralia thought, considering she'd extinguished it moments before pulling Sascha into her arms and onto her bedroll. Oralia freed herself from the curl of his heavy arm and stood, moving swiftly for the door.

She snatched her tunic from the pile of scattered clothes and tugged it over her head and shoulders. From the doorway, she could see the firepit outside was alive and licking upward with tongues of wispy orange flame. Also not how she left it. Oralia's sharp eyes scoured the surrounding darkness for whomever had lit the signal. Through the trees, she saw campfires in the distance and heard the drunken whispers of the soldiers huddled around them. She neither saw nor smelled the interferer.

Drawing her arms tighter over her thin tunic, Oralia settled onto the ground alongside the fire and waited, confident the intruder would make their presence known eventually.

Her encampment was in the wooded lot that straddled the road to Belfast Manor. White spruce and paper birch loomed overhead, their branches rattling in the soft breeze. The sky was dark and moonless, with small stretches of speckled starscapes peeking through the cottony gray clouds. In the distance, she heard the babble of a stream trickling over stone and the soothing croak of frogs.

"Old friend," a soft, singsong voice called to her. "I would have messaged the usual way. But, given that you have company, I thought it best not to raise unwanted questions with your paramour."

Why the heirloom she wore around her neck not only glowed, but also communicated telepathically with its beholder, were questions Oralia hoped to never address with anyone. Especially not the orc currently occupying her bed. Across the fire, Oralia saw a shadowed figure materialize from the gloom. "I did not expect to see you so soon, Dear Whisper," she replied, purposely steering the conversation away from the details of her personal life. "Do you have news for me already?"

"Your soldiers celebrate. Captain Monk has defeated the mountain man."

Not the news Oralia wanted, but a small relief nonetheless. It was useful to know that Faris—and, by some minor extension, Rasp—could be counted on to follow instruction when necessary. At least when there was payment involved. "And what of my rat problem? Have you discovered anything during your travels?"

"Your spy is lying low. I suspect they will scurry from their nest once the expedition is underway. Until then, I will keep my ear to the ground." The soft voice carried to her on the breeze. The air stirred, intermingling the smell of smoke with the subtle notes of wintergreen and spruce. "What makes you so certain there is a spy?"

An insect buzzed near her ear. Oralia ignored it, keeping her gaze fixed on Whisper. "I am to retire at the end of this expedition. The Speaker of the People has agreed my debt is settled."

"Ah," Whisper said, thoughtfully. "And you, the natural skeptic, have no faith in the word of your compeer."

Oralia gave up trying to make out Whisper's shifting form and stared into the flames instead. "Geralt promised to release Ashwyn in exchange for the trade routes. I should be relieved, and yet I cannot help but wonder what trap he is setting. I know he is waiting for a slip-up so he can use it against me."

Again.

"Dear Ashwyn. Seventy-three years locked away in that dungeon. Forced to sit idle while you chip away at her penance from the outside," Whisper tsked. "She is fortunate to have such a devoted sister. Most failed revolutionists don't live long enough to regret their poor decisions."

Ashwyn was not the only one with regrets. Had Oralia any inkling how the events following the uprising were fated to unfold, she would have done everything differently. That was in the past, however, and she had since learned to be cleverer. Soon, she would put it all behind her. Provided she could outwit Geralt one final time.

The breeze blustered across the flames, wafting smoke into Oralia's eyes. She blinked the ash from her vision as Whisper's voice encompassed her. "You look more troubled than usual, old friend. Outfoxing the Speaker of the People should be second nature by now. Do you know something I do not?"

We are being set up for failure, Oralia thought.

"The troops I have been assigned have never served directly under me. My next-in-command is a halfwit and our guide is blind. I am not naive to the fact that this mission has all the makings of a disaster." Oralia's shoulders sank. The weight of her burden had grown unbearable in the recent years. She attempted, without success, to control the unnatural waver in her voice. "I cannot afford to have this go wrong, Whisper. I have given everything to get to this moment. I cannot give any more."

Two centuries. That was how long Oralia had served as the realm's enforcer. A figurehead was expected to last fifty years, sometimes twice that, but never this long. Geralt dangled her sister on a string in front of her, forcing Oralia to soldier on. Disaster or not, this mission would be her last. Oralia would secure their damn trade routes, return to the capital to collect Ashwyn, and then disappear into obscurity forever.

The soft, singsong voice whispered into her ear. "Well, it is good you have me on your side then, isn't it? I will see it through to the end with you, dear friend. As promised."

Not that Whisper had much of a choice in the matter. Like Oralia, they were bound by obligation. Whisper's release from service depended on the success of the mission as much as Oralia's. It was a sensitive topic Oralia knew better than to bring up.

"Have you thought about what you will do afterward?" Oralia asked.

"I may have found a promising prospect."

The wind stirred the dirt into the air around her, muddying her vision. Oralia felt the chain tug against her neck. For a brief moment, the stone caught the firelight, casting an unearthly glow.

"I look forward to reclaiming this as well," Whisper's voice said. "Until then, do take better care of it. I can see the dwarf's grubby little fingerprints from here. A little polish now and then wouldn't hurt, you know."

The breeze dropped. Rubbing the dust from her eyes, Oralia glanced downward. There was no trace of Whisper, only the opal pendant hanging over the collar of her tunic. Oralia tucked it back out of sight.

"Oralia?"

The sudden, deep voice from behind caused her teeth to snap together.

Turning to look behind her, Oralia found Sascha's large head peeking out of the front of her tent. His dark eyes shifted, surveying the surrounding trees with the marked care of someone in the habit of watching where they planted every careful step. His large nostrils flared in and out as he tested the cool night air. Oralia remained calm, knowing any trace of Whisper would be disguised by the smoke of the fire.

Having confirmed they were alone, Sascha strode from the tent draped in her blankets. He wore them proudly, as though her old furs were the robes of royalty. "Still talk to yourself, I see," he said, flashing his spade-like upper teeth in a teasing smile.

Towering a head taller than her, with shoulders as wide as a double doorway and tusks the length of gardening shears, Sascha cut an intimidating sight. Intimidating, however, could not have been any further from the truth. Sweet, endearing Sascha had the gentlest nature of any person Oralia had ever met. Everything about him was soft, from his touch to his words to the way his doughy stomach rolled when he laughed. She found it all strangely intoxicating.

She stabbed the hot coals with a stick. "Did I wake you?"

"I'd rather be out here, anyway. Sleep's no fun if there's no one to elbow me in the face when I snore." Sascha settled onto the dirt beside her, managing to net her with the blanket in the same, sly move. He pulled her closer, murmuring, "What's got you on edge, Moonflower? It took me a good hour to knead the tension from your shoulders."

Oralia was not particularly fond of his pet name for her. Hated it, to be exact. She had attempted to illustrate her point by calling him Sunflower in retaliation, but like everything with Sascha, it did not go as planned. He loved it so much, he refused to answer to anything else for several weeks afterward. Thus, Moonflower stuck. But only in private and certainly not when any of her four were within hearing. That was not something they would have ever let her live down.

She tore herself from her thoughts, remembering that he'd asked a question and it was considered common courtesy to answer those. "I am not on edge."

"Your jawline begs to differ."

Oralia gazed across the dancing flickers of red and orange flame as she took one final sweep of the surrounding forest. Whisper was probably halfway across camp by now. Once certain there were no onlookers, she leaned into Sascha and closed her eyes. Situated so close to the fire, she didn't need the added warmth, but it felt nice all the same. His comforting scent washed over her, battling the thoughts raging behind her eyes for her attention. "We are attempting to overthrow an enemy we have never fought on home territory before. You know the stakes as well as I do. It would be foolish not to be on edge."

"Hmm." Sascha scratched his left tusk thoughtfully. "Now that you mention it, I did find it strange none of the other cooks bid on this posting."

"So you *did* volunteer."

"I leveraged a deal. At triple my usual rate, it was an opportunity too good to pass." Sascha laughed. The sound echoed in his chest, close to her ear. "Besides, I couldn't have my Moonflower off starving on the Iron Ridge without me."

"Do you plan to feed me rocks when we run low on rations?"

"Remember the mud pies we used to make as younglings? I've since perfected the recipe. A pinch of gravel. Half a grub." Sascha kissed his fingertips. "Like a symphony in your mouth. You'll never go hungry again."

Oralia smiled in remembrance. "You made the pies, not me. I recall building the fortifications."

"And then you and Ashwyn slung my creations at the local soldiers. I remember. They never caught you two, either. Just me. The one that couldn't fit through the gaps in the fences." Sascha worked his strong fingers through her hair with a chuckle. "Little fire starters, even back then."

The mention of her sister stirred an old ache in Oralia's heart. With Whisper, it was different. The [voice? entity?] knew only the failed revolutionist. Sascha had known Ashwyn before the realm had placed a bounty on her head. He talked as if she were still the rambunctious youngling from their childhood. That version of Ashwyn existed only in memory now. Oralia blinked away her guilt, knowing it was her hand that had placed the final knife into Ashwyn's back.

"There I go opening my big mouth again. I didn't mean to upset you, Moonflower."

Oralia wasn't sure whether she was more impressed or annoyed by Sascha's uncanny ability to tell her mood from a single stretch of silence. Ultimately, the use of her pet name was what helped sway her decision. She kept her voice flat and free of the pain that hung heavy in her heart. "I do not start fires. I put them out."

"Hmm." If Sascha didn't have an immediate answer or, as in this case, if he knew his answer would be met with a differing opinion, he simply substituted words for sounds. It allowed the listener to draw their own, often wrong, conclusion. From his half-assed attempt, Oralia suspected he disagreed, but did not have the desire to make an argument of it.

Unfortunately for him, she was in the mood for one. Oralia locked eyes with him. "You think I am trouble?"

Sascha's knowing smile said everything his confounded tongue didn't.

The warmth of his smile combated her icy expression. The two battled without speaking until Oralia was forced to concede her silence. "You are one bad apology away from sleeping under the stars tonight."

"You are the worst kind of trouble." The flickering firelight bathed his broad, handsome features in an orange glow. She hadn't noticed before, but the reflection from the fire highlighted the few silver hairs that hid among the tangle of his black beard. Sascha's soft, rumbling voice continued. "The type that inspires a lovestruck fool to lug his ass up a cursed mountain just so he can be near you. My own mother begged me not to go."

Oralia unclenched her jaw and stood, muttering, "You are a hopeless romantic."

"Well, at least the two of you finally agree on something."

Senseless fool. She would only break his heart, as she had done countless times before. Sascha was a glutton for punishment. He always came back. Maybe it could be different this time. Maybe when the expedition was over and Oralia was released from the realm's service, she would take Sascha with her. And together, they could spend the rest of their lives basking in the firelight beneath the stars.

Good gods. She was as hopeless as he was.

Oralia tugged the blankets from his body and strode into the tent, calling over her shoulder, "Unless you want to see firsthand what trouble I am capable of, you will extinguish that fire and get your carcass swiftly back to my bed, where it belongs."

CHAPTER TWENTY-ONE

All Things Stupid and Boring

Two days. That's how long his injuries delayed the expedition. Rasp wasn't solely responsible for the setback, either. Captain Monk's, whose condition was equally severe, was laid up in the makeshift infirmary beside him for the duration of his stay. Rasp drifted in and out of consciousness most of the first day. He caught the occasional grumblings from his roommate, mostly about the perpetual ringing in his right ear.

Sadly, Rasp didn't have the strength to taunt him.

On the third day, the protector shoved his ass onto a horse and the traveling party departed Lonebrook. Mount Hook was the second tallest of the Iron Ridge peaks and home of the Stoneclaw clan. The journey there would take four days. At Rasp's insistence, they would ascend from the west, the steeper, more dangerous, nearly impassible cliff face. It would go unsuspected by the mountain folk for one, and two, it would hopefully be hazardous enough to make the convoy question the sanity of their leaders. Until then, the most important factor was to avoid the foothills. Rasp chose the road that snaked along the Byorne River instead. The trek consisted of long stretches of realm forest and the occasional farmland. Uneventful. Safe. Time consuming.

Two days on the trail came and went without incident. With each day's passing, Rasp found himself longing for the stiff infirmary bed with disturbing frequency. It smelled better than his musty horse. Moved less, too. Every step and jostle was agony on his bones. There was the added complication that Rasp didn't know how to ride, either. Stoneclaws didn't use horses. The animals ate too much, broke too easily, and had the unfortunate habit of attracting dragons. The raiding parties only ever brought them back to stock the meat larders. And even then, horses weren't very good tasting. Not unless you were a dragon, maybe.

To make matters worse, the realm emissary, Daana, seemed to be under the misguided impression that he wanted her company. Her horse bobbed alongside his as she babbled endlessly about the history of the realm and all things stupid and boring. "Interestingly, the realm isn't a single territory. It's actually a set of individual territories united under the protection of a governing body . . ."

They clearly had differing opinions of what qualified as interesting. The United Territories of the Realm. It was in the fucking name. How daft did she think he was? "Faris!" Rasp shouted, searching along the horse's neck for something to steer it with. "How do I make it go faster?"

". . . It's ruled by three main branches of government, each with its own figurehead. The Leader of the Realm, the Protector of the Realm, and the Speaker of the People," Daana continued. "Each territory has elected representatives that travel to the capital to . . ."

"Yaw, Oralia! Yaw!" Rasp remembered his lessons from the day before and squeezed with his legs. "Run, you stupid horse!"

"You named it Oralia?" Faris's blurry shape appeared alongside Rasp's right, about knee level. Unlike him, the blasted faun was allowed to walk. As the guide, they insisted the horse was for Rasp's protection. He was less likely to injure himself and, in the event there was trouble, the protector could have him swiftly escorted to safety.

"I regret that now. Clearly it's living up to its namesake." Rasp squeezed again to no avail. The damn thing plodded along uselessly. "Why won't it run?"

"It's a pack horse, Dinglehead," the faun replied. "You're not going to get it to run. Not unless the front one does."

Of course the protector had given him a defective horse. Rasp wouldn't get very far on his own. A horse, however, could carry him a greater distance if he were to slip away into the night unnoticed. Clever Oralia. Rasp leaned over in the saddle and spoke in a hushed tone. "Have you found anything yet?"

"What was it I was looking for again?"

Rasp clenched his teeth together, hissing, "The witch, Dingle. The witch!"

"Not this again," Faris groaned. "There's no shame in admitting Monk beat you. You don't need to save face. No one respected you to begin with."

"You should be taking this seriously! Someone used magic against me, Faris. They could do the same to you."

"Oh, right. Definitely witchcraft and not because you got your ass beat."

With a groan, he shifted back into the center of the creaky saddle and sank lower, allowing his thoughts room to run. The magic hadn't come from

Captain Monk, Rasp was fairly certain of that. He suspected the witch had been hidden among the audience, using their powers in a manner that slipped the notice of the bloodthirsty crowd.

The question was, who? There hadn't been a magic user listed among the specialists in the travel party—Rasp would have raised an uproar, otherwise. And why had they interfered? Admittedly, he didn't care so much about that last question. The moment he discovered the identity of the witch, he planned to move on to the part where he ensured they didn't disrupt his plans a second time.

"What's this about magic?" Daana's voice roused him from his internal stewing. Rasp's resulting silence only furthered the nosy elf's prompting. "Go on. If you're not going to pay attention to your lesson, then you might as well tell me what the two of you are whispering about."

Blasted elf ears. Another reason the emissary was steadily wearing on Rasp's nerves. Her heightened sense of hearing allowed her to catch every insult uttered under his breath.

"Dinglehead here thinks the realm secretly planted a witch in the traveling party," Faris said, unaffected by the cutting glare Rasp shot in his approximate direction. "He still can't give me a good reason as to why they would do that. So far, logic hasn't swayed him."

Stupid, stupid Faris. The witch could be Lady Lazuli herself for all they knew. "That's it! I'm renaming the horse Faris."

"And what makes you think that? You aren't magic-sensitive, are you, Rasp?" Daana asked. For whatever reason, her voice lowered to a level that might have qualified as teasing had Rasp not suspected she was one hundred percent serious. "Did you feel a magical tingle down your spine recently?"

Rasp bared his teeth at his keeper. "Remind me again why I'm not allowed to hit her?"

"Easy, Rasp." Faris gripped his arm preemptively. "It's an innocent question for realm people, you know. The emissary didn't mean anything by it."

The use of his real name helped stifle the fury brewing behind his eyes. With the citizens of Lonebrook behind them, Protector Dawnsight had allowed him to ditch the ridiculous cover name. There was a small minority of soldiers that did not appreciate learning they were helping to reinstate a former Stoneclaw enemy, but Oralia had assured him that so long as he kept his infernal mouth shut, they would keep their grudges to themselves. And, in the event Rasp picked a fight he couldn't win, she made it very clear that she would wait until the absolute last moment to intervene on his behalf.

With the pain of defeat still fresh in his mind, Rasp vowed to keep his sparring matches strictly to the verbal variety. At least until he had healed sufficiently, anyway. It was a prospect that drew nearer with each passing day.

Daana's grating voice startled him from his thoughts once more. "Oh, right. I forgot the mountain folk have the whole anti-magic thing. Sorry." There was a brief, lovely pause before she launched into a barrage of questioning. "Why is that? And is it true anyone caught using magic is thrown from the cliffs?"

Rasp set his jaw so tightly his back molars ached. Barbarians, that's what she thought of his people, thanks to misconstrued realm propaganda. His people understood the risks of magic. Unlike the realm, which openly encouraged the dark arts. Anyone in the United Territories found to possess magical abilities was taken from their families and delivered to the Division of Divination for training. The realm had an entire education system specifically designed to weaponize witchcraft.

"No," he said, "it's not true."

"But I heard—"

Rasp whipped his head at her, snarling. "Then you heard wrong!"

"I didn't mean to offend."

"Well, you did."

"I'm sorry," Daana said, after a pause. "That was assuming of me, wasn't it?"

She was . . . apologizing? Rasp didn't know how to respond. Or if he was supposed to. No one who ever apologized to him ever actually meant it. Maybe this was simply a ploy to entrap him. He clamped his jaw shut and said nothing. No good would come of this, anyway. Magic was not something to be spoken about so openly. Everyone knew drawing attention to these sorts of things would only make the temptation stronger. Harder to resist.

His hand curled into a fist as the little voice in his head whispered, *You can't hide it forever. They'll find out eventually. They always do.*

The hot afternoon sun beat down overhead without mercy. From time to time, the road would snake closer along the dense tree line, the overreaching boughs offering a brief respite from the sweltering heat. The welcome shade would stretch for a short distance before the forest receded and Rasp's horse plodded along an exposed length of road once more. Even surrounded by an army, he felt strangely vulnerable. The urge to duck and roll from the horse and dart into the protection of the trees was ignored only because he wouldn't get very far.

Perhaps he would have felt less on edge if the emissary weren't still talking.

"I want to know more," Daana prodded kindly. She sounded genuine, too. Somehow that made it worse. "In all of the realm, we have but one book on your people. I've been attempting to translate it, but progress is slow. As I have been sent as the liaison between our territories, it only makes sense that we understand each other. So please, teach me. Why is it that the mountain folk have such a strong aversion to magic?"

Rasp wanted to snap how obvious it was. How anyone with half a brain knew the answer to that. But he didn't. Instead, he simply, shortly, replied, "Magic is inherently bad. It doesn't matter if you start out with good intentions or not. Eventually, all who use it are corrupted."

Faris cut in. "Weren't you accused of being a witch?"

His shoulders stiffened. "What's your point?"

"Well it's the reason they threw you down the mountain, yeah?"

"For the gods' sakes, no one gets thrown from the mountain! There are consequences to using magic, yes. As there should be. And, for the record, since no one seems capable of remembering this very vital fact—I was not thrown from the cliffs. My brothers chased me off the mountain *and then* tried to kill me. Big difference."

"Because they thought you were a witch," Faris concluded.

"No!" Rasp said. "They accused me of killing our father so I could take his place! It just so happens they also thought I was a witch. And anyway, you don't kill a witch on the mountains. That's just asking for a warbear. Gods, do either of you know anything?"

There was an air of confusion in Faris's voice. "Are you trying to say *werebear?*"

"No! Warbear. As in *war-lock-bear.*" Rasp added the extra syllable for emphasis. The same way certain ignoramuses spoke to him when they confused blindness with a head injury. "Except you don't say warlock on the mountain without someone throwing accusations your way. So you shorten it to warbear and pray to whatever gods you align with that you don't encounter one. Clear enough for you, Dingle?"

"That's so oddly specific. Why warlock-bear? Why not witch-bear? Wibear?" Faris contemplated this for a moment. "You know what, I can see why you went with warbear. No one who shouts 'Watch out for the wibear!' would be taken seriously."

"Are you finished?"

"How do you tell a warbear from a regular bear? Does it wear a pointy hat and robe?"

Rasp swiveled his head in Faris's direction and narrowed his eyes. "It's the reanimated soul of a witch born into a bear. No, it does not wear a fucking hat, Dingle. It's got red eyes and teeth the size of blades and can walk through walls."

"Oh, so you've seen one, have you?"

"No," Rasp grumbled as some of the fire left his belly. "But my brother Lingon did."

"And just how drunk was he when the magical bear walked through his wall?"

"Oh my gods. Just shut up already."

"Thank you for your input, Mister Belfast. I would like to ask some questions of my own, if you don't mind," Daana said, sounding every ounce like the envious sibling who'd been eyeing your new lizard-on-a-string all morning—or whatever toys realm folk played with.

Rasp wondered, briefly, if the emissary even knew the joys of playing with other children. Hitting your brothers with rocks, putting snakes in each other's boots, slipping slugs in their trousers, and so on. Daana spoke with the entitlement of an only child who learned a little too late in life that no one wanted to play knife-knife-who's-got-the-knife with her. Daana's voice brought him back from his reverie, and Rasp caught the tail end of her blathering about magic, or witches, or something. There was probably a question in there somewhere, but he didn't care to answer any more of those.

"Why are you so fixated on this?" Rasp remembered the etiquette instructor, who smelled vaguely of camphor oil and mothballs, advising him to address a person by title. It demonstrated respect, after all. Something someone in his Rasp's position would benefit to show more of. So Rasp added, voice dripping sweet and sticky like fresh fir sap, "Lady Lapissy."

"Lazuli."

"I'm certain that's what I said."

"I believe you were telling me how the mountain folk deal with witches, yes?"

Rasp should have stuck to daydreaming about rocks and slugs and fighting over whose turn it was to poke the wasp's nest with the burning stick. Maybe if he indulged the emissary it would help dispel the "thrown from the cliffs" nonsense. He doubted it would prevent her from continuing to talk, unfortunately. That would have been too merciful.

"The first time you're caught meddling in the dark arts, it's a warning. The second time, you lose an eye. And, if you're stupid enough to keep doing it, the third and final offense is met with banishment. Harsh, yes. But like I said, no throwing anybody off anything."

The explanation was all but lost on Faris, who promptly replied, "Is that why they took your eyesight, then?"

"Oh dear gods." Rasp slumped forward in the saddle and drew his hood over his head. "Go back to boring me to sleep, Lady Lazily. I'm done."

After another firm correction on the pronunciation of her name, the emissary continued her lecture, explaining that unlike their mountain folk neighbors, the realm celebrated the diversity of its citizens, including those that demonstrated magical abilities. Throughout history, many great wizards and sorceresses had served the realm. Daana went on to name them, gushing over each with enough details to fill a book. Ozgard the Great. Merrista the Wise. Bobart Who Gives a Flying Fuck.

Croak!

Rasp jerked upright in the saddle. "Dragon?"

CHAPTER TWENTY-TWO

Dragon

Get into the trees!" Rasp tried once more to urge his horse forward without success. "Faris! Faris, for fuck's sake, get them off the road!" This was the time of the year the swift tails and sky shrieks emerged from their winter lairs with empty bellies. But the dragons weren't supposed to be here. It was too far south. Rasp had avoided the foothills for just this reason. A large caravan traveling along the exposed road was a dinner bell to a hungry dragon.

"A dragon?" Faris sounded torn between being legitimately concerned and not wanting to fall into Rasp's latest prank. "Where?"

Croak!

"Above, you idiot. Get us into the tree line, now!"

"Move off the road there's a—"

Rasp never heard the last of Faris's words. An ear-shattering screech thundered from above. Sky shriek. He knew it by its call. A thirty-foot winged monster with claws, teeth, light blue and white scales, and an appetite for flesh.

Rasp's horse reared in terror and bolted. He lurched forward, clinging to its mane with all the strength in his hands as the frightened animal galloped across the uneven terrain. Rasp heard screams as the caravan devolved into chaos behind him. Suddenly, the air moved overhead in mighty gusts as two, no three, additional cries echoed the hunting call of the first.

Not just a dragon. Several dragons. A mother and her hatchlings, judging from the eager, hungry shrieks that rang out above him.

Without knowing the terrain underfoot or even which direction his horse was bolting, Rasp slid from the saddle. He hit the ground and rolled, abruptly slowed by a thorny shrub. Groaning, Rasp gathered his cloak over him and crawled further into the brush. Sky shrieks hunted by sight. If he kept low and stayed still, there was a chance he might be overlooked.

The ground trembled as the others stampeded past. Someone tripped over him and fell. Rasp cursed and rolled with them, semi-grateful it hadn't been a horse. The blood curdling shriek of a nearing dragon prompted the soldier back onto their feet.

"Stay down!" Rasp tackled them. He pinned the squirming soldier against the dirt and felt something sharp prod the center of his chest. "Good gods, tell me that isn't a hatchet I'm laying on top of."

A muffled voice, female, gasped beneath him, ". . . Can't . . . breathe."

He lifted a fraction higher, allowing her room to breathe but not enough to bolt. If they were still, the dragon would pass over them unnoticed. "Would you like to live?"

The head bobbed rapidly beneath him.

"Great, from this point forward, you are my eyes. I've done this before, understand? Stick with me and we'll make it together," he said quietly. "Now look around us. Do you see cover? A ledge, hole, den, anything?"

The further underground the better. Sky shrieks were aerial hunters. They wouldn't bother to dig up prey with this much food around them.

Her short, gasping breaths began to slow. "I—I see a ditch. There might be a burrow there, I think."

"How far?"

"I, uh . . . twenty yards? Oh gods, it's coming back! We won't make it."

"Get a hold of yourself, soldier!"

"I'm not a soldier," she whimpered, her body quaking beneath him with muffled sobs. "I'm the herbalist."

Rasp's mind raced to place her. The herbalist, a faun, he recalled. She'd been among the unlucky few taken from Lonebrook to accompany them up the mountain. If he didn't get her to calm down quickly, neither of them would make it past the road. "The forest hermit, I remember. Remind me of your name?"

"Briony," she wailed.

A dark shadow passed overhead. Loose dirt and debris pelted Rasp's shoulders, stirred into the air by the dragon's mighty wake. "Alright, Briony. We're going to do this together. First, I need you to make sure there isn't another one nearby. Do you see anything?"

He felt Briony shift her head to look. The point of her left horn dug painfully into his shoulder as she did so. "The others are back over the road.

A hundred yards. Oh my gods, they've got someone. They're eating—"

Rasp jumped onto all fours, pulling her with him. "Stay low. Get us to that ditch. That's all you have to do."

Briony took his outstretched hand and together, crouched low, they raced forward. Weeds and thorny branches whipped Rasp's unprotected face as he stumbled alongside her. The rocky terrain sloped suddenly and Rasp lost his footing, slamming hard on his ass and skidding the rest of the way down. Briony, acting as a counterweight, heaved against him, grinding Rasp to a halt. With a final, agonizing pull, Briony dragged him under the ledge with her.

Rasp scuttled as far back as the narrow burrow allowed. He didn't stop until his shoulders hit earth. The space was small, so much that even crouched on all fours, he was forced to lower his head to avoid hitting the ceiling. He released the breath that had caught in his throat with a giddy sigh. "Oh my gods, that actually worked. We're alive!"

"You said you'd done this before!"

"To be fair, those times usually involved cutting someone down as bait," Rasp said. "Anyway, you're welcome."

She shushed him. "Listen. Do you hear that?"

Frantic footsteps thumped against the ground overhead. Rasp heard a muffled cry followed by the thud of a body slipping from the ledge. There was another sound, too. The steady beat of monstrous wings as one of the dragons drew closer.

"It's Willem!" Briony darted forward before Rasp could stop her. "Willem, in here! Hurry!"

Rasp pressed his shoulders as far back against the side as he could, allowing room for the third body. Willem collapsed against them, whispering through his heavy, panting breath, "Blessed be, miss. Thank you."

"Quiet!" Rasp hissed, listening. The others instinctively pressed into him, as far from the entrance as physically possible. He was too preoccupied by certain death to be bothered by the overwhelming smell of camphor oil that buzzed irritatingly close to his nose.

Clumps of dirt fell loose from the low-hanging ceiling as giant footsteps thundered outside. For a few seconds, everything went still. There was a low, guttural growl followed by a torrent of hot air that filled the den. In-out, in-out, the dragon's musty breath sniffed for its prey. The walls trembled, dirt falling faster, as the hatchling began to dig.

A Stoneclaw was many things, but not an easy meal. "Briony, the hatchet!"

Rasp barreled to the mouth of the den and swung. The blade buried into something thick and hard before he wrenched it back in a spray of hot dragon blood. Spurred by the hatchling's scream, Rasp hacked blindly. He hit rock and dirt mostly, but was rewarded with the dragon's pained shrieks thrice more. Rasp felt the poison churn in his gut. He swallowed it back down, skin burning as the magic pulsed through every stretch of muscle and sinew. He couldn't, not here. It was too cramped. He'd kill the hermit and the oily mothball man. Probably himself, too.

"Rasp!" Briony shouted for possibly the third time. She reached out and grasped his shoulder, staying his swing. "Rasp, wait! The birds. They're attacking!"

With chest heaving, Rasp realized he could hear the fierce echo of the flock outside. The ravens would only be able to keep the hatchling at bay for a few minutes at most. They had to move quickly. "Briony, lead," he panted, hoarsely. "Willem, you next. I'll bring up the rear."

"Are you mad?" Willem said.

Rasp listened, realizing he heard more beyond the ravens. "The river, is it far?"

"Forty yards at least," Briony said grimly.

"Sky shrieks don't swim. On my mark, we run for it."

"Fauns don't swim either!" Briony protested.

"Then you'd better fucking float." Rasp ushered her to the front. "Now go!"

Briony's hooves scraped against the hard ground as she hurtled out in front of them. Rasp grabbed Willem by the arm and propelled him out after her. With the hatchet gripped in his left hand, he sprang free, realizing too late that he should have grabbed onto one of the others first. Birds swooped around him in the bright, unfiltered light as he ran. Their frantic calls, mixed with the deafening roars of the dragon, drowned out the sound of the river. With panic rising, Rasp realized he was turned around and didn't know which way to run.

An arm hooked under his and jerked Rasp backward. "Running in the wrong direction," Willem grunted. "You really are mad."

Rasp's boot caught on a rock. He tripped but didn't fall, yanking hard on Willem. "You're my eyes, idiot! Use them."

"Do you want me to be your feet too?" There was a waver in Willem's voice now. "Pick them up, boy! It sees us."

"Good, hopefully it chokes on you first!" The dirt terrain underfoot turned to loose stones. Rasp slipped again but kept his footing this time.

River rock. They had to be close. Rasp raised his voice to be heard over the roar of the water. "Tell me we're not far."

"Only a few yards," Willem panted. "Terrible news, though."

"What?"

"The bank's too steep. We'll have to jump."

Rasp suppressed the whimper that rose in his throat and hooked his arm tighter. In his younger days, he would have tripped Willem to ensure a clean getaway. Being a good person came with a whole host of inconveniences. Avoiding murder, mainly.

Rasp felt the heavy draft from the dragon's wings at his back. The hatchling was gaining. Spurred by his terror, the poison surged through him a second time. His fingertips pulsed, skin buzzing. Of the two evils, magic was lesser than murder. Surely fate would see it that way.

"Mother!" Rasp whistled loudly between his teeth, releasing Willem's arm. "Kill shot!" It reeked of desperation. Their hunting technique was for vermin, not killing dragons. But Rasp would be damned if he didn't at least try.

"What?" Willem screamed.

"Not you. Just tell me when to jump." Rasp called again to the raven. "Any time now, Mother!"

"Jump!"

Rasp turned, pushing off from the bank with both heels, throwing arm locked in position and legs coiled beneath him. On Mother's call, Rasp whipped the hatchet in her direction, channeling all of his power into the throw. There was a ghastly scream and the air whipped and churned in mighty gusts, buffeting him further out over the river. Rasp fell for several heartbeats before he plunged beneath the surface. A silent scream caught in his throat. The water, cold and crushing, stole the breath from his lungs. He fought to the surface, managing a gulp of air before the current ripped him back under.

CHAPTER TWENTY-THREE

Witch Hunter

Dinglehead, where the muck are you?" Faris shouted from below, bounding through the thick underbrush. From Daana's position in the treetops, he appeared like an erratic white blur against the green landscape. She understood now why the faun refused a horse, opting to walk along the traveling party instead. He would have put Uncle Geralt's prized race team to shame.

Curly, less enthusiastic in his search, leaned against the birch tree Daana was currently using as a lookout point. He peered up at her through the spindly branches, speaking around a mouthful of wild raspberries. "See anything yet?"

"No," she grumbled, clinging to the rough trunk as she began her shaky descent. It had been years since she'd climbed a tree of this height. Daana took it slowly, testing each branch underfoot before committing her full weight to it. "We could cover more ground if you helped search, you know."

"Eh, Rasp will show up when he gets hungry enough."

"Not if he's injured," Daana countered. Or worse, dead. A possibility she didn't want to consider at the moment. She was nearly to the base of the tree. Only a few spoke-like branches separated her from the fern-carpeted ground below. "And he's not the only one we're looking for, either. Willem is still missing, too."

"And, if we're lucky, they're both dead and we can go home."

Daana considered dropping her boot on top of Curly's unsuspecting head and claiming it was an accident, but she probably wouldn't get it back. Besides, if Willem were here he would remind her that she was supposed to be making nice with the faithful four, not inciting war. Biting back her temper, Daana slid from the lower branches onto the ground and fixed Curly with her most disapproving frown. "Did you really just say that?"

Curly wrinkled his nose at her. His broad, square teeth were stained red from the berries. "Do you always ask such stupid questions?"

Faris came barreling through the forest at them, unknowingly sparing Curly from a well-deserved earful. The faun leaned forward and rested his arms against his knees, chest heaving. "Anything?"

"No." *Alright, Daana, say something that demonstrates you're in charge. With confidence, like you mean it, and you're used to people listening.* "But Curly has volunteered to go check by the river's edge so you can take a rest."

"I did *what?*"

"I'm fine," Faris insisted.

"Slow down and use your head, Mister Belfast. You may be fine for the moment, but you're going to be a lot less useful when you succumb to exhaustion two hours from now." *So far so good.* Emboldened by her new-found confidence, Daana shoved her waterskin into Faris's hands and glared fiercely at Curly. "Are you waiting for a formal goodbye? Go!"

The scorn that curled over Curly's lips caused her to take a step backward. *Okay, maybe too much.* ". . . Please?"

The orc adjusted his travel pack over his shoulders and grabbed another fistful of raspberries before he stomped away, shaking his head. "Search party, my ass. Everyone else gets to take care of the damn dragon and I'm stuck with you twits."

Rasp's horse had bolted when the first dragon attacked. Forced to scramble for cover, they'd lost sight of him altogether. Faris, with Daana's help and Curly's presence—as the orc was absolutely no help whatsoever—scoured the meadow and surrounding woods for him. So far, they had yet to find a trace of either Rasp or Willem.

"It's Faris, by the way." The faun sat, reluctantly. "Mister Belfast makes me sound like my father."

Finally, a first-name basis with someone. The young Belfast may not have been one of the faithful four, but he was a step in the right direction. Faris traveled in and out of Oralia's inner circle as if he was the unofficial fifth member. Daana had not yet pieced together how he, not a soldier, not a killer, not particularly anything, according to her uncle's intelligence officer, fit in their ranks. Faris provided the faithful some sort of benefit, surely. The sooner Daana discovered exactly what that was, the sooner she wouldn't have to linger as an outsider on the sidelines.

Daana massaged her temples with her fingertips, sighing, "Why Dinglehead?"

He nearly spit the water from his mouth, surprised. "What?"

"That's what you call Rasp, isn't it? A nickname like that has to have a story."

The surprise left his face and was replaced with something else. From the way his fair-colored eyes narrowed around the edges, Daana suspected it was suspicion. Faris wiped his mouth with the back of his hand, grunting, "Not really."

A cautious individual, evidently. She wondered if he would respond to authority. "I am the emissary, you know. I could demand you tell me."

Faris gave a disgusted snort. "Don't do that."

"Don't do what?"

"That's not how you throw your weight around. Do you think Oralia travels the realm announcing she's the protector wherever she goes? No, because it's stupid and it looks weak."

Daana felt a sudden heat flush across her cheeks. "Oralia doesn't have to. Have you seen the size of her? When she wants something, she looks you straight in the eye and speaks in a tone that makes you grateful not to be dinner."

"If that's all you see, then you're not looking hard enough."

A cautious, strangely insightful individual, it seemed. Faris may not have wanted to be mistaken for his father, but he had certainly learned a few things from the judge. "And what would you have me do?"

Faris picked up a stone and turned it over in his hand. "I don't know. Are you good at anything?"

Before Daana could recall the finer points from the dossier, her mouth opened and words sprang forth in an order that, if not accurate, were at least arranged in the correct sequence. "Of course I am. I'm a diplomat. I'm versed in realm history, speak seven languages, and am trained to handle even the most tense of political situations."

Faris produced a harsh laugh as he stood, shaking his horns slowly. "And they sent you out here? Gods, someone must be trying to get rid of you."

The heat on her face now burned like a fire. Luckily, she remembered she was supposed to be playing the role of a well-mannered court member and, instead of cursing him to the seven realms of chaos and back, lifted her nose into the air with a huff and said, "I will not be spoken to that way."

"Can you catch?"

"Can I what?" Daana turned her head in time to see something hurtling at her. Her hands shot into the air, fingers crossed at the knuckle. Before she could stop herself, Daana uttered the deflection spell. Magic coursed through her arms and burst from her fingertips in a concentrated blast. "*Prohibere!*"

The stone dropped harmlessly to the ground in front of her.

From the way his eyes narrowed and mouth pulled at the corners, Faris looked smug, not surprised. "Now that's good at something. Interesting you didn't mention it."

Daana felt immediately dizzy. Her legs were as wobbly as the gelatin tower desserts that were left untouched after every banquet. She was supposed to remain hidden, dammit! It was, what? Hardly the third day on the road to Mount Hook, and already she'd been pushed from hiding. She did not want to imagine what Uncle Geralt would have to say.

Fear gave way to anger, dispelling all sense of prior diplomacy. "Why the fuck did you do that?"

Faris's reply was surprisingly simple. "I wanted to know what I was dealing with."

"I'm not what you think."

"You mean a witch?" the faun said, circling her cautiously. "Oh no, you most certainly are not. Those fancy bands on your arms, they hold power, but not your power. Because you're not a witch. You're a witch hunter."

Daana rolled her eyes at the archaic term. "I'm a seeker."

"There's no need to be modest, Lady Lazuli. You're not just any witch hunter, you're *the* witch hunter, aren't you?" Faris slipped in and out of the overgrown brush, disappearing from sight one moment and then popping up again somewhere else the next. "You go by a different name in the field, but I know a parasite when I see one. Tell me, is it true you can drain a witch of their powers simply by touching them?"

Faris whipped Daana's waterskin from out of the trees at her. Daana dodged the projectile and then dropped swiftly into a crouch. She locked her forefingers together and waited for his next attack. "You know an awful lot about my business, Mister Belfast. Why is that, exactly?"

"I find it never hurts to be informed." Faris's voice called to her from a different direction than she anticipated. "Why are you here?"

She'd never had prey toy with her during a game of cat-and-mouse before. Daana was the damn hunter, not him. The situation was as confusing as it was unusual. Feathery, dark green ferns crumpled underfoot as she shifted her weight to her back leg and gazed up and down the needled tree forms, scouring the shadows for her quarry. "If you were intelligent enough to figure out what I am, then I suspect you already know."

"Fair point," Faris said from behind her.

Daana spun around on her heel, cloak swirling in her wake. She saw nothing. Over the fast in-and-out of her own breath, the only other sound she heard was the wind rustling the treetops overhead. *Where did he go?*

From the direction of his voice, Faris had once more managed to change locations without giving himself away. "*Who* are you looking for then? I thought you seekers went after little kids and those that can't defend themselves. I don't know about you, but no one here seems to fit that bill."

First of all, she did not hunt helpless little kids. She helped locate fledgling witches to offer training and a better life through the Division of Divination. Secondly, this exchange was obviously going nowhere. With a groan, Daana stood straighter, throwing her hands out at her sides in the universal sign of defeat. "Faris, really. If I knew who my target was, don't you think I'd have them apprehended and halfway back to Sunstorn by now?"

Daana was magic-sensitive. Unable to produce a power of their own, those gifted with magic sensitivity could usually do little more than detect its presence. Daana's abilities went a step further. She could draw magic from its source and, after years of practice, had learned how to manipulate it through spell commands. Had this been an ordinary mission, it would have been over and done with by now. The ghost, her current target, was as unordinary as they came. Among a multitude of powers, the ghost was capable of disguising its trail. Whenever Daana sensed she was getting close, the ghost's magic would vanish and reappear again on the very edge of her range.

Apparently the ghost and Faris had that in common. For the life of her, Daana could not get a handle on the faun's ever-shifting position. As she had seen from her lookout position in the tree, Faris was obviously the faster of the two. If he intended to turn her in, he would have done so already. She raised her voice, calling out to him. "Why haven't you run back to warn the protector?"

"Because you haven't told me what I get for helping you yet. The Director of Magical Affairs pays two hundred silver a head for an unregistered witch. If they sent you, that must mean this catch is bigger. It would be stupid to choose a side without knowing the stakes first."

Not a soldier, not a killer. Faris was an opportunist. A scavenger looking for its next meal. Daana considered her options for a moment. She couldn't afford to have him warn the protector. Oralia despised magic in all its forms. If the protector found the ghost first, she would destroy it. Daana with it, if given the chance.

Faris may not have been an accomplished witch hunter, but he possessed an advantage Daana did not—he had already wormed his way into Oralia's inner circle. With Faris's help, she could insert herself into their ranks much quicker than she could on her own. He had the potential to get her closer to Protector Dawnsight, too. Then, and only then, did Daana have a chance at discovering what Oralia was plotting.

First, capture the ghost. Second, learn the intimate details of Oralia's plan to undermine Uncle. And third, return to the capital as a hero. From there, Daana would rise to the highest ranks of the Division of Divination and, when the time came, take over for Uncle Geralt. Gods, it sounded so easy in her head.

Daana's mind was made up. "I'm hunting the Palace Ghost."

CHAPTER TWENTY-FOUR

Over the Edge

The tips of Daana's ears burned as Faris's snorting laughter filled the damp forest air. Her big reveal had not only fallen short, but landed on its face and was now writhing pitifully in the dirt. "Are you finished?"

"The palace ghost?" The faun wheezed between words. "What kind of name is that?"

"Look, I'm not the one that named it, alright? All you need to know is that it's something the Director of Magical Affairs will pay handsomely for."

Nobody knew what the Palace Ghost was. Only that it resided in the capital palace and laid dormant most of the time. But, every so often, once or twice a decade, it would go active again. The magic was unlike any ordinary power. It was something old, something forgotten, something that, in the right hands, could raise a nation. And, in the wrong ones, level it.

For the greater part of a century, it had been the same. The ghost would awaken, triggered by an unknown circumstance and, without warning, leave. Sometimes it moved alone and sometimes, as in this case, it followed a realm caravan to its destination. What purpose the ghost fulfilled by doing so was a mystery, as every seeker sent after it never returned—except Willem, which Daana didn't think counted as he had technically been an apprentice at the time. And then, weeks, months, or even years later, the ghost would reappear within the walls of Sunstorn and once more return to its slumber.

"I'm still waiting, witch hunter."

Daana snapped from her thoughts, glaring in the direction of his voice. At least he'd finally stopped laughing. "What's your price, Faris?"

"Oh, you know, the usual. A title, land, a big vault of silver and gold."

"How do I know I can trust you?"

Faris stepped from one of the many flowering white and green thickets beside her, grinning at the way she jumped. "I was wondering the same thing about you. I guess I'll just have to assume if the speaker sent his own blood after this thing, he's willing to pay. You'll have to trust that I love money enough not to turn you in to Oralia."

"I don't work for Uncle Geralt. I work for the Division of Divination."

"Oh, right. Like the two are mutually exclusive," Faris said with a wink. "Everyone knows the Speaker of the People is the division's biggest sponsor. I'm surprised the order hasn't changed their motto to 'We lick Lazuli boots the best' yet."

This clever faun knew entirely too much. Daana furrowed her brow at him. "If you want a family to return home to, you will tell no one. Especially not Oralia."

"Much better, Lady Lazuli. That's how to throw your weight around. I actually believed you this time, see?" Faris held his hands wide, flashing her another toothy smile which looked strangely predatory on a vegetarian. "What about the protector makes you so jumpy? I mean, besides the whole 'eat you for dinner' look she's so fond of."

"Oralia would rather kill a witch than turn them over to the Division of Divination. She's done it before. I need the ghost alive," Daana said, ignoring the way something inside her was performing acrobatic somersaults. Oh gods, Willem was going to be so cross when he found out. This was breaking every secrecy rule in the order. But that's why Daana would succeed where no one else had before her. Uncle Geralt had taught her all about bending the rules.

"So," Daana said. "About that nickname, then?"

Either he sensed she was testing him or he had simply grown bored of his games, because Faris answered without any of his former caution. "Rasp calls me Dingle. Which I think is a reference to his genitals, but I'm not going to humor him by asking. I started calling him Dinglehead in retaliation, hoping he would stop. It stuck, instead. And now here we are."

Faris was half-right. It was an insult, albeit a lighthearted one, used exclusively between the Stoneclaw brothers. It was almost flattering. Faris wasn't just his keeper, Rasp fancied them brethren. Such information could prove useful.

"You're right," Daana said, glancing down her nose at him. She borrowed one of Willem's expressions, attempting to appear simultaneously cold and disinterested. Somehow she managed to miss both targets and landed squarely in the "unnecessarily cruel" category. "It wasn't that interesting."

Dammit. That wasn't intimidating, it just sounded mean. Willem makes this look easy.

A powerful whistle cut through the trees before Faris could say something clever in return. The faun's ears flickered in the direction of the sound and his expression dropped. "That's Curly. He must have found something."

Faris was gone in the time it took Daana to sling her waterskin back over her shoulder. Stifling a groan, she started after him, but soon lost the faun altogether. Dried spruce needles crunched underfoot as Daana padded along the dense forest floor, pausing every few minutes to detangle herself from the sprawling plant life. The whistle led her up a fern-covered hill. Daana shifted her weight to her toes and climbed, mindful not to disturb the devil's club that blanketed the lush hillside. The trees began to recede until she reached the peak where only a few sickly, splintered evergreens stood tall against the elements, their scraggly branches whipping in the wind. Daana spied Curly's burly form first. Faris was beside him, crouched along the edge of a ravine, gazing down at the raging waters below.

"What is it?" Daana panted, trying to make her lapping breaths less obvious. Her lungs were burning, and already there was a cramp in her ribs. Despite their reputation, seekers did very little to no hunting, at least not anymore. Their primary duties were to travel from village to village across the territories testing the young for magical abilities. Very few dared run from a seeker. That probably had more to do with the overall decline in witches, and not so much the peak form of the magical order. Daana made a silent vow to work on her endurance. After all, a huffing and puffing hunter would not be impressive to anyone, especially not the ghost.

"Down there," Curly yelled, his voice barely heard over the rush of the river. "There's no telling how long she's been trapped, but she won't last much longer. She's as pale as death."

"It's Briony." Faris's white hair blew across his face as he spoke. "She's the herbalist from my village."

Cautiously, Daana edged out near where they stood. The harsh wind stung against the exposed skin on her face and neck. Below, a good ten-yard drop by her estimation, a small form huddled against the cliff face, half submerged in water. Daana saw the tan and brown faun looking at them, eyes wide with terror and shaking. Alive, at least. But Curly was right, not for long. With nightfall quickly approaching, the temperature would drop and Briony would freeze to death.

"Dear gods," Daana cursed. "There's got to be a low spot near here some-where. Maybe one of us could wade in and get her?" Not her, obviously. She didn't swim.

"Don't get any bright ideas about swimming, princess." Curly knelt beside his pack and began tossing random items onto the ground beside him. "The current's too strong. It'd drag you three miles downriver before you even got a paddle in. She's lucky she got washed onto that ledge."

"So you have a better plan then?"

The orc produced a braided rope from his bag. "I'm going to lower one of you two cocksuckers down there. You tie her on. I hoist her up. Once she's secured, I throw you the rope again and you climb back up praying the cliffside doesn't give way under all our weight."

"Not it," Faris said.

"Me?"

"You're the elf. Aren't you supposed to be light as birds or something?"

"Do I look as light as a bird to you?" Daana gestured to her figure. She was not the long, straight-haired wisp of an elf that the court artists loved to depict in their paintings. Daana had full hips and a belly, and a chest that made her back ache most of the time. "It should be you. You're smaller."

Faris jutted his jaw at her, scowling. "I am shorter, not smaller. My bones weigh twice what yours do. Rasp threw out his back trying to toss me into the pond once."

"I'm about to shove you both into the river and call it a day," Curly snarled.

"Fine!" Daana snapped.

As an elfling, she used to climb from her window onto the palace roof. Surely this wasn't any different. Minus the whole raging river and having to trust the orc, who wasn't overly fond of her to begin with, to not drop her to her death. She was suddenly grateful she hadn't thrown her boot at him, after all. "At least tell me you have a harness."

From Curly's disconcerting smile, Daana knew her answer. "Oh gods," she groaned. "I'm dead."

"It's time for a little lesson in rope tying, princess. For your sake, I hope you're a fast learner. I can help with yours, but you're gonna have to secure Briony on your own. Faris," Curly called. "Play dead."

"What? Why?"

"You're the dummy, dummy."

With Faris reluctantly serving as their rescue victim—who had to be reminded several times that he was unconscious and therefore could not complain—Curly demonstrated the process. Three fathoms of rope, he explained, using the length of Faris's arm span as a guide. He showed Daana how to make a bowline knot and how to reinforce it. Next, Curly strung the loop between Faris's legs, around the upper torso and then fixed the two ends into what he referred to as a sheet bend. Once everything was tightened, he demonstrated the makeshift harness's durability by lifting Faris into the air.

"Put me down!" the faun shouted, kicking.

Curly obliged him, dropping Faris back onto the ground into an undignified heap. "Hope you got all that."

Daana sorely wished she'd brought along something to take notes with. "I think so."

"Good," Curly said, unstringing Faris from the rope. "Because down there, if the faun slips, you're breaking her fall."

He made Daana practice five times, until the last two emergency harnesses were tied to his satisfaction. And then, before she knew it, Curly was fixing Daana into a harness of her own and guiding her over the edge of the cliff. She wriggled over the ledge on her stomach, inching backward until her body swung down. From there, Daana descended with her legs braced against the rock and feet shoulder width apart. She took it slow, one shaky step at a time as Curly gradually fed her more rope from his position above.

The wind howled around her, threatening to shake her footing and slam Daana against the cliffside. There wasn't time to stop and consider the easiest way down. Without control of the rope or the speed at which she was rappelling, Daana was at the mercy of the rockface. To her relief, the ledge below grew closer. Until at last, with two final, trembling steps, her heel struck stone.

The ledge wasn't large, barely a two-foot lip of jagged rock that jutted out from the cliffs along the water's edge. There was room to stand, but not enough to lie down without being partially submerged in water. The faun barely noticed Daana. She was curled into a small ball with her head resting between her arms, shivering. Briony's strength had to have given out hours ago. Daana dragged Briony from the water, as far onto the narrow ledge as she could, before untying her lifeline. With her hands wet and shaking, Daana spoke Curly's directions out loud as she followed them.

"Through the loop . . . around . . . back through and tighten."

The wind raged through the ravine, chopping the rough waters and stealing the words from her mouth. With her coiled brown hair snapping in front of her face, threatening to block her vision, Daana finished tying the sheet bend and tightened it. She stood back and tugged the lead three times as dread filled her belly. Several heartbeats later, the rope pulled taut and Briony was slowly lifted in the air. The faun's head rolled backward and she ascended, limp and lifeless. Daana watched helplessly from below, hoping the harness would hold better than her first two attempts.

Daana flinched the few times the poor faun rocked into the cliffside. Slowly, painstakingly, agonizingly, death-defyingly slowly, Briony inched toward the top. Faris's hands reached over the edge and heaved Briony the rest of the way. The last of the faun disappeared over the lip of the cliffside.

Daana, realizing she'd been holding her breath the entire ascension, forced the air from her lungs. It was over. Briony was safe. Wrapping the cloak tightly over her shaking shoulders, Daana pressed her back to the rock face and tried to tune out the sound of the rushing water. She had a deep distrust of any body of water deeper than a bathtub. Ocean, river, lake—she would walk around before she entrusted her life to a boat, or worse, her own poor swimming abilities. Fortunately it wouldn't matter, Daana thought, as she gazed across the river with an involuntary shudder. Because any moment now the rope would slither down to her and she would be pulled free without even getting her boots wet.

And so Daana waited. And she waited. And waited some more. She craned her head upward as the gnawing sense of dread flooded her gut a second time. Maybe they were attempting to revive Briony first. Maybe Curly needed to rest his arms. Maybe Faris convinced Curly to leave Daana at the bottom and they were both already halfway back to camp, perfectly content to let her die.

"You two didn't forget me, did you?"

The blistering howl of the wind was the only reply that reached her ears.

Her unease grew heavier, like a weight in her chest, steadily crushing any lingering hope of a rescue. She slammed her fist against the rock, suddenly wishing she hadn't. Daana bit her lip, blinking back tears of anger and pain as she filled her lungs with air. "This isn't funny! Throw the rope down this instant!"

CHAPTER TWENTY-FIVE

Hurt

Wind whipped through the ravine. The howling torrent of frigid air chopped the river's glistening silver and gray surface, kicking up gusts of wet spray. Willowy green and yellow reeds bent against the onslaught. The tops of their leafy stalks rattled in a chorus of flimsy twists and snaps. Daana's wool cloak flapped above her head, threatening to rip free of its clasp and take flight. Wide-eyed, she drew it tighter over her trembling shoulders as the festering dread in the pit of her stomach spread outward.

Daana shut her eyes, trying unsuccessfully to block out the swell of dark thoughts that lapped along the rim of her mind like the water's edge. "Benton Cortair! This is your last warning! If you don't lower the rope I'll . . ."

Scream some more? Pace uselessly until the ledge gave out beneath her? Daana's options were regretfully limited. Alone, without rope or anyone to assist, she had three choices: stay put and hope someone came along and found her, attempt to brave the river, or, lastly, climb the cliff face on her own without a safety harness. All three would end in death, undoubtedly.

Visions of her childhood flashed before her eyes. She remembered how her academy mates used to lock her in the supply closest between classes. The time they convinced her to join them on an outing into the haunted woods and left her. She sank down, squatting with her back still firmly pressed to the cliffside as the old feelings stirred from the dark recesses of her memory. Abandonment. Betrayal. Hurt. Always on the outside, never in. The cornerstones of her formative years.

Uncle Geralt was the only reason Daana had survived her training at the Division of Divination. He hadn't been overly affectionate or encouraging, not like the other parents, but he had been there. The only constant in Daana's life. Swooping in at the last moment, righting the wrongs, ensuring justice was carried out. As Speaker of the People, Uncle Geralt had the power to bring the entire wrath of the realm down upon anyone who hurt her. Except Uncle wasn't here. He wouldn't know who to blame for Daana's death. Or even how she died, for that matter.

"No, no, no," Daana whispered around the tightness in her chest as her breaths grew short and shallow. Despite the chill, her forehead felt inexplicably hot. "It's not like that. You're okay. You're going to be okay."

Troubled thoughts swept across her mind uninhibited. They would not be stifled. They would not be shoved into the dark. They would not be silenced, or repressed, or forgotten. Not this time. Her anger and despair transformed to grief. Daana buried her face in her hands as realization gripped her. She would be another headstone erected over an empty plot. Just like her parents. Insignificant. Meaningless. Forgotten.

She had no memories of her father. And over time, her mother had grown faceless. Daana had been so young when they died. She could recall Mother's voice, sometimes, but even that slipped from her memory like loose sand between tightly clenched fingers. Nobody talked about them, not even Uncle Geralt. The family portrait was removed from the great hall and the rest of the realm moved on, as if they had never existed.

Would she be treated the same?

All her life she'd wanted to be someone important. Someone respected and revered, like her dear uncle. It was her entire reason for joining the division. Her parents had left behind enough funds to support her for life, but Daana didn't wish for simple existence. She wanted her name on the wall of the greats. She wanted to be remembered. To be loved. She wanted everything that her parents had been denied.

And now she was going to die alone and cold in the uncaring wilderness. Destined to carry on the family legacy, after all.

There was something else buried in those memories. Like Mother, it was distant, fuzzy, and felt more like a half-forgotten dream. All Daana had was a blurred outline of a face. For some reason she remembered small glints of light reflecting from it, like stars peeking against the black velvet night. That, and fragments of a nursery rhyme. It came to her in moments like this, when she needed little glimpses of starlight to illuminate the dark.

Little tadpole, little tadpole,
What do I see?
Little tadpole, little tadpole,

Ya not like me.
Can't swim, can't hop,
Ya talk nonstop!
Little tadpole, little tadpole,
Don't ya see?
Little tadpole, little tadpole,
Don't belong ta me.

A piercing whistle disrupted her thoughts. Daana whipped her head upward and watched as the slack end of a rope sailed over the edge, uncoiling like a great serpent as it plummeted toward her. Choking back her tears, Daana wiped her nose against her sleeve and grabbed the lead. Three fathoms of rope tied into a bowline and then reinforced. She took the loop and doubled the end and strung it between her legs and around her chest. Despite the tremble in her hands, she secured the final knot and then took a step back from the ledge. She sucked in air through her nose and held it, steadying her shaky nerves. Finally, calm enough to begin the ascent, she tugged on the rope thrice.

The harness lifted her body from the ledge and, once she had her footing, Daana braced her legs against the jagged cliff face and began to climb. Going up was significantly more strenuous than going down. Several times Daana felt the rope drop and for a few panicked heartbeats, thought she was going to plummet to her death. The harness held, however. As did Curly, who dutifully pulled her one arm's length of rope at a time. With trembling hands, Daana reached the top at last. She heaved her upper torso over the edge, fingertips grasping for whatever handholds she could find as her feet dug at the cliffside for traction.

Curly maintained the tension on the rope until she was all the way over. His lower jaw hung slack and his breaths were heavy and strained. He looked across at her wearily, chest and shoulders heaving, seemingly debating whether he wanted to maintain his bravado or drop to the ground with exhaustion.

Daana stood, managing several wobbly steps, before she collapsed into him, wrapping him in her arms. Every muscle in Curly's chest flinched against her. The obligatory "thank you" turned to ash on her tongue as Daana felt something sharp prod her just under the armpit.

She shoved away from him with all the speed and none of the grace of a cat. "Did you just pull a knife on me?"

"You attacked me first!"

"It was a hug!"

"Oh. Eww." Curly's suspicious glare shifted from her to the blade in his hand and back again, as if debating whether to slip it back into its sheath or keep it out in the unlikely event Daana attempted a second embrace. "Why?"

"For not abandoning me?"

"Well, excuse me for not realizing that was an option."

For several pained seconds, the pair stared each other down with eyes locked and arms crossed. What in the seven realms was going on? In the span of a single event, she'd gone from terrified, to grateful, to furious. If there was such a thing as emotional whiplash, Daana was certain she was experiencing it now. Still maintaining her withering expression, she unclenched her jaw and conceded the argument. "Thank you."

Apparently that wasn't what he was expecting either. Rather than acknowledge her gratitude, he stuck his tongue out at her with a sneer instead.

Oh my gods. You just put your life in the hands of a giant baby. "How very mature of you."

With a shrug, Curly coiled the braided rope over his arm before returning it to his pack. Daana set about collecting her own belongings. A few curious glances over her shoulder confirmed that he was still staring at her with a look she could not quite pin down. A second wave of heat flushed across her reddening face. "What?"

"I can't say letting go didn't cross my mind as I was pulling you up." A grin pulled across his mouth and spread to his eyes. "But then I'd lose my favorite rope. Couldn't have that. So if any of the others ask, *that's* why you're still here."

"That would be tragic for you, I'm sure," Daana said, forcing an exaggerated eye roll. She made a mental note to add "rock climbing" to her growing list of activities to never attempt again. It ranked lower than swimming and getting attacked by a flight of hungry dragons, but not by much.

It was then she noticed they were the only two on the ridge. "Where are the others?"

"Faris took the herbalist back to camp already." Curly finished rearranging the items into his pack and stood, arching his back until it produced several sickening pops. "Gods, I'm starving. Tell me you caught a fish while you were playing in the water down there."

"Catch a fish? With what?"

"I dunno. You're the emissary, aren't you? Can't you just order one to jump out onto the bank?"

Emissary was better than princess, Daana decided. Besides, he had a point. She hadn't eaten since breakfast, and after several hours of searching and one death-defying climb, they'd earned a break. "Maybe not fish, but it works surprisingly well on kitchen staff. Come on, leave the talking to me. All you have to do is stand there and look scary."

He shouldered his pack and began the long trek back to camp. "Me, scary? You ain't seen scary. Try reorganizing Snag's vials sometime. That'll get you scary."

"Isn't that your primary function of the four? The scary muscle?"

"I wish. Rali says I've got too much of a baby face to be believable." Curly's dark eyes grew wide, as if realizing he'd shared too much. "Don't tell anyone I said that. It's bad enough the others treat me like a fucking tot. I don't need the realm catching on."

"I can't picture anyone babying you."

"Oh, yeah? Then why am I out here lookin' for Rasp when I could be helping fight that last dragon, eh? I always get the shit duty."

"Constantly underestimated. Story of my life." Daana saw her opportunity and seized it, adding with a smile, "I won't tell. *If* you stop calling me princess. Surely you can come up with something more clever."

Curly made a face like he'd eaten something sour. "Then what am I supposed to call you?"

"My name, preferably."

"Queen, got it."

"That's not any better!"

"What's that?" Curly shifted his pack higher and broke into an easy trot, his strides growing longer as he disappeared down the fern covered hill. "Sorry, Your Highness. Can't hear you!"

"Keep it up and by the week's end you'll forever be known as Benton Baby Face Cortair!" Daana summoned the last of her strength and took chase. She may not have been as fast as Faris, but there was a chance she could catch Curly. "Scratch that. I'll tell Rasp, and the whole realm will know by sundown!"

CHAPTER TWENTY-SIX

Like a Greased Sausage

There were thirteen species of dragon in the known world. Of those, five species resided within the realm. Over the years, Oralia had encountered four of those five, as well as a non-native grabble horn that had been smuggled in as a pet and later escaped the basement after devouring its owner. Sky shrieks lived in the Iron Ridge. On the *other* side of the Iron Ridge. They terrorized the flatlands, not the United Territories. There was no precedent for sky shrieks being anywhere near the realm. They were big. They were mean. And they were so well camouflaged that unless you heard their telltale scream, not even the best elf scout could see the beasts coming until they were dropping out of the sky on top of you.

The convoy had been prepared for raiders, swamplanders, and even the illusive swift tail attack, but not blasted sky shrieks.

"Left wing's broken. It can't fly." Ellisar's stale voice broke Oralia from her inner raging. The elf stood beside her, surveying the creature from afar. They were on the opposite side of the road, tucked along the dense tree line. Anyone not on dragon duty had been ordered to stay out of the open.

"How in the seven realms of chaos did that happen?" Captain Monk demanded. He was seated on an overturned tree behind them, freeing his facial hair from the debris collected during the scuffle. He pulled a twig away with a twist and grimaced. As usual, his voice was a half-step below a scream. "An arrow wouldn't do that kind of damage, would it? The archers are the only ones that have gotten even close to hitting that thing!"

Ellisar's ashen face didn't turn in the captain's direction. Her words mirrored her expression, flat and without emotion. "An experienced archer with a longbow, maybe. By definition, that rules out your people. And I certainly didn't do it."

Captain Monk stopped pulling at his beard and glared at her. "Insults at a time like this? Show some blasted respect!"

Oralia was too consumed with thought to prevent Ellisar from baiting the captain into an argument she would inevitably win.

The adult dragon had grabbed its kill—two horses, one of which still had its unfortunate rider tangled in the stirrups—and disappeared over the trees. It was the hatchlings that caused most of the damage. They roved up and down the meadow, scattering the convoy, chasing the horses and terrorizing the soldiers. Oralia regrouped, and with the help of her faithful four and a handful of the others, chased off two. The third wouldn't leave. It stomped along the road, snapping at anything that neared. Presently, her soldiers had it cornered near the river, driving it back each time it tried to cross the meadow back toward the traveling party.

Judging from Ellisar's haughty stance, she was already proving victorious in the battle of wills taking place between her and the captain. The fact that she was doing so without saying a word was a small feat in itself. Oralia interrupted the pair, sparing Captain Monk from the humiliation of his impending defeat. "Ellisar, have you dealt with one of this species before?"

"That depends. Are we including today?" A cold look from Oralia prompted a more helpful response from the elf. "No. But if you want it dead, I have some ideas."

"You will take the lead, then. Bring it down as safely as possible."

Captain Monk rose tentatively. "Is this wise, Madam Protector?"

Letting Ellisar lead? Certainly not. The elf had grown careless over the years and took to chance like a bird to wing. Captain Monk spoke of killing the dragon, however, which was absolutely necessary. On its own, flightless, the hatchling would either die of starvation or take to raiding the nearby farms. The only dragons farmers ever contended with out here were swift tails. Which, not much bigger than a dog, really just meant raising your pitchfork at it and yelling until it scampered off with a mouthful of squawking chicken. A sky shriek, thirty terrifying feet of pure monster, would just as likely eat the farmer and pick its teeth with the pitchfork afterward.

Killing the hatchling had to be done. Even if Oralia didn't particularly want to be the person to do it. Or anywhere near the person doing it.

"I cannot risk it following us. Take the rest of the traveling party a mile up the road, Captain. Make camp in the trees and get the medic on her rounds. Ralizak, I want a full damage report when we are finished with the hatchling." The distance was for safety. In the event the carnage attracted something bigger, Oralia wanted to be as far away as the injured could travel before nightfall. There wasn't supposed to be anything bigger out here, but there weren't supposed to be sky shrieks, either.

"Get a letter to the nearest city, Captain," Oralia added. "Tell them to send a squadron of dragon hunters immediately. The sky shrieks cannot be allowed to settle."

"Yes, Protector." Captain Monk, looking somewhat relieved, departed to do her bidding.

Ellisar still had her eyes on the hatchling. "The medic was eaten."

With a sigh, Oralia started across the meadow. With her forces scattered, it was impossible to know how many of the missing were dead, lost, or in hiding. Among those unaccounted for was the Stoneclaw. His horse had been found grazing down the road, riderless. Knowing Rasp, he'd dismounted and was probably still up a tree somewhere. He likely didn't want to be found, because then he would have some very serious questions to answer. For example: Why in the seven realms of chaos were there sky shrieks this far south? And, possibly more terrifying: Did you summon them, Rasp?

It was rumored that several very ambitious mountain folk had discovered how to tame dragons. The method involved snatching the egg from the nest before it hatched and raising it by hand. But in all her years fighting the mountain people, Oralia had never seen a dragon heed anyone's command. When one of the beasts arrived during a skirmish, it very indiscriminately ate whatever enemy was closest, including Stoneclaws.

At the moment, Rasp wasn't her primary concern. The dragon first and then she'd deal with him.

Oralia didn't normally mind silence, but it felt necessary to say at least something in the event this was the last time she and Ellisar spoke to one another. "One last hunt for the glory days?"

Ellisar's straw-colored hair caught the waning sunlight as she strode casually alongside Oralia. The terrain between the road and the river was flat with tall, flowering grasses and fireweed. "To which lifetime are you referring? I found more glory in piracy, personally."

"That is not something you say aloud."

An elf could be many things in its lifetime. Ellisar had been a few too many: mercenary, pirate, revolutionist, and—the only career choice the realm advertised to its adoring populace—renowned dragon hunter. Unlike the others, Ellisar's participation in the faithful four was not voluntary. Rather, an alternative to serving a life sentence.

Oralia ignored the fleeting smirk that crossed the elf's harsh features. "I am giving you free rein. Do not abuse it. I will not risk lives because you like to play fast and loose."

"That is the definition of dragon hunting, Protector."

"No, it is not. I visited the dragon exhibit in Sunstorn when I was there last and had a very interesting conversation with the curator. It turns out, whenever the name Ellisar Farrow is mentioned in the record books, it is followed by an asterisk labeled 'what not to do.'"

While effective, Ellisar's methods were questionable. Apparently the dragon slaying community had thought so, too.

"I'm still alive, aren't I?"

"It is the safety of those around you that concerns me, not your own. If you could do the takedown with less . . . collateral damage?"

"No one died last time."

"Yes, you are correct. And I appreciate that. I was thinking more along the lines of less broken bones and missing appendages."

"Fine." The elf's golden eyes narrowed, either annoyed or deep in thought. Her controlled reactions often made it difficult for Oralia to decipher her mood. "I'll need Snag, then."

"You cannot use Snaglebrag as bait." Not after what happened last time. It had taken weeks for him to speak to Ellisar again, and many months more before he stopped spitting in her food.

"A tempting idea, but I require his skill, not his hide. A beast this size will need something potent to bring it down."

"Poison?"

"Boring, isn't it?" Ellisar said flatly. "Just the way you like it."

Oralia was relieved. Boring meant safe. *Safer*, at least. Taking down a sky shriek was, by definition, the complete opposite of safe. It bordered on madness. Fortunately for Oralia, Ellisar thrived on madness.

The pair were across the meadow now, nearing the line of soldiers armed with pikes barring the hatchling from the road. Snag was not difficult to locate. He was with the others—as much as someone like Snaglebrag could be among others, Oralia supposed. Standing a sensible distance from the danger of both the dragon and the pikes, Snag fiddled with his pipe, producing sharp, horribly offkey sounds.

"I thought you burned that," Ellisar said.

"So did I."

Snag's head snapped up at their approach, hoops jangling softly. He slid the pipe into his back pocket, likely to prevent Oralia from destroying it as she had the three that preceded it. Unlike his playing, the craftsmanship improved with each model. "Oi! Dragon duty, really?" He tapped his clawed foot at her. "Curly should be here, not me. He volunteered, for the gods' sakes."

"Curly wants to make a name for himself. I trusted you were smart enough not to get eaten. Prudent it seems, as Ellisar has use for you."

Snag's yellow eyes shifted between them suspiciously. "You're not using me as bait."

"That was one time," Ellisar said.

The goblin's ear flattened against the back of his head. "It was three! And that last one nearly got my skull split! Your arrow caught me in the ear, remember?" He crossed his arms and jutted his lower lip, adding, "Which you never apologized for either, by the way."

"I remember splitting my winnings when I didn't have to." Ellisar flicked her chin in the direction of the hatchling. "What do you have that will bring it down long enough for me to sever its head?"

Snag only scowled at her.

"If I were you, I would go with the option that does not involve live bait," Oralia said. It was not uncommon for her and the faithful four to come across varying beasts from time to time. It was also not uncommon for Snag to find himself as the lure for whatever it was they were trying to trap. Accidents happened, unfortunately. At least that's what Oralia had written in her report, choosing not to mention it had been a bet that prompted Ellisar to award Snag with what she insisted was a "new ear piercing."

"I'll see what I have on me," the goblin muttered.

"Thank you."

Snag's spindly fingers unclasped the pouch slung across his scrawny hips. He mumbled to himself, sorting ingredients as he considered their options. "Oh, the mighty sky shriek. I lost my uncle to one of them, you know? I mean, it wasn't a surprise. Auntie slathered him in hog fat and tossed him out of the cave with a torch first. He went down like a greased sausage."

An unfair comparison to sausages, Oralia thought. A goblin was anything but appetizing. They were all skin and bones and little bits of metal. There didn't appear to be an ounce of spare fat on Snaglebrag, either, which everyone knew was the best part of sausages. It must have been a very desperate dragon.

"Sky shrieks are resistant to most plant-based toxins, but a highly concentrated venom might do it." Snag selected a glass vial and held it out to Ellisar. "Crypt spawn, freshly milked. A single drop can stop a troll dead in its tracks. May not be enough to kill your beasty, but it'll—how do the humans say? Make it sleep like a tree?"

Oralia didn't think that was how the saying went.

Ellisar studied the clear liquid, unimpressed. "How does one milk a dragon?"

"You pay someone an arm and leg to do it for you. And don't ask where I got the arm and leg, 'cause you don't want to know." He watched Oralia from the corner of his eye, adding, "I expect to be reimbursed for the poison. It's a personal item. Hard to come by. Not exactly realm-issue, if you catch my drift."

Which meant expensive and quite possibly—no, definitely—illegal. Oralia sighed. "I will have Ralizak add it to the expenditures."

She had half a mind to list it under "hog fat."

"Excellent. A final question for the hunter." Snag held his gnarled fore-finger aloft. "How do you intend to administer toxin to a dragon?"

"Poison-tipped arrow to the mouth."

"Ah. No scales, direct access to the bloodstream. Smart." The goblin clasped his pouch shut and retreated several steps, offering a half bow. "Best of luck then. I'll be jeering you on from the tree line."

"Still need you," Ellisar said.

"Dammit."

CHAPTER TWENTY-SEVEN

Disturbingly Sentimental

The sky shriek hatchling stomped along the river's winding edge, snapping at the wall of pikes that impeded it from crossing the meadow and disappearing into the protection of the trees. It would charge on occasion, gaining a few yards of ground before being driven back once more. The imminent danger of the situation was all but lost upon Snag and Ellisar, who stood with crossed arms and fixed expressions, each attempting to stare the other into submission.

Ultimately, it was Ellisar who won the battle of wills. She extended her quiver in Snag's direction triumphantly. "Mix the venom into a paste and apply it to the arrowheads. I will need you at the ready to bring me more if necessary."

"Oh, a blasted delivery service, is that it? Why not just coat me in the paste and ring the dinner bell?" Snag's glare lessened when Ellisar's silvery eyebrows perked at the suggestion. "Don't look at me like that! I wasn't serious."

"You're my backup, Protector." Ellisar turned her attention to Oralia. "I don't trust any of these halfwits to get there in time. Tell the line to retreat halfway to the road. They are to hold there with pikes at the ready."

Oralia had only ever seen sketches of a sky shriek prior to this. There was a very nice skull on display in the exhibit in Sunstorn. Shy of wondering what they'd done with the body, Oralia hadn't given it much thought. Now she found herself wishing she'd bothered to read the little plaque below the display to see if it had offered clues on how it died. "Any tips for sky shrieks? I am dangerously out of my element."

She could admit things like that to Ellisar, because from the elf's definitely-not-smirking face, she already knew Oralia was well out of her depth.

"Avoid looking like a sausage?"

"Thank you, Ellisar. Helpful as always."

The elf then gave some actual instruction which, while morbid, at least gave Oralia a faint idea of what to do in the event the dragon slaying turned to dragon escaping. "Sky shrieks are hydrophobic. If things go sideways, save my ass in the direction of the river. Remember your three vulnerable points. And, if all else fails, try to let it eat Snag first. He might be toxic enough to give it a stomach ache."

"Hilarious," the goblin muttered.

When the others were in position, Ellisar strode amid the waist-high grass to where the dragon paced along the water's edge. The sight was reminiscent of the famous painting that hung in the east wing of the capital palace. A tall elf warrior, long hair billowing behind them, bow in hand and sword at their side, stalking their deadly prey. It was almost as picturesque up close, minus the one glaring distinction. Paintings were soundless. The ruckus Ellisar was making was loud enough to wake the dead.

Oralia could only catch pieces of what the elf was shouting. The few verses carried to her on the wind were vulgar enough to make a seasoned streetwalker blush. Effective, though, as Ellisar had the dragon's attention now. It whipped its neck about, long body uncoiling, as it lumbered in her direction. The first arrow whizzed across its snout, bouncing harmlessly off the hatchling's scaled hide.

"She missed!"

Oralia knew better. Ellisar never missed, not unless she was taunting her prey. "She is goading it into position."

Enraged by the assault, the dragon charged, its mouth agape and hooked fangs bared. Ellisar corrected her aim to account for the wind and waited. Oralia's hand instinctively hovered over the hilt of her blade as her feet shifted into position, ready to sprint at a moment's notice. From forty yards, there wasn't anything she could do but watch and wait as the dragon barreled toward the brazen huntress. Ellisar held steady, waiting until the hatchling was nearly on top of her before letting the arrow fly. It struck deep into the beast's gaping maw. In the time it took Oralia to blink, the elf was gone, vanished into the overgrown landscape.

The hatchling whipped its head back and forth as it charged along the riverbank, scaled sides heaving. At last, the beast's steps grew heavier. The right wing flapped, pummeling great gusts of air across the sea of quaking green and yellow grasses. The left wing hung slack, broken and useless. With a pitiful squeal, the dragon staggered a few clumsy steps more and collapsed. Its head struck the ground and, with one last tremble, went still.

Ellisar emerged from the brush near the tail. She inspected it first, circling the fallen beast, mindful to stay out of range. Satisfied, the elf drew nearer. Having traded her bow for the longsword at her hip, she jabbed at the dragon's exposed underbelly. Nothing. A second and third test confirmed the results of the first. Finally, Ellisar approached the head. She raised her blade over her shoulder the same moment the wing stirred.

"We've got movement!" Snag cried. "Ellisar, tail! Watch the—"

Ellisar's sword buried into the dirt where the neck had been only seconds before. The dragon lurched, rearing its head into the air as its tail whipped the elf's back in a blur of blue and white scales.

"Drive it back!" Oralia shouted to the pike bearers.

She was already halfway there, running at full speed with her broadsword gripped in both hands. The dragon staggered onto all fours in front of her. Its body swayed, tail swishing as it lumbered forward. Oralia lost sight of Ellisar. Judging from the way the hatchling stomped at the ground, the elf was using the grass as cover.

Oralia was not a dragon slayer by any means. She'd *helped* slay dragons, but that mostly involved deferring to Ellisar and stabbing when the elf said "Stab!" But Oralia knew the basics: aim for the eyes, nose, or mouth. As she had no intention of approaching a sky shriek headfirst, Oralia settled for the less deadly option. Slash where it would hurt. Dragon scales, similar to armor, were weakest at the joints. Oralia dodged the tail and drove her blade into the thick webbing between the rear leg and underbelly. The hatchling shrieked and whipped around, but Oralia was already gone. She darted beneath it, ducking along the shifting legs, around the tail, and out the other side.

Half hidden by the trampled brush, Ellisar saw her coming and started to rise. Oralia heaved the elf's light frame the rest of the way, still running. She sprinted for the river, supporting Ellisar under one shoulder, painfully aware of the deafening howls of the dragon at their backs. The ground shook behind them as the great beast gave chase. Oralia didn't dare look behind her.

They slid down the sloped bank into the tangle of reeds and debris collected by the water's edge. Crouched in the shallows, hidden by the cattails, they watched with bated breath as the dragon slowed its ungainly gallop. It sniffed the air, jaws held open loosely. Dark purple blood dripped from its mouth. The dragon eased one heavily clawed foot down the bank, testing whether the dried mud would give way beneath it. The second foot tentatively followed.

Oralia glanced warily over her shoulder. The river flowed too swiftly to swim. The current would pull them to a cold, watery grave. Their best chance was to hunker down and wait, hoping the pike bearers could drive it from the water's edge.

Ellisar slid the bow from her shoulder and notched an arrow, whispering, "If you make it out alive, tell Ashwyn how I died."

Oralia grimaced, feeling her boots slowly fill with cold water. "How disturbingly sentimental of you."

"Spare no detail. Tell her how my eyes bulged and the blood poured from my screaming mouth. As graphic as possible. I want her to feel bad. She's the reason I'm here."

"And *I* am the reason the two of you skipped your date with the gallows. Now, if you could feel as strongly about the dragon as you do my sister, perhaps you will live to tell her yourself. Feet shoulder-width apart and knees bent, Sergeant Farrow. You are not dismissed from my service yet."

The edge of Ellisar's mouth curled as she corrected her stance. "Oh my, Protector. You've given me the flutters."

A sudden, earsplitting trill prevented Oralia from giving the impudent elf a proper dressing-down. She covered her ears instead, watching helplessly as Ellisar was forced to do the same. A scraggly figure raced along the slope toward them, blasting another round of shrill, headache-inducing sounds. Snag weaved in and out of the tall grasses near the dragon's feet, luring it away from the water's edge. The dragon snapped at him, but the goblin was already dancing out of range, still producing torturous notes from his pipe. Incensed, the great beast pulled its front legs back onto the ledge and gave chase.

Once certain it would not double back, Oralia slogged through the thick reeds toward the riverbank. The soft mud gave way underfoot with a slippery squelch. "Dammit. He has an argument for keeping that wretched thing now."

Ellisar scrambled onto the bank ahead of Oralia. In two awkward leaps, she cleared the pebbled slope and disappeared into the overgrown greenery, calling over her shoulder. "Only if he survives!"

"He just saved your life. For the gods' sakes, kill the dragon, not Snag!"

Oralia half expected a reply of *"I can do two things at once!"* to carry back down to her. She heard only silence instead. Somehow, that was even more unnerving.

CHAPTER TWENTY-EIGHT

Still Alive

Oralia, more than twice the weight of her elf soldier, did not ascend the steep riverbank as easily. She dug the toe of her boot into the loose gravel, grasping whatever handholds she could find to pull herself the rest of the way. A pike bearer met her at the top and lent her a welcome hand. Once clear of the embankment, Oralia shakily stood. She gritted her teeth, ignoring the heavy ache in her knees. She was entirely too old for this.

"Status?" she huffed.

"Uh, still alive, madam?" the young dwarf stammered.

From his confused expression, Oralia was unsure whether he meant her, the dragon, or himself. Perhaps all three. She shielded her eyes against the setting sunlight to see for herself. The rest of the soldiers were in a half circle formation, keeping the dragon at bay. Snag marched along their ranks, utilizing the bone handle of his dagger to press the more nervous ones back into position. An occasional trill from his pipe kept the hatchling focused in his direction.

Ellisar stalked the beast from behind. She crept along the tall grasses in a half-crouch, sword in hand, timing the rhythmic sweep of the dragon's tail. She saw her opening and broke cover, sprinting up the dragon's tail and onto its back. Bounding past the wings and over the shoulders, she planted her feet firmly against its neck and, in one mighty thrust, drove her sword behind its skull. With a mangled scream, the hatchling's body convulsed and then went limp, collapsing in a scaled heap onto the ground.

Silence descended over the meadow. No one dared go near it. Not until the huntress decapitated the beast.

Oralia breathed a sigh of relief as she started toward them, fighting the stiffness in her bones. Her hips hurt. Her legs cramped. And her feet were wet and miserable. Still, not their worst monster hunt, all things considered.

Snag waited for her by the dragon's head. He extended his wineskin to Oralia as his jagged mouth pulled into a smug smile. "Why yes, Protector. I do believe that was some of my best playing. Thank you for noticing."

"You may keep the pipe." Oralia took a grateful swig. The flavor was earthy, eerily similar to dirt or moldy sock. Tastes she was regretfully familiar with, as her faithful four had snuck both into the evening meal on more than one occasion. Oralia managed to hold the swallow down, wincing with disgust. "Have you poisoned me?"

"Nettle tea," he said, toying with the ring in his lip. "It'll help with the inflammation."

Gods, how old was she? Even her poisoner was adjusting his elixirs to cater to her aging needs. Oralia shoved the wineskin back into his hands. "Stick to spirits."

"If Ellisar can drink a cupful every morning without complaint, so can you."

"Do not compare me to someone who licks toads for recreation. It is a wonder she can taste anything at all." There were many things Ellisar did that Oralia simply would not, including drinking something that had the flavor profile of a damp sock. A sudden expletive from above caused Oralia to lift her gaze. She watched as the elf in question placed one foot in front of the other, edging ever closer to the left wing of the dead beast. The spectacle reminded Oralia of a tightrope walker—minus the flashy costume and fire breathing, of course. "Find something?"

Ellisar reached beneath the scaled joint and, after several vigorous pulls and a plethora of elven curses, dislodged a bloodied hatchet. She turned the weapon over in her hands, puzzled. "I have seen everything now."

The tall grass rustled behind them. Snag whipped his head in the direction of the disturbance, reaching for his dagger. "Oh, look," he snarled, curling his upper lip as his hand returned to his hip. "Late to the funeral as always, Rali. Where were you when the damn dragon charged?"

Oralia furrowed her brow and looked to Ellisar, who had a better grasp of human sayings than she did. "Funeral?"

"Rasp's teaching him idioms." Ellisar's expression was impossibly blank. "Don't say anything. It's better this way."

Rali clomped toward them, barely visible over the flowering landscape. She was either unaware or unfazed by the spiderwebs in her hair. "Where was I? Watching from the road, obviously. Someone had to record your deaths." She waved her writing slate at Oralia. "I have the damage report you requested, Madam Protector."

Oralia eased onto the grass and removed her boots, emptying their wet contents over the ground. "Read it to me."

"Of the original fifty-eight, we have fifty-two alive and accounted for. Chief Medical Officer Tarvy and Privates Strong and Dixon were eaten. Sergeant Rosenfall was carried off with his horse by the mother dragon and is assumed dead. We have two members still unaccounted for. Willem Foss and Rasp Stoneclaw. The herbalist, Briony Blackwater—who was until just recently missing herself—claims the pair were swept downriver." Rali looked up from her notes, bored. "Do you wish to hear the tally of horses next?"

Oralia's jaw lowered, aghast. "They fell into the river?"

"Not that I'm aware. Of the five missing, at least two were eaten and—"

"The people, not the horses, Rali!"

"Oh, right then." The dwarf consulted her indiscernible scribbles. "They did not fall into the river, boss. They jumped. According to Blackwater, Willem and Rasp were pursued by a hatchling." She looked up at no one in particular, wincing. "Oof. Between drowning or dragon fodder, I'm not sure which I'd choose. Tough call."

"Can humans swim?" Orcs couldn't. Not for any significant amount of time, anyway. They were too heavy, weighted down by muscle and bone. An orc could manage a slow, shallow river perhaps, but not the mighty current of the Byorne.

"Willem is half elf," Snag reminded her.

"Can they swim?"

"Humans can better than most, I'd say," Rali said. "Elves tend to float. Neither was wearing armor. They've got that going for them, at least. A proper soldier would have sunk straight to the bottom." The lieutenant illustrated her last point with her hand, dropping it from head to hip with a sliding whistle.

Oralia glared at her callousness. "There is a chance they survived, then?"

"I suppose." Rali shrugged, impervious to the ferocity of Oralia's stare. "They won't last the night, though. Not once the chill sets in."

There was a chance, at least. Without their guide, the mission was dead in its tracks. "Return to camp and assemble a search party immediately."

"I already sent Curly and Faris downriver, boss."

"Good." Four dead. Two swept downriver. Gods help her, they weren't even to the blasted mountain yet.

Rali cleared her throat, casting a distrustful glance around them. "There's something else that may interest you."

Oralia recognized Rali's worrisome tone and promptly ordered the pike bearers back to camp, motioning for Snag to stay. She waited until the soldiers were well out of hearing, suspecting she already knew what was on the lieutenant's mind. "Rasp has been trying to stall us from the beginning," Oralia said. "Is this sabotage? Did he pick this route because of the dragons? I have never put any credibility to the myths, but is it possible he could have summoned them?"

"I thought it was sabotage at first, too," Rali said, wisely steering clear of the dragon-summoning part. Lieutenant Ralizak planted her feet firmly in fact and preferred to keep them there. "But now I'm learning the back of the convoy had prior warning. They were halfway into the trees when the mother beast came out of the sky. According to several sources, including the keeper himself, it was Rasp who raised the alarm."

Snag squinted at her. "It did shriek, didn't it? I mean, he's got ears. Doesn't take much brainpower to shout 'Dragon!' when you hear one."

"He sounded the warning *before* it shrieked." Rali met his disbelieving look with one of her own. "Look, I know how it sounds. But it's the same story every time. And the people I asked were very insistent no matter which way I asked them. If by some divine power it's true, then it rules out sabotage. If this was malicious, Rasp would benefit from the most destruction possible. Defeats the purpose of drawing the dragons in just to sound the alarm the moment one of them shows."

"Or," the goblin countered, "it's a ploy to make us think it's not sabotage."

"Are we discussing the same mountain man? You are giving him entirely too much credit. That is something *you* would do. I don't think Rasp's got the brains to think that many steps ahead."

Their best lookouts had been stationed two at the front, two at the back, and two moving inconspicuously ahead of the convoy along the tree line. Not a single one of them saw the dragon until it was upon them. Sabotage or not, how a blind man knew before any of them was suspicious. Oralia looked to Ellisar. "Thoughts?"

The huntress balanced the hatchet against the flat of her palm. "Willem is kind of cute. Shame for that to go to waste."

"Were you not just pining over your wife back at the river?"

"Mrs. Farrow and I have an arrangement. So long as I don't get anyone knocked up, I'm free to hop into whatever bed I fancy." From the slight curl at the edge of her mouth, Ellisar was enjoying this. When it came to the intimate details concerning her marriage, she took every opportunity to make Oralia as uncomfortable as possible. "She only asks that I detail my exploits in letter form for her afterward. Got to get the wife her kicks too."

"We know!" Snag said. "You insist on reading them to us."

Rali looked up over her slate through furrowed eyebrows. "Can we circle back to the pregnancy part real quick? Please tell me you know that's not how procreation works."

Ellisar flipped the hatchet into the air and caught it, ignoring the contribution of her teammates. "If it's answers you want, Protector, I say we go ask the mountain man ourselves."

"Then we are in agreement." Oralia decided she didn't want to be involved in Ellisar's relationship with Ashwyn any more than she already was. Some things were better left a mystery. "Snaglebrag, follow the water's edge. Ralizak and I will take the road. Ellisar, you may do as you wish." The huntress's body had taken a beating from the dragon tail. As Ellisar would never admit to weakness, Oralia trusted she could decide her own limitations.

Snag twisted his head in Ellisar's direction with a devious smirk. "Two silver says I get there first on foot."

"I'm faster than you by far."

Snag slammed his foot just below her knee. He was gone before she could react, already running in the direction of the waterway in a zigzag pattern. "Not now, you're not!"

Rali tilted her head, watching his progress with mild interest. "He never specified you had to be on foot."

"No, this will be more fun. The idiot has forgotten I have poison tipped arrows." With golden eyes gleaming, Ellisar slung the hatchet into her belt and sprinted after him with more spryness than Oralia had felt in years. Hit with a blasted dragon tail and already back on her feet again. Madness had upsides, she supposed.

"Do not shoot him!" Again. Oralia went in the opposite direction toward the road, feeling some of her energy return. "How quickly can you ready the horses, Ralizak?"

Rali gestured to the tree line, where her gray pony was tied alongside Oralia's black charger. "You mean those horses, boss?"

"Exceptional as usual, Lieutenant." Oralia cut through the tall grass as dusk settled over the land. The sky was ablaze in striking hues of orange and red over the western wood. Already, the temperature was dropping. The honeyed fragrance of evening primrose carried to her on the wind.

Behind her, Rali's baritone voice rang out across the meadow in song:

"She's the first, the original, the best.
Above and beyond the faithful rest.
The brilliant, the conniving, the daringly, sparingly divining.
Who's called upon to get it done?
Quartz Ralizak, she's Oralia's number one!"

CHAPTER TWENTY-NINE

Fever Dream

Rasp awoke suddenly. There was a fire beside him, alive with the crackle and pop of flames. He rolled to the side and felt something shift over his body. His fingers explored the edge of the material, realizing it was a cloak—velvet, thick, warm. Definitely not his. His skin tingled. Not from the warmth of the fire, either. This was something else. Something terrifyingly familiar.

Magic.

He heaved into a sitting position, grimacing at the searing pain that surged up his spine. The sudden chill rolling across his skin made him painfully aware his clothes had been stripped away. At the moment, nakedness wasn't his main concern. Rasp lowered his head, growling, "*You.*"

He waited with bated breath, but the only sounds to reach him were the snap of the hungry fire and the distant roar of the river somewhere below. As the fog lifted from his weary brain, other details began to slip into place, allowing him to piece together his surroundings. He heard the creaking groan of poplar trees swaying in the wind overhead, and the fluttering rattle of their paper thin leaves. There was the pungent stench of wet moss and forest rot, too. He was a fair ways away from the riverbank, he concluded. Tucked out of sight in the trees with an unknown magical presence.

Fan-fucking-tastic. He was either about to be dinner or an unwilling participant in a summoning ritual.

"I know you're there!" Rasp's throat was dry, like he'd swallowed weathered limestone and helped it down with a shot of sand. The hoarse voice emitting from between his tightly clenched teeth did not sound like his own. "I can feel you, witch. Just like I could feel you the night you fucked over my match."

"I have been called many things in my lifetime," a hauntingly beautiful voice called to him. "The wind, ghost, whisper, but never witch. Tell me, why is it you see what no one else does?"

Against the brightness of the fire, Rasp saw a blurred shape approach. He instinctively reached for the blade concealed in his clothes, only then remembering he wasn't wearing any. His hands searched the ground around him and grasped the closest object he could find. A spined weed, he realized too late. Rasp rolled backward with a mangled scream, clutching his throbbing hand and trying not to think about how stupid this looked.

"Stay back!"

"Spirited little bird." From the witch's tone, Rasp suspected "spirited" was a polite substitution for "stupid." The voice carried on talking in soft, silken words that were already beginning to soothe Rasp's blistering temper. "Spirit is good. You'll need an edge if you wish to survive your training."

Training? The realm sent a witch to . . . train him? He was dreaming, surely. Rasp's body was crumpled along the cold riverbank somewhere, dying a slow death. This was a hallucination brought on by the fever dream, nothing more. Rasp's thoughts raced, struggling to reconstruct his last moments. He recalled the icy river and fighting the current to stay afloat. And then, when the last of the strength left his weighted arms, he'd heard Willem's voice. The next moment Rasp was pulled from the water and dragged onto the bank. Everything was a muddled blur after that.

"You are not dreaming," the voice said, as if it had read his thoughts. "I helped fish you from the river. Your companion succumbed to exhaustion shortly after you did. You are fortunate I was feeling generous."

Well, shit. So much for the hallucination theory.

"Where's Willem?" Albeit mostly useless, Willem *had* saved him from drowning. Rasp supposed it was only fair to return the favor by not throwing him to the witch as a blood sacrifice. This was twice now Rasp had refrained from senseless killing in order to save his own skin. It was a shame the only person he could brag to was the witch. Rasp doubted they cared all that much for the ways of morality and being a better person, being an agent of the dark arts.

Where was Faris when you needed him? Oh, that's right. Probably still back at the road kicking himself for not reacting faster to the damn dragons. Stupid Faris.

I still wish you were here right now. But only so I could feed you to the witch.

The witch's blurred form knelt down and took Rasp's hand. The searing pain in the center of his palm subsided to a dull throb. "Fear not, little bird. The etiquette instructor will not disturb us. I made sure."

Rasp's voice cracked. The effect, alas, sounded nothing like the deafening crack of a whip or someone's femur snapping in half, but that of a prepubescent boy stepping barefoot onto a porcupine. "You killed him?"

Evidently his self-control had been for nothing. Damn.

"I put your companion in a deep sleep, nothing more. I needed to speak with you alone."

Rasp pulled away, drawing the cloak tighter over his shivering body. The fabric was unlike anything he'd felt before. It was warm, as if producing a heat of its own. More magic, probably. A prospect he wanted to spend as little thought on as possible. "The realm is out of their fucking minds if they think I'm going to have anything to do with a witch. Be gone, foul demon. I'm not interested."

"It does not work that way," the voice tutted softly. "First, you will answer my questions. And then I will decide if you are worth saving. Let's start with the ravens. What power do you possess over them?"

Rasp felt compelled to answer, if only to make it clear he was not involved in witchcraft. "It's not a power. They're family."

"Elaborate."

"When my people die, our spirits come back as ravens." So long as they passed on the mountain—the reason why his brothers had driven him from the cliffs before attempting his execution. Rasp's punishment wasn't just death, it was being denied an afterlife with his family. "They're supposed to guide the lost back onto the right path."

"Can all of your people speak to them?"

"Of course they can." Anybody could *talk* to the ravens. It was the matter of the ravens talking back, however, that posed a problem. Most realm folk, like Faris, assumed Rasp was either crazy or pulling their leg. The mountain clan hadn't been as accepting of his odd ability.

"Ah, this raven must be your mother then. She watches over you often. Hello, Mother Stoneclaw."

Mother? Rasp tilted his head and listened. He could hear a bird in the boughs above him, shifting nervously from foot to foot. "How did you . . ."

A finger pressed against Rasp's forehead. Magic sparked between their skins. "Mother has one eye. Meddled in magic too many times, I suspect. You must have inherited your abilities from her, then."

Rasp's blood ran as cold as a fireless winter night, the kind where nobody wanted to go fetch more wood in the raging blizzard outside. The witch knew who Rasp was. And what he was. They knew the consequences for using magic, too. They had to have been someone close to him during Daana's lecture. But who? "Don't say that. I'm not a witch. I'm not like you!"

"No, you're not like me," the voice agreed. "You are unpracticed, under-trained, and reek of raw magic. It's a small wonder you were able to hit that dragon at all."

Shit. Shit. Shit.

"That was the last time!"

"No. It wasn't. It will happen again, and at some point you're going to get unlucky and kill someone."

Rasp wanted to shrink away. To hide. To be anywhere but here. He willed his body to become the size of an ant. His body decided being a below-average-sized human was close enough, and ignored him.

"Denying what you are has done yourself a great disservice, little bird. How do you expect to achieve harmony if you hate what cannot be changed?"

"I didn't ask to be cursed! It has brought me nothing but pain."

"Ignoring a wound will only cause it to fester. Accept what you are and learn to wield it. Only then will you realize this is a gift, not a curse." The voice paused for a moment before saying, "You are not yet beyond help. Will you accept mine?"

"Do not tempt me, witch. I will not succumb to your evil."

"Not all magic is evil." The voice was less beautiful now. It sounded weary. "Of course you're scared of it. All your life you've been told it's wrong. But the more you suppress your magic, the more control you lose. You've only ever seen it do bad things, reinforcing the idea that magic is bad. That you are bad."

Rasp focused on his breathing. He was too weak to escape, but that didn't mean he had to listen. The witch would not manipulate him with its soft words. He drew inward, as he had done many times before. His heartbeat slowed. Senses dulled. Soon, the only sound he heard was the steady in and out of air from his lungs. He was safe. No one would reach him here.

The witch's soft voice rippled over his quieted mind, sparking every sense back to life like a jolt of invisible lightning. **I see you are not completely without control. Tell me, why does the truth make you so uncomfortable, little bird?**

CHAPTER THIRTY

Whisper

Leave me alone!" With his concentration broken, Rasp was back on the outside, exposed and angry. "I won't be put under your spell!"

"I have no desire to control you. I wish to help."

"Why?"

"Because you're not, as you say, a witch. You're a baby bird that's fallen from the nest. Without someone to teach you to fly, you will be consumed by the dark."

The poison seething beneath his skin subsided. "You know about the darkness?"

"It left its mark on you, Stoneclaw. You tapped into a source that didn't belong to you," the voice said. "You're stupid, but resilient. Not many walk away from that kind of power. Fortunately for you, I can fix stupid."

Rasp felt his weariness pull at him. Whatever energy the witch had sparked in him was fading. The weight in his limbs doubled, and it took all of his willpower not to flop over and wave the white flag of "fuck this, I'm done." His words came out sounding more whiny than he'd meant them to. "Can't you just take the curse away, instead?"

"There is only one sure method to do so. Is that what you wish?"

Rasp eased onto the ground. With his anger gone and energy lagging, the irresistible call of sleep pulled at him. He rested his head in the crook of his arm, mumbling, "You mean kill me? Pass."

"You have two choices then. You may either accept my help and learn to use your gifts in a productive way, or you can refuse."

"I get the feeling if I refuse, you're still going to kill me."

"Afraid so, little bird," the voice said with what might have been sympathy. "Without proper guidance, your power is too unwieldy. You are a danger not only to yourself, but others. The consequences would be devastating if you were to be found by someone with the means to extort you. Believe me, a quick death is a kindness by comparison."

"The realm doesn't get their trade routes if you kill me." Rasp managed a weak smile. The witch's threat was an empty one. Oralia wouldn't allow anyone to kill him. After Rasp took her up the mountain, maybe, but not until then.

"A compelling argument. Unfortunately for you, I regard the realm the same way you might an insect bite. A fleeting annoyance. Here today, gone tomorrow. I care nothing for trade routes."

Of all the things the witch had said so far, this was the most intriguing. Gritting his teeth, Rasp forced his aching body upright once more. Rest would have to wait. This was an unexpected turn. One that, just maybe, he could use. "You're not with the realm?"

"Not any more than you are."

Was fate finally taking pity on him? If the witch wasn't with the realm, what reason would they have to be here? Him? Rasp thought for a moment, wondering who else could possibly know about him and his curse, and be motivated enough to prevent him from fulfilling the prophecy of the sixth son. His brain offered nothing in the way of an answer.

Rasp had no doubt the witch intended to corrupt him. Considering his limited options, he could at least ensure it happened away from the Iron Ridge. "What happens if I agree? Do you take us away from here?"

"No. We return to the travel party and you speak of this to no one. I will find time to train you along the way."

The sudden lift in Rasp's spirit shriveled. Fate was unmerciful, after all. It intended to deliver him to the mountainside more dangerous than ever. "Why?" Despite the chills that racked Rasp's body, his face radiated unnatural heat. "If you have no loyalty to the realm, why stay? Wouldn't it be safer to train me away from their prying eyes?"

"I have an obligation to fulfill."

"Is your obligation to get everyone on this trip killed? Because that's what's going to happen. You said you knew about the darkness, but if you had any inkling of what it's capable of, then you would take me as far away from the ridge as possible!"

It wasn't enough. It was *never* enough. The others knew the prophecy and didn't care to prevent it. Why would the witch be any different? If this was going to work, then he had to say the other part, too. The part that stepped from superstition into nightmare territory. "Do you know why my people called me the Iron Devil? It wasn't because I was some fucking merciless cutthroat like everyone thinks. It's because I couldn't die. And believe me, my father tried. Every damned battle, you can bet your ass he put me out front and center. When that didn't work, he started sending me on suicide missions. And each time, I returned alive. The elders said I couldn't die because the mountain wouldn't let me."

Rasp hadn't believed the rumors at first. Sure, he might have made it back after a few bloody encounters when no one else did, but that was because he was practical, not cursed. He may have had a reputation for bloodlust on the battlefield, but he wasn't an idiot. Why go for the strongest opponent straight away when you could let the others wear them down first? Besides, he'd started to enjoy the look of horror on his father's face each time he returned to the village coated in blood with barely a scratch. While others might have fought for glory and conquest, Rasp lived only to displease his father. It wasn't until his assassination attempt that he realized he was wrong. No one should have survived that, not even him.

The witch was still painfully silent, prompting one final plea from Rasp. "The darkness has designs for me. If I go back to the Iron Ridge, you will be playing right into its hand."

"Then I will teach you to resist the darkness."

"You're not listening!"

"I *am* listening. Your survival was not tied to the darkness. You lived because, intentional or not, your magic saved you. Just like it did with the dragon."

The heat from Rasp's face flushed to his ears. The urge to argue was strong, but he locked his jaw and waited for the inevitable. His magic or dark magic, what did it matter? It would all end the same anyway.

"So you do not wish to be trained. Is that your decision, little bird?"

He didn't dare open his mouth. Doing so would all but guarantee some pitiful excuse would come tumbling out, and all the nerve he'd worked up thus far would falter.

"Very well. Old friend, forgive me." A rough hand wrapped over Rasp's forehead and yanked backward. Cold steel pressed against his exposed throat. "You have my sympathies, little bird. May you find your flock in the afterlife."

Instinct kicked in. Rasp's feet pawed at the dirt as he reached behind him for something to grab onto. He caught the witch's arm and dug his fingernails into their scaled flesh. His mouth curled open to scream, but the words died on his tongue. This was what he asked for, wasn't it? Killed by a witch. There was probably some irony in this somewhere, but at that moment the panicked thoughts flashing bright colors behind his eyes couldn't be bothered to piece it together.

There was a flutter of feathers as Mother descended from the branches in a frenzied panic. Her cries were so loud they rang in Rasp's ears, drowning out the sounds of the fire, the river, and the stream of curses rampaging through his head.

The cold blade tapped lightly against Rasp's neck, as if to garner his attention. "What does Mother Stoneclaw say?"

"That she's going to peck your eyes from your face while you sleep!"

Croak!

This time, the flat of the blade snapped against his cheek with a painful *whap*. "Why do you insist on making things so hard on yourself?"

Rasp winced, managing through clenched teeth, "She says I should stop being stupid and accept your help." *Traitor.*

"You are supposed to listen to her, are you not? You said so yourself that the ravens steer the lost back onto the right path. The fact that you require an entire flock is an indication that perhaps you have still not found your path, yes?"

Gods dammit. He hated it when people used his own words against him. Rasp had been prepared to die a few seconds ago, but that was the funny thing about living. The more you did it, the more attached to it you got. Maybe he could appease the witch and Mother, at least for a little while. Surely another opportunity to cut and run would present itself before they were all the way up the mountain.

"Yes," he grumbled.

The hand on his head released him, but the blade remained. Once more, it tapped against his jugular as the voice tsked its disapproval. "Then accept your path, little bird."

"Fine! I'll learn to be a fucking witch." Admittedly, he could have said that with a lot more dignity and grace, but he didn't have much use for dignity anyway, sitting sprawled in the dirt without any clothes and every body hair standing on end.

"Learn from this, little bird, because I will not hesitate next time." The witch lingered, a dark, shifting form in the center of Rasp's blurred vision. "Alas, your indecision has cost us time. I will have to put you back to sleep soon. The search party is not far."

Rasp felt along the side of his throbbing face with his fingertips. "You just tried to slit my throat. I'm not sleeping anywhere near you."

The voice sounded amused. "You don't trust me?"

"Are you fu–"

Before Rasp could finish his words, something blew into his open mouth. The fine powder tasted like soap and smelled sweet and subtle, like the fruit blossoms Rasp's mother used to thread into her hair. It dissolved into a thin, fragrant film over his tongue. Rasp's eyes watered along the edges as his eyelids grew inexplicably heavy. "Gods, I already hate you," he gagged, attempting to spit the floral taste from his mouth.

"If you would bestill your flapping lips, I will delve into your first lesson. The old ones."

"Is that what you are? An old one?" Rasp wiped the film from his tongue. His mouth had started to tingle. The spot on the back of his hand too, where he licked.

The witch wasn't a mortal, at least not any Rasp had encountered before. He'd felt their skin when he reached for the witch's arm. It was like tiny, hard-toothed scales against his hand. Smooth to the touch when brushed in the right direction and, like bristled armor, capable of inflicting incredible pain when not.

"I am not anything," the witch said. "Not anymore."

"Fine. What do I call you, then?"

"A name holds great power. I no longer use mine. To some I am known as Whisper, but you may call me whatever you wish."

Several highly inappropriate suggestions crossed Rasp's mind. Still feeling the sting on his throbbing cheek, he decided he didn't want to risk sounding clever. "Whisper, it is," he said with an unexpected yawn. "Oh gods, that flowery stuff is working."

The ache in Rasp's back dulled. His head felt light, as if it would suddenly lift and float free of his body. The thrum of magic numbed the sensation in his fingertips. His other senses blurred, slowing down, as if trapped in time as his body slumped over. Rasp hit the ground, but felt nothing except the slow trickle of saliva from the corner of his mouth.

"Fuhh . . . k . . .you . . ." was all he could manage before his tongue failed him entirely.

"Hush." Whisper's soft voice was in his ear. "Close your eyes and listen."

Whisper's soft, lulling voice rippled across Rasp's mind, summoning dreams that did not belong to him. Rasp saw the land before it had been given names. Before it had been divided into imaginary sections and fought over with the blood of thousands. It was rich and lush, untouched by mortal hand.

This world was not always ruled by elf, orc, or man, Whisper began. **There were great beings in the before, powerful, godlike. The old ones. They survived not on food, but magic. As time drew on and the spark of the early world faded, so did they. With their lifesource dwindling, the old ones consumed one another until only a few remained. When the age of mortals dawned, the last of the old ones slunk away into the far reaches of the land. Without magic to sustain them, their bodies died. Only their power, corrupted from their all-consuming lust, remained. The darkness leached into the ground, and to this day it waits for an unsuspecting vessel to fall prey to its siren song.**

Many misguided souls have sought the dark to wield power beyond their limits. The darkness gives at first, to draw the vessel in. And then it takes. You've glimpsed the darkness, little bird. The corruption will consume you if you give in to it again. It will take your body and hurt everyone you've ever loved. To avoid the dark, you must first learn what power belongs to you, and what to leave alone . . .

CHAPTER THIRTY-ONE

Hammer and a Horn

"Come on, Dinglehead. You're not wimping out on me now. Wake up!"

Rasp awoke to the sting of someone slapping their palm firmly across his face. Groaning, he pushed the persistent hand away and tucked his chin back into the warmth of his arms. "Go . . . a . . . way . . ."

"Move aside." This was a different voice. Harsher, like steel against a sharpening stone. It made the hairs on Rasp's arms bristle. He heard the rustling of a leather bag and then a sudden snap beneath his nose. A revolting smell invaded his nostrils. Rasp lurched back, gagging, unsure whether he'd inhaled sweat or piss. As consciousness slowly returned to his body, he realized he was still draped in a cloak. His own, this time. Made evident by the fact that the material was thin, scratchy, and a little damp.

"There." The harsh voice sounded pleased with itself. "That's got the little maggot coming around."

There was only one person who called him maggot. Rasp did not have the strength to raise his head, much less his fist. He settled for a curled upper lip instead. "Pet."

"Welcome back to the land of the living. For now." Snaglebrag's fingertips explored Rasp's face uninvited, checking the skin around his eyes and gums. He reported his findings far louder than necessary, indicating there were others around them. "He's got a bad case of the shakes. He needs fluids and could probably do with some damn clothes, but he'll live. Whichever one of them lit the fire saved them."

"Will . . . em."

"The manservant saved you? How embarrassing."

The next thing Rasp knew, the goblin was prying his jaws open and slipping something under his tongue. Rasp tried to pull away but Snag snapped his mouth shut again and held his head. "Don't spit it out. Let it do its work. You'll come around faster."

His mouth flooded with a sickly sweet flavor. It was thick and viscous, like warm honey, and dripped down his throat. Rasp struggled to swallow. For a panicked moment, he couldn't breathe. And then the syrup slid down his gullet and hit his empty stomach like fire, jolting his senses back to life.

Rasp shoved away from Snag, hacking and coughing, trying to get his airways clear. "Oh gods," he whimpered. "I'm going to vomit."

"Faris, get his clothes. I've seen enough of the maggot to give me nightmares." Snag said under his breath to Rasp, as if imparting a grave secret, "You are aware of the—uh—on your?"

"Yes. I put it there." The words came easier now and Rasp no longer felt like his insides were going to liquify and ooze out his nose. Maybe from other places, but on the bright side, he wasn't wearing pants. "Well, I paid someone to. My hands weren't steady enough."

"Why?"

"Didn't want to maim myself."

"You know that's not what I meant."

"Oh, you meant the—" Rasp replaced the word with a wink. "To identify my body. In case I ever lost my head."

"Of course you did."

The next thing Rasp knew, someone was easing him upright and tugging his shirt back onto him. The fabric was warm and tingled against his clammy skin, as if it'd been hung by the fire. Rasp wasn't sure whether it was Willem or Whisper who had the forethought to dry his wet clothes. He should have felt grateful and yet, his cheeks burned with embarrassment instead. He wasn't a damned toddler! He could dress himself . . . once he regained control of his limbs, of course.

With some effort, Faris managed to wrangle Rasp's trousers over his unresponsive legs. "Why is it even on the brink of death that I find you with your clothes off? I swear, half this job is keeping you from strutting around in the nude."

"I will leave this world as I came into it! Naked and scr—" Rasp gasped, barely able to breathe around Faris's sudden, crippling embrace. "Are you . . . hugging me?"

"Don't ruin the moment."

If anything, at least the faun was warm. Rasp leaned into him. "What, no kiss?"

"Rali," Snag called. The proximity of his voice was entirely too close for Rasp's comfort. "Give me a hand here."

Rasp recognized Lieutenant Ralizak by the loud stomp of her footsteps. The dwarf walked as though she was perpetually trying to squash something smaller than her. "Which do you want? The left or the right?"

The goblin forced a noise through his nostrils, which sounded more like the last desperate wheeze of a dying animal than a laugh. "Hilarious. I want your waterskin, not your appendages. Give it here."

"Why? What's wrong with yours?"

"I can smell your breath from here. It's obviously not water you've been sipping all day."

"Sorry, bucko. Afraid that's not going to happen. This is the last of my good stuff, you see. And I aim to make it last for as long as possible."

"Uh, if I could interject for just a moment," Faris said in that tone of voice that suggested he was holding a finger aloft. Not the middle one, though. Probably. "Contrary to popular belief, alcohol won't warm him."

The faun's body shifted toward the bickering pair, releasing Rasp under the poor assumption he could hold his own body weight. Rasp flopped over with a squawk, prompting Faris to quickly pick him up again. "Sorry."

Snag produced a gravelly knock deep in his chest. If this were the battlefield, this would have been the exact moment Rasp ducked behind someone taller, allowing them to take the brunt of the goblin's wrath. When push came to shove, goblins, despite their diminutive size, had an explosive temper like no other. As this was not an active battlefield, Rasp assumed Snaglebrag merely resented the fact he was being asked to explain his process to simpler minds.

Simple minds called for an equally simple answer and, after a muttering sigh, Snag said, "It won't be alcohol when I'm done with it."

Rali stomped her foot with such force, it sent Rasp scuttling into Faris's lap. Faris didn't appear to mind, considering there were more pressing matters at hand. Avoiding the wrath of the rampaging dwarf, for instance, which seemed to be occupying the majority of his attention.

"You want to turn the last of my booze into snake oil?" Rali hissed under her breath. "Forget it!"

"Fine. You got any cheap swill on you then?"

"Do I look like a tavern to you?"

Rasp was about to point out that she smelled like one, but was prevented from saying anything by Faris's hand clamping securely over his mouth.

"No? Then it's settled. Hand it over"—here the goblin lowered his voice so only those closest to him would hear—"or I tell Oralia. She knows you're back on the bottle, but not about the powder. Is that what you want?"

"I swore off that shit! One intervention was enough, thank you."

"Yeah, but who's she going to believe? Me or you?"

Rali produced an odd sound from her throat. It might have been a 'harrumph,' if said harrumph had come from a bear currently debating whether to kill you outright or just dig in and let the inevitable take care of itself. The dwarf said nothing more. Rasp, however, did hear the muffled slosh and subsequent thump of the waterskin exchanging hands in a very fast, possibly violent, manner.

"I'll get you more. Just put off murdering Snag until he's done, alright?" Faris said in his *come on now, we're all friends here* voice.

Rali offered another grunt. This one, thankfully, less murderous than the first.

"Alright, danger's over. You, *off.*" Faris picked Rasp from his lap and deposited him back onto the ground beside him with more gentleness than Rasp expected. "So if the alcohol's not to get him plastered, what are you using it for?" Rasp assumed Faris was speaking to Snag, as Lieutenant Ralizak was resigned to the silent treatment and Rasp used alcohol exclusively for drinking and setting things on fire.

Snag uncapped something and in the next moment was shaking Rali's waterskin with great vigor. Rasp could hear the slosh of the liquid within. A sour smell soon permeated the air. It was similar to fermented fruit, but the kind that promised stomach cramps and not the benefit of intoxication. "Alcohol serves as a carrier agent. The compound doesn't distribute as well in water."

"You're an alchemist?" Faris's tone made the transition from mildly concerned to *"ooh, something shiny!"* in the span of a heartbeat.

"Think less magic, more science. But if it helps you wrap your brain around it, sure."

"Faris," Rasp groaned. The inside of his skull throbbed like someone was hitting it with a hammer. Several hammers, in fact. And maybe a horn for good measure. "If Oralia's pet poisons me with science, gut him."

"I should get the honors," Rali grumbled. "It's my booze he's wasting."

"This is why I prefer making people dead, and not the reverse. There's so much less complaining involved." Snag ceased his shaking and shoved the waterskin into Rasp's hands. "Keep an eye on this one for me, Faris. I've got to see if the manservant is going to be as fortunate. Slow sips. Don't let him drink all of it at once or it will make him sick."

"Willem better come around," Rali said, her clomping feet following after him. "Ellisar gets all stabby when she goes unravished for too long."

Rasp took a swig of the mixture and nearly spat it back out. It was sour and kicked like a mountain goat, burning the back of his throat on its way down. His arm was already coiled behind him, preparing to fling the offending concoction as far as he could throw, when Faris caught his wrist. "Don't make this like the vitamin tablets," his keeper warned. "I got you to choke down those. I can make you take this, too, if I have to."

Rasp reluctantly lowered his arm. "This is worse than those."

"Yeah, and I can't disguise it in nut butter for you, either. So deal with it."

Groaning, Rasp leaned his full weight into Faris and nursed the drink, making sure that each foul sip was followed by an exaggerated gag. Not too exaggerated, unfortunately, as the concoction was horrid enough to elicit actual gagging. As much as he would never admit it, the medicine was working. Rasp could feel the tips of his fingers now, in that unpleasant, buzzing sort of sensation that happened right before the pain kicked in. It wouldn't be long before he could sit on his own, unassisted. But Faris was warm, and Rasp was going to take advantage of his body heat for as long as the faun would tolerate the unnecessary cuddling.

Rasp's sense of hearing returned to its former sharpness, along with touch, and, unfortunately, taste. He could hear the dying crackle of the fire, the wind in the trees, and the rush of the river in the distance, but it was the conversation across from him that he was most interested in. Specifically, if Willem was alive.

"I still don't understand what you see in the old prune, El," Snag muttered.

"Some of us like the strict schoolmaster quality. Mister Foss's disapproving scowl doesn't make you weak in the knees, Snag?"

"I believe you're describing rickets."

"Unbelievable!" Rali said. "Don't tell me you two bought that pile of horseshit. Look at his boots, you twits. Those are the shoes of a professional. Good leather, worn in, and they don't make that awful creaky sound when he steps. Willem's not an etiquette instructor, he's somebody's plant."

Curly joined the conversation, calling from across the fire, "Doesn't look like a flower to me."

"Not that kind of plant, stupid. An infiltrator. Someone up top placed him in the traveling party for ulterior reasons. Whose pocket he's in, exactly, I haven't figured out yet. I don't think the emissary has any clue he's not who he says he is. Which means Daana either isn't in on her uncle's plans, or Willem works for someone else."

"You have said enough, Ralizak," Oralia's stern voice cut in from farther away. Sneaky Protector. Oralia had put off speaking for as long as possible to keep Rasp unaware of her presence, he was sure of it. "I will remind you there are others listening," she said. "Possibly Willem himself."

"He's out frozen," Snag replied. "You want me to snuff him while we've got the chance?"

Rali could not contain her outburst and said, "How are we supposed to find out who he's working for if you kill him? We wait for him to make his move, coerce him to talk, and *then* kill him."

"Ralizak!"

"Apologies, boss," the lieutenant huffed. "I'm trying to preserve the integrity of the information flowing in and out of the camp. If we lose Willem, they may find someone else and I will have to start all over again."

"Keep him alive, Snaglebrag. He is not the focus of my questioning tonight."

The fiery liquid churning in Rasp's belly lurched upward. Forcing the acidic taste back down with a difficult swallow, Rasp leaned closer to Faris and whispered, "Is it just me, or did that sound ominous to you, too?"

Pressed against him, Rasp could feel Faris's shoulder was more rigid than it'd been mere seconds before. "Considering they're all staring this way, I'm going to go with yes. Very ominous."

"Fuck."

CHAPTER THIRTY-TWO

Witch Killer

The glowing red and orange embers burned lower, allowing the advancing dark to tighten its stranglehold over the makeshift campsite. Long shadows danced on the edge of Rasp's blurred vision. Unlike the rhythmically swaying trees, the five threatening shapes that loomed in a strategic formation around him and Faris stood fixed in place. Rasp hadn't noticed when exactly they'd slunk into position, but the intent was clear. Oralia's goons had just cut off any chance of escape.

"Faris." He leaned closer as the rampant drum of his heartbeat filled his ears. "What the fuck is going on? What's the protector want to question me for?"

Faris gripped his forearm so tight, Rasp could already feel the tiny, crescent-shaped bruises beginning to form under the skin. "Shit. I think they might know."

Might know? Might know *what?* The panic surging through his veins slowly awakened his mind in the same way a teaspoon might stir a vat of cold molasses. There was movement, just not enough to make a difference. "Stop being cryptic and tell me!"

Gods, he hoped Faris had an answer, as going into an interrogation without knowing why was really going to suck. Not that it didn't seem to be headed in that direction already. He hadn't done anything wrong, had he? Rasp dredged his memory for a few painstaking seconds as he tried to recall exactly what he was guilty of. He *had* ran, but that was to escape the dragon, not Oralia. And last he checked, jumping recklessly into a raging river was criminally stupid, not the other way around.

"I think they know what you are."

". . . Wildly incompetent?"

"A witch, idiot."

Rasp choked on his surprise. He thumped his chest with his fist, attempting to dislodge the spittle trapped in his windpipe. "You knew?"

"Of course I mucking knew! That's the least of your worries right now." The direction of Faris's voice shifted, as though he was moving his head to make sure no one had changed position without his notice. "Protector of the Realm isn't the only name Oralia's made for herself. Behind closed doors, she's called the witch killer."

Oh fuck, fuck, fuckity, fuck. "And you didn't think to tell me this sooner?"

"So you could do something stupid? No. I thought letting you live in denial was a safer bet."

"Snaglebrag," the protector's calm voice called from across the fire. "Can you decipher what they are whispering about?"

"Something about you being a killer bitch?"

"Hey! You take that back." One of the warriors took a daring step forward. Rasp may not have been able to distinguish the shadowy figure from the others, but the voice told him it belonged to Rali. "Only we're allowed to call her that!"

If Oralia was insulted, her words certainly didn't reflect it. Her tone was calm, confident, and left no doubt as to who was in charge. "Mister Belfast, please assist Curly and Snaglebrag with taking Willem back to camp."

Rasp threaded his arm through Faris's and tugged him closer. "Don't you fucking leave me."

"Last I checked, I'm not Willem's keeper. Being as this is my realm-appointed position and all, I think I'm going to stay where I am, thanks."

"Rasp and I need to have a private conversation. Rest assured, I will return him to your care when we are finished. How long that takes depends entirely on him."

Oh no, no, no, no. This was bad. *Really* bad. Rasp tried to gather his knees beneath him, but lost his balance and collapsed against Faris instead, nearly biting his tongue in half. Gods damn this blasted chill! At the moment, he couldn't think any straighter than he could walk. And Oralia knew it. She was planning to use his own weakened state against him. After having stared down death several times that day, the constant reminder of his impending mortality was starting to wear thin.

Oralia's voice snapped Rasp from his panicked thoughts and back into the present. "I will not ask again, Faris."

"No."

"No?"

"I'm not leaving him."

"Very well," Oralia said after a moment of quiet deliberation. "Curly, remove Faris."

The closest shadow broke from its position and was upon them before Rasp could begin to formulate an escape plan. Curly lunged for Faris, but the faun was faster, spinning from his grasp in a maneuver that sent Rasp sprawling backward into the dirt. Heat flushed across his clammy face. They could try to kill him all they wanted, that wasn't anything new. But threatening Faris crossed a line Rasp hadn't realized existed before.

Gathering his strength for one final act of desperate stupidity, Rasp pounced. He wrapped his arms around the leg he hoped belonged to Curly, in an attempt to drag him to the ground. He'd barely gotten his teeth sunk past the thick fabric of Curly's pant leg when the orc's boot caught him in the chest. Dazed and unable to fill his deflated lungs, Rasp dropped. Hot tears filled his eyes as he gasped uselessly for breath.

"Come on, Faris. Don't be stupid. He's not—ah!" The ground shook with a heavy thump as Curly's body landed next to Rasp, writhing uselessly in the dirt. "Seven realms, somebody kill him! Little fucker just kicked me in the balls!"

Two more shapes darted forward to assist. Against the contrast of the dying firelight, Rasp saw one of them grab Faris from behind. "Gods, for your own good, Faris," Rali grunted over the sounds of struggle. "Quit while you're ahead! That's a poison-tipped arrow you've got pointed in our direction, bucko!"

A *what?*

Morality be damned. Just because he didn't have full control of his limbs didn't mean he was going to sit back and do nothing. Gritting his teeth, Rasp pulled unsteadily to his knees. Sweat dripped from his forehead as his breaths grew shorter. Magic stirred inside him. Already, he could taste its venom on his tongue.

I see you are about to do something foolish. Whisper's harmonic voice was suddenly in Rasp's ear. **Would you like assistance?**

"You're still here?" And why weren't the others reacting? Was the witch invisible? Never mind, it didn't matter. Saving Faris was his first priority. Rasp could sort out all the other details afterward. "No. I've got this."

He threw his hand out in front of him, fingertips fully extended. The surge of magic crackled down his arm and gathered into the center of his palm before sputtering out in an anticlimactic puff of nothing.

In case you are wondering, you look very stupid right now.

Why wasn't this working? No matter how hard Rasp tried, he couldn't will the magic from his body. From the sounds of it, Faris was still putting up a fight, but for how much longer, Rasp didn't know. Defeated, the words tasted like soot on his tongue as he rolled his head back, snarling, "Fine. Yes, help me!"

You are an elemental, one with nature. Listen to what is around you. Find your nearest source first.

Rasp closed his eyes and drew in. All grew quiet except the crackle of the dying fire.

Your objective is to get your point across, not kill anyone. Focus on a non-lethal target, say the elf's bow. Picture it in your mind and then let your instincts guide you.

Rasp felt the burn of his magic build in his hand. His skin was hot, fingertips curled and scorching. With his target burning bright in his mind, he released. Rasp screamed, but the sound was in his head, not his throat, reverberating deep in his skull to the sounds of hammers and a horn.

"Sweet goddess!" Ellisar shouted. Something struck the ground with a soft clatter, followed by a storm of elvish cursing.

"Your bow's on fire!"

"No shit, Snag! So are my fucking sleeves!" There was stomping and furious patting as Ellisar's tall frame did a sort of awkward, twisting dance on the edge of Rasp's muddled vision, attempting to smother the flames.

Rasp couldn't take credit for the attack, at least not completely. He'd felt the witch's power intermingle with his own, guiding the blaze. He was lucky he hadn't caught himself on fire. Rasp clenched his trembling hand, forcing the words through gritted teeth. "Let Faris go or it will be your face next!"

Light from the firepit flared several feet into the air. The heat burned twice as hot against his face. He hadn't meant to do that, but he supposed it looked more badass if he pretended otherwise.

"Alright, alright!" Rali talked him through what was happening. She probably didn't mean for it to be helpful, but with the afterimage of the fire still dancing across his vision, Rasp could no longer distinguish the blurry people shapes from the blurry tree shapes. "There, your boyfriend's free. Just don't do me like you did Ellisar, you hear? I prefer my facial features unsinged, thank you."

Faris bounded over and pulled Rasp into a more stable sitting position. The faun sucked in breath through short, panicked gasps. "Please don't let me do anything that stupid again."

"Don't worry. I'm sure they won't let us live long enough to try." Rasp flexed the pain from his fingertips. "They've gone quiet. What's going on?"

"Ellisar's disappeared, probably working her way through the trees to catch us from behind. Curly and Rali are staring daggers at you, and I don't think Snag has moved since the action started."

"I'm allergic to fire!" the goblin called from what sounded like a sensible distance away.

Ellisar's disappearance was troubling, but it was the main member of the party that worried him. "And Oralia?"

"Oh gods, she's drawn her sword and is . . . putting it down?"

"Rasp Stoneclaw." Dirt and gravel crunched underfoot, marking the progress of the imposing form that drew nearer, seemingly unafraid. "I am approaching unarmed. Do not set me on fire."

"Call off your elf first! I want her out in the open where Faris can see her."

A twig snapped to their left. Cursing, Faris hooked his hands under Rasp's arms and dragged him several feet across the leafy ground behind him. "Too close, too close! Back the elf up."

"Ellisar, stand down!" Oralia cut through the commotion with a single, deafening command. Rasp's spine straightened not out of volition, but instinct. "Move to the other side of the fire with the others, *now*."

After several seconds of nauseating silence, Oralia spoke again with an edge so sharp, it made him wish she'd go back to yelling at him instead. "You are full of an alarming number of surprises, Rasp. Unfortunately, they will not save you. You are unarmed and outnumbered. How do you want this to end?"

Rasp wriggled free of Faris's grip and landed on his ass harder than he'd meant to. If he was going to die, he'd at least prefer to do it while not being carried around like a limp ragdoll. He slowly drew one knee under him, and then the other. "Is there an option that doesn't involve you murdering us?"

"Or torture," Faris added. "Maybe rule out pain altogether while we're at it?"

"Fuck that. I'm going to peel his fingernails off one by one and cram them down his gullet until he chokes!"

A loud click of Oralia's tusks silenced Ellisar's protests. From the protector's voice, she seemed to have aged several decades in the span of one evening. Her normal rolling, rumbling speech was noticeably frayed. "We will address what just happened soon enough. For the moment, I want to know why the two of you are acting like imbeciles. I expect this from Rasp, but not from you, Faris."

"I'm not going to let you kill him."

"Why would I terminate the one person I am relying upon to get me into the Iron Ridge?"

Faris's former resolve sounded as though it had just wilted like a lily under the full force of the afternoon sun. "Then why were you so bent on separating him from me?"

"My intention was to be discreet. Clearly that is no longer necessary, as your ward just lit a member of my team on fire. If you did not know what he was prior to this, I am certain you have some idea now."

Faris nudged Rasp with his hoof. "I think this is the part where you're supposed to grovel."

He was already on his knees. What more could Oralia possibly want? He'd never been very good at the whole repentance thing, but Rasp supposed there was a first time for everything. "Look, I almost got eaten by a dragon and then drowned in a river. And now I'm cold and sick and I think I hit my head at some point. I'm *not* thinking, okay? Just leave Faris out of this. I'll even let Ellisar hit me if it'll make her feel better."

"It's not fun if you want it," Ellisar retorted.

A cool breeze swept over Rasp, bringing a hint of familiar magic. If one of the others was speaking again, Rasp was unable to hear. His body shivered as Whisper's voice rippled across his mind. **I'm afraid saving your companion came at the cost of revealing your secret, little bird. The best you can do now is to accept what you are and speak to the protector truthfully.**

"Are you crazy? I'm not telling her I'm a—" Rasp stopped mid-sentence, remembering too late that Faris and Oralia could hear him just as clearly as Whisper.

A tad late for that. Alas, this is as far as I can help for the moment. The rest is up to you. Good luck. Before he could protest, Rasp felt Whisper's presence leave him. Apparently even the witch had the sense not to pick a fight with the Protector of the Realm.

"Showing up just long enough to get me in trouble, is that how it is?" As usual, his need to have the final word served only to bite him in the ass.

"Rasp, to whom are you speaking?" From her exasperated tone, Rasp suspected Oralia didn't want an answer so much as she wanted the hushed, maniacal whispering to stop. When he impressed everyone involved by keeping his infernal mouth shut, she continued with a sigh. "If I agree to overlook tonight's rash behavior from you and Mister Belfast, will you speak to me truthfully?"

"Yes!" Fortunately for him, Oralia's version of what constituted truthfulness was vastly different from his. Surely he could find a way to spin this without fully incriminating himself. "But only if Faris stays."

The protector's great, blurry shape loomed over the top of him, poised to squash him like a cockroach beneath her heel. "In that case, I will insist on having Ralizak present during the questioning as well. Fair?"

Dammit. While human phrasing went over Oralia's head unnoticed, Lieutenant Ralizak was more on the up-and-up. Even Faris couldn't talk circles around her. Judging by Oralia's terms, she was well aware of the obstacle Rali posed to the two.

"Totally fair. No complaints here," Faris said before Rasp had a chance to set her olive branch on fire.

"Ralizak, over to me. Curly and Snaglebrag, take Willem back to camp alive," Oralia said, with the sort of tone that emphasized "alive" was an absolute and not a suggestion. Her next words sent an icy prickle down Rasp's spine. "Stay within earshot, Ellisar. In case I have need of you."

CHAPTER THIRTY-THREE

Don't Be Crow

Curly and Snag departed for camp without any of their usual grumblings. If Rasp were a betting man, he'd wager the pair was probably relieved to put as much distance between them and whatever was about to go down. Sometime during the shuffle of moving bodies, he had lost track of Ellisar again. The fact that she was still lurking nearby twisted his intestines into knots. The added knowledge that she was using this time to plot her revenge ensured the knots were double and triple tied.

"Ralizak," Oralia addressed the hazy shadow that was currently dumping loose dirt over the smoldering coals. "If you are quite finished, I would like to get this over with sometime tonight."

"Yeah, yeah, give me a minute. Just taking some precautions first." Having extinguished the fire, the dwarf's clomping footsteps approached with just enough drag to demonstrate her reluctance. "I don't know about you, boss, but I have no intention of being turned into a living candle the moment someone loses their temper again."

"Sit." Oralia's order must have been aimed at Rali and Faris, because Rasp was barely managing to hold himself semi-upright as it was. He heard the rustle of chainmail as the protector eased onto the ground in front of him. True to her nature, she got right to the point. "Thanks to tonight's complete overreaction, I suspect I have some of my answers already. Regardless, we are going to go through today's events thoroughly. If you are smart, you will give me the truth. I am choosing to hear you out instead of awarding the kick to the head the two of you rightfully deserve. Do not test my generosity any further."

Rasp only nodded, knowing any answer other than "Yes, Protector" would likely be testing her patience. And "Yes, Protector" was, of course, much too obedient for Rasp's nature.

Oralia continued, "Sky shrieks are not supposed to be in realm territory. And yet they are. On the road that you chose, of all places, right before we reached the mountain. Why is that, Rasp?"

"I don't know. I chose the road for its length, not danger." Rasp flinched, realizing he'd already shared too much. He could feel the weight of Oralia's glare settle over the top of him. "What? You asked for honesty, didn't you?"

With an irritated exhale of breath, Oralia jumped into her next question without giving him time to prepare. "Did you summon the dragons?"

"Gods, no! That's just something we tell outsiders to keep them away. It's not real."

The eldest of Rasp's siblings, Crow Stoneclaw, was a non-living testament to the ridiculousness of such a claim. Theoretically, you could tame a sky shriek. In the same vein of thinking that if you threw yourself off a cliff, you might learn to fly before you hit the bottom. It could happen, maybe, but most people weren't stupid enough to try. Crow, in an attempt to prove all the naysayers wrong, decided he would try his hand at raising a freshly hatched dragon. Alas, the enthusiastic Stoneclaw was devoured by the mother beast before he could so much as sneak the egg from the nest.

If nothing else, Rasp's brother lived on in infamy. "Don't be Crow" was now a very popular mountain folk saying.

A threatening silence passed between them, and Rasp wondered exactly what information the protector was gathering from his petulant expression. Oralia let the quiet linger a few dreadful seconds longer before moving her interrogation along in a voice that, if Rasp didn't know any better, might have passed for friendly. "I have been informed it was you that sounded the alarm. Is that true?"

"Alarm?" Rasp searched the area to his right for Faris. His hand brushed against what he assumed was the faun's knee and gripped his tangled fur. "Did I do that?"

"Yeah, actually you did. Something about 'Dragon! Get off the road,' I think."

Oh, damn. He did, didn't he? It had all happened so fast Rasp barely remembered. "It seems I did do that, yes."

"You can stop touching my leg now." Faris lifted Rasp's hand away with the care of someone trying not to contract the spotted plague, and let it drop onto the patchy ground between them.

"I'm not going to set you on fire!"

"Didn't stop you from torching my sterling reputation."

"Oh, please. You did that yourself."

Rather than wait for their petty squabble to draw to a close, Oralia merely spoke louder over them. "How did you know about the dragons, Rasp, if you cannot see your own hand in front of you?"

That was a question he was not prepared to answer. The first of many, probably. Once more, Rasp tried to obtain a clearer picture of the situation from Faris's posture. He meant to place his hand on the faun's shoulder, but overshot and made contact with the side of Faris's scruffy face instead.

"Can I help you?"

"Touching your face helps me remember."

Faris, aside from some slight annoyance at being touched, wasn't nearly on edge as he had been previously. Had the danger passed? Oralia said she needed him alive in order to reach the mountain. Maybe that outweighed the whole witch-killing thing. Rasp stewed on this for a moment, wondering if her leniency was about to change. Surely there was a way to offer Oralia the truth without outing himself as a witch in the same breath. "I knew about the dragon because of the birds."

This served only to elicit an exhausted sigh from his interrogator.

"You mind if I step in here?" Rali asked. Having received some unseen command from Oralia, she continued in an inquisitive tone that was alarmingly genuine. "The birds, you say? How does that work exactly?"

"Uh, they um . . ."

"It's obvious you have a unique relationship with the birds. We've all seen the way you talk to them, and give them bits of silver, and pull off that little hunting trick you do." Rali scooted closer, lowering her tone in a concerned manner. "Do the birds talk back to you?"

"Does 'chirp-chirp' count?"

"Oh my gods." From the sounds of it, Faris was burying his face hopelessly in his hands.

Rali continued undeterred. "So, controlling fire and talking to animals, are those your only abilities?"

"Not animals. Just the ravens." Oh shit. Rasp physically cringed, wishing he could shrink into himself. He'd walked right into that one.

"Oh, okay." There was a rustle of chainmail as Rali, having gotten exactly what she wanted from him, leaned back into a more comfortable position. "You hear that, boss? It's just the ravens then."

For a short while, the only sounds between them were the wind rattling the leaves overhead and the soft scrape of someone sharpening a blade further away. Oralia's voice was harsh in comparison. "So you are a witch then. Is that what you are trying so desperately to avoid saying?"

Rasp recalled the terminology Daana used during her lecture. "I prefer 'magically inclined person.'"

"I think I'm starting to get a better picture here. He's got all the powers and none of the abilities. Like a baby witch. Is that right, bucko?"

Rasp wasn't sure why he felt suddenly insulted by that. It was true. By all accounts, he was a terrible witch. Still, she didn't have to say it like that.

"He prefers 'wildly incompetent,'" Faris contributed helpfully.

"Faris," Oralia's rumbling voice shifted directions, as if suddenly remembering something. "You overreacted before you even knew what my line of questioning was about. Did you already know?"

"I had a feeling, yes."

"And what prompted you to keep it to yourself?"

"He's not big on sharing his feelings," Rasp blurted out before Faris was given the chance to remind Oralia that she had a murderous reputation to uphold.

Faris, fortunately, was more strategic in his reply. "Like I said, it was just a feeling. I don't ruin people's lives over a hunch."

Whether she believed their flimsy excuses or not, Oralia didn't say. "Do you have your magic under control, Rasp?"

Whisper had warned him not to mention his training. At the moment, he wasn't sure which of them he feared more. He would have to find a way to appease both sides. "I've managed this long without anyone suspecting, haven't I?"

Oralia was ready with another blasted question. "And what happens when you cannot manage anymore? When it becomes a problem. *My* problem."

He thought back to the knife held to his throat. Whisper had offered a swift death. Perhaps Rasp's cowardice had done nothing but stall the inevitable. He wondered if the protector would be as merciful in executing him. "What am I supposed to say to that, Protector? The last time it caused a problem my family chased me down a mountain and tried to kill me. If I slip up, are you going to do the same?"

"No. Chasing you first would be tedious."

A cold breeze blustered between them and he shivered, drawing the damp cloak further over his quaking body. Rasp's shoulders slumped so low, they nearly matched his dwindling hope of survival. "Still on thin ice over the whole living thing, got it."

He heard Oralia shift across from him, her voice marked with confusion. "There is no—"

"It's a figure of speech," Rali whispered.

The protector recovered remarkably fast, continuing as though Rasp's words hadn't shot so far over her head that they were currently soaring through the clouds. "From this moment onward, you will come to me before there is a problem. No more managing on your own." Oralia must have seen the surprise on Rasp's face, prompting her to explain, "In our negotiations you asked for my ear. You have it. If there is an issue, I expect to be the first to know. Agreed?"

This was entirely too easy. There had to be a trap laid out for him somewhere. Before Rasp could seal his fate, Faris butted in. "I'm sorry. I think I missed something here. Can we back up for a moment?"

"Did something I say confuse you, Mister Belfast?"

"I'm not questioning your judgment by any means. It's just, last I checked, you're pretty well known for killing witches. It's kind of your thing." He must have regained some of his confidence, because he was now asking questions a more sensible person would have kept to themselves. Faris pressed on, slapping away the fingers Rasp was using to pinch him. "Is Rasp not witchy enough for you? Do you have some moral aversion against killing incompetent witches, maybe? It just seems kind of like you're doing the opposite of your reputation here."

"He's witchy enough!" a voice called from farther away.

"Oh look, Ellisar's weaving a noose. How sweet. Normally she just sticks an arrow in their gut and lets them die nice and slow like." Rali's hand patted Rasp's knee affectionately. "Someone's certainly made an impression."

"An arrow's no good when your bow's been burnt to a crisp," Faris reminded her.

"Oh, right." Rali's voice was magnified now, probably from cupping her hands around her mouth as obnoxiously loud people do in order to become obnoxiously louder. "Looks good, Ellisar! See? Crafting *can* relieve tension."

As he did not wish to hear any more details concerning Ellisar's impending revenge, Rasp surprised everyone, including himself, by turning in Oralia's direction and grumbling, "You were saying?"

"I only remove witches that stand in my way. Do as you are told, and I will ensure Ellisar's noose goes unused."

Naturally, Rasp was wary. "I don't understand. Why would you want to help me?"

The protector went unbearably quiet, as if considering exactly how much to tell him. Finally, Oralia said, "We would be helping each other. I cannot afford to lose passage through the ridge and you cannot afford to be discovered. My faithful will keep their mouths shut, but I cannot guarantee the same of anyone else. Keep your abilities hidden. The Speaker of the People values power over trade routes. If he learns what you are, he will take you and come after your people looking for more."

"He'll be wasting his time. I am the only one like me. The mountain folk want nothing to do with magic."

"That is not the point." Oralia's tusks clicked softly against her teeth. "It has been a long day, and I am tired. Will you assure me that you will continue to keep your abilities a secret so we may be done here?"

"You have my word."

"And you will seek my help when needed?"

Hiding his magic was the easy part. Letting someone in would be less so. "Yes, Protector."

"As for you, Faris Belfast." Oralia's rumbling voice shifted directions once more.

"I had nothing to do with it!"

"You noticed what nobody else did. Going forward, if you see something the rest of us miss again, for your sake and Rasp's, report it. I told your father I would keep you safe. Your cooperation ensures I will not have to break that promise. Understood?"

"From now on, I report all of Rasp's business directly to you. Understood loud and clear."

"What transpired here will not be spoken of. That includes you two," Oralia said to her remaining warriors. Her large, blurry shape grew taller in Rasp's vision as she stood. "Rasp will ride double with me back to camp. Faris, I will need your assistance getting him onto the horse."

Oh, great. Another horse. As much as Rasp appreciated the still living part, his last encounter with the species had left him leery of climbing back into the saddle. And now he was getting to share one with the single person he was terrified of most. Well, aside from Ellisar maybe.

Hurray.

CHAPTER THIRTY-FOUR

Deceived

After some effort, with which Rasp's wobbly legs were of no help whatsoever, they got him situated on the back of Oralia's horse. He was certain she could have thrown him over the top of it single-handedly but, seeing as he'd already set one member of her team on fire, was probably using Faris's help as a friendly buffer. The horse itself was a huge, smelly, monstrously sized beast that could probably trace its ancestry back to the mammoths. It made sense, he supposed. A regular horse would have broken its back merely looking at an orc.

The worn leather creaked as Oralia mounted and slid into the saddle in front of him. "You will have to put your distrust of me aside long enough to hold on, Rasp."

Hesitantly, he clasped his arms around her. The heat radiating from her back was disturbingly pleasant. It took effort not to slump against the protector and leach her warmth. Suspecting she wouldn't appreciate the closeness as much as him, Rasp abstained. Oralia clicked her tongue and the horse lunged forward uphill. Rasp nearly slid off the damn thing. He gripped Oralia tighter, wiggling his hips back into the shared saddle.

For some time, the only sound between them was the steady footfalls of the horse. Just as Rasp was about to nod off, Oralia's voice startled him awake.

"Ride ahead, Ralizak. I will catch up in a moment." The protector waited until the pony's hoofbeats were faint in the distance. When she spoke again, her voice was low and carefully guarded. "I know you had help."

Startled, Rasp groggily lifted his head. "What?"

"That stunt with the fire. If you actually knew how to use your magic, you would not be here."

Rasp wasn't sure if her statement meant, "If you actually knew how to use your magic, you would have thwarted me by now." Or if it was, perhaps, the protector's vague way of saying, "If you actually knew how to use your magic, I would have already left you dead and in a ditch somewhere." Given the circumstances, Rasp decided the safest option was to say nothing at all.

He glanced over the side of the beast, attempting to gauge the distance to the ground. The moon above was hidden behind a thick shroud of clouds and, without a proper light source, he couldn't see shit. Although he'd survived one dive from a horse so far, that horse had been significantly smaller than Oralia's charger. On the off chance Rasp managed to land without breaking his neck, he'd probably get crushed to death.

She needs you alive. She needs you alive. She needs you alive. As far as personal mantras went, it wasn't the best. But it was successful in keeping his ass planted in the saddle, at least. A second, unhelpful thought popped into his head. *Or this was a clever ploy to separate you from Faris. He's got to walk back. And you're gods-only-know how far away, alone on the road, with the enemy.*

Rasp's guts lurched, attempting to upend a hot bellyful of tonic and stomach acid. *Shut up, brain!*

Oralia's voice disrupted his panicked thoughts. "You were conversing aloud with thin air earlier. I am going to give you the benefit of the doubt and assume that you are not suffering from a psychotic break. Rather, I suspect you have met Dear Whisper. And, from your sudden and uncharacteristic silence, I also suspect you were instructed not to speak of it. That rule does not apply to me. When you hear from Whisper again, tell my dear friend I expect to be included in whatever it is you two are doing."

"You?" Rasp managed, at last, practically choking on the damn word.

"Me, what?"

"Whisper said they weren't loyal to the realm. Loyal, my ass. You represent a third of the ruling power!" Rasp sank lower in the saddle as a second realization struck with the force of a sledgehammer. In the midst of the crisis, there hadn't been time to consider why the witch had helped him only to turn around and leave the moment the consequences for acting like an idiot started to roll in. Now it made perfect sense. Whisper hadn't been helping *him*, they'd been helping Oralia. "That little shit deceived me! No wonder they didn't try to stop me. Your witch tricked me into showing my powers to you, didn't they?"

"Although I doubt it took much trickery, I suspect that was Whisper's intention, yes."

"They let me set Ellisar on fire."

"Whisper and Ellisar have a complicated relationship. Truth be told, that was not the worst one has done to the other. Allowing you to take the fall was rather clever on Whisper's part."

"Gods dammit!"

"Lower your voice."

Rasp obeyed, hissing, "Why? Who do you not want to overhear? Your people obviously already know the big, scary witch killer has a witch up her sleeve. Don't want the rest of the realm to catch on that you're a hypocrite?"

"Only Ralizak and Ellisar know. My remaining warriors are currently unaware and I aim to keep it that way. My immediate concern is not for them, but Faris. Whisper guards their existence very carefully. If someone who is not meant to know finds out, I cannot guarantee how Whisper will react. You obviously care for your friend. Keeping your confounded mouth shut is the best way to ensure his safety."

The bubbling sensation from earlier had finally settled in the pit of Rasp's stomach. Except it didn't stop once it bottomed out. It sank lower and lower, threatening to drag him down with it into the churning depths of bile and acid. Preventing the traveling party from accessing the ridge was still priority number one, but finding a way to accomplish it without compromising Faris's safety was a complication he hadn't considered before. Gods dammit. Life had been so much easier back when he didn't have friends.

A solution to his problem existed. Like an annoying insect, it buzzed just on the other side of the window, trying to get in but unable to penetrate the glass. And, had his brain not been a pile of congealed mush, he might have come to an eventual, possibly groundbreaking, conclusion. Alas, in that moment all he could think about was how damned cold he was.

He had already lost all sensation in his fingertips. Rasp feared it would not be long before he started to lose other things, too.

Unfortunately, the protector was not finished with what was swiftly becoming her second interrogation of the evening. "The fact that Whisper revealed themself to you is telling. Of what, I am not sure. What is Whisper attempting to accomplish with you?"

The cold was affecting other parts of Rasp's being as well. Primarily his sense of self-preservation. To be fair, that one had always been somewhat underdeveloped in the face of authority. Thus, his reply was not so much an answer as it was a silent plea to be ejected from the horse. "Why don't you ask your 'dear friend' yourself?"

Rasp felt Oralia shift in the saddle. Based on the contortion of her body, she was peering over her shoulder at him. Rasp envisioned the protector viewing him in the same way someone with a scalpel might study the hapless test subject writhing on their examination table. Finally, after extracting whatever information his defiant expression offered, Oralia said, "You do not know. Interesting."

"Of course I know what your witch wants!"

"No, I meant why I cannot ask Whisper myself."

"Oh." Rasp was grateful when the protector returned to her forward-facing position. The few, brief moments his body was unshielded by her from the wind left him chilled and shivering. Propriety be damned, he needed to get warm. Rasp pulled his arms tight and hugged her.

The muscles in her back tensed and he felt her reach across for her weapon. Oralia must have realized his intentions were to steal her body heat and not to throw her from the horse, because she relaxed back into the saddle. She spared both of them the awkwardness of addressing it and said instead, "Once more, Rasp. Why did Whisper approach you?"

He thought back on his conversation with the witch and offered a suitable, if vague, answer. "Because I'm a baby bird, apparently. One who's to be trained into a proper witch. Something about learning to use my powers before they get me killed and whatnot."

Rasp took a breath, wondering if she would return the favor and answer one of his questions. "Why is it you can't ask?"

To his surprise, Oralia was forthcoming. "It is not a matter of can or cannot. Whisper is a shapeshifter. I would not know *whom* to ask. Whisper once rode from Adderwood to Castle Bay disguised as a mouse on a supply cart. For their safety, it is best I do not know what form they have taken."

"A shapeshifter?" Rasp drew his breath in through his teeth with a hiss. "I thought those only existed in faerie tales."

"You used magic to light my sergeant on fire, yet question the existence of a shifter?" Rasp swore he heard a note of amusement in Oralia's tone. It was as fleeting as it was unexpected. "I may not believe in fate or prophecies, but I am not ignorant to the powers that shape them. You should not be, either. Someone as old and cautious as Whisper does not risk revealing themselves for nothing. My dear friend either pities you enough to spare you from the fate of their people, or is attempting to fulfill a destiny of their own."

Rasp suspected the latter. Wondering, if for once in his fucking life, it would be possible to meet someone who didn't try to use him for their own purposes. He rolled his head back and groaned, "Please tell me this destiny doesn't bring on the end of times."

"No. Just that of the realm."

The what?

"Gods, Protector. Did you really just say that out loud? To me?" A sworn enemy? Or, at least, a former sworn enemy. Now Rasp wasn't sure what they were. Unsworn enemies? Temporary allies? Convenient saddle buddies? He didn't want to dwell too much on that last one. "If you were anyone else, I would assume you're joking. But you're not, are you?"

"So long as they are in my debt, Whisper is powerless to enact their revenge. What happens afterward, I cannot say. I will be free of my service by then. The remaining heads of the realm will either rise to the challenge or fail. Perhaps failure will weed out the corruption that I, myself, could not."

". . . You're not going to try to stop it?" He'd mistakenly assumed that was the point of having a Protector of the Realm. Maybe, you know, to protect the fucking realm. Not that Rasp was one to talk, being the fate-appointed leader of his people and still trying to find a way to get out of it—a way that skirted around the gruesome death part, preferably.

Still working on that one.

"The last revolution I tried to stop nearly cost me everything. I have no intention of repeating that mistake."

A very optimistic and possibly concussed portion of his brain volunteered its worst idea yet. *You could run away together! Problem solved.*

Somehow, he didn't think she'd go for it.

"The reason I tell you any of this, Rasp Stoneclaw," Oralia said, "is because Whisper does not yet realize how difficult you are to motivate. You were born a witch, and with time and effort, Whisper may be able to mold you into a decent one. But a revolutionist, I think not. You balk at the idea of helping anyone who is not yourself. I find it difficult to believe you would risk your life for the cause of a stranger."

"Said with such confidence. Careful, I could surprise you."

"Then stave off your change of heart until after I have my route through the Iron Ridge. It would be a shame to kill you prematurely."

He rested his cheek against her back, head jostling in time to the horse's rolling movements, and smirked. "Oh, good. There's the threatening Protector I know. I was beginning to think you liked me."

CHAPTER THIRTY-FIVE

Upside Down and Drunk

Daana was reading under the cook's lean-to, sitting as close to the roaring fire as she could without getting a faceful of smoke and ash. It was the day after the dragon attack. Fog had rolled in and hung low in the trees, making for an especially cold morning. The wind picked up every now and then, threatening to rip the canvas that stretched above her from its poles and into the air like a sail.

With the breakfast rush over, Daana felt a calm settle over the tent. The cook busied himself doing what seemed to be a thousand tasks all at once. He was a cheery fellow and, unlike everyone else in the camp, did not object to Daana's presence. The two shift workers busied themselves with cleaning, keeping the kindling well stocked, and disputing whose turn it was to lug fresh water from the river. It may not have been as cozy as the division library, but the kitchen was a good second best. Warm, with just enough noise to not be bothersome, and of course, well stocked. Sascha was always jutting a spoonful of something in her direction, insistent on her thoughts. Not because the dish needed fixing, Daana realized after about the fifth time, but because he genuinely liked feeding people.

Sascha was sorting through a basket of mushrooms the foragers had brought when a harsh sound disrupted his work. "You again?" he said with a sudden warmth in his voice. "Not a fan of the radishes then, huh? I have some bacon trimmings you might like better."

Daana peered over the top of her book to see who he was conversing with. The person in question was not actually a person at all, but a raven. Had this been the first time she'd witnessed a grown adult conversing with a bird, she might have found it unusual. As Rasp regularly carried on one-sided conversations with an entire flock, Daana considered that perhaps it was she who was missing context. Given the lack of local entertainment, this may very well have been how citizens outside of the capital passed their time.

How terribly sad.

"Friend of yours?" she asked.

Sascha lumbered past, placing a bowl of scraps onto the floor near the edge of the lean-to. "We're getting there. Some of the flock hang around the back hoping for handouts, but this one is bolder than the others."

The raven skittered closer, but did not venture all the way in. It tilted its head at Daana, eyeing her warily. This was not the raven Rasp referred to as "Mother." This one was significantly larger, with a handful of white feathers in its tail.

"Oh, come now. It's her you're worried about. Really?" Sascha tutted, rubbing his left tusk. "Stop your bellyaching and come sit by the fire. It's miserable out there."

The raven produced a guttural click from the back of its throat. This, coupled with a dramatic head dip, communicated something that, even to the untrained eye, could not have been mistaken for anything but blatant disapproval.

"I haven't named you yet. Any more of this and you'll be called Chicken Liver."

Croak!

With a halfhearted sigh, the large orc lifted the corner flap of the tent and strolled out of sight. A few moments later, Daana heard a splintered *crack* and Sascha returned, carrying what looked to be half of a tree over his shoulder. He drove the large branch into the ground by the firepit as easily as one might cut through soft butter with a hot knife.

"There." He stooped, picking the bowl from the floor and setting it into the branches with a delicateness that seemed uncanny for someone who could level an entire forest with his bare hands. "Good enough for you, Your Highness?"

Ruffling its feathers in what Daana assumed was gratitude, the raven fluttered up to its new perch and began picking through the scraps for the tastiest bits.

Was it strange that she felt a sense of shared comradery with a damn bird? Daana had been encouraged into the safety of the tent under eerily similar circumstances. Minus the raw bacon trimmings, of course—she had standards, after all. It had started only a few days ago when, desperate for somewhere warm to read, Daana had found herself huddled by the fire in the

main canteen area. It was unprotected from the elements, however, and she
soon found herself even more miserable than before.

Making enough noise to be noticeable but without actually saying anything, the cook placed a crate near the sheltered edge of his lean-to and went
back to business. Daana would have thought nothing of it had not one of
the kitchen hands gone out of their way to explain it was an invitation to
sit. The next morning the crate reappeared, but this time further inside. By
the third day, Daana was fully inside the enclosure and had gained enough
confidence to attempt polite conversation with her gracious host. Despite
his intimidating size, Daana quickly realized Sascha's personality was the orc
equivalent of a teddy bear.

Having returned to his prep, Sascha was a blur of constant motion, flittering from one station to the next and humming a tune she did not recognize.
He had the mushrooms cleaned, diced, and into the soup in the time it took
Daana to finish her page. He paused, drying his hands against his sunflower
apron, and frowned at the journal resting in Daana's lap. "This is the third time
I've seen you with that book and you still look like you want to burn it. Is this
an emissary thing? Or are you always this hostile with your reading material?"

"I don't normally advocate the destruction of literature, but for this one
I might make an exception." Daana set the journal into her lap and massaged
her aching temples, groaning, "The protector kindly tasked me with translating it. Normally I wouldn't object, but the damn thing is written in stolac. A
language I don't even speak!"

"Hmmm." Half of Sascha's responses were indistinct noises left entirely
to Daana's interpretation.

Today he was interested, she decided. Mostly because she didn't have
the heart to stumble through another page of useless translations, but also
because it was nice to talk to someone about something other than customs
and diplomacy or whatever the fuck an aspiring emissary was supposed to
care about. And, seeing as Daana couldn't discuss magic, her one true passion, complaining was an acceptable alternative.

"The protector thought, once translated, it could serve as a sort of common ground between us and the mountain folk. Stolac is a bastardization of
laftak, the language of the flatlands—which I can read. The idea was that I
could use laftak as a foundation to build upon."

"I'm sensing that's not been the case."

"I've barely made it past the front cover. No matter what I try, I can't get
a grasp on it. I swear, it reads like the author had written it upside down and

drunk." Which, if Rasp was an accurate representation of his people, was a strong possibility. The passages Daana had translated so far were disjointed and made very little, if any, sense. She would have given up days ago had it not been for the fact that Oralia was awaiting her report.

"If only there was someone who was already versed in the written language of the mountain folk," Sascha said. "How helpful that would be."

From his easy smile, Daana suspected the cook was teasing her. She had originally hoped to garner Rasp's help translating the text. That no longer seemed a viable possibility now, considering the mountain man was one, blind, and two, made it his personal mission in life to be as absolutely unhelpful as possible. "The last time I tried to have an intelligent conversation with that man, he ran off and tried to get eaten by a dragon."

Sascha only laughed.

Sudden movement from the nearest corner of the tent caught her attention. As soundless as a shadow, a dark shape slipped beneath the canvas siding and slunk swiftly toward her. Daana was already halfway off her crate, startling the black-and-white raven from its perch, before realizing the intruder was not some ax-wielding maniac.

One look at his narrowed eyes and Danna found herself almost wishing it had been a madman with an ax. "Willem?"

He threw a finger to his lips, signaling for her to keep quiet.

With her heartbeat still pounding in her ears, Daana sat back down onto the wooden crate with force. Her back end regretted the dramatic landing, but at the moment, there were more serious matters to address. Why her partner was acting like a nutcase, for instance, currently topped the list of "things I wish to yell at you about."

"What are you doing here?" she hissed. "You're supposed to be in the infirmary."

Before Willem could reply, the black and white raven dropped to the ground and hopped in their direction. It fanned its wings wide and screeched at Willem, like some sort of feathery guard dog.

With the deafening racket sure to draw unwanted attention, Daana snatched the remnants of a biscuit from her mess plate and flung it across the lean-to, near the entrance. "Go, shoo!"

With a final, threatening hiss, Chicken Liver fluttered to the front, grabbed the offering in its beak, and disappeared into the surrounding trees.

Checking to be sure no one saw, Willem positioned his body against Daana's makeshift chair in a way that would obscure him from the kitchen staff. "I'm sorry for the surprise entrance, my dear." He searched the tent with his eyes as he spoke, as if making a mental note of every available entry point in the event he was forced to make an equally hasty exit. "I would have sent for you had I found someone willing to carry the message."

"Are you alright? What's going on?"

"There isn't much time," he whispered. "I got here as soon as I could. The protector has—"

"This is a waste of my talents!" A booming voice preceded the two figures, one large and the other small, that entered the lean-to from the wind-ravaged doorway, drowning out Willem's words.

"Oh, dear." Willem clamped his eyes shut and pressed further into the crate.

Swiveling her head in the direction of the entryway, Daana spied Curly's hulking form first. His scowling companion was recognizable to Daana only because he happened to be a goblin. For a fleeting moment, a spark of excitement rose above her growing dread. Snaglebrag Flint was the only member of the faithful four Daana had not yet met. Not for her lack of trying, of course. Snag avoided others as much as others usually avoided him.

But what were they doing here? Breakfast had ended an hour ago. Were they after Willem? Whatever for? Daana, checking her expression, fanned out her cloak to better conceal Willem and returned to the journal in her hand, listening for further clues.

"Catching dysentery isn't a talent," she heard Snag mutter. His voice was gruff and scratchy, and made the back of her throat tickle with sympathy pains.

"Act natural," Willem hissed under his breath. "I'm not here."

To Daana's horror, Snag's ears pivoted in her direction and his unnerving yellow stare followed. There was a flicker of recognition in the goblin's eyes as he took her in. Why it was there, Daana couldn't say. Only that it left her suddenly queasy.

CHAPTER THIRTY-SIX

Wipe the Blood
From Your Feet First

Gentlemen, welcome," Sascha greeted in his *all are welcome but kindly wipe the blood off your feet first* voice. He set aside his prep work and stepped toward the pair, wiping his gargantuan hands against the front of his flowery apron. A cold gust of wind blustered through the canvas flap doorway, stirring loose dirt and ash into the air as the cook approached the new arrivals. "Can I assist you with something?"

The unnerving look vanished from Snag's face as his gaze shifted from Daana to Sascha. A new expression slid into place and suddenly, he was all business. Snag cracked what was probably supposed to be a friendly smile but looked more like he was fighting the urge to bite something. "The herbalist is running low on supplies. You got any extra you're willing to part with?" He waved his clawed hand at Curly. "Don't just stand there. You're the assistant. Deliver the list."

Curly pulled a slip of parchment from the inside of his jacket with such force it crumpled. "I'm starting to think you made up this assistant-to-the-medic position just so you don't have to do any grunt work."

"And that's why I don't pay you to think."

"You're not paying me at all!"

Sascha seemed to sense a fight was about to break out and diffused it with practiced ease. "That's right. I heard about the promotion to chief medical officer. Congratulations, Mister Flint."

Evidently redirection worked just as well on cutthroats as it did unwieldy toddlers. Snag opened his mouth and then caught himself. Whatever nasty thing the goblin intended to say crawled back into his cavernous maw and died. With a grudging sigh, Snag grumbled his thanks instead.

With Medical Officer Tarvy deceased, together, Snag and Briony had been put in charge of the infirmary on the grounds that they had the closest experience to anything resembling medical work. Based on his reaction, it was a decision the goblin appeared to loathe more and more with each passing breath. There were those that would do nearly anything for a position of power, no matter how small. Snaglebrag was not among them. Daana suspected he fell into the significantly more terrifying *why would I need a false sense of power when I could just kill you* category.

"Hey, you nearly took my head off when I congratulated you!" Curly placed his hands on his hips in a gesture that might have unconsciously been borrowed from one of the female members of the faithful four. "Why's he get a free pass? You're being sizeist, aren't you? Bigger doesn't mean better, you know. I could squash you just as easily as Sascha can."

Snag's ears pinned against the back of his head. The ring strung through his lip shook as he spoke, brandishing a mouthful of pointed, needle-like teeth. "Because unlike you, he actually means it! Besides, I am in the process of asking a favor. You don't eat the hand that feeds you."

Sascha furrowed his eyebrows but, after a moment of quiet deliberation, appeared to have decided against correcting him.

Curly made no indication that he even noticed. He tilted his head in Sascha's direction, explaining, "Snag told Oralia he was going to walk into the river if she expected him to take on the responsibilities of chief medical officer by himself. She recruited the herbalist to split the duties with him as a compromise, and he's *still* acting like a baby over it."

"That's it!" Snag ripped the list from Curly's hand and delivered it to the cook himself. "Consider yourself officially demoted from assistant to intern."

"Thank gods. Does that mean I can go now?"

"No, it just means I'll be withholding your wages."

"For the last time, scribbling faces on rocks is not payment."

Ignoring them, Sascha held the parchment a few inches from his face as he skimmed the list. "Such neat handwriting. Can you ask the herbalist to teach the rest of camp penmanship? It's not often I get a note I can read without the aid of a strong drink first."

Curly's neck shrank into his shoulders as a red tint crept across his cheeks. Sascha was too absorbed in the list to notice, but Snag did. The goblin's lips pulled back into a toothy, knowing smile. "Lovely, innit? All the loopy letters. Dotting the i's with little hearts was a nice touch, I thought."

"Mhmm," the cook murmured, half listening. "Make yourselves comfortable, gentlemen. I'll see what I have in the back for you."

Curly waited until Sascha had disappeared before pivoting in Snag's direction, swinging his outer leg with impeccable speed. "I didn't draw any damn hearts!"

Snag sidestepped Curly's kick as easily as one might dodge a three legged turtle. "What are you blushing for? Afraid I'm going to embarrass you in front of the emissary?"

"The wha'?" Curly whipped his gaze up and down the poorly lit tent before, at last, it settled on Daana. A mischievous smirk pulled at the corner of his lips. "Hello, Your Majesty. I didn't realize you were even in here. What with you not talking my ear off and all."

Shit. You've been spotted. Just play it cool and maybe they won't catch on that your partner has lost his mind and is currently using you as a barricade.

"Hello," Daana managed weakly. She debated calling Curly by his newly bestowed nickname, Baby Face, but decided she didn't want to draw any more unwanted attention to herself than necessary. Snag was staring at her with far too much interest as it was.

Snag's yellow eyes glistened in the flickering firelight as he studied her with a blank, unblinking stare. "Curly, do you remember how I keep telling you the importance of body language?"

"Yeah, what of it?"

"What's the emissary telling you right now?" The goblin lifted his hands the moment Daana instinctively began to shift position. "No, no, don't move. Stay just as you are. Let's give him a chance here."

"Do I have to?" Daana squeaked.

The orc's sly smile widened as his half-slit eyes roved between them. "She thinks you're creepy?"

"Start at her feet. Her toes are pointed in our direction, but her body is shifted away. Notice the position of the arms. One crossed over her chest and the other covering her neck. What's that say to you?"

"She's confused goblins with vampires and is covering her throat so you don't drain her blood," Curly said with unfounded confidence.

"I wasn't thinking that!" Daana squeaked.

Snag's mouth curled open as he glared up at his counterpart. "Deception, you dolt! It means she's hiding something." When it became abundantly clear Curly wasn't going to get any further with the lesson, Snag raised his voice, even though the proximity of the tent didn't require it. "You can come out now. There's no point in hiding. I smelled you the moment we walked in."

In a flutter of black coattails, Willem was up, over, and seated on the opposite side of Daana, as though he had been there the whole time. Some part of his brain clicked back into place and he sat straighter, remembering perhaps too late that he, an aging etiquette instructor, was not supposed to be as nimble as a cat. "Mister Flint," Willem said, feigning a friendly smile. "Enjoying your break, are we, sir?"

"Not particularly." Snag's ensuing scowl was severe enough to curdle not only milk, but any liquid, even those previously thought incapable of curdling.

At the moment, Daana was too preoccupied to fret over the meaning behind such threatening facial expressions. Willem's unexpected display of agility stirred a nagging feeling in the back of her mind. A half-formed thought, shrouded in darkness, pulled at her. *Something . . . something about yesterday. Think, Daana, think! What was it?*

"You have not been released from the infirmary yet," Snag said matter-of-factly. "What are you doing here?"

"I heard fresh air does wonders for the body."

For a few terrifying breaths, Snag only stared with his sharp mouth pressed into an unamused line. "You know, it's a shame I didn't diagnose that broken wrist earlier." He signaled for Curly to move in with a tilt of his clawed forefinger. "How about we assist you back to the infirmary and I'll set it for you?"

"Finally!" The orc rubbed his hands together as he started in their direction. "You know that crackling sound a hardboiled egg makes when you roll it over a counter and press a little? I'm gonna do that with your bones."

"How dare—" Daana leapt upright, the words already spilling from her tongue, when Willem pulled her back down onto the crate with a rough jerk.

"Your point is taken." Willem kept one hand locked firmly on Daana while holding the other over his head to demonstrate his compliance. "It was foolish of me to lie. I see that now. If you could find it in your heart not to break an old man's bones, Mister Flint, I would forever be grateful."

"I believe you were telling me what you're doing here."

"Ah, yes," Willem agreed, shrinking back down. He straightened his gloves as he spoke, keeping a wary eye on Curly in the event he suddenly closed the gap between them. "I was making sure Lady Lazuli was prepared for the upcoming officer's meeting. Going over potential talking points, reminding her to stay on topic, proper etiquette, that sort of thing."

"I do have a habit of going off topic," Daana volunteered. "Thank you, Willem. I will make an effort to keep my talking points short and concise."

"Ugh." Curly rolled his head backward with a groan. "Even their lies are boring. Can I break his arm now?"

Snag's gaze shifted, watching as Sascha returned with an armload of supplies from the makeshift storeroom. "Finish your preparations, manservant. But make it quick. You'll be returning with us as soon as we're done here."

While Daana was grateful her partner's wrist had been allowed to remain intact, the insult still stung. Seven realms. This was the second person now to mistake Willem as her personal manservant. She wasn't *that* pampered!

"Thank you, Mister Flint." Willem waited until the pair moved further away before pulling Daana closer. "We will speak in depth later. For now, you need to get yourself to Captain Monk's tent on the double."

Daana glanced over her shoulder, noting Snag's ears were flared in their direction. If the goblin's hearing was anywhere as good as his sense of smell, there wasn't any point in whispering. Nevertheless, she matched Willem's example and kept her voice low. "Why? What's happening?"

"I told you. The protector's called an emergency meeting with the top officers."

"That was real? I thought you made that up."

"They were going to break my wrist. I wasn't going to lie!" Willem silenced her with a cutting glance. "There is no time for questions. As emissary to the Iron Ridge, you have every right to be present. Browbeat your way in if you have to. Don't take no for an answer." Willem paused, tsking under his breath as he straightened Daana's clothes. "This is your one, and possibly only, chance to be accepted into her ranks."

Curly's blasting whistle caused both of them to cover their ears. "Time's up, servant man. We're headin' back. Let's go."

"Remember your training, my dear. I'll come find you later." Willem's gaunt face grew noticeably paler as he rose shakily to his feet. "Provided they don't decide to snap my legs instead."

"I'll manage, thank you." Daana caught his elbow, preventing him from leaving. She searched his expression for answers she did not find. "Are you going to be alright? I've never seen you like this before. It has me worried."

And there's something you're not telling me.

CHAPTER THIRTY-SEVEN

Can't Go Blind Twice

Daana watched as Willem shuffled out of the kitchen lean-to along-side Curly. The bitter wind howled outside, catching the edges of his dark clothing and whipping it behind him as he moved, bent against the elements. She had to get going herself, but for a few heartbeats she found herself unable to look away, wondering exactly what trouble her partner had gotten himself into.

The cook's deep voice startled her from her daze. "You know, I find snakes get an unfair reputation. Most people dislike them because they don't know any better. But, give them a little space and watch where you step, and they'll keep the rats from overrunning the place."

To her horror, she realized Sascha was watching her. Daana quickly replaced the look on her face with something less repugnant. "I thought orcs didn't do metaphors."

"Maybe I just like snakes," he replied, returning to his prep station. "A word of advice. If you're really serious about getting that book translated, then making nice with Snag is your best bet."

Daana tossed the journal, loose parchment, and chalk sticks into her bookbag with less care than they rightfully deserved. "He speaks stolac?"

"He and the guide go at it from time to time. I can't speak for Snag's fluency, but whatever it is he's shouting at the mountain man seems to get a rise. I might be able to arrange for his help, you know. If you want it."

"Why?" Crap. That probably wasn't what an aspiring emissary would say. Definitely not with such an accusatory tone. "I mean, you would do that for me?"

Additionally, why was Oralia having her translate a language one of her own faithful was already versed in? Dear gods, was this just busywork? A means to keep her occupied while Oralia went about her business undisturbed? Daana's brow furrowed at the realization. *Touché, Protector. Weaponizing my own made-up backstory against me. You get points for that one.*

"In my experience, most dignitaries are too busy playing the political game to give any real thought to their duties," the cook spoke as he worked. A white root vegetable of mysterious origins was halved, diced, and then scraped into a separate bowl in a matter of seconds. A second specimen took up its place on the chopping block and disappeared just as rapidly as the first. "They spend all of their effort getting ahead of the competition and never actually accomplishing anything. Your dedication to establishing common ground between us and the Iron Ridge is refreshing. That seems like a cause worthy of helping, if you ask me."

Daana's stomach sank. The pit she was steadily digging herself deeper into felt like it had just swallowed her whole. It was one thing to deceive the enemy, but doing it to the only person who was actually nice to her didn't settle well on her conscience. "Thank you." She attempted to mask the sudden hitch in her voice, but probably not well enough to fool anyone. "I appreciate your vote of confidence, sir. But I would hate to take the new medic from his duties."

"I just gave him enough medicinal herbs to resurrect a horse. It's safe to assume he owes me." Sascha happened to look over his shoulder at her, noticing her mad scramble to gather her belongings. "I'm sorry. Here I am rambling and you have places to be. Where are you off to this time?"

"My first officer meeting." Should she have said that with more enthusiasm? At the moment, that was the last thing she was feeling.

"An occasion indeed." Sascha bustled over to one side of the lean-to and promptly returned bearing a weathered tray with a matching tureen and several empty bowls. "I hate to ask, miss, but my help seems to vanish the moment there's any mention of work. This is supposed to be on its way to Captain Monk's tent. I don't suppose I could trouble you to take it with you?" He paused, adding slyly, "They will be hard-pressed to bar you from any meeting if you come bearing gifts."

"Oh," Daana said. "I mean, yes, of course. An emissary helps all her subjects."

He awarded her the tray and then said, tilting his finger at her for good measure, "If the protector is cold to you, just remember, she was young and new to a position once, too. Everyone starts somewhere. Don't let it get to you."

"Thank you!" Daana scurried away into the roiling fog, balancing the tray between her hands, and realizing too late that was probably not the right response either. Oh well, at least she got the enthusiastic part right.

Captain Monk's pavilion was not difficult to find. It stood in the center of camp, towering above the modest soldier tents like a garish tan and brown steeple. Such luxurious accommodations seemed impractical for one person, but Daana doubted anyone was bothered enough by it to object—except for maybe the person tasked with carrying it. Or the ones responsible for assembling it, just to turn around and tear it all down again. Actually, the more she considered it, the more impractical it became. Whose bright idea was it to send him on the mission again?

The same people who thought sending you was a good idea.

You knew it was going to be an especially good day when even your thoughts were against you. Rude.

Daana approached the entrance and slowed her step. Chin up. Shoulders back. Walk with a purpose. Confidence was half the battle, her old academy trainer had told her once. Perhaps if she had confidence in her ability to feign confidence, she could fool herself, too. Two soldiers posted as sentries at the door stepped dutifully aside as she approached. The one on the left drew back the canvas flap that served as the entryway and gestured her inside.

"Lady Lazuli," they murmured in unison, heads bowed.

Daana offered them a nod of acknowledgment before passing though into the tent, fighting the inappropriate urge to smile. Ha, it was working!

The air within the dim tent was warm and thick with the aromatic notes of burnt ginger and cardamom. The spiced incense was almost overpowering enough to disguise the smell of old mildew. Almost. There was a small folding desk in the corner, along with a pair of thin, collapsible chairs, and a single oil lamp that burned just low enough to keep the darkness at bay. Monk's bedroll was twice the size of her own, complete with a mound of patchwork blankets that looked warm enough to brave even the hardest winter.

Yep, she was definitely not the pampered one, Daana decided. Her accommodations were a hovel compared to this. Not that she minded. In fact, she was beginning to miss her little ramshackle tent already. The hot, buzzing smell had already infiltrated her sinuses and was starting to bring tears to her eyes. Its potency reminded her of those obnoxious scented pine cones the head housekeeper used to put out around the winter solstice.

"Lady Lazuli!" Captain Monk stepped into view. The edges of his ears turned an unusual shade of red as he glanced hurriedly around the tent's interior. "I wasn't aware you would be joining us. I would have tidied up more beforehand."

"Not at all, sir. Your tent is lovely." Daana forced a sweet smile, blinking back tears as she lifted the tray a fraction higher. The irritation had since migrated from her nose to her throat. "Where might I put this, Captain? The cook sends his regards, by the way."

"Oh, of course! Over here, please." The captain hastily cleared his writing desk for her. He met her halfway, relieving her of the tray. "Forgive my manners, my lady. I should have offered to take this the moment you walked in."

It was difficult for most to work past the captain's unnecessarily loud volume. Those who could, however, soon realized there was more to the man than over-enunciated words and well-groomed features. In today's case, there was *a lot* more going on. From his bright red face and jittery movements, he was clearly in a flutter about something. Daana wondered what it was he didn't wish her to see. She glanced up and down the thick canvas sides, feigning interest in its unimpressive construction. There, tucked away in the corner, she realized what she had missed. Whom, actually.

"Faris?"

The faun sat cross-legged on the ground by the bed. His dark hood, coupled with the poor lighting, made him nearly indistinguishable from his surroundings. Judging from the bags under his eyes and the way his head drooped, Daana guessed he was on the verge of falling to sleep from sheer exhaustion. Faris shifted his gaze in her direction and offered an insincere smile. "Lady Lazuli."

Daana instinctively stood straighter. She had not seen him since yesterday's encounter in the woods, where it had taken him all of five minutes to figure out what she was. "I was told this was a meeting of the top officers. What are you doing here?"

"Oh, did they make you an officer? I must have missed the ceremony."

"Mister Belfast," Captain Monk said. "Mind your tone, sir."

"My apologies, Lady Lazuli. The lack of sleep makes me forget myself." Faris kept his expression impossibly blank. She suspected there was a threat hidden in his words. What exactly it was, Daana was having trouble deciphering. When she made no move to respond, he lost interest, returning his dead-eyed stare to the billowing doorway. "I will be out of your hair once my relief gets here."

Daana kept her voice sugary sweet. Faris wouldn't buy her act, but her efforts were for Captain Monk, not him. "Relief for what? You still haven't said what you're doing here."

Faris kicked the bedroll. "Don't be impolite. Say hello."

The mound of blankets shifted and Daana swore she heard it growl.

"Oh." She took a startled step backward. Daana glanced at Captain Monk, who had returned to his previous state of embarrassment. "I didn't realize you and Rasp had become an item. Good for you, Captain."

"A what? Gods no, my lady. Perish the thought! There's a simple explanation, I assure you." The tips of the captain's ears had gone from pink to crimson again. "As the infirmary is currently at capacity, Protector Dawnsight graciously volunteered my tent for overflow. My guests arrived very early this morning."

Captain Monk's harsh glare settled on Faris as he spoke. "Normally I wouldn't mind the intrusion, but I was under the impression they would be bringing their own bedding. Not sharing mine!"

Faris coughed into his hand in order to disguise his snorts of laughter. Composing himself the best he could, the faun awarded the mound of blankets another lackluster kick. "You told me humans slept in a giant pile."

Not yet ready to face the trials of the day, the form beneath the blankets rolled out of reach with an unintelligible grumble.

Daana's attempt to mask her own amusement was apparently unsuccessful. Captain Monk glanced her way and his scowl deepened. "There is nothing funny about it, miss. No respectable officer should ever wake up next to a stranger! Especially not that one."

"Our saddlebag got misplaced during yesterday's move. The horse, too, come to think of it. I'll find them when I'm off duty." Faris said, yawning, "*After* I've slept."

"Ahoy!" an overly cheerful voice called from the outside. "Permission to come aboard, Captain?"

Seemingly grateful for the change of subject, Captain Monk peeked out of the doorway. "Lieutenant Ralizak, of course, come in. Welcome!"

Rali appeared at the entrance and snapped a short bow before she swaggered inside, brimming especially bright for someone who had probably slept a handful of hours at most. Like Faris, Lieutenant Ralizak had been among the search party that returned in the early hours of the morning with the missing camp members. Rali bent so far forward, the top of her head nearly scraped the ground near her toes. "Emissary Lazuli."

"Lieutenant Ralizak." Daana returned the gesture with a polite curtsy. She suspected the exaggerated bow had been mocking, but supposed it was better to play it safe.

"I've got it from here, Faris. Go ahead and get yourself some winks. I'll send Curly to peel you off the floor when it's your shift again."

Faris shuffled out, stifling another yawn as he called over his shoulder, "He needs feeding and can't do it himself. Something about his hands being numb. I don't know. I wasn't really listening."

Rali's mouth twisted to the side. "What? He wank it too hard again?"

"Lieutenant!"

"Don't fret, Captain." Rali waved her hands in a calming manner. "It's perfectly natural. Can't go blind twice, you know."

Lieutenant Ralizak, the legendary warrior who single-handedly held off an entire squadron of invaders during the Red Rock breach, was far less intimidating than her reputation had led Daana to believe. Uncle's information had painted the dwarf as the supposed mastermind behind Oralia's faithful four. From what Daana had witnessed so far, Rali seemed nothing more than a functional drunk with a passion for writing lewd songs and inciting belching contests.

Rali wore traditional dwarf chainmail, but had ditched the heavy helm and battle ax. The steel-toed shoes were missing, too, having been traded for a pair of lightweight boots. She lived above ground, unsheltered from sunlight, kept unusual company, and fought not only dirty, but with a short sword—a typically human weapon. By all rights, Quartz Ralizak was the most un-dwarfish dwarf Daana had ever encountered. According to Uncle's advisors, Rali's radical lifestyle was tolerated by dwarfkind on the basis that it kept her from returning to the underground cities and corrupting the younger generations.

Rali tilted her head, smelling the air. "Is that leek and mushroom soup? Gods, I haven't eaten since yesterday. I don't know about you two, but I'm famished."

"It would be polite to wait for the protector," Captain Monk reminded her.

Rali produced a jolly laugh, as if the captain had imparted a particularly clever joke. "Have you seen how much an orc can put away in one sitting? I swear, between her and Curly, it's a small wonder the rest of us haven't starved to death. Take it from an expert, you both should eat while you have the chance."

"I'm not hungry, thank you." With Daana's luck, she'd probably spill it down the front of her tunic. Today had to go smoothly. No slip-ups. This was her only chance to prove to Oralia that she was more than a simple, starry-eyed elfling.

Lieutenant Ralizak ladled two steaming bowls of broth and took up Faris's former position alongside the bedroll. She threw her head back and drained hers without bothering to chew. Finished, she thwacked the unused spoon against the other bowl, calling. "Up and at 'em, sunshine! It's chow time."

The form beneath the quilts shifted, heaving upright until the top of his head loomed over the dwarf. Rasp, working from within, rearranged the blankets into a sort of cocoon, leaving only a small opening for his mouth and nose. "If it's that gods awful nettle tea, don't even try. Shit tastes like musty ballsack."

Rali raised one bushy eyebrow at him, grinning. "Do you prefer your ballsacks freshly powdered?"

In lieu of a verbal reply, Rasp made an obscene gesture with his tongue instead.

Captain Monk covered his face, wincing. "I should not have to remind you there is a lady present! Keep your lewdness to a minimum."

Rali took advantage of Rasp's open mouth and shoveled a spoonful of broth inside. "Don't give me that face, mouse muncher. This came straight from the cook. It's good."

"It's fuhkin hot'th!"

"Oh." Rali's gaze dropped to the bowl, watching the stream waft into the crisp air above its oily surface. Dwarfs were used to eating petrified bread and molten stew. The idea that it had been too hot probably hadn't even occurred to her. "Sorry. You want me to blow on it for you?"

"No." Rasp's mouth drew into a tight line. "I want you to stop," he muttered. "This is infantile."

She ladled another spoonful in his direction. "I could make little dragon noises for you if it'd help." When Rasp made no attempt to open his mouth a second time, she prodded at his face with the spoon, making horrific screeching sounds that Daana assumed were supposed to be her impression of a dragon. To no one's surprise, her efforts were wildly unsuccessful. "Huh, always works on Curly."

Captain Monk was red in the face and looked to be on the verge of leaving. Which was saying something, really, considering it was his tent. Daana could not afford to have the meeting over before it had even begun. She attempted to distract him instead. "Do you know what the meeting is concerning, Captain?"

"I do not. If it were up to me, we would have been on the road hours ago."

A screeching roar from the other side of the tent stole the polite response from Daana's mouth. In a dramatic flurry of patchwork blankets, Rasp ripped the quilt from his body and flung it over his shoulder. The front of his clothes were wet, and for some reason the wooden soup bowl now rested upside down on the ground, empty. He lunged, seized Rali by the braid, and yanked the squealing dwarf backward over the bed.

"The fuck is wrong with you?" he shouted.

"It's so dark in here, I thought your mouth was closer!"

Lieutenant Ralizak rolled the moment Rasp descended on top of her, sending both of them tumbling over the side of the bedroll and into the dirt. Over what had been a supposed accident, she seemed keen for a fight. She was back up the same time he was, and the two bodies collided once more.

CHAPTER THIRTY-EIGHT

Warpath

The two fighters rose and fell over one another in the dimly lit tent like undulating waves that somehow lacked both rhythm and flow. Without vision to guide him, Rasp's entire strategy revolved around getting his opponent to the floor. It seemed somewhat cruel that the moment he finally got Rali down and halfway into a decent chokehold was the same moment Captain Monk chose to intervene.

"Enough!" Instead of attempting to pry the fighters apart, the captain retrieved his waterskin from the small pile of neatly arranged belongings and dumped its contents over their heads. "Show some blasted restraint, both of you!" His shouting voice was somehow even louder than his normal, headache-inducing volume.

With her opponent's grip loosened, Rali struggled free. She shoved Rasp to the side and staggered to her feet, but he wasn't finished with her yet. He latched onto her leg and started to drag her back down. Lieutenant Ralizak rewarded his efforts by giving up on gravity altogether and sat, pinning the struggling human beneath her. "Apologies, Captain," she huffed, crossing one stubby leg over the other as she fought to catch her breath. "Yesterday's events seemed to have rattled Rasp's memory. I find it helpful to remind him of the pecking order from time to time."

Rasp flailed uselessly beneath her, gasping, "You started it!"

"Well, if you'd been more helpful with the eating part, you wouldn't be wearing the soup right now, would you?" Rali snapped back.

"I see." Captain Monk stroked his beard and nodded. The fact that one of the faithful four was actually listening to him for a change was apparently enough to soothe his former outrage. "I can only hope I do not have to remind him of the pecking order again myself!"

Rali tossed the quilt over Rasp's head to muffle his heated reply. Once certain the others couldn't distinguish whatever horrific things the mountain man was shouting, she offered the captain her most charming smile yet. "Well done, sir. You've gone and put the fear of the gods into him now!"

This was absolute madness. And to think she had been concerned about blending in before. At this rate, Daana may very well have been the most normal-acting person in the room. That realization was somehow more terrifying. Surely this had to be some sort of joke, even if only on a cosmic level.

Daana glanced over her shoulder, noting it would take but a few steps to slip away. To be clear, she wasn't leaving. She was simply going to stand closer to the door. That way, if things continued to get out of hand, she could waltz free unscathed.

It was a good idea. A *great* idea. It was too bad her feet hadn't gotten the message, because they seemed perfectly content to remain in place. *Will you two move it, please? Shuffle over there, by the door, now!*

Alas, just as her legs started to respond, Captain Monk remembered she was present and that, for some gods awful reason, he wished to speak with her. "Did the protector tell you how long she would be, Lady Lazuli? I'm a man of action! All this sitting and thumb twiddling is bad for the blood."

Daana froze in place as her mind strung together an answer that was both believable and skirted around the fact that she had not technically received an invitation. "No, sir. I didn't ask, either. It's not my place to question Protector Dawnsight."

"I see, understandable then. For the best, I'm sure. The protector was in an especially foul mood when we spoke. Well, she spoke. I don't think I got a word in." The captain, desperate for some sort of civilized conversation, carried on obliviously. "How have you been faring, miss? Yesterday was a traumatic day for us all."

Six steps, Daana calculated. That was all that stood between her and a nice, cozy spot by the exit. "As well as can be expected, sir."

"Has the break in travel given you time to update your log?" Captain Monk bellowed. "Your uncle would be delighted to read how well you handled yourself yesterday. I know how much the speaker enjoys your letters."

Daana did not like how Lieutenant Ralizak was watching her with such sudden, fixed interest. She had been right in her original assessment of the captain. Captain Monk was a clueless, driveling dunce. He wasn't even aware of her true purpose, and still, it didn't stop him from spelling it out for more prying minds to put together on their own. "No, sir. I won't have the means to update Uncle Geralt until we're settled on the mountain."

"The protector sends her correspondence by bird," Rali said. "I could arrange to fly yours as well, if you would like."

"An excellent suggestion, Lieutenant!" Captain Monk congratulated.

Down to three steps now. Progress. "We didn't bring any birds."

"Of course we did. What did you think all of these ravens fluttering around are for?" Rali, still seated on Rasp, patted his shoulder affectionately. The mountain man, unbeknownst to her, was in the process of working her knife from her belt. "Have you seen some of the tricks Rasp's taught them? Couldn't teach a wild bird that."

"Thank you, Lieutenant. I will be sure to tell Uncle how helpful you've been." Damn. On top of tracking the ghost, reviving her failed attempt to befriend the faithful four, and making sure Faris didn't turn on her, Daana now had to write some stupid letter. "He's got your knife, by the way."

Cursing, Rali leapt off of Rasp and kicked the knife from his hand. He might have lost his weapon, but it did nothing to temper his foolhardiness. Rasp tackled her, and the pair rolled across the floor, hitting, spitting, and yelling the filthiest sentiments Daana had ever heard uttered. Captain Monk fluttered uselessly along the sidelines. Each time he attempted to separate the fighting pair, he was nearly caught by a flailing arm or leg.

"Now, see here! Both of you stop this instant!"

Rali had shorter reach, but she matched the Stoneclaw punch for punch. A clip to the jaw left Rasp momentarily stunned and Rali kicked out from under him. She rolled onto her feet, breathing heavily and her forehead beaded in sweat. Rasp recovered faster than expected and surged forward in a streamlined blur of lean muscle and raw fury. Rali dodged and Rasp slammed into Monk instead, dropping the captain flat on his back.

"Not him, idiot!" Rali slung her arm around the Stoneclaw's neck and ripped him away before he could inflict any serious damage.

Daana saw her opening and took it. She turned swiftly on her heel and reached the doorway the same moment it flung open and the protector stormed inside. Cursing her luck, Daana scuttled backward out of the way. A second officer followed Oralia inside and took up a position alongside the entrance, effectively cutting off any future escape.

"Quartz Ralizak," Oralia ordered. "At attention."

"Shit." Rali shoved Rasp to the ground as she leapt upright. The dwarf lifted her chin, squared her shoulders, and pressed her feet together before Daana even had time to shut her mouth.

Oralia took in the Stoneclaw's disheveled appearance first. Rasp was crouched on the ground, blood trickling from his mouth. From the corner of her eye, Oralia must have seen the way Rali's lips began to move, because the orc swiveled her head in the lieutenant's direction, snapping, "If you even think of opening that confounded mouth of yours, Ralizak, I will demote you this instant."

Oralia circled her soldier. The orc's fearsome form loomed an entire head, shoulders, and chest over Rali. The difference in height hadn't struck Daana until now. Anyone who had to crane their head that far up to look their commander in the eye was already at a poor disadvantage.

"Captain Monk, explain to me what I have walked in on?"

The captain stood, hesitantly, not bothering to straighten the creases in his uniform jacket. "A fistfight, madam! Between Lieutenant Ralizak and Mister Stoneclaw. I attempted to separate them and was, uh—"

"Unsuccessful?" Oralia ventured.

"Caught off guard, madam. I was calling for assistance when you arrived."

"Thank you, Captain." Even in the foulest mood, Oralia did not forgo her formality. It was terrifyingly effective. The protector continued to circle her lieutenant, and Daana realized Oralia was only getting started. "I expect such ludicrous behavior from Rasp, but not you, Ralizak. You are my highest-ranking officer and a direct reflection of me. I should not have to tell you that, at this moment, you are making a very poor one."

Daana, not even the subject of the protector's wrath, flinched with each word. It was as if the breath had been sucked from the tent. According to Uncle Geralt, Oralia could do the same to an entire council chamber with a single look. Where Uncle relied on favors and alliances to further his position, Protector Dawnsight needed nothing of the sort. She wielded a natural power of her own, something that couldn't be bought or bribed. When Oralia spoke, even the enemy listened. Especially when she was on the warpath.

"I have half a mind to send you back to Sunstorn. Regretfully, due to yesterday's catastrophe, I cannot afford to lose another body. Not even yours. Do not misinterpret my refusal to dismiss you for anything but sheer necessity. Make no mistake, there will be consequences. For now, understand this: If there is another incident like today, you will be making the rest of the journey in fetters."

From the dwarf's wide eyes and trembling mouth, she looked to be on the verge of tears. Rali managed to keep her eyes forward and not wince each time Protector Dawnsight crossed her line of sight.

"Do we understand one another, Ralizak?"

"Yes, Madam Protector," Rali said quietly.

"As for you." Oralia turned her attention to Rasp.

He instinctively shrank closer to the ground. "She threw hot soup over me on purpose! I'm allowed to defend myself."

Oralia was quiet for an unnerving amount of time. Finally, she said, "Just as I thought we had reached an understanding, you disappoint me once more. I have nothing left to say to you that has not already been said. You will do better."

Rasp opened and closed his mouth several times. It looked as if, just as he'd finally thought of something clever to say, the more sensible portion of his brain had retracted it from consideration. Eventually, with the angry look of a dog caught eating from the waste bin, he settled into a quiet, stewing huff. Daana was grateful. Rasp possessed an inexplicable gift for igniting already flared tempers beyond repair. She did not want to see firsthand what extremes the protector was willing to take to ensure he knew his place.

"I will deal with the both of you later," Oralia said. "For now, sit down, keep your mouths shut, and speak only when spoken to."

Rali, hastily wiping under her eyes, pulled Rasp back over to his blankets and sat, refusing to make eye contact with anyone.

"Do you have anything you want to add, Captain?"

Captain Monk's facial expression was remarkably blank. For the first time since Daana could remember, his voice softened to a normal conversational level. "Uh, no, madam. I think you dealt with it sufficiently."

"That etiquette instructor will earn his keep yet." Oralia's gaze shifted to Daana. For a few sickening heartbeats she thought the protector was going to question her presence, but Oralia didn't. Instead, the protector launched into her meeting, either ignorant or uncaring to the fact the entire tent had forgotten how to breathe.

"While setbacks are to be expected on the road, yesterday was inexcusable. We are fortunate to have lost only four members. From this moment forward, I will not have this convoy caught off guard again. Disorganization was our biggest downfall yesterday. Your forces did not know whether they were coming or going, Captain. For the remainder of today and tomorrow, anyone not on duty will be running emergency drills with Sergeant Farrow. She will ensure that every soldier from here on out, no matter the circumstance, will react without hesitation. The journey is only going to get more dangerous. I will not lose any more lives to unpreparedness."

"It was a sky shriek, madam," Captain Monk said. "No one could have expected that!"

"I am told humans have a saying for this type of situation, Captain. What was it again, Lieutenant Holt?"

All eyes looked to the officer standing inconspicuously by the door. Lieutenant Isadora Holt, Captain Monk's second-in-command, was the human equivalent of a rock. She was stiff in places that were not supposed to be, had all of two facial expressions—unamused and highly unamused—and could stand in the same position for hours without garnering notice. Daana assumed Holt's ability to meld into any background was the reason she'd survived serving under Captain Monk so long.

"Expect the unexpected, Madam Protector," Lieutenant Holt said while managing to avoid direct eye contact with every single person in the tent.

"Yes, that is the one, thank you. As oxymoronic as it sounds, we are going to henceforth expect anything and everything that can go wrong." Oralia, stifling any argument on the matter from Captain Monk with a single curl of her lip, turned her attention to Rasp. "Mister Stoneclaw, you are the most familiar with mountain dragons. What is a flight of sky shrieks doing on the wrong side of the ridge?"

"Hunting, madam. Successfully, I might add."

Oralia only waited, allowing her silence to draw the rest out of him.

"Look," Rasp said, "I'm not on the ridge, I don't know. I could speculate for you all day why they're here, but it boils down to one basic answer. They're desperate. Something drove them out of their usual hunting grounds."

"A bigger dragon?" Captain Monk suggested.

Rasp shrugged. "Sure."

"Now is the time to speculate, Rasp. While your punishment is yet undecided."

Rasp hung his head, sighing, "Another predator, yes. Lack of prey, famine, blight, maybe. Or it could be raiders making a territory grab. Every year we've got flatlanders hitting us from the north, swamplanders to the west, and you lot always trying to push up further from the south. The mountain patrol usually keeps everyone from getting too far into the foothills, but it's the first year without dear old dad to run things. My brothers may not be as organized as previous years. The dragons might just be trying to stay out of it."

"A raiding party would be an easy win compared to another dragon," Captain Monk said, inadvertently missing the highly unamused expression that flickered across his second-in-command's stony face. "My soldiers are at least equipped to handle swamplanders."

Rasp snorted, but kept his mouth shut. A remarkable improvement, Daana noted.

"Do you have something you wish to share?" Captain Monk asked him. Again, no reply.

"Speak, Rasp," Oralia ordered.

"Without the regular mountain patrol to keep the swampies back, they're probably in a mad dash to expand their borders. There could be hundreds of swampland soldiers swarming the foothills as we speak. And your plan is to, what? Fight them? Decimate half your army before you even get partway up the damn mountain? I may not be an expert on military strategy, but even I have the sense to know that is a terrible plan."

The tips of the captain's ears were bright red once more. He started to protest, but Oralia interrupted, consequently sparing him from whatever embarrassment was about to spew out of his mouth. "Have the swamplanders ever come this far inland, Rasp?"

"No. But like I said, these aren't normal circumstances. I would go so far as to use that oxymoronic phrase about expectations you seem to love so much."

"We've already scouted the area, Protector." Captain Monk gestured to Lieutenant Holt for backup. "Tell her!"

Holt looked to be skimming a stack of mental documents before offering her reply. "As of two days ago, the foothills were clear, Madam Protector. There were no signs of either the mountain patrol or swamplanders."

The captain nodded approvingly. "There, see? Does a flight of dragons really warrant all of this extra precaution? Is it not possible they simply got turned around?"

"Then we scout again to be sure. Is that alright with you, Captain?"

Captain Monk set his jaw, frowning. "Yes, madam."

"Emissary Lazuli, do you have any input? I assume you must have something to contribute, as I did not invite you here."

Apparently Daana was not to be spared from the protector's wrathful mood after all. "No, Madam Protector," she said. "I am only here to learn. 'Be seen, not heard,' as Uncle Geralt always says."

Oralia's steely expression did not change. "How fitting."

Dammit. Daana flinched, only now realizing her blunder. As if Protector Dawnsight didn't think of her as a child enough already. Her only consolation was that the rest of the gathering was too consumed with dread to notice. Lieutenant Ralizak had gone catatonic, Holt was doing her best impression of a tent wall in hopes of not being called upon again, while Rasp had his head craned in the direction of the door, as if calculating whether or not he could make it out before someone grabbed him.

Oralia turned to the only member of the meeting she had not yet ground into unrecognizable little pieces beneath her metaphoric heel. Not for lack of trying, Daana noted. "Select your five best scouts and send them to survey the foothills again, Captain. Thoroughly. If there is so much as a single goblin in that area, I want to know about it. The rest of the party will remain here running drills until they return. We will not blindly walk into another massacre."

"Yes, Madam Protector."

Unwilling to waste anymore of her time with an insincere farewell, Oralia strode from the tent, cloak snapping behind her. "Ralizak and Rasp, with me, *now*."

CHAPTER THIRTY-NINE

The Final Act of a Dead Man

His first instinct was to fight. Not because he would win, but because a sudden death would spare him from whatever vile consequences the protector was currently running through her head. The mountain folk had a word for this type of last-ditch-thinking, which roughly translated to "the final act of a dead man." Alas, the final act wouldn't work. Oralia still needed him alive. If anything, it would only worsen his situation.

With fighting out of the question, Rasp's second instinct was to leg it. Again, not entirely helpful given his present circumstances. But such was the nature of instincts. They existed because at some point in the past, buried deep in the ancestral bloodline, it *had* worked.

Lieutenant Ralizak clomped dutifully along beside him. She tightened her grip on Rasp's elbow, as if she could hear his thoughts.

Rasp could take her on his own, he was certain. He'd been playing nice in the tent, but if she stood between him and his freedom, a little twist and pop of the neck would—no, Rasp cut himself off with a wince. That was his old way of thinking. He was reformed now. According to Judge Belfast, life was precious. Even to those Rasp didn't find all that precious. It wasn't his right to take it. Gods forbid, that's how he'd ended up in this mess.

No more killing. Fighting, yes. Acting like a downright menace to everyone and everything, yes. Sabotage, most certainly. But no murder. Besides, Rasp kind of liked the dwarf. She gave as good as she got, and when you were done beating each other bloody, she would smile and say, "Thank you, sir. May I have another?" It was commendable, in a way.

The frigid wind whipped at Rasp's face, snapping him from his thoughts.

Oralia was parading them through camp. Rasp couldn't see this, of course, as his eyesight picked up nothing more than varying shades of passing gray shadows. The biggest of which being the protector herself, who loomed several paces ahead of him. Rasp knew because he could feel every pair of eyes watching them with dread-filled curiosity. The soldiers, huddled beneath their tents to escape the elements, had no doubt overheard Oralia's raised voice. Rasp was certain the entire territory had heard her, and were similarly cowering for reasons perhaps they themselves didn't fully understand.

The protector's path was intentional, Rasp concluded. She wanted the troops to see that no one, not even her number one, was spared from her wrath.

Eventually the blurry outlines of the surrounding tents receded as they pressed onward into denser forest. The sparse light above grew noticeably dimmer and the vegetation underfoot was suddenly waist-high and grabbing at him with invisible claws. At first, he suspected Oralia was taking them somewhere into the wilderness to dispose of their bodies. But then he remembered this was Protector Dawnsight. Killing would have been too easy for her, and again, she still needed him alive. She was taking them to her and the faithful four's personal encampment, which was set slightly apart from the rest for the simple fact that space benefited everyone.

Traditionally, a commander kept their quarters stationed within camp. Usually located near the heart of the sprawl for protection. Clearly, this wasn't necessary for Oralia and her warriors. They were the protection.

Rasp breathed in the smoke of a nearby fire. As they drew closer, he could hear its gentle, crackling burn, accentuated by the occasional pop of wood being consumed by hungry flames. He assumed there was someone tending it, as leaving a fire to tend itself often resulted in disaster. And, judging from the eerie quiet, also assumed this person was Ellisar. Curly would have at least offered a dull hello, and Snag made soft, jangling sounds wherever he went on account of the collection of miniature wind chimes strung through his ears.

Oralia's strident voice broke the silence. "Keep watch. No one comes in or out until you have heard from me."

There was no answer, which probably meant the elf had found some other way to demonstrate her acknowledgment. A nod, tilt of the head, or Sergeant Farrow's favorite good ol' one-finger salute.

And then Ralizak tugged his arm and they were walking again. Tripping, actually, in Rasp's case. It was a small wonder he'd managed the entire trek without twisting his ankle. The dwarf pulled him upright and into a sort of musty darkness, which Rasp suspected was the protector's private quarters. The abrupt and almost immediate stop upon entering also led him to believe this tent was smaller than Monk's. The tight quarters made the tinge of cheap barley ale wafting off of Rali all that more noticeable. This, alas, was the more innocuous smell compared to the heavy undertones of sweat and body odor that hung thick in the dingy air.

Attempting to distract himself from the sudden, salty film that coated the inside of his mouth, Rasp raised his hand and realized he could reach the sloped ceiling. Definitely smaller, he concluded. By his guesstimation, there was barely enough room for Oralia to come and go without stooping.

"Do you have a question?"

Rasp swiftly returned his arm to his side, trying not to flinch. An impossibility, at the moment, as his entire body trembled. To his credit, it wasn't all fear. He'd woken up with the shakes and his hands seemed to enjoy the sensation because no matter how hard he willed it, they kept shake-shake-shaking. The tremor spread to his legs and Rasp felt his knees buckle beneath him.

He pondered this sudden betrayal by his extremities. Why now? He'd been in this situation before, hundreds of times, in fact. How was this any different than all the others? And then that annoying little voice jumped in. The one he ignored most of the time, but regardless, it hung around waiting for the day he eventually learned to listen. Too little, too late, it seemed. The voice shouted, *Because you trusted her, idiot! You lowered the barrier and now the enemy's over the wall. Stupid, stupid, stupid!*

"He is trembling." For whatever reason, Oralia's observation seemed to be targeted at Rali and not Rasp.

"Oh, are we playing another round of state-the-obvious, boss? That means it's my turn then. Right, let's see. Your tent is, uh . . . dark."

"Why is he shaking, Ralizak? You insisted you could pull this off with minimal damage."

"Please, the worst I did was sit on him a little. Nobody's ever died from that."

Rasp jumped when he felt Oralia's heavy hand on his shoulder. "Are you ill?"

Confused, more like. Regardless, it didn't stop his confounded mouth from blurting out, "No! I mean, yes! I don't know, okay? I'm angry and I don't know what the fuck is going on right now!"

He crossed his legs and sat, searching the floor around him for something warmer to wear. His fingertips brushed against her blankets and he yanked them free of the bedroll. Rasp wrapped the thick covering over his trembling body and hunched his shoulders.

"See?" Rali said. "Still feisty as ever."

It was Oralia's turn to sound confused. "Rasp, what are you doing?"

Despite his efforts to clench his jaw, his teeth chattered. "Getting warm. If you're going to draw this out then I'm at least going to spend my last moments comfortable."

"Drawing this out, am I? Would you have preferred this to be carried out in front of everyone?"

"Do you do this on purpose?" Rasp said before his brain could catch up with his mouth. Alas, the damage was done. Unfortunately, his infernal mouth wasn't. The words spilled from his tongue unchecked. "You're bearable one moment and then like ice the next. Just as I think I'm finally starting to get a grasp on you, you go and prove you're nothing but a raging asshole! It's messing with my head."

"Are you finished?"

"No, I'm not," Rasp said. In the battle of supremacy between self-preservation and the need to have the last word, the latter won out, as usual.

"If you're going to fuck me up, I might as well earn it and say everything. You want to kick me around to make your point? Go ahead, have at it. You can't do anything to me that hasn't been done before. But Rali didn't deserve what you did in there." This was taking an unexpected turn. Rasp's inner dialogue was on a roll, however. One he couldn't derail and in a matter of seconds his inner dialogue became outer. "I threw the first swing. She did what anybody else in her position would have done. Threatening to demote her, that's low, Oralia. Even for you. Rali is the most loyal person you've got. You should be grateful you have someone like that in your corner!"

What in the realm was this? Apparently he'd gone mad somewhere in the last two days. Making bargains with witches, disclosing secrets to the Protector of the Realm, defending people other than himself. Dear gods, this was all so incredibly wrong. Which of course, probably meant it was right, because that's how morality seemed to operate. Rasp had the sudden urge to scrub his skin with a metal scouring brush.

Fortunately, the torrent of excrement from his mouth had ceased at last. Nay, not a torrent, it had been a rockslide. A metaphorical avalanche of one stupid thought tumbling from his tongue and dislodging bigger, stupider thoughts until everything was pouring out at once in a single, thundering—

And then it hit him. Like taking the first swig of fermented goat milk, Rasp's head swam for a few dizzying moments until everything pieced together. The answer to his dilemma had been in front of him all along. For a few heartbeats, Rasp dared not breathe as he ran several scenarios through his head. It would require precautions, of course. But nobody would get hurt. He could make sure of that. It would put him in Stoneclaw territory, a prospect he wasn't thrilled about. On the other hand, it was a land he was familiar with. In, out, and then he could slink away forever.

Yes, yes it could work. It *would* work! Rasp could escape and thwart the realm in the same move. All without fulfilling the curse, too. Thus appeasing morality and setting his life back on track. For the first time in months, Rasp's soul did more than lift. It fucking soared!

Remembering where he was, Rasp carefully checked his expression and made sure his ass was still planted firmly on the ground. An escape plan was no good if he was back to square one with Oralia. It was a little late to beg for forgiveness now. He'd said his piece. All of it, regretfully. Perhaps it was time to do that thing he wasn't very good at, and listen.

CHAPTER FORTY

The Warm and Fuzzies

Around him the stillness stretched like a never ending cavern. The air was thick and heavy, and Rasp didn't think anyone had moved since his outburst. The tension broke, finally, with a playful shove from Rali. "Oh, come on. Keep going," she snickered. "Tell me how great I am some more. I was starting to get the warm and fuzzies over here."

What. The. Fuck.

It was settled then. Rali had gone mad. There wasn't any explanation that made sense other than—dear gods. Wait, was this on purpose? Was this sabotage? Everyone knew Lieutenant Ralizak was Oralia's number one. The damn dwarf had composed an entire song about it! But Rasp wasn't a threat. He barely skirted the line between helpful and utter nuisance on a good day. Just because he and Oralia had shared a moment together on the road didn't mean . . .

Oh damn. That was it, wasn't it? Rali hadn't been privy to that conversation. She suspected something was amiss and had staged a fight to make him lose all credibility with Oralia. Right? That made sense, didn't it? What was sense again? And did he have it? Damn this blasted brain fog! His poor body wasn't the only thing unsuited for this situation. Rasp decided to keep listening, if only to prevent his mouth from releasing another embarrassing deluge of half-formed thoughts.

The voice of the glum, despaired soldier from before had vanished. Here, in the protection of Oralia's tent, away from prying eyes, Lieutenant Ralizak dropped her act. "It really warms the heart knowing just what you think of me, bucko. Sorta makes me feel bad about pouring hot soup over you."

"I knew it! This was a setup, wasn't it?" Rasp dropped his head into his hands as a nagging thought wormed through several layers of sludge soup to the forefront of his mind. "Are you going to tell me what I did? Or is it just straight to the stockades from here? It's not very fair when your boss is judge, jury, and executioner, you know."

"Not to upset your fragile ego, Raspy my boy, but you aren't the target here. You are merely a convenient means to get me closer to the real mark." Rali trapped him under her sweat-soaked arm and ruffled the top of his head in a rough, almost endearing manner. "If it makes you feel better, all of the supposedly smart ones fell for it, too. Not that it's much of a surprise, really. I'll have you know I personally planned and orchestrated the whole thing."

"Did you?" Oralia's tone swung somewhere between amused and annoyed.

"Yes, yes, you helped some, I guess. But my performance carried it. I mean, real tears? Come on. You wouldn't get that kind of quality from any-one else."

"Your humbleness is refreshing as always, Ralizak."

Was that a joke? If there was one thing Oralia Dawnsight was incapable of, it was humor. All the signs were there, Rasp decided. This wasn't madness, after all. Somewhere in the past hour he'd died and gone to some demented afterlife where everything was topsy-turvy. Rali orchestrating her own fall. Oralia cracking jokes. And him, in the middle of it all, discovering the solu-tion to his problems. He knew the afterlife wasn't supposed to be rainbows and sunshine for people like him, but this was bordering on sadistic.

"Aw, that face," Rali cooed. "Poor thing looks like someone swindled his sweeties and he's only now figuring out how. Breaks my heart."

Not dead, apparently. Just very, very confused. Rasp softened the biting edge of his tone. "Are you going to tell me what's going on?"

"Nah."

"Ralizak."

"He's too much of a risk, boss."

"He attacked you over soup, Ralizak. You assumed the risk the moment you involved him." Oralia added, almost reluctantly, "As I have learned the hard way, you cannot drag Rasp into your plan and expect him to sit quietly in the dark. If you wish to mitigate the risk, then you start by telling him what is going on. I have no doubt he will set himself on fire to burn his enemies."

"Me? Never," Rasp scoffed. Oralia hadn't meant it as flattery, but Rasp couldn't help but feel a small swell of pride. It was nice to be recognized for your destructive tendencies for a change. He may have been a flaming pile of horseshit, but at least he had potential. Setting other things on fire, namely.

"For the record," Rali said to Rasp, "I'm against this, but apparently whatever touchy-feely moment you two had on the road the other night is making the protector all sentimental. She wants to preserve your new line of—what'd you call it again, boss? *Openness?*"

Rasp heard the orc's tusks click together, followed by an exasperated, "I believe you were explaining."

"Fine," Rali huffed. Despite her initial reluctance, she sounded genuinely pleased with herself. "Yes, I planned this. I had to find a way to get in trouble that was both public and believable. Thankfully, you're as easy to play as a fiddle. I knew if I needled you a bit you would blow up eventually. Cue fistfight in front of the captain and the emissary, and ta-da, you and I are in deep, my friend. Getting the captain involved was genius, by the way. Really sold it."

"But why?"

"Because if you are cruelly pragmatic like the protector, you're going to pick a punishment that fits the crime. In this case, given our atrocious lack of manners, we're being sentenced to etiquette sessions. I mean, obviously that's not all we're getting. After a show like that you've got to look firm and—"

There was that little sound in his head again. *Click!* As the final pieces of the puzzle nestled neatly together. Rasp understood the scheme now. "You caused a fistfight just to get closer to your plant?" he said, realizing he was, in fact, shouting.

Rali reached down and squished his face between her hands. "Now he gets it! I knew there was a brain somewhere under all that rage."

"Are all your schemes this impractical?"

"Theatrical," she corrected with a patronizing pat to the head.

"Please stop." He wasn't sure theatrical was any better, but at least he didn't appear to be in as much trouble as he'd previously thought. "Anyway, you obviously got what you wanted. You can manage the rest of this without me, right? Just pretend you beat me or something. I'll walk with a limp for the next few days."

Rali went back to smooshing his face between her tiny hands. "Sorry, no can do. Subterfuge will be easier with Willem's attention on someone else. Normally I'd use Ellisar for this sort of thing, you see, but she's been off her game ever since a certain someone tried to fry her nice and crispy-like. Now all she wants to talk about is untimely demise this, and unsuspecting revenge that. You were the best alternative."

The dread that had finally settled to a still calm fluttered back to life in his rolling stomach with a vengeance. Rasp batted Rali's grubby fingers away and moved his head in Oralia's direction, searching unsuccessfully for her among the gloom. Without light to guide him, the inside of the tent was one muddled blur. "If I do this, it means we're even for last night, right? And all the consequences from today are just pretend consequences?"

And just maybe, it'll keep your elf from skinning me alive? A decent trade, all things considered.

"If you can manage to keep it together, then yes. The consequences from today bear no actual weight on your current standing. For future note, however, I could have done without the assault on Captain Monk. That was unnecessary."

Rali leaned closer and whispered loud enough for the entire countryside to hear, "She's a little miffed you didn't prune his mustache, to be honest. But she's not allowed to say that, so I will."

If words could imply winking, Rasp was pretty sure the dwarf was doing so right now, vigorously. Possibly with both eyes.

"Officially, I am gravely disturbed by today's events. As Lieutenant Ralizak suggested, etiquette lessons are most definitely in your future." And, with an inflection he could not quite pin down, Oralia added, "Among other things."

"I don't know if this is a good time to remind you or not," Rasp said, "but I am the only one who knows the way up the mountain. In case that affects your decision at all."

"As a matter of fact, it does. Thank you, Rasp."

He shuddered, feeling as though he'd not only fallen into her trap, but threw himself wholeheartedly over the edge.

Oralia continued, "As our guide, your continued safety is imperative. Therefore, you and Lieutenant Ralizak will spend the rest of the afternoon practicing emergency drills with Sergeant Farrow. With Ralizak serving as your temporary keeper, her duty will be to assist you to safety no matter the circumstance. You will be heartened to know Ellisar has not taken on this responsibility lightly. From what she has outlined so far, I am confident it will be an illuminating experience for all."

Shit. So much for escaping Ellisar's wrath. She couldn't kill him outright, but that probably wouldn't stop her from trying.

"Afterward—"

"You mean there's *more?*"

"—you both will report directly to the kitchen for the evening rotation. Any questions?"

Rasp feared if he piped up again Oralia would take it as an opportunity to bestow more work upon him.

"No, Madam Protector," Rali answered for both of them.

"Good." Oralia's voice lowered to a menacing snarl. "This should go without saying, but I will say it so we are one hundred percent clear, Rasp. This conversation never happened. And if you blow Ralizak's cover, there will be actual consequences."

"You say that like this isn't punishment!"

"You did assault the captain," Oralia reminded him. "And by your own admission, threw the first swing. If these were normal circumstances I would be staking you to a post outside."

His own admission—curse his stupid mouth! Rasp had never been very good at holding his tongue. He was going to have to get better at it, especially if he hoped to enact his plan. That was days away, though. And in the meantime he would have to toe the line if he wished to wiggle out from under the protector's scrutinizing stare. That meant no more fires, of both the figurative and not-so-figurative kind.

Still, how did they expect him to run drills if he couldn't even walk straight? Not to mention the whole not-being-able-to-see business. This was downright cruel. Rasp doubted he would receive any mercy, but tried anyway. "Aren't I supposed to be recuperating? Look at me! I've got the trembles."

Rasp lifted his palms from the blankets, painfully aware the shaking was getting worse.

"We got Snag whipping up something special for you." Rali's clomping footsteps retreated in the direction of the doorway and she hollered at a volume that seemed unnecessary, "We're ready for you now!"

The tent flap drew back moments later and Snag padded inside, hoops jangling, and smelling strongly of sage and horse—the latter for a reason Rasp decided he did not want to know. The smell grew irritably closer until it buzzed under Rasp's nose. Through the gloom, mere inches from his face, Rasp could just make out the goblin's blurry shape.

Snag took Rasp's trembling hands into his own and twisted them this way and that way. With an edge to his tone that sounded more irritated than concerned, he said, "When was the last time you ate?"

"Uh . . ." That was a question Rasp was not prepared for. "When did a dragon try to eat me?" Was that yesterday? Two days ago? A week? A year? Rasp's sense of time was not conforming to the normal standards as of late.

"Yesterday."

"Before that then. Breakfast, I think?"

"Seven realms." This time, Snag's irritation seemed to be targeted not at Rasp, but the other two. "Did it occur to either of you that maybe the human should be fed before you march him out onto a training field? He's not an orc, you know. Humans are fickle. They need regular tending or they wither and die!"

"In my defense, I did try to feed him earlier," Rali replied.

"Pouring soup on my head does not count!"

"Look," Snag interrupted before a second fistfight broke out. "I threw together the tonic you asked for. If you want me to give it to him as is, fine. But without food in his gut, it'll kill him. Which, if that's what you're going for, also fine. I'm just trying to make sure we're on the same slate here."

"Uh, no," Rasp said. "Not fine."

Oralia cut in before her dwarf lieutenant could say something smart-assed. "What are you recommending?"

"Food, fluids, and some decent clothing to start. The tonic will give him the kick he needs to get through Ellisar's playtime, but it'll take a full night of rest to sleep off the aftereffects."

"I will see to it," Oralia assured him. "Any further instructions before you go?"

Snag's voice dripped with the sort of sticky sweetness you'd expect to find on a carnivorous plant. "Administer it to the mouth end? I know with the amount of shit that dribbles out his orifices it can be hard to tell which is which, so look for teeth."

"Har-har-har!" Was it National Pick On Rasp Day? Because it was certainly starting to feel like it.

"Thank you, Snaglebrag. I imagine there is plenty for you to do at the infirmary. I would hate to keep you." Oralia waited until Snag's muttering died away in the distance before saying, "If you would stand and relinquish my bedding, Rasp."

Reluctantly, Rasp shrugged off the blankets and rose on wobbly legs.

"I will now deliver the two of you into the capable hands of Sergeant Farrow."

Rasp wasn't sure if the protector was giving them the polite boot or if they were waiting for something. And then he heard it. The harsh, somewhat melodic clink of metal against metal. Rasp instinctively shied away, inadvertently backing into Oralia's outstretched arm. She ushered him several forceful steps forward. Rasp couldn't see Sergeant Farrow, but the elf had a presence and he knew she was waiting for him in the doorway. Not smiling, because Faris said Ellisar never smiled, but probably doing the facial equivalent of whatever a smile was to her.

How the fuck did she even get in here? His keen sense of hearing usually made it next to impossible for anyone to sneak up on him. This sudden realization, alas, wasn't even the most troubling one. "Why do I hear a chain?"

"Manacles, actually," Rali contributed helpfully. She raised her voice and Rasp noted the small, nearly indiscernible edge of apprehension. "Tell me you're not making me run drills with my hands shackled."

"No," Ellisar said with no inflection in her voice whatsoever. "I'm making you run drills shackled together."

"You can't do that to a blind person!" Rasp said.

Something cold clamped over Rasp's wrist with a soft *clunk*. "What you're describing is discrimination," Ellisar replied flatly, as she tightened the iron band until it was impossible to slide over Rasp's hand. "As a respectable torturer, I take pride in my ethics."

"Drill sergeant," Oralia corrected.

"That's what I said."

"You heard Snaglebrag. Get him fed and properly dressed before you have your fun. Is that understood?"

"Mhm."

There was a pause before Oralia felt the need to make one final clarification. "Slugs do not count as food."

Rasp swore he heard a stifled snicker as Ellisar set about connecting the other end of the manacles to Lieutenant Ralizak. Rali leaned over, whispering hoarsely into his ear, "Probably shouldn't have lit her on fire, bucko. She looks as happy as a dwarfling that's just unwrapped its first pickaxe."

CHAPTER FORTY-ONE

Rabid Dog

It was official. Ellisar Farrow was a lunatic. A creative one, wrapped up in a layer of ruthless wickedness and slathered in an unending supply of energy. She not only ran the gaggle of off-duty soldiers through every emergency drill imaginable—she did it while running *with* them. For someone who ordinarily handled speaking as if it were a chore, she certainly had the voice for it. Rasp wouldn't have classified Sergeant Farrow's voice as booming, because it didn't boom. It snarled like a rabid dog. Foaming at the proverbial mouth and ready to sink her fangs into you, the elf followed at your heels and no amount of kicking could get her to leave you alone. Ellisar was here, there, and everywhere at once. And by gods, if you made a mistake, she announced it for all of creation to hear.

She didn't know names, either. And obviously had no intention of learning them. As a result, most of the troop was awarded such endearing nicknames as "Knob Slobber," "Giblet Brains," and Rasp's personal favorite, "Mommy's Disappointment."

Ellisar started the session with a run-through on dragons. All thirteen species, in fact. Rasp was convinced she'd made up a few but, like all the other fear-stricken soldiers, dared not question it. As he did not have to partake in the actual soldiering side of things, Rasp's role as the guide was fairly straightforward: Don't die. Partway through, he made his own addition to the rules, which comprised entirely of: Whatever you do, stay as far from Ellisar as possible. With such a vast array of hapless victims to distract her, this plan would have worked remarkably well if it were not for the fact that he was chained to a shit-stirring loudmouth.

Each time he nearly managed to escape a run-through by the skin of his teeth, Rali had to go and blow it by provoking Ellisar. For some inexplicable reason, most of the dwarf's taunting involved a colorful range of seafaring vernacular. Had Rasp been able to do more than breathe and wait helplessly for the next nightmare to begin, he might have asked about it. He didn't though, because breathing was the only thing he was doing with moderate success, and there wasn't any sense in trying to jinx it.

Eventually, even Rali grew weary of having to repeat drills and got with the fucking program. Together, they navigated Ellisar's perverse playground, ducking, running, hiding, whatever it took to escape the field without making a mistake. Anyone unfortunate enough to fail the drill was sentenced to wait out the rest of the exercise in horse stance along the sidelines. This in itself didn't sound too bad. That is, until Rali explained to Rasp what a horse stance was. And then he decided he would just rather fall off a cliff and get it over with.

Once satisfied most of Captain Monk's soldiers would survive another dragon encounter, Sergeant Farrow moved on to swamplander ambushes, then troll attacks, and then threw in battling wizards for none other than the simple fact she enjoyed the suffering of others. Captain Monk came by at one point to supervise the antics, though he suddenly remembered he had something more urgent to attend to when Ellisar invited him to join.

By mid-afternoon Rasp had reached his exhaustion point and could barely remember to pick up his feet, let alone recall what scenario they were playing through for the thousandth time. Something was attacking them—goblins, trolls, angry ducks perhaps—when Rasp lost his footing and hit the ground and rolled, taking Ralizak with him. When he refused to get up again, the disgruntled dwarf hooked her hands under his armpits and finished the drill by dragging him along behind her as if Rasp was a human-sized sack of potatoes.

From what he could tell, the safe zone was nothing more than a random ledge of rock. Upon reaching it, Rali collapsed on top of him in an unceremonious heap. "You don't have any more of that tonic, do you?" she managed between labored breaths.

"No."

The concoction Snag had given him did the job, certainly. But it turned out Rasp hated the job, possibly more than dying, and found himself wishing it'd been poison instead. Despite the pain coursing through his body, he could not help but twist the metaphorical knife deeper into Rali's side. "What, having second thoughts already? Maybe if you gloated about how incredible your plan is some more, you'd feel better."

"For the record, my plans *are* incredible. My ability to follow through, not so much." Rali rolled off of him and lowered her voice to a suspicious whisper. "Hold on. Faris just darted across the battlefield and appears to be negotiating with Drill Sergeant Power Trip. Any idea what that little devil might be up to?"

"Mff . . ."

Lacking the energy to care, much less form proper words, Rasp curled into the fetal position and died. His body shook its last feeble tremble and went still. Death was not as he expected. In fact, it was a lot like living. His feet still hurt and his bones ached. Alone, in the dark, Rasp's only companion was the steady, agonizing throb that beat the inside of his skull like an overworked drum. Time blurred as days crept into months, and months into years. Before he knew it, entire centuries had passed. This was it. The beyond. He was dead—no matter what the voices on the outside said.

"You're not dead." One in particular, which sounded strangely like Faris, insisted for possibly the third time.

"I am," Rasp heard his own voice whimper weakly.

Faris let out a long, wearisome sigh. "Would you come back to life knowing you don't have to run drills anymore?"

"Don't waste your breath, Faris. We can raise the dead later. Go ahead and grab his ankles, I'll get the bitey end." Rali hooked her hands under Rasp's arms once more and lifted. "Lead the way, quickly. Before Ellisar changes her mind."

Had he not been dead, Rasp might have found this method of travel humiliating. His head bobbed with each jostling step against the dwarf's sweat-soaked chest. His left arm hung slack whereas the right was bent awkwardly, as it was still securely shackled to Rali's own wrist. Rali and Faris each moved with their own, mismatched stride, which only increased the unpleasant jostling. Time sped forward once more and the next thing Rasp knew, his corpse was being propped against a tree with his legs arranged on the ground in front him. Still drooling, because surely that's what corpses did, his head slumped lifelessly onto his chest.

Rali was panting heavily next to him. "Alright, Faris," she said between ragged breaths. "What are you two up to?"

It was strangely generous of her to assume Rasp's involvement in this scheme extended beyond playing dead. In regards to what Faris was doing, Rasp was as much in the dark as Rali was. Still, it felt nice to be included. The fuzzy warmth swelling in his chest shriveled when he caught the subtle notes of lilac and rosewater on the breeze. That wasn't right. Faris's scent of choice was an irresistible combination of honey and almond paste. A fact he knew well, as he'd irresistibly taken several bites from Faris's soap bar before realizing his error. The perfume wasn't coming from Rali, either. The dwarf regularly smelled like his shoes the morning after a fun night of drinking. Despite some light scrubbing and a spritz of pine, the funk of stale alcohol lingered.

Focus, Rasp's maybe-not-so-dead brain commanded. Slowly, he tuned back into the world of the living, if only to satisfy his growing curiosity. Lilac and rosewater. He'd smelled this person before, but who? And, more importantly, why were they here? And since when did Faris work with anyone else? *He* was Faris's right hand, or vice versa, or however their arrangement worked. It was what, barely halfway through their first day apart? Had Rasp been replaced already? The nerve!

He listened, realizing his suspicions were correct. There was a second voice. This one was softer, sweeter, possibly female. Finally, the name settled on his tongue and Rasp choked back his surprise. "Hermit?"

"Briony," the voice said, not-so-sweetly.

"What are you doing here?"

"Returning the favor and saving your butt, apparently," Briony replied. She added, with an air of bitterness this time, "For the record, I maintain that jumping into the river was a horrible idea yesterday. I'm still fighting off this damn chill."

"You know where it's not chilly? Inside a dragon."

"Don't bite the hand that saves your ass," Faris said, clipping Rasp lightly on the ear with the back of his hand. "She's here to help."

And then, as if Rasp and Ralizak suddenly vanished from the face of the known world, the fauns proceeded to ignore them. Their blurry forms huddled a few feet away, speaking in hushed mumbles and the occasional grunt of agreement. Faris, the little sneak, was up to something. In an effort to thwart his father, the cunning young Belfast had developed his own coded language used to run his small network of underlings. Back at the village, Faris could convey an entire message using nothing more than a series of snorts, an ear flick, and the occasional stomp of a hoof.

Whatever Faris was up to had to be clever. Rasp wasn't sure in what way, exactly, but the fact that Rali was equally clueless counted for something. The dwarf leaned into Rasp, whispering, "I haven't spent much time around fauns. Is this normal behavior? All that ear twiddling and whatever that lovely husky sound is?"

"It's a mating ritual. Pretty standard from the sounds of it." Rasp fought the wicked smile that threatened to break across his wind-blistered face. "Actually, since you're here, would you mind describing it to me? The constant stomping and snorting just isn't painting the right picture in my mind."

"Bucko, don't make me sit on you again."

Faris's secret code was not without flaw, however. And, eventually, the pair reached a point where a well-timed ear flick simply could not convey their position in the same way that words could. "Rings are too noticeable," Briony said. "What's wrong with the iron tokens? One for each pocket. Inconspicuous."

"Tokens only work if you're in the habit of keeping your clothes on."

Briony gagged a little. "Please don't put that image in my head."

"You two make a darling couple, really, you do," Rali said with such force, air whistled between her tightly clenched teeth. "But I just watched you bribe Ellisar with a bag of gods-knows-what and—"

"Poisonous mushrooms," Faris said.

"Hallucinogenic mushrooms," Briony corrected. Rasp couldn't see her shaking her horns, but he knew she was. It was the kind of tone fauns used when they were the authority on the matter and were too polite to say it in words, but nevertheless wanted you to know.

"Right, hallucinogenic mushrooms. That's brilliant of you, no doubt. But please, before I lose my fucking patience here, will one of you tell me why you bribed Ellisar to release us early? I'm in enough trouble as it is, thank you. If Oralia finds out I weaseled out of her punishment, I'm going to have to do it all over again. There are only so many drills a dwarf can run in a day before her legs turn to nubs, you know."

Grudgingly, Faris obliged her in the most uninformative manner possible. "We're taking precautions."

"How dandy," Ralizak said. "Against what?"

"The ears," Briony hissed under her breath to Faris. "Unless he's in the habit of taking those off, too."

Faris made a noise, a bizarre combination of a grunt and a snort at the same time. If Rasp didn't know better, he would have assumed Faris had swallowed something down the wrong pipe and was attempting to dislodge it in a single heave.

"It'll work," Briony insisted.

"He's got half an ear on that side!"

"Exactly. I'll put two on that one. Balance him a bit."

Rasp did not like where this conversation was going. Before he could protest, Lieutenant Ralizak's voice cut back in like a roll of thunder. "Precautions against what, Faris?"

"Evil spirits. I don't mind them so much myself, but you know how superstitious Rasp is," Faris said tiredly. From the strain in his voice, Rasp wondered if Faris had skipped sleep in lieu of side work again. Not that it was all together surprising. But the damn faun had to know when to quit. He was already stretched thin and, with the added antics of last night, was due to drop dead any moment now.

Captain Monk hadn't been particularly thrilled about sharing his quarters with them after their return from the river. To put the captain at ease, Faris insisted he would keep watch to ensure there wasn't any funny business. Funny business of course being the key word for "Rasp, sleep next to the dear ol' captain to keep him distracted while I rifle through his things. Oh, and if he happens to wake up, be an angel and bite him for me so I have enough time to put everything back." Rasp didn't know what Faris had found. Did it have something to do with this? And exactly what was this? Rasp hated *witches*, not evil spirits. They were two very different things.

"Faris, I'm not an idiot. You're not an idiot. He, well, he might be," Rali said, thumping Rasp's leg. "But that's a debate for another time. Whatever's going on right now isn't up to your usual caliber of underhandedness. So you can either level with me here, or I'll drag your ass to Oralia and she can beat the truth out of you. And believe me, bucko, she's in the mood for a good knuckle buster."

"This is about the jacket, isn't it?" Faris said. "Look, I already told you, come up with my twenty silver and you can have it back. Until then, I'm going to keep making this shit look good."

"Faris, for shame." Briony clicked her tongue in disappointment. "You should charge at least three extra for getting the blood out of the collar. Don't undervalue your work."

"How hard do you have to scrub to get blood out of white fur, I wonder?" Rali said, with the sort of thoughtfulness that made Rasp double-check his pockets for a knife.

Faris sat quiet for a few harrowing seconds as he mulled his options over. "You know what, you're right. I'm sorry. Friends shouldn't keep secrets from each other. That's on me." And then, with a voice that might have passed for sincere had Rali been born yesterday, he said, "We both can agree Rasp is the opposite of subtle, right? I've heard aggression like his can be due to too much toxin in the blood or something. Anyway, these little charms here are supposed to help with that. While they won't necessarily suppress his fiery outbursts, so to speak, they will make his aggression a little less obvious to others."

Gods dammit. Faris was doing that thing where the real message was sandwiched somewhere in between meaningless words. As the inner mechanisms of Rasp's brain hadn't fully resurrected from the dead yet, he was now completely lost. His only hope was that maybe Rali was following along and would spell it out for him in tiny words.

"Aggression, you say?" Her tone had abandoned all sense of cheerfulness. "You know, I've heard castration can work wonders in that area."

That he understood. No tiny words needed. "Unnecessary!"

"True," Faris agreed with the marked calmness of someone whose testicles were not on the chopping block. "But, last I checked, your boss needs him travel-worthy. My way ensures he can still ride a horse. Plus, there'll be a lot less complaining."

"So this is like preemptive damage control?" Rali said.

"Commonly referred to as a safety measure, yes."

"Splendid! I have to say, I really appreciate the level of openness we share, Faris," Rali said in a tone that Rasp suspected meant she didn't necessarily believe the bullshit Faris was peddling but, nevertheless, seemed to realize the truth was of no consequence to her. "Now, if you want me to keep this little scheme of yours under wraps, I'll gladly take your bribe now. No mushrooms, thank you kindly. After the soup incident this morning, I don't think I'll be able to look at another one of those for a while."

Rasp heard Faris throw something at her. It sloshed as it sailed through the air. Rali caught it, causing the chain between them to rattle against Rasp's wrist. With another customer satisfied, Faris spoke in Rasp's direction—in that particular voice he used when what he was suggesting wasn't for your benefit, but his, but somehow you still wanted to do it. "Now, how much do you trust me?"

CHAPTER FORTY-TWO

Anti-Magic

How much do I trust you?" Rasp repeated. *Less and less with every word out of your mouth.* "That depends, Dingle. Are you going to tell me what you're actually doing?"

"I'm going to pierce your ears. Well, actually, Briony's going to. I'm just here for moral support and to handle all the bribery."

"No."

Briony placed her hand on Rasp's knee in what was supposed to be a reassuring manner. "But you'd look so fetching with earrings."

"No need to be cruel, Briony," Faris said. "Besides, if you want him to do something, you tell the truth. He'd rather be used knowing what you're using him for."

Rasp wasn't sure he agreed with that, but Faris was pretty good at getting him to do things. Was that really all it took? No! The very idea was preposterous. Then again, that was how he'd ended in his current debacle. He'd only agreed to Rali's stupid plan because she'd explained to him the bigger picture and, more specifically, his role in said picture. Crap. He really *was* that easy to play. Well no more. From here on out, he'd be Rasp the Unusable! The Unworkable! The Unnecessarily, Uncompromisingly Unbendable!

Maybe not that last one. He was going to have to give his new title a little more thought. Later, perhaps, when there wasn't a pair of crafty fauns trying to rope him into their schemes.

"Have either of you ever fought with metal in your ears? One good yank, that's all it takes. Pass!" Rasp would know. He had given lots of good yanks to lots of unsuspecting ears over the years. It was an especially good day if he walked away with the matching pair in his pocket. The rings, not the ears—those he left on the ground where their owner could find them when they came around again.

"Trust me," Faris said. "You want these."

Toxins his ass. Faris's weak answer may have been enough for Lieutenant Ralizak, but Rasp wasn't agreeing to anything until he understood the specifics. If Faris was going to play dumb, then so could he. It was a role Rasp was significantly better at. "Do I, though?" he said, rolling his unshackled wrist innocently. "I feel like earrings aren't going to fix the toxins in my blood. Maybe I should try eating a diet of those horrible leafy things first?"

"Vegetables?" Briony ventured.

"I mean, if it's between that and unnecessary body modifications, then I'm willing to give spinach another try."

"You want to talk about unnecessary body modifications? You, of all people?" Faris thumped his hoof against the ground in irritation. "These are not unnecessary. They are, in fact, very necessary. Possibly even lifesaving. These charms confuse evil spirits. I would say they work like magic, but obviously you hate magic and I know you would never want anyone to ever think you'd use magic. So let's just say then, they work like anti-magic."

"To keep the spirits away," Rasp said, marveling once more at Faris's ability to explain something without actually saying what *it* was.

"Exactly."

His brain was slowly catching back up to speed. If Rasp was following correctly, Faris intended to charm him. Not in the smooth-talking "let me buy you a drink and then we can go back to your place" sort of way, either. This sounded more like a means to hide his magic from others. Unfortunately, there really wasn't much of a point anymore. Whisper had already found him. And yet, the words "reek of raw magic" drifted back through Rasp's brain. A little insurance wouldn't hurt, he supposed. Gods forbid, he couldn't handle being exploited by two witches at the same time. Besides, if nothing else, maybe the anti-magic would annoy Whisper into giving him some distance. He was going to need every advantage he could get at this point.

Reluctantly, Rasp sighed. "You do know how much I hate ghosts."

"Spirits."

"Right." Gods, the inane things he did for the sake of friendship. Faris was lucky he was reformed now. No respectable brawler put little metal pieces in their ears, no matter how anti-magical they were. "Fine. As long as it doesn't kill me, I guess."

"You're going to have to be quick about it," Rali's singsong voice called. She sounded farther away for some reason. Which could not have possibly been the case, considering only a small length of chain connected them. "We're expected at the kitchen for the dinner shift soon."

"Maybe don't drink all of that at once then?" Briony said. "You do want to be able to walk there, I imagine. Maybe avoid accidentally cutting your hand off while you're at it?"

"Don't fret your head, miss. Everyone knows the best way to ward off spirits is with more spirits!" Rali was highly amused by herself, as made evident by the bout of snorting laughter that followed.

Briony worked quickly. She started with Rasp's right ear, or what was left of it anyway. She swabbed something wet across the lobe and allowed it to air dry for a moment. "Little pinch," she said, as not one, but in fact two little pinches pierced Rasp's ear. She threaded something cold into each opening and then finished with another swab that stung this time.

"Aren't you supposed to be a herbalist?" Rasp said, probably with too much accusation in his voice. He knew Briony did odd jobs for Faris from time to time back home, but this one seemed especially odd.

"It's a profession with many hats," she replied.

"Does warding off spirits bring in much business?"

"Oh, yes. Sage prices are through the roof right now. I could give you a little to burn later if you'd like."

Briony repeated the process on his left ear, this time awarding him only one piercing. Rasp felt the earlobe, noting to his relief that the studs were small. They weren't rings, either. Which meant it would be nearly impossible for an opponent to get a finger hooked through the jewelry during a fight. Rasp ran his thumb against the flat head of the post and felt something etched onto the metal brush against his skin. It was a symbol of some sort. Anti-magic, according to Faris.

Briony slapped his hand away. "Don't irritate it."

"They feel funny." He was certain they were emitting a low frequency buzz, but perhaps that was simply an aftereffect of breathing in Rali's under-arm odor for too long.

"Good. That means they're working. Leave them alone. If I have to come back again, I'm stringing the next one through your nose."

An impish smile pulled across Rasp's lips. "If you're in the mood for a real challenge, I've actually been wanting another—"

Faris placed his hand against Rasp's mouth. "Gods no, please. You don't need any more excuses to remove your pants."

The nerve! Not only had Rasp been replaced, but Faris was oddly protective of her, too. He was not going to take this lying down, or sitting, or whatever the fuck he was currently doing. "Since I'm attached to . . . that"—which was the least offensive way Rasp could describe Lieutenant Ralizak—"does that mean you get the evening off, Dingle?"

"What's it to you?"

Time to head this off at the pass before things escalated too quickly. Rasp bent forward, searching along the moss covered ground until he found Briony and grasped her hands. He stared somewhere in the vicinity of her blurred face and adopted his most concerned voice. "I can tell when Faris likes someone. And I know for a fact he likes you because he called you by your name and not just idiot, like the rest of us."

"What the muck are you doing?" Faris demanded with none of his usual tact.

"Do be gentle with him." Rasp continued, "I suspect it's his first time. And if he cries afterward, well, just hold him for a little while. Tell him it wasn't that bad and that nobody gets it right on their first go."

"That's very, um," Briony paused, searching for the right words, "assuming of you?"

"On the flipside he's a topnotch cuddler. Tucks me in almost every night. Not much of a kisser, though. Who knows, you might be able to set him straight." Gods, what he would give to see her horrified expression right now. Faris was seething. Rasp could practically feel the heat radiating off of him.

Lieutenant Ralizak produced a belch that would've drowned out a stampede of trumpeting elephants. From the way the chain rattled, Rasp assumed she was now standing. There was a disturbing lack of sway in both her stance and speech. "Alright, Raspy, my boy. You done playing matchmaker, yet? We've dillydallied enough. Time to set sail."

"Faris, Hermit, please use your heads, okay? I'm not ready to be an uncle." Rasp stood, fighting a smile as he searched the space around him for Rali's shoulder.

"I think they call that using your hands," Rali said with another of her whooping laughs.

The dwarf grasped Rasp's fingers in her own crushing grip and started in the direction of what he could only hope was the kitchen. His walking stick had disappeared after yesterday's speedy dismount and nobody seemed to be in any hurry to replace it. Thus, he was forced to depend on Lieutenant Ralizak to get them to and fro safely, which was unfortunate as she seemed to have a very loose interpretation of what *safely* meant. She also insisted on holding hands. Rasp didn't dare protest this time, fearful she might take it as an opportunity to start acting weird again.

The recollection of running drills with Rali singing and skipping alongside him, hand in hand, was going to haunt him for many a sleepless night to come.

Rasp picked his way through the underbrush back toward the bustling sounds of camp. Dread pooled in his stomach once more. As much as he'd hated it, the drills had been a convenient means of distraction. He'd been able to set aside his thoughts for a few hours and focus solely on surviving Sergeant Farrow's wrath. Now, without a psychotic elf nipping at his heels, his mind was free to wear holes into his already paper-thin escape plan.

The plan would work. It *had* to. Else, in a matter of days, they would all be dead.

CHAPTER FORTY-THREE

Shadowman

Do we have to do this right now?" Willem dragged his feet behind Daana as if each leg weighed twice what it should have. A handful of silver strands had escaped his hair tie and whipped across his face like frenzied insects caught in a web. Willem smoothed the stubborn flyaways against his scalp, grumbling, "The infirmary put me to work, you know. I spent all day boiling bandages and grinding herbs into paste. I can barely feel my fingers."

Daana pulled him along by the elbow, ignoring his meek protests. Tent walls were thin and, as she'd learned from that morning's officer meeting, voices carried—particularly those of the loud, angry variety. She needed to speak with Willem privately. Which, alas, meant dragging him out into the woods where her loud, angry conversation would not be overheard.

Daana marked the trees with her charcoal stick as she walked, leading him deeper into the forest. Satisfied with the distance between them and camp, she stopped and faced him. "You owe me answers."

It was nearly nightfall. The last of the brilliant red-orange light danced across the tops of the towering conifers as the sun settled beyond the horizon. Darkness carpeted the forest floor in long, deep shadows. The damp earth around them smelled of mud and old spruce needles. Already, swarms of buzzing insects had begun to cloud the cool evening air.

Willem's sharp eyes flickered up and down the thick, needled boughs overhead, looking for something Daana did not see. His downturned mouth appeared more severe than usual. "Answers about what?"

It wasn't until a few hours ago, when Daana's head stopped spinning, that she remembered what had been driving her mad all morning. "You can stop with the harmless old man act. I saw you follow Rasp's horse across the meadow during yesterday's dragon attack."

A flicker of annoyance crossed his harsh features. "You saw that, did you?"

In that moment, in the midst of chaos, there hadn't been time to consider how wrong that was. Now Daana suddenly had all the time in the world. "And the way you moved in the kitchen this morning? This whole time I thought the council had paired me with a grumpy old librarian. But that's not the case, is it? What are you really? And why in the seven realms of chaos did you put yourself in that kind of danger yesterday?"

Willem didn't answer. In fact, he didn't appear to have heard. His entire concentration was focused on something above her.

"Now what?" Daana craned her neck back in order to see what was so damn important. Chicken Liver, the white-tailed raven, was perched in the branches overhead. It watched them with its head tilted to one side, curiously. Daana spoke through clenched teeth. "Is that bird giving you trouble, Willem?"

"It's been following us since camp." He waved his hand at the raven. "Move on, already. Shoo!"

With a harsh croak, the white-tailed raven fluttered upward and found a more suitable roost near the top of the tree. It preened its long pin feathers which, in the waning light, looked more dark blue than black.

"Oh my gods, you've gone and lost your mind, haven't you?" Daana dug a square of cloth from her pocket and unfolded the edges, tearing the corner from her stash of cured salmon. The meat was overseasoned and left an oily aftertaste, but she doubted the raven was picky enough to care. "Is this what you want?" She tossed the morsel above their heads. Chicken Liver swooped from its branch, caught the fish midair, and fluttered out of sight. "There. It's gone. Will you stop acting strange and talk to me?"

"Great. Now you've taught it to come back every time it's hungry." With his head still tilted upward, Willem's eyes moved in her direction, watching her from beneath heavy lashes. "To answer your question concerning yesterday's break in character, I thought I sensed something. Instinct took over and I followed. Admittedly, I should have been more careful, but you know how it is. Sometimes the pull of magic is so strong, you get caught up in the chase and all else fades away."

Willem's dour personality made it easy to forget that he could detect the presence of magic just as easily as she could. Like the two of them, all seekers were magic-sensitive. And although a seeker would never ascend to the lofty ranks of a witch, they still held a key position within the Division of Divination. The magic-sensitive were trained in the art of detection, able to pick out those lucky persons born with natural talents for the art of witchcraft. It was not glamorous work by any means, and seekers often felt overshadowed by their magical academy mates, but their role was vital nonetheless. After all, it was seekers who ventured out across the seven territories of the realm in order to keep the division's numbers strong.

Magic-sensitive or not, it still didn't explain Willem's sudden shift in behavior. Her partner was many things, but she had never known reckless to be one of them. Thus far, Willem showed more enthusiasm for lamenting over their assignment than he had about actually participating in it.

"You were chasing magic?" Daana repeated. "During a dragon attack? You can hear yourself, right?"

In the diminishing light, Willem's pale skin had taken on an eerie glow. An uncharacteristic smirk danced across his sour lips. "Do you suppose that's why the council forced me into early retirement all those years ago? I've come to appreciate my stuffy library, but there was a time when I was just as hungry for the hunt as you."

Forced into retirement? She hadn't heard any mention of that before.

Daana gnawed her bottom lip, all while wondering if dragging him into the woods with her alone was perhaps a poor idea, after all. "Well, did your recklessness pay off? Did you discover anything?"

"Alas, no. I can remember the dragon, and jumping into the river, but everything after that"—he made a halfhearted fluttering motion with his hand—"gone."

"That doesn't alarm you?"

"Of course it's alarming. The only other time I suffered memory loss was during my first encounter with the Palace Ghost. I suppose, if anything, this means I'm on the right track."

"The ghost *was* highly active last night. More than I have sensed in a long time." She had his full attention now—both eyes boring into her with the intensity of two burning blue suns. "Don't get your hopes up. Thanks to our dear friend, Captain Monk, I couldn't get away to investigate." With Willem swept downriver, and concern about the potential of another dragon attack, Monk had assumed protection over Daana. The overzealous captain had assigned her not one, but two escorts, making it impossible to slip away unnoticed.

Daana asked, "Do you think it could have saved you?"

"Why would it do that?"

"I don't know. The ghost spared you once before, didn't it?"

For whatever reason, among all the mighty seekers ever sent after the ghost, it had revealed itself to only one person. A lowly apprentice at the time, Willem had journeyed with his master to track the Palace Ghost through the Adderwood territory. The correspondences stopped shortly afterward. And then, two months later, Willem limped back to Sunstorn on his own, injured, half-starved, and clinging to his rapidly unraveling sanity.

"Spared? Gods, no. The damn thing got bored of chasing me. I may not look it now, but I was a spry young thing back in my day." Willem must have seen something in her expression, because he lifted one graying eyebrow higher than the other. "You're doing that thing with your face again. What is it, my dear? Finally having second thoughts?"

The nagging feeling that had been slowly eating away at her all day was back with twice the intensity. Daana attempted to quell the sudden dropping sensation in her gut by crossing her arms. One thing was becoming increasingly clear: Willem wasn't here simply because he was the authority on the ghost. He was something more. "You're not a seeker, are you?"

"Don't be preposterous."

"Preposterous? Me? For the gods' sakes, Willem, no one goes gallivanting off under the nose of a dragon unless they have some sort of hidden talent or they're just plain crazy. And while the latter might be true in this case, I suspect there's more you're not telling me. For the last time, what are you?"

What little light filtered in from above cast Willem's face in long shadows. His eyes glistened against the gloom, watching, uninhibited by the growing dark. Finally, after a moment of deliberation, he gave in. "If you must know, our employer has two solutions for these types of problems. Sometimes, all that's needed is a show of brute force. Precisely what we have seekers for. For the more delicate situations, when it requires a level head and methods that do not draw unwanted attention, that's when someone like me is sent in to take care of matters."

Daana considered pointing out his actions had drawn plenty of unwanted attention yesterday—that of a hungry dragon, and not the protector, fortunately. She decided now was not the time to be pedantic and said instead, "You're a shadowman?"

Willem snapped a branch from a nearby tree and dragged it mindlessly behind him as he strolled past. His limp from before was suddenly absent. "Now you're just being insulting."

Daana had only heard them referred to as shadowmen, a somewhat childish take now that she was face-to-face with one. "Magic-sensitive hitman" was probably a more apt description, but Daana doubted Willem would like that any better. The division had several of the kind employed in its service. Too cutthroat to function as ordinary seekers, the division tucked them away like ugly handknit sweaters, hoping they would never see the light of day but keeping them stashed in the far reaches of the closet for the rare instances their function outweighed their unsightliness.

The intelligence report had conveniently failed to mention her partner in crime was quite possibly an actual criminal!

Unrelated, how far away was camp again? Too far, unfortunately. Besides, she was still angry and wanted to shout some more.

"Were you planning on telling me?" she demanded.

"Eventually." He glanced over his shoulder as he walked, shrugging. "We used to be closer, you and I. But ever since you joined the magical program, you've acted like a stranger. I had to be sure your reasons for being here were your own and not your uncle's."

"I am here because I am the most capable for the task."

A task that, as of late, had grown unbearable. It had been easier separating herself from the work in the beginning. But as time progressed and her assignments grew more complicated, the lines had started to blur. Capturing the ghost was her way out. Her way of proving, once and for all, that she was above the duties of a seeker. It was a line of work she no longer had the stomach for.

Willem's voice pulled her from her thoughts. "Most capable, you say? Oh, the confidence of youth." He strutted past, still dragging his infernal stick through the soft dirt behind him. "You've got an advantage, yes. But between you and me, you're a bit of a one-trick pony."

"Excuse me? In case you've forgotten, I have the power to drain the Palace Ghost."

Each word was spoken with the same crisp, rage-inducing emphasis. "One. Trick. Pony."

"Fine." She could already feel the heat of her anger working up her ears. "And what does someone like you bring to the equation?"

Willem's face lit eagerly. "I'm so glad you asked. You might have the means, but I have the experience. For example, take the seer's trap I've drawn into the dirt around you. Not my best work, but for the purpose of demonstration it will suffice." He tossed the branch aside, explaining, "Now, normally this symbol wouldn't have an effect on a non-magical person, but because of those pretty little stones of yours, you'll find getting out of it rather tricky."

"A what?" Daana attempted to step over the ring and found her foot fixed in place. Her runestones flared violet as power surged down her forearms and gathered in her fingertips. The ring responded, glowing the same color as her magic.

Oh fuck.

CHAPTER FORTY-FOUR

Excessively Stabby

The seer's trap shimmered in a ring around her, casting the surrounding trees in a ghoulish violet glow. While Daana's upper body was unaffected by the power of the symbol, her feet were rooted to the ground. Her increasingly undignified efforts to squirm free were unsuccessful.

"Willem, so help me gods!"

"Ah-ah-ah." Willem tilted his finger at her. "Magic powers the trap. A witch, even a pretend one, cannot leave the circle. Come now, girl, I'm disappointed. While you were busy dazzling the division council with your stolen magic, I spent all those years trying to teach you to wield the greatest power of all. Did you even read any of those books I gave you?"

"Of course I did!" This, specifically, was not in any of them.

Willem continued to circle her, patiently placing one foot in front of the other. While his posture remained as pristine as ever, something about the way he carried himself was different. As if, in the span of one conversation, he'd somehow regressed in age. "Being relegated to the library came with some unexpected benefits, I'll admit. I never imagined how much I would learn combing through the old spellbooks the council deemed too outdated to teach. Naturally, I kept all of the better findings to myself. Would you like to know more about this one?"

"As a matter of fact, I would." Daana closed her eyes and focused her concentration inward. With a flick of her fingers, she extinguished the power in her armlets. She took a deep breath and held it. And then another, and another, until the heat raging inside of her had settled enough to continue the conversation without profuse amounts of screaming. There would still be screaming when Willem was finished making his stupid point, of course. This calming measure simply ensured there would be less of it.

Daana opened her eyes again and glared in his direction. "I'm particularly interested in the part where you tell me how to get out of it."

"A seer's trap, while a useful trick, only works on low- to mid-level witches. Attempting to capture anything stronger would overpower the symbol. This caveat, unfortunately, does not apply to you." Willem came to a halt in front of her, clasping his hands behind his back. "You were always a quick study. Tell me, how do you get out?"

By smacking that smug look from your face!

Not helpful. Also likely not the correct answer. But a tempting idea nonetheless. Daana gnawed her bottom lip as she considered a more well-thought-out response. "The trap is powered by magic?"

"Yes."

"Then it's a trick question. I'm not actually stuck."

That damn smile was back, hovering over his thin lips like a moth to a candle. "Because?"

She took one more slow breath to keep from spitting the words at him. They tasted bitter regardless, like raw dandelion greens on her tongue. "Because I'm not a witch."

Daana grudgingly unclasped her armlets and let them drop. Free of the source of magic, she stepped from the circle, smudging the symbol from the ground with her boot as she did so. The shimmering violet light gradually faded until all that remained was a broken rune etched in dirt.

Willem tilted his head at her curiously. "Then why do you act like one? You may be the first magic-sensitive person accepted into the division's gifted program, but your peers will never consider you one of their own. Your power comes from siphoning the magic of others. By definition, your very existence is a threat to them."

"Look, I get your point, alright? I got too big for my boots. My power isn't my own and no one at the division actually likes me. Thank you for pointing all of that out. I will value your input from now on." Daana scooped her armlets from the dirt, snapping, "Are we finished?"

"No. You've been snubbing me this entire trip because you think I betrayed you. I wasn't the one who changed, Daana. You lost sight of what was important. No amount of power, not even from the ghost, will turn you into what you want. You will never be a witch."

"I know that!" Daana struggled to refasten her armlets. The hurt in her chest bubbled to the surface and before she could stop herself, she blurted out, "I thought you were my friend. When I started at the division, you were the only one that treated me like I wasn't a fraud. After years of working my ass off, the council was finally starting to see that I could be something more than just another seeker."

She took a shaky breath, fighting the tears that threatened to fall. "And then this mission came up and I saw my chance to prove myself once and for all. Instead of supporting me, you, in front of everyone, told them I wasn't good enough. Can you blame me for being mad?"

"I only said—"

"'Has this council grown so desperate that it is willing to put its fate in the hands of a magical anomaly, when all the power in the realm has yet to bring the ghost to heel?'" The words were burned into Daana's memory. Hot tears slipped down her face, unchecked. "Those were your words. Your only kindness was that you said anomaly, when you meant mistake."

"I do not think you are a mistake. I had to be dramatic to make a point. And I was never against you being sent on the mission, Daana. I was against you being sent alone. They were throwing you to the wolves, girl. Can't you see that?"

Daana didn't offer a reply, because she didn't have one. What was she supposed to say to that anyway? That maybe he was right and she was wrong? For the gods' sakes, he'd trapped her with a stupid symbol etched in dirt! How could she possibly take on the Palace Ghost when she couldn't even handle Willem?

"Put aside your pride and think logically. If the Palace Ghost could be captured by magic, then it would have happened by now. Witches, stronger than you and I and all of the seekers in the realm combined, have gone after the ghost and failed." Willem pinched the bridge of his nose, sighing. "Knowledge is more powerful than magic. It's what I've been trying to teach you all along. Between the two of us, we might have what it takes. But in order for this partnership to work, I need you to remember that your value is not found in a handful of shiny stones."

That was . . . actually kind of nice. Nice as far as Willem was concerned, anyway. He was still willing to work with her, too. The right thing would be to set her wounded pride aside and accept his peace offering. The right thing, however, also felt gross and Daana wanted to revel in her petulance a few seconds longer before growing the fuck up. "Was that your attempt at a compliment?"

"It's the closest to one you will ever hear." He paused, grimacing. "Gods, I can still taste it. It's like a lingering foulness on my tongue."

"I still think you're a bastard."

"And you're still a spoiled brat. One, who, if she remembers to stop and use her brain every once in a while, might just make me the second most famous seeker in realm history." Willem offered her his gloved hand. "I need a partner, not a competitor. Can we leave the pettiness behind us?"

Daana wiped under her eyes with the back of her sleeve. "Did that compliment hurt as badly as the first? Or does the exposure lessen the sting each time?"

Okay, maybe just a *few* more seconds of petulance. And then it would be out of her system for good. Or at least until tomorrow. Baby steps, after all. Growing up was hard.

"It was exponentially worse," Willem said.

"And we're talking actual partners here? Equal say, equal sway? No more pointless power moves? You tell me everything, the good, the bad, the unsightly. And I, in return, do the same?"

"This is starting to feel oddly specific."

Daana seized Willem's hand before he could reconsider. "Good, because there's something I need to tell you."

Dragging Willem into the trees to yell at him for acting like an idiot during a dragon attack was not the only reason for her being out here. The second reason was arguably the more important one. Earlier, the mere thought of sharing this would have reduced her lower intestines to knots. Perhaps she was drunk on a misplaced sense of camaraderie, but Daana no longer felt the need to curl into a ball and scream. Just screaming would suffice now. No ball needed. Progress!

"Yesterday, while you were away, things got complicated. I had to make an executive decision. One you're not going to agree with."

Willem closed his eyes and lifted his chin skyward, running his fingers through his frazzled hair. "I'm regretting this already."

"There was an incident with Faris Belfast, the Stoneclaw's keeper. He knows what I am." Daana added, quickly, before Willem could berate her, "I mitigated the damage as best I could. I promised him land and a title for his cooperation."

Willem's eyes snapped back open. "You did what?"

"He only knows about me, not you." Which went without saying, really. Considering that until only mere moments ago, she had no idea what Willem was either.

"And, pray tell, how did he find out?"

"I don't know. He saw my armlets and put two and two together, I guess." Daana ground her heel into the dirt, feeling the dry crunch of the pine needles underfoot. "He's clever, Willem. Enough that he immediately jumped to blackmail instead of running to Oralia."

"Oh, dear gods."

By his tone, Daana suspected Willem was already considering ways to remove the pesky faun. "I don't want him hurt. I know it's not ideal, but I think we can make it work to our benefit. We need more eyes and ears in the camp. If Faris's loyalty is dependent on the highest bidder, I can't be outmatched."

Willem spoke through his hands, which were currently slamming into his forehead. "Straight to blackmail? And that somehow makes him trustworthy? Do you hear yourself, Daana?"

Seekers weren't killers—with the exception of Willem, apparently. That wasn't part of the work. Daana was supposed to locate the magically gifted and help them realize their potential. Sure, the well-intentioned citizen got in the way from time to time, but there were protocols for dealing with them. The situation with Faris had been so completely out of Daana's league she'd frozen. She couldn't damn well kill him. For one, she wasn't sure she could, as Faris was a devious little bastard, and two, murder definitely fell outside of the rules even she was willing to break.

"Willem, whatever horrendous skills you possess, I'm asking that you don't use them. Not yet. Give me a chance to get ahead of this. I'm the one that caused the issue, I'd like to be given the opportunity to fix it before you take it upon yourself to do something—" Daana found some difficulty choosing the right word. Murderous? Cutthroat? Excessively stabby? "—extreme?"

An earsplitting whistle broke through the trees, scattering the birds from their evening roosts. "Hey, Your Highness!" Curly's bellowing voice rang out in the distance. "Where in the seven realms are you?"

"If you think you can manage Mister Belfast on your own, have at it. It's high time you learned to clean up your own messes anyway." Willem's eyebrows twitched as he tilted his head ever-so-slightly, listening to the bumbling antics of the loud orc with a purposefully blank expression. "I see you have been making progress in one area, at least."

"Daana!"

She tried not to wince at Curly's volume. "He's not calling me princess anymore, if that's what you mean."

"Oh, please. I know a familiar tone when I hear it," Willem said, shooing her away with his hands. The gesture appeared alarmingly harmless for a hitman. Daana wondered if he practiced in front of the mirror for it to appear natural. "Go. See what he wants. I'll find my own way back to camp."

"My dear partner, was that an order?"

"It was a plea. As someone who desperately needs to rest his aching head, I beg of you. Make it stop."

"Well, in that case, sweet dreams then." Daana's gaze dropped to the thin dagger strapped to his side. What she previously mistook for a precaution was starting to look more like a tool of the trade. And he wore it outright! Surely Willem wasn't advertising what he was. Was he? Did anyone else notice, or were they all just as caught up in the harmless old man act?

Willem caught her looking. His stony expression remained unchanged, save for the small curl at the edge of his mouth. "Do me a favor and don't get lost on the way. I can't watch the search team fumble through another rescue. There are only so many times I can say "Is that a footprint? She must have gone that way," before it starts to look suspicious."

Daana turned around and started back toward camp, rolling her eyes. "I only got lost one time."

"It was three!"

"You're three!" She was *totally* nailing this growing up thing.

Daana didn't wait for his reply. She darted through the dark forest with her hood pulled over her head, unaware of the black-and-white raven that soared soundlessly over the treetops above her.

CHAPTER FORTY-FIVE

The Game

For the first time in many nights, Oralia found herself alone with her thoughts. With Rali and Sascha working the kitchen shift and the other three having conveniently disappeared, her camp was empty. These moments were few and far between, and Oralia normally enjoyed them. The quiet gave her a chance to think. Regrettably, tonight she had too many thoughts. There were too many questions, too many theories, too many possibilities swirling around the inside of her aching skull. Each thought scrambled over the others, clawing its way to the surface of her mind and screaming to be heard.

There was only one way to drown out the noise. Something so meticulously mind-numbing it required her full attention—mending. She liked mending. What's more, she liked that she was good at it. Somewhere along the way the others had picked up on this and now snuck their own garments into her repair bag when she wasn't looking. Except Snag, the only one of the four content to wear a uniform until it had surpassed the threadbare stage and bordered dangerously on see-through. Most of his clothing skipped the mending pile and went straight into the fire, often resulting in a dazzling display of green and purple flames that smelled of sulfur and made you light-headed if you stood too close.

Oralia didn't mind the extra work. She wasn't an expert hunter. She couldn't whip together a soothing tonic with a handful of wilted leaves and boiling water any more than she could haggle circles around the local merchants until they gave up out of sheer frustration. But she was good at this. And it felt nice to contribute something outside of being the responsible one who put out the fires, handled more paperwork than should legally be allowed, and occasionally slipped defeated merchants a coin or two when no one was looking.

The sound of a twig snapping underfoot caused her to look up from reattaching what was to be her third button of the evening so far. Oralia hadn't bothered with a fire and, alone, sitting quietly in the dark outside her tent, she would be difficult to discern from her surroundings. A warning shout would only call attention to herself. She waited instead, watching as a cloaked form stole from the opposite side of camp toward her.

The hood helped, but there was no mistaking that white hair. His stealthiness wasn't for her benefit, however. From the way Faris approached, not bothering to duck or creep between the trees, his trek around the backside of her camp had been to ensure he wasn't followed, not to catch Oralia by surprise. Fauns did not possess superb night vision. Their eyesight was a step above humans at best. But Oralia was certain Faris Belfast saw nearly everything, including her position on the ground.

He stopped short of her and pulled a match from his pocket, lighting the cigarette hanging from his mouth. For a brief moment, the flare of flame highlighted his broad nose and scruffy jawline. "Evening," he greeted as enthusiastically as someone learning dinner was watered-down cabbage soup for the fifth day in a row.

Oralia unclasped the needle from between her lips and commenced her stitching. "Mister Belfast."

"You know, this is not how I pictured you spending your nights," Faris said, cupping his elbow in one hand and holding his cigarette shoulder-height with the other. His glassy gaze swept across the dark tree forms. "It almost makes you relatable. Is that why you're doing it in the dark? Wouldn't want anyone to suspect beneath all that gruff, you're just an ordinary person. Split seams and all."

"I do not require light. Orcs possess excellent night vision."

"Still, shouldn't you have a designated person to do this for you?"

"Are you volunteering?"

"You know I don't do actual work," he snorted. "I could have Rasp take a crack at it for you. That is, if you don't mind your entire wardrobe being reduced to cut-offs."

It couldn't be any worse than Rali's needlework. The few times the dwarf had been left in charge of her own mending, she'd managed to stitch her sleeves shut. "My aunt was a seamstress," Oralia said. "When she learned I had been named the next Protector of the Realm, she swore she would die of embarrassment if I was ever seen in public with split britches. She claimed her reputation was at stake and made me vow to carry a needle and thread with me at all times."

Poor Aunt Maeve had done the best she could. She'd taken Oralia and Ashwyn in when their father passed and raised them as the unruly daughters she never wanted. Set on teaching them an honest trade, Maeve spent many an afternoon attempting to impart the importance of a well-executed back-stitch. Oralia picked it up naturally, even helping with the influx of orders during the busy season. Ashwyn proved incapable of learning anything outside of stabbing Oralia in the thigh with pins. Aunt Maeve eventually gave up and sent her to go terrorize the baker boy next door instead.

Satisfied with the sturdiness of her button stitch, Oralia clipped the excess thread and selected a pair of trousers from her work pile that were far too small to be her own. "Did you find anything in Monk's tent?"

Faris took another drag from his cigarette and held it. He expelled the sweet cherry smoke through his nostrils and after a moment said, "Not anything incriminating. There were a few letters." Faris produced a slim stack of folded parchment from his pocket. He regarded Oralia's wary expression as if it were an insult to his intelligence. "I made copies on my own paper, obviously. I didn't take the originals."

"Thank you, Faris. Well done. You may put them by my finished pile." Oralia watched to see if his expression would change. Rali thrived on the compliment, whereas Ellisar operated best with a stern rebuking. Snag preferred favors over words, and Curly simply wanted to feel important. Everyone had something that made them tick. Faris acted like money was his primary motivation, but Oralia suspected otherwise. He played the game because he liked the game. What's more, he was *good* at it. A skill that would either make him an exceptional ally or an exceptionally brief hindrance.

She was hedging her bet on the former. Enlisting Faris had been a gamble, she knew that. But tasking him with sleuthing through Captain Monk's belongings had been a matter of testing the waters rather than an actual assignment.

Faris pawed the dirt with his hoof. Not one for compliments, it seemed, as his reaction was a snort shy of disgust. Interesting. He wasn't leaving, either. Which was unusual, given his aptitude for unspoken commands.

"Is there another reason you are here, Faris?"

Faris gnawed the rolled end of his cigarette paper, still refusing to make eye contact with her. "You said to tell you if I noticed something."

She was surprised, actually. Oralia hadn't expected him to keep to his word. Either his information was nonessential, or it was just troubling enough to involve her. Judging from the deep rings under his pale eyes, it had been keeping him awake. "Telling involves speaking, Faris," she reminded him after a stretch of silence passed between them that tested even her appreciation for stoic pauses.

"Look, I don't like this, okay? I prefer being the one holding all the cards. Trusting someone else to know what I know and not bend me over a barrel with it—" An involuntary shudder worked down his neck. "I don't know you. Protector Dawnsight is a carefully constructed façade. She is a handful of different things to different people and I haven't figured out which of those are real, if any."

Nor would he. In the unsteady world of shifting alliances, secrets, and betrayal, staying aloof was the only way to walk away unscathed. Oralia said none of this, of course. She only had to wait—all while wishing she wasn't currently sewing a patch to the torn seat of someone's thermals. The mending made her silence seem less hostile. Perhaps she could find a knife that needed sharpening. Intimidation was so much more impactful when you had a blade in hand.

"I've already made up my mind," Faris said. "I'll tell you what I know, but I want honesty in return."

"What you ask is fair."

"Noncommittal answer. Don't think I didn't notice." He eyed her for the briefest of moments. Either unwilling or incapable of holding her stare, his gaze drifted aimlessly once more. After another puff on his cigarette, he continued. "The emissary is a seeker. The division's best one, I suspect. Capable of draining a witch of their power and using it for herself."

Oralia kept the surprise from her face. She kept personal tabs on the Division of Divination, particularly their more powerful members. Seekers warranted less attention. As a whole, they were several steps less useful than a full-blown witch and were, consequently, easier to dispose of. Oralia knew most of the active seekers by name in the event she had the misfortune of encountering one. Daana Lazuli had never appeared on any of Oralia's lists. Daana certainly played her part of the fumbling, clueless girl well. Oralia had suspected some form of underhandedness, but she assumed it was Geralt exploiting the girl's naivety. Apparently, Oralia was the naive one.

"We have seekers come to our village," Faris carried on. "It used to be every third spring, and then every other, and now, with the shortage of magic, they come the moment the pass clears. There are ways to hide a witch. I'm doing what I can to keep her off Rasp's trail."

"Is she here for him?"

"I don't think so. From what she said, she's hunting something called the Palace Ghost. Heard of it?"

Whisper.

The steady weave of the needle in Oralia's fingers paused. Was this why her friend was avoiding her? Perhaps the seeker was getting too close for comfort. Surely Whisper already knew about Daana. Whisper meddled so deeply in the Division of Divination, they knew more about the inner workings than its own members. Why hadn't Whisper said anything? While Oralia allowed considerable leniency with what Whisper did in their own time, this was something she should have been made aware of.

Oralia, remembering she promised transparency, offered it to Faris in the most vague manner possible. "I have heard of the ghost, yes. Anyone who steps foot in the palace has the misfortune of hearing the speaker's theories on the subject. He can go on for hours." If Oralia was better humored, she might have enjoyed listening to Geralt's irrefutable "facts" about the Palace Ghost. She had a reputation to uphold, however, and was expected to shut him down the moment he opened his mouth. A task Oralia treated with great relish. "Tell me, Faris, how did you come by this information?"

"Daana told me." He grinned, adding, "After I threatened to blackmail her."

"With what exactly?"

"Telling you. Consequently, I'm working for her now. Ghost hunting, fun, right?"

Not if Faris actually understood what he was up against. Whisper enjoyed their games, but the moment they got bored, or worse, stopped winning, the fun turned deadly.

Faris pawed at the ground, oblivious to Oralia's thoughts. "Call me crazy, but I think there's something to this ghost stuff. In fact, I suspect whatever it is Daana's chasing might be throwing her powers off. Rasp's decent at hiding what he is, but no seeker should be this incompetent at their job."

"You think it is hiding him? Why would it do that?" The question was for Faris's sake, not hers. His observation, astute as it was, was supposed to come as a surprise, after all. Oralia already knew the answer. Whisper was interfering because they'd already found Rasp and did not wish to share him.

"I was hoping you could tell me, actually."

Oralia lifted her eyes to meet his unusually calm stare. Faris was getting better, she had to give him that. A week ago, he would not have been able to hold her steely gaze for more than a few seconds. "I am not the ghost, Faris."

"No, you're not. That would be ridiculous. You're an orc. A species not generally known for their ability to wield magic." He tilted his horns at her. "But you are good at telling other people what to do. Does it apply to ghosts, I wonder?"

In all her years—Oralia thought—over half a century of careful, careful planning, and it had finally come to this. For the first time, someone on the outside had seen past the masquerade. That was the thing about good people, or at least those that fancied themselves good. They thought they could recognize good from bad. Say the right words, behave the way they expected, and you could fool almost every one of them. A crook, though, a decent one—suspicious and cunning, someone like Faris—they didn't have that problem. They noticed the discrepancies that no one else did.

Faris Belfast saw Oralia as only few had. Humans had a saying for this type of phenomena: takes one to know one.

"I've got to give credit where credit is due, Protector. This reputation you've manufactured, it's genius, really. You've got everyone, including Daana, so utterly convinced you hate magic, no one's ever stopped to wonder why you carry a powerstone around your neck."

Oralia set aside her mending and rose. It wasn't a threatening gesture, but when you towered nearly two feet over your adversary, it could easily be mistaken as such. A glimpse of moonlight broke between the clouds and filtered through the treetops, illuminating the ground around them in patches of eerie, pale light. The boughs rustled overhead in the wind as Oralia took her time, allowing the sounds of the night to fill the silence.

"It's good Daana won't start to wonder then, isn't it, Faris?"

"Did you just use contra—" Faris's head lifted as the words trailed from his open mouth. He stared up at her, eyes wide with awe. "My gods, this is the real you, isn't it? Finally!"

Oralia lifted the corner of her lip. A flash of her upper teeth conveyed her position more effectively than words.

"Alright, alright. This should go without saying, but if it makes you feel better to hear it, I hereby solemnly swear not to tell Daana." Faris shifted his weight from one hoof to the other. He seemed to have realized he'd reached the end of her leniency and offered a fleeting smile in return. "But I am curious. How do you do it? That stone controls the ghost, I know that much. How come I'm the only one that seems to have noticed? I mean for gods' sakes, the answer is right in front of them and nobody sees it. Is it enchanted?

Or are people so afraid of the truth they'd rather close their eyes and believe what you want them to?"

"My, oh my. Clever little cuss, isn't he?"

Faris, unequipped with night vision, had not seen the shadow that slunk from the underbrush toward them. The faun whipped his head in the direction of the voice and froze, finding himself eye-to-eye with another. The indigo-colored face smiling back at him was elfin, with pinched features and long, elegant ears.

The blue lips peeled back in an even broader smile, revealing teeth that had no business being in an elf's mouth. "It's fae magic, if you must know. Impossible to see unless you are expecting to see it. You see a powerstone. Everyone else sees a pretty little pendant." Whisper's silvery eyes darted in Oralia's direction. "Curious little lamb, no? Might be time to consider slating this one for the slaughterhouse."

"Faris." Oralia gazed deep into the faun's terror-stricken eyes. She spoke the words firmly, giving him time to carefully consider them. "Do not run."

CHAPTER FORTY-SIX

Spy

O h, come now, old friend. Don't ruin my fun," Whisper tutted. They leaned closer, whispering into Faris's ear loud enough for Oralia to overhear, "Do it. Run. You're quick, no? Let's see which of us is faster."

"Whisper, *no.*"

The fae ignored Oralia, watching Faris like a cat debating whether it wanted to devour its prey or bat it around between its paws first. "Go on. I'll give you a head start."

Oralia could smell the sour stench of fear and sweat emanating from Faris. Against every prey instinct screaming at him to bolt, the faun remained where he was. He tore his gaze from Whisper long enough to search Oralia's face. "If it's all the same to you, I'd like to go with the option that doesn't involve being hunted. If I move, it's only to stand a little closer to you, yeah? Your ghost looks hungry."

Whisper did not eat their victims. And yet, there was no mistaking the carnivorous gleam in the fae's eager expression. No doubt it was intentional. Between the three of them, the fae was outmatched in both size and strength. A stiff breeze could have lifted Whisper from the ground. Whisper's unnerving smile made it clear that any lack of physical prowess would not be an issue. It was not often Whisper had an audience, and they seemed hellbent on making the most of the opportunity.

Oralia placed her hand on Faris's shoulder. It served two purposes. Firstly, to ensure the faun did not have a sudden change of heart and break for the trees. Secondly, it was to make it clear that Faris was under her protection. A nonverbal marking of territory, as it were. Minus the scent marking, of course, because no respectable person went around pissing on things. Except that time Ellisar got Curly very, very drunk and he mistook someone's battle helm for a chamber pot. But that was once, and respectable wasn't a word that applied to either of them anyway.

Focus! By the gods, her thoughts really were all over the place tonight. "Dear Whisper, heed my words. Faris is not to be harmed. Do you understand?"

"Irrefutably." Whisper selected a quill from the cascade of white, spined hair spilling down their shoulders and flicked it at Faris. The projectile stuck into the faun's thick neck with ease. Choking on his gargled protest, unable to form the sounds into words, Faris staggered a step and then dropped.

Oralia should have tried to catch him, but at the moment she dared not lift her gaze from Whisper. "That is the exact opposite of what I just said!"

"You said not to harm. There was no mention of incapacitation." Stooping, the fae plucked the white quill protruding from Faris's neck with what might have been painstaking care. Whisper's scaled hand disappeared into their cloak and reappeared seconds later, sans quill. Oralia did not care to guess where exactly the projectile had gone. When it came to magical cloaks, it was best not to employ logic.

Faris didn't move. Couldn't, actually. Every muscle in his body was coiled tight, like a spring-loaded trap rusted shut. Wide-eyed, he stared up at Oralia. His mouth parted, but all that came forth was a pitiful squeak.

"Temporary paralysis," Whisper explained with a roguish smile. Even standing in a pool of filtered moonlight, they were difficult to see. The fae's scaled hide did not reflect light, but absorbed it, making them appear nothing more than a shadow. A useful trait when one spent their life moving in darkness. "You'll regain muscle control shortly. If you're lucky, that is. In the meantime, try not to swallow your tongue."

"Has your mind finally slipped?" Oralia demanded as heat leapt to her face. Her skin was molten to the touch. Any moment now, she was certain she would feel steam pluming from her ears. "You were supposed to remain hidden. This is the second person you have revealed yourself to in as many days."

"Come now, old friend. Many have seen me over the years." The quills running down Whisper's neck rattled in a disquieting manner. "The trick is to ensure they don't live to talk about it."

"You cannot kill Faris."

"But I can. It would be very easy, in fact."

This was the problem when working with fae. If there was a workaround, you could be damned sure they would find it. Oralia clicked her tusks. "No harm will come to Faris. You are forbidden from killing, maiming, or influencing his death. And in the future, do not incapacitate him without my permission. Do you understand?"

Faris emitted another squeak.

"Congratulations on finding the Palace Ghost, Mister Belfast. Grunt once if you agree to keep this information between us. I would hate to retract my prior statement."

Still glaring, possibly with twice the fury as before, Faris managed a weak sound that Oralia took as a yes.

"I really do dislike that name," Whisper said. "Ghosts are spiritual, not magical. It's entirely illogical."

Oralia pinned Whisper beneath her stare. "You still have not given me your word."

"About what again? Good grief! How do you deal with all of these stickers?" Whisper said, picking the thorns from their sleeves with annoyance. The fae's thin, wispy body was hidden beneath a strange assortment of loose garments. The only article of clothing Oralia could identify with any certainty was the velvet cloak that shifted color with a will of its own, ranging from deep maroon to purple to black. "I can't step one foot into the trees without coming out looking like a pin cushion."

The irony was not lost on Oralia that even without the aid of stickers, Whisper already resembled a pincushion. "Do not deflect."

Whisper smoothed the scales on their arm, sighing, "I did what you asked. It cannot be helped if you disagree with my results. My answer is what it is."

Whisper could talk riddles around her all night. Straight to the point was the only way for Oralia to gain ground. "First, assure me that you understand Faris is off limits. And then you may tell me why you broke your cover."

"Oh, very well." Whisper gestured to the faun with an overly extravagant and completely mocking bow. "I give you, the spy. And let me tell you, this one is a slippery devil. Should have been born a trickster."

Oralia tilted her chin upward, fighting the sudden urge to rip her hair out by the handful. "Well done, Dear Whisper. I have a few notes. Perhaps next time you could start with finding a spy that is *not* one of my own?"

Whisper tilted their head curiously. The effect was something akin to an owl rotating its neck until its mouth was nearly level with its large, intelligent eyes. "Not just yours, old friend."

There was a ragged laugh and, to Oralia's surprise, she discovered it was coming from Faris. Judging from the perplexed expression stretched across

Whisper's face, the fact that Faris could already produce such a noise was highly suspicious to them, too. Whisper's incapacitation spell usually took hours to wear off, not minutes.

Faris rolled forward. He still did not have full command of his body, but the fact that he was able to push himself into a half-sit was highly impressive. He noticed their stricken faces and offered one of his winning smiles. "Funny thing about iron." He reached into his coat pocket and produced a rusted token, rolling it between his fingers in a manner that might have been mesmerizing had his movements not been so painfully slow. "It's brittle as shit, but surprisingly effective against fae magic. Mum never let us go into the woods without it."

Whisper's silvery eyes flared as they looked to Oralia, finally spilling what they knew. "The faun is colluding with the emissary. He takes your money and he takes hers. On top of that, he's been making secret deals with your faithful four. And he has the Stoneclaw so wrapped around his finger he could turn the boy on you in a second. The faun is not on your side, old friend. This one has no side. He works them equally."

Oralia held up her hand, staying Faris before he could spoil her questioning. "Emissary, you say?"

"Yes."

"And if I asked if Lady Lazuli was here for any reason other than as emissary to the Iron Ridge, what would you say then, Whisper?"

"I'd say that was a very open-ended question, and you could do better," Whisper replied smartly.

Ah, equivocation. A fae's favorite tactic when they didn't want to answer directly. "I know what Daana is. And I know what she is looking for here. Why did you hide this from me?"

Whisper dropped uncharacteristically silent.

Due to the nature of their contract, Whisper could not lie to Oralia. That didn't mean they told the truth; not all of it, anyway. Her friend omitted information when it suited them. It wasn't personal. When the system was inherently flawed, you learned to work it. Oralia did the same with her fellow figureheads. It was simple survival. The point of survival, however, was to do it better than everyone else and reining Whisper in was proving more difficult than usual.

"Faris already told me about his deal with Lady Lazuli." Oralia watched Whisper's stony expression for tells. "You were not expecting that, were you? Did you really think I would kill him for conning her? Conning is what

Mister Belfast does. A skill I find useful, by the way. Why did I have to learn Daana is a seeker from him, when it should have come from you?"

The fae threw their arms into the air dramatically. "She isn't your concern! You asked me to find your spy, nothing else. The young Lazuli is a pet project. I would appreciate it if you didn't interfere."

"Is your pet project a threat?"

"She is a necessity." It took only a few moments for Whisper's resolve to wilt into submission. "Fine. You're not going to let up. If you must know, there is an inordinate amount of magic on the ridge. I lured the young Lazuli onto the trip in order to keep my own powers in balance. If at any point the magic becomes too much for me to take on, I can channel the excess to her."

Magic was a give and take. And in Whisper's case, a quite literal one. Their kind did not feed in the same way as mortals. They survived by absorbing the magic around them. Too little, and a fae would wither away to nothing; too much, and their power became uncontrollable. In an effort to avoid following the path of their predecessors, the old ones, Dear Whisper's kind had found creative ways to maintain the balance. This included sharing their magic, which, alas, had led to the eventual downfall of the fae species.

"And you can do this without her suspecting?"

Whisper's white spines rattled down the back of their neck with disdain. "Do not treat me like a child, old friend. I know what I am doing."

"Very well." For the moment, Oralia conceded the matter. Concession, however, did not spare Whisper from the rest of her questions. "Then you may enlighten me about the Stoneclaw. I know you helped him set Ellisar on fire. And while I am certain you could weave a very convincing excuse for doing so, I am more concerned with your motivation. What are your intentions with Rasp?"

Apparently, under the right circumstances, even a several-thousand-year-old fae could look like a street rat caught picking your pocket. Whisper's petulant expression dropped as a hint of panic swept across their scaled face. They chose their words with slow, methodical care. "My intention was to save him and keep your mission from falling to the wayside."

"You are going to do better than that."

CHAPTER FORTY-SEVEN

The Trickster Pair

Whisper opened and closed their mouth several times as they chose an answer and then immediately withdrew it from consideration again, reminding Oralia of some kind of blue, spine-covered fish. At last, the fae settled on an answer that was as truthful as it was impossibly vague. "Fine. If you must know, I wish to train him."

"Why?"

This time their reply was prepared. Whisper stood straighter, clasping their hands behind their back. "I've decided to take on an apprentice."

"Why?" Oralia's part was easy. She only had to repeat the same question until the fae offered a satisfactory response. "You hate people," she added. Particularly those of the mouthy variety. And Rasp Stoneclaw was nothing but mouth.

"Nonsense, old friend. I don't hate all people. Only the annoying ones."

As far as Oralia was aware, that still included nearly everyone.

Further silence prompted more out of the reluctant fae. "I am the last of my species. And I am old. I never understood why the others insisted on helping mortal-kind. But the realization that if I don't, my people's knowledge will be lost forever, weighs on me."

"So you chose Rasp?" Faris cut in.

He was still seated on the ground, staring at his unresponsive legs with absolute concentration, as if sheer willpower alone would be enough to get them moving again. Faris's tone sounded torn between laughing and screaming. "Who, one, hates witches possibly more than he hates himself and, two, is human. Humans have a life expectancy of what? Eighty years? Ninety, maybe? What's the point of having an apprentice who, by the time you finally get him to learn anything, will keel over of old age?"

Whisper squinted sharply at Faris, attempting to dissect him with their eyes from the looks of it.

"He has a valid point," Oralia agreed. "Several, actually."

"Yes, I too can count." The edge of Whisper's mouth was lifted in a half-snarl, revealing several pointed teeth. "Hatred can be softened. Ignorance corrected. And, as far as lifespans are concerned, my kind is the expert at stretching those beyond mortal means. So long as the little bird is willing to learn, I am willing to teach."

"Does that include shapeshifting?" Faris wondered. "How about your dragon form? Can you teach him that?"

Oralia tensed at the word *dragon*. No wonder Whisper wanted the faun dead.

The early world had been populated by many types of fae. Most of them died out around the dawn of mortal-kind. The survival of those who still walked the land was dependent on two cardinal rules: Never disclose your true name, and never disclose your species. Knowing their name meant a fae could be controlled. Knowing their species meant they could be killed. Faris, somehow, some way, knew what Whisper was. There was such a thing as too clever, and Faris Belfast was currently skirting that line.

"No." Whisper exchanged an accusatory glance with Oralia. They were undoubtedly thinking the same thing as her. They were also, very likely, already running scenarios through their head that both appeased Oralia's "do not kill" order and rendered Faris dead. "The Stoneclaw is not fae, don't be daft. And if what you are suggesting was true, a shapeshifter would need to be in possession of their full power in order to assume their dragon form."

"I see. Can't perform without your stone, is that it? They've got herbs for that, you know."

Whisper's quills rattled, warning Faris to quit while he was still ahead.

The daring faun continued anyway. He lifted a finger, asking, "Quick question. Can you communicate with other dragons? Like, I don't know, say sky shrieks, for example?"

Abandoning all sense of subtlety, Whisper looked directly at Oralia, almost pleadingly. "It would be so easy. One little nick to the throat. Gone forever. He won't feel a thing, you have my word."

"No, Whisper. You cannot kill him. And Faris brings up a point I had not yet considered. You did not trigger the dragon attack yesterday, did you?" Was it mere coincidence that Rasp had been separated from the main party? It suddenly seemed highly suspicious that Whisper found him along the river first.

"No! I did not!" Whisper stomped away and returned as angry, if not more than before. The white quills on their head were bristled high in the air, making them appear several inches taller. To an outsider, this might have appeared threatening. To Oralia, it looked more like a toddler having a tantrum. "I had to break my cover in order to save the little bird. And because of it, I've now got a blasted seeker hot on my tail."

"If you had told me about Daana sooner, I could have helped. In the future, I will do my utmost to keep her distracted." Oralia realized they'd not only gotten off subject, but had drifted entire continents away. "We are not finished discussing Rasp. I am reluctant to let you train him. He can be a nuisance when he wants to be. Teaching him to use his power has the potential to elevate him into something more."

"A dull knife is more dangerous than a sharp one. My training ensures not only his safety, but that of the entire party. Unless he is taught proper control, the little bird will present a problem the moment we reach the mountain." Whisper tried, without success, to smooth the raised indigo scales on their armor-plated arm. "I know your reluctance to believe in superstition, but there is something ancient and powerful that lurks on the ridge. The darkness calls to him, old friend. I can feel it. It will only grow stronger as we draw closer. If you would like for the old stories to stay just that and not become reality, you will not hinder my work."

The sixth son, born of a mighty Stoneclaw leader, shall inherit the silver-hair and bring destruction and darkness to the world. Oralia had never put any faith into prophecies. But if it had Whisper on edge, perhaps it was time to start. Was this it? Was the mission over before it had even started? Of course it would be a blasted witch that sparked the apocalypse!

"All is not lost, old friend. People only ever remember the token prophecies that come to fruition, never the hundreds that do not." Whisper said, as though they'd read Oralia's thoughts. "Allow me to mentor the boy and I will ensure he does not become a problem. You get your escape route through the mountains and I get my apprentice."

She decided against correcting Whisper's use of "escape route" for fear of drawing attention to it.

Unfortunately, her hesitation allowed Whisper the opportunity to follow up with something substantially worse. "You are afraid of his power, understandably. Fear not. I will not hesitate to cut him down if the little bird proves too unwieldy."

Oralia did not miss the flinch that could be glimpsed on Faris's face.

Dammit. Why couldn't Rasp have stuck to being an ill-tempered political puppet? Oralia had enough difficulty maintaining control of one magical nuisance. She loathed the idea of adding another to the already unstable mix. She sighed, digging her knuckles deep into her temples. "Rasp set Ellisar on fire. That makes him a fire elemental, yes?"

"Yes," Whisper said, perhaps too quickly.

"What else is he?" She peered down at Whisper from between her hands, narrowing her eyes. "That is not the limit of his powers. You would not be so interested in him if it were. Spare me the runaround and tell me what he is. In *detail*, please."

One by one, the quills on Whisper's head flattened against the back of their head. With a grudging sigh, the fae gave in. "Traditionally, when a human elemental is first trained, they are taught to hone one element. They spend years learning to wield it, shutting their powers off to all of the others. Sometimes, a very talented elemental can pick up another later, but the older they get, the more difficult it becomes to reopen those pathways. The little bird never learned to draw from a single source. He can pull from all of them. Granted, he has no idea how to use it once he does, but the potential is there."

"I have never heard of such a thing." Oralia did not doubt Whisper's words; if her dear friend said it was possible, then surely it was. It was merely a disturbing realization that such power existed. More so, that it was in the hands of Rasp Stoneclaw. Oh, how the end of civilization seemed to loom but a little bit closer.

Faris had gone strangely quiet, Oralia noticed. She wondered what was running through his head. Nothing good, from the looks of it. "Am I to believe that you truly have Rasp's best interest in mind, Dear Whisper?"

"Yes."

"And if it conflicts with my best interest?"

Whisper's eyes said, *"You're the one holding my powerstone."* Whisper's mouth offered a more diplomatic, "I will defer to you, as always."

It would have to do. Whisper would do as they promised, Oralia had no doubt. She also did not doubt there were many things Whisper intended to do which they were not saying. Oh well. With any luck, she would be long gone before the spark hit the tinder. It would be Geralt Lazuli's fight by then, not hers. One he'd had coming for a long time.

In the meantime, Oralia would have to settle for keeping Whisper on their toes. "Good, because if you truly want what is best for Rasp, you will acknowledge that Faris plays a vital role in his wellbeing."

"I could—"

Oralia silenced the fae with a stern look. "No. You are forbidden from killing Faris and assuming his likeness. Do not bring it up again."

Faris swiveled his head at Whisper, mouth slack with horror. "You were going to do *what?*"

Whisper offered what Oralia swore was a shrug. It appeared entirely out of place on an immortal being. "You would be dead. You would have no further need of it."

"People would notice."

"You would think. So far it has yet to be a problem."

"Except we're talking about Rasp here. Believe me, the moment you miss one dick joke, he's going to know you're not me."

Whisper's expression was that of someone who'd just bit into a lemon, expecting an orange. Although their gaze had not lifted from Faris, their words were directed at Oralia. "I still vote we kill him."

"I have a better idea," she said. "The two of you will work together. I have full confidence that as a team you will be able to root out the actual spy and keep Daana at a heavily distracted distance, all while preventing Rasp from becoming a problem." Oralia realized they could plot together against her. But that was the magic of it. Whisper and Faris were of the same mind—trickster through and through. They'd be too preoccupied outwitting one another that there wouldn't be time to involve her. It was chaotically beautiful, really.

That, or she'd just united two agents of chaos into a single, unstoppable force, paired them with an overpowered witch, and released the trio onto an unsuspecting world. That scenario would be all chaos, none of the beauty. Unfortunately, the only way to know for certain was to throw the dice and hope everything didn't go up in flames the moment the pieces settled.

CHAPTER FORTY-EIGHT

First Blood

The moon hung high overhead by the time Daana reached the edge of camp. The front of her cloak was encrusted with spruce sap, needles, and more than one spiderweb—whose creator she feverishly hoped was still back in the trees and not crawling down the inside of her hood. Checking to be sure the watch was focused elsewhere, she slipped between the rows of drooped tents, listening for Curly.

It didn't take much effort. She found him, several bellows later, moving along the main pathway with the confident swagger of someone used to garnering unwanted attention. Pausing only to catch her breath, she stepped out into the open and adopted her best look of innocence. Mildly annoyed innocence, at least. Curly enjoyed making her mad. It was all part of the game.

Was she breathing too hard? Most definitely. Gods, Daana hoped he didn't notice. "Are you"—*huff, huff*—"trying to attract"—*gasp*—"another dragon? Lower your voice."

"You're looking awful flushed. I didn't disturb something private, did I?" Curly asked with a toothy smile. Hopeful, probably, that he had.

The barrage of volatile replies stampeding through her thoughts were all too wordy to get out efficiently. Daana settled for something less verbose and to the point. "Do you want something, Baby Face?"

"I told you to stop calling me that."

"You did, didn't you?" She paused for a few thoughtful seconds, making it clear that she would not be offering an apology on the matter. The effect probably would have been more impressive if she wasn't currently sucking in lungfuls of cool night air like a fish out of water. "I'm still waiting for you to tell me what you want."

"You got your bookbag on you, right? Why am I even asking? Of course you do. You're a little book grub."

"That's not even a thi—"

"Yeah, yeah, come on." Curly turned and gestured for her to follow. "Sascha sent me to fetch you. You can yammer my ear off on the way."

Reluctantly, Daana fell in step beside him. "The cook? Since when do you take orders from him?"

"I don't!" His dark scowl faded away almost as quickly as it had come. Curly lifted one massive shoulder in a shrug, mumbling, "He asked nicely, is all. Even called me sir."

Ah, motivated by authority then. When he was the authority, at least. That could be useful when it came to gathering further information. *Dear sir, do tell me all your secrets. Sir, what is your boss planning? Sir, why do I feel warm and fluttery when I call you sir?*

Daana's eyes snapped wide open, horrified by her own thoughts. Nope, nope, nope. She was going to bury that last one way, way deep down and never think about it again.

The makeshift canteen was much more crowded than it had been that morning. Curly pressed through the cluster of soldiers and Daana hurried after, trailing in his wake. Unlike her, the orc simply moved in whatever direction he wished and the crowd parted around him, sometimes by choice and sometimes by the orc's preferred method, force. Curly made good use of his broad shoulders as he plowed through the dinner mob, employing a diplomatic elbow to an unsuspecting ribcage when necessary.

They were about halfway to the kitchen lean-to when some sixth sense demanded Daana's attention. She turned and watched, mystified, as several soldiers ganged up around a solitary figure near the edge of the gathering. She normally stayed out of soldier politics, but the sixth sense tugged harder. Something about the situation was off. And, after a careful reexamination of the scene, she realized why. The victim, a poor, wide-eyed wretch, wasn't a soldier. It was Rasp Stoneclaw. He stood with his back bent and teeth bared, pulling at something in his hands and looking every ounce like a cornered animal.

Why wasn't he backing down? Surely even the mountain man knew when the odds were stacked too high against him. And then, to Daana's horror, she realized Rasp's left hand was shackled to a log, unable to escape the impending beating. The only reason the others hadn't lit in on him yet was because no one wanted to be the first. The soldiers were still measuring each other up, silently drawing metaphoric straws to determine who among them would take the first broken nose in order to get Rasp down.

The situation was downright unfair. Daana did not know Rasp well enough to say what exactly he deserved, but surely it wasn't this.

Heat leapt to her cheeks. Before Daana could stop to consider a more tactful approach, she pushed her way through the bustling crowd. Her progress was slowed by several accidental elbows to the stomach and chest, but she made it, huffing and puffing with her sticky hair clinging to her damp forehead. Daana drew herself to her full height, which still seemed depressingly diminutive in the presence of the taller soldiers.

"Leave him alone!"

There was a moment of uneasiness as the group all looked from one to another, attempting to decipher exactly what sort of threat, if any, presented itself. Between the soldiers, there were two humans, an elf, and an orc. Daana felt her ears burn as a sudden sheepishness crept over her. Perhaps it would have been wiser to have barged into the assembly armed with something other than her bookbag.

"Yeah, leave him alone!" Rasp echoed. "Or the emissary is going to see to it you all hang!"

Oh, now the wrath of the soldiers was pointed in her direction. Great. Daana took an involuntary step backward, wringing her hands. "Uh, no. Probably not that, but—"

"Thirty lashes!"

"You're not helping," she hissed, before adjusting her expression to something that looked more diplomatic. "May I enquire as to what the problem is here, gentlemen?" A glare from the orc prompted the addition of, "And lady."

"They're pissed that they had to run extra drills because the person I happened to be chained to couldn't keep her confounded trap shut," Rasp explained, still pulling futilely at his bonds. "And now they're going to take it out on me, completely negating the fact that I was just as much of a victim as them!"

The closest human soldier bridged the gap in a single step, jabbing a finger into the center of Rasp's chest. "You're the reason we had to run drills in the first place!"

Rasp didn't flinch. Strangely, he didn't retaliate either. He only titled his head in the offender's direction and said, "Maybe the next time the guide shouts 'get off the road, there's a fucking dragon,' you'll listen."

"Fuck you!"

Daana screamed at the swinging soldier to stop, but Rasp needed no saving. With a resigned roll of his eyes, he ducked the swing and slammed his elbow into the man's gut. Seizing him by the back of the neck, Rasp shoved his opponent's head down and lifted his knee. The impact itself was relatively soundless, unlike the soldier's gargled screams. With blood streaming down his face, the man crumpled into a whimpering heap at Rasp's feet.

"Look what you made me do! That was my longest pacifistic streak yet, and you broke it!" Rasp's fingers clenched and unclenched in frustration as his eyes searched the space around him, attempting to find the others before they found him. "I am seriously not in the mood! Now kindly fuck off, the lot of you!"

The orc was halfway into a lunge when a heavy hand clamped over her shoulder, fixing her in place. The snarl vanished from the soldier's twisted mouth when she glanced behind her into the bigger, far more menacing smile of Curly. "Three-on-one's not very fair," Curly said. "Why don't you invite a few more of your friends so I don't have to do this with one arm behind my back, yeah?"

"Hey!" Rasp stomped his heel, narrowly missing the soldier curled into a ball at his feet. "You couldn't have intervened any sooner?"

"And get accused of drawing first blood? Not after what happened to you and Rali. I figured there should be at least one body on the ground before I started cracking skulls."

"You know what? Just for that, I changed my mind. Start your own damn fight. This one's mine."

"You're unarmed and chained to a log. What are you going to do, give them splinters?"

"Parasites, actually. Your goblin friend says I'm teeming with 'em. I just got to break the skin with my teeth a little, and bam, they'll have hookworms munching pathways through their brains in no time. Now . . ." Rasp clapped his hands to draw the attention of the others. "Are we going to do this single file, or will all of you rush the blind man at once?"

Everyone else dropped silent as Curly argued over why he should be allowed to partake in the impending bloodbath. From the corner of her eye, Daana did not miss the way the soldiers began to slowly inch backward. Ganging up on a shackled mountain man was one thing. Willingly facing down the largest member of the faithful four was something else entirely. Suicide, probably.

"Come now, Curly. I'm sure skull-cracking won't be necessary." Daana seized upon their hesitation, ignoring the waver in her voice. Her legs wobbled like jelly and the inside of her stomach was performing acrobatic flips, but she damn sure wasn't going to let anyone else know that. Daana fought to keep her tone flat, ignoring the urge to duck behind something more solid. "Now we all clearly saw this poor man slip and hit his head—"

"And land on my foot." Rasp pressed his boot into the downed man, producing another pained whimper. The soldier was lucky the Stoneclaw was blind. Daana suspected Rasp's heel would have gone straight for the groin had he been capable of finding it.

"—and land on Rasp's foot," Daana said, shooting daggers at him with her eyes. A futile effort, she remembered too late. "Now, before anyone else has a similar accident, I think it would be best for the three of you to pack up your friend here and get him examined. That nose looks like it could be a serious break."

Nobody moved. Except for Rasp, who had since replanted both feet firmly on the ground and was shifting his weight from one leg to the other, smiling like a madman. Curly was processing the situation at a more thoughtful rate. His lips moved as he silently repeated her words in his head, having trouble deciphering whether or not there was going to be any actual action.

Daana decided it would be best to move things along before he realized she was giving the soldiers a way out. "Did I mention Curly here is on excellent terms with the new medic? No? Oh, well let me tell you, Chief Medical Officer Flint is brilliant with the scalpel. He'll have your comrade right as rain in no time."

Curly suddenly felt eager to contribute. "She's not kidding. Have a look at this!" He peeled back a layer of chainmail and thick wool to reveal a hideous scar snaking from sternum to navel. "Impressive right? I mean, Snag's the one that gutted me in the first place, but it's neat patchwork, yeah?"

Daana tried not to look at it for fear of turning green. Whether the underlying threat in Curly's message was intentional or not, it was having the desired effect. The elf soldier was looking at the others and shaking his head in a not-so-subtle manner. Realizing that in order to collect their fallen companion, the trio would have to move within Rasp's range, Daana decided an olive branch was in order. "Mister Stoneclaw, if you would kindly step away from that poor man, they'll be able to drag him away much easier."

"Easy? Why would I make this easy for them? You want him?" Rasp lowered his stance into an eager crouch. "Come get him."

This elicited an unexpected laugh from Curly. He bent at the knees, gathered Rasp's log in his arms and walked it several paces backward, pulling the struggling Stoneclaw with him. "Gods, all this rage from someone who's so itty bitty. Where do you contain it all?"

"No, no, no, dammit!" Rasp dropped to the ground and flailed with his legs, attempting, and failing, to kick the soldiers while they were still in range. "Alright, alright, we'll share! You get one and the rest are mine!"

With Rasp removed from striking distance, the elf and human darted forward, gathered the fallen soldier under the arms, and heaved his whimpering body away. The orc trailed after them, casting infuriated glances over her shoulder at Rasp as she went. The ordeal had not gone unnoticed, though with the promise of a show fading, the attention of the curious onlookers soon drifted elsewhere.

When a sufficient amount of time had passed, Rasp stopped flopping like a landed trout on the bank and whispered, "They're gone now, right?"

Daana felt her lungs fill with air for what felt like the first time in minutes. "Yes."

"Oh thank gods. I thought I was going to die."

"What are you talking about?" Ensuring Rasp was out of the way, Curly dropped the heavy branch back onto the ground with a solid thump. "I just had to drag you out of a fight like a mad dog on a leash!"

"It's called intimidation, dum-dum. I get to save face and they might just think twice about starting shit next time. Besides, it wasn't them I was worried about. Do you know what would happen if I got caught fighting twice in the same day? It'd be your boss who did the killing."

"Who are you and what have you done to Rasp?"

"I don't know. I just don't have it in me anymore. I think I might be broken." Rasp gathered his knees to his chest and slumped into them. He stared straight ahead, as if in a daze. "Emissary Lazuli—"

Dear gods, this was the first time he had used her name correctly. Irrefutable proof that the little fiend had been saying it wrong on purpose all along! Realizing she was probably supposed to be listening, Daana tuned back in to catch the rest of Rasp's words.

"—stupid of you. Like really stupid. You know those were soldiers, right? Armed to the teeth, looking for any excuse to fight? Anyway, I guess I should probably say thanks for what you did, but I'd hate for it to go to your head so . . . good job finally being useful, then?"

Apparently he wasn't *that* broken. "You're welcome, Rasp."

Curly wiped the dirt from his hands against his trousers, glaring at the hunk of rotted wood as if it had personally insulted him. "Who'd you piss off to get chained to a log anyway?"

Log was perhaps an oversimplification. In truth, it looked as though whoever had put him there had found the largest, heaviest tree branch unsuited for firewood and secured the chain around it in a fashion even Rasp couldn't wriggle his way out of. Short of giving the man an ax, the only way to get loose would be to gnaw his hand off. An option Daana did not necessarily put past him.

Naturally, Rasp tried breaking free anyway. He gathered the chain in both hands and pulled with all of his might, managing to drag the log a fraction of an inch. "If you must know, I am currently boycotting the kitchen's hostile work conditions."

Considering the man was a hostile work condition in his own right, Daana suspected it was the kitchen doing the boycotting. Their line of questioning was cut short by the large form that waded through the crowd toward them like a slow-moving iceberg. Unlike Curly, Sascha picked his way along with the care and thought of a giant trying to navigate a beach full of turtle nests without crushing any eggs.

"Mister Stoneclaw." Sascha had a blanket slung over his shoulder and a lantern swinging from one hand. "You were left unsupervised for two minutes. Have you gone and started another fistfight already?"

"I can assure you, there were no fists involved," Rasp said from between gritted teeth. Having already given up on dragging the log with him, he now seemed set on breaking the chain. Rasp had his feet braced against the wood and was using his body as a counterweight against the manacles.

"He was getting picked on by soldiers," Curly said, conveniently leaving out the more damning portion of the incident. "It didn't get far. Her Highness went and scared them off with words."

Sascha's stare shifted to Daana and gave her an approving smile. "Did you? Well done."

Of course the first thing she'd managed to do right the entire trip so far was by complete luck. "Thanks," she murmured. "Curly says you sent for me?"

"Yes. Mister Stoneclaw was assigned to me for kitchen duty. Unfortunately, I keep finding him underfoot, which is not a good place to be when you're his size and it's my foot. I thought perhaps he could be of better use to you. Help you and Mister Flint translate that book of yours, maybe?"

"Oh, that," was all Daana managed before her better sense returned. Glancing around the crowded canteen, she was relieved to see Snag was nowhere in sight. He seemed to be a sensible fellow. Perhaps the goblin had already run for the hills. Why hadn't she thought of that? "Well, it doesn't look like he was able to make it. So I think I'll just—"

"Hold this for me, thank you," Sascha deposited the glowing lantern into Daana's hands before twisting his upper body into the direction of his lean-to. With hands cupped to his mouth, he called, "Over here, please."

A scrawny figure, backlit by the kitchen fire, stepped reluctantly from the tent. Snag trudged toward them with his arms wrapped protectively over his chest and eyes cast downward. He paid no mind to the soldiers who, like a shoal of nervous anchovies, parted to give the approaching barracuda a cautious berth.

"What do you say?" Sascha grinned, somehow missing the sudden despair that flooded Daana's face. "Ready to make some real progress on that book of yours?"

Daana offered him a brimming smile, feverishly hoping there wasn't anything green stuck in her teeth. "I feel like I couldn't possibly say no even if I wanted to."

CHAPTER FORTY-NINE

The Human Curse

Excellent! They're yours for the evening, then. Simply return the lantern when you're finished with it. As for you, Mister Stoneclaw." Sascha unslung the blanket from his shoulder and dropped it over the top of the struggling human. "Mind that tongue of yours or I will be serving it to you as breakfast."

Rasp fought his way out of the blanket. His head broke from the covers, gasping, "Yes, sir! As you say, sir! Sorry again about the potato peeler, sir!"

Daana's mouth pulled to the side quizzically. "Potato peeler?"

"A temporary lapse in judgment is all. Nothing an evening spent with the emissary can't fix," Sascha chuckled, slipping among the throng of bodies back toward the lean-to, sidestepping a very slow-moving Snag on his way.

Daana followed Sascha with her eyes, mouth agape and trembling with sudden fury. "I'm his punishment?"

Curly swiveled his head around at Rasp and placed his hands at his hips. "You shanked Sascha?"

"Accidently!" Rasp managed between heavy breaths as he braced himself against the log in another futile attempt to break the chain. His efforts, alas, were for naught. The iron, old and tarnished, held strong against his struggle. "He stepped on me and I reacted. Honestly, I felt horrible afterward. Like I'd kicked a giant, mountain-sized puppy. I might have cried more than he did."

There was a sharp pain behind Daana's eyes that hadn't been there before. It made her forehead hot and left a sort of soft buzzing in her ears. If she didn't know better, she would have sworn it magnified with every word out of Rasp's belligerent mouth. She watched the pair in the sort of way one might watch two runaway carriages barreling down a narrow street at one another. It was disastrous and yet, she couldn't look away. Alas, she was stuck with

Rasp for the moment. It would be prudent to make the most of her predicament and get some part of her assignment translated, busywork or not. Her gaze transferred to Curly, noting that he'd found a comfortable position on the ground beside Rasp.

Daana pinched the skin between her eyes and sighed. "Are you helping, too?"

"Wouldn't dream of it." The orc thumped the patch of dirt beside him, calling to Snaglebrag, who had since started to drift in the wrong direction. "Hey, don't you try to slink away! I didn't get to watch Ellisar's drills because of you. I'm getting my entertainment tonight one way or another."

Like a stray dog skulking along the edges of the communal cook pit, Snag inched nearer, but dared not draw close enough to sit. This was remedied by Curly, who seized him by the belt and yanked him roughly to the ground. "Why are you so jumpy all of a sudden?"

"We are sitting out in the open surrounded by a bunch of stab-happy halfwits. This might be your wet dream, but it's not mine. I've spent my life avoiding these types." Snag struggled free of Curly's grip, grumbling, "The village loses *one* damn chicken and it's all pitchforks and torches until my livelihood is up in flames and I'm escaping into the night with nothing to my name but the clothes on my back."

Curly placed his broad hand on Snag's shoulder, practically engulfing it. "Anyone even looks at you wrong and I'll shove their pitchfork in one ear and out the other, alright? The only one that gets to pick on you is me."

Daana placed the lantern onto the ground and set about gathering the necessary supplies from her bookbag. She reached inside and felt a tingle run up her arm as her fingertips brushed against an unfamiliar object. Checking to be sure the others were too preoccupied with their bickering to notice, she pulled the small journal free. It was bound in faded green leather and the corners of the pages had yellowed with age. She tentatively peeled the front cover back.

The first thing that struck her was the artistic scrawl of the handwriting. The curved, looping letters danced across the page in neat lines. The second thing that struck Daana was that she recognized the handwriting. *Willem?*

What the devil was this doing in her bag? Had he put it there without her noticing? But how? Her bookbag never left her side. And what was it, anyway? Daana peered closer at the first paragraph and her heart nearly leapt into her throat. She closed the book with a slam, fighting to contain the giddy smile that pulled at her lips. *Spells!*

"Don't tell me I came all this way to read your diary."

Daana's eyes grew wide, suddenly remembering there were others around her. Her gaze lifted from the spellbook to the person sitting across from her. While Rasp and Curly were still having a go at each other, Snag had his jeweled ears perked in her direction, watching Daana's every move like a grumpy alley cat disturbed from its afternoon nap.

"Oh. Uh, wrong book." Daana tucked the journal safely back into the confines of her bookbag. It took all of her willpower not to dismiss the meeting and scurry back to her tent to pore over every yellowed page until dawn. Back at Sunstorn, she had read every spellbook in the division's library thrice over and had never once come across this particular one. Meaning, of course, this was from Willem's private collection. And he'd shared it with her! They really were partners.

Snag gave up trying to pry Daana's secrets from her expression and ran a clawed hand over his face, groaning, "Explain to me what it is I'm supposed to be doing here? Sascha mentioned something about a report and my soul left my body until he was done talking."

Right. *That.* Back to work, then.

"I need your assistance translating this." After a few moments of searching, Daana withdrew the correct journal and extended it in his direction.

The book appeared substantially larger in Snag's gnarled claws. He turned it this way and that, studying the front cover with a perplexed expression which, for whatever reason, prompted him to sniff it. Whatever olfactory conclusion he came to, he didn't say. Snag laid the leather-bound journal across his knees and opened it with noticeable care. "I'll be damned. This is from the ridge, isn't it?"

"From what I was told, yes."

"The mountain folk are very protective of their things, particularly the ones that actually belong to them. How'd you get it?"

"I didn't steal it, if that's what you're implying. It was given to me by the protector to translate." Daana leaned forward, as if imparting a grave secret. "I can't help but wonder why I was awarded this assignment when you were the better choice. You do speak stolac, don't you?"

The goblin studied her for an alarming breath, his jaw locked in silent deliberation. Finally, he said, "Better choice for what? Busywork? I don't do busywork. That's what we've got Curly for." His lips drew back in an unfriendly smile. "And now you, apparently."

Called it!

An emissary couldn't say that of course, so Daana opted for an innocent sounding, "It's not pointless busywork. It's to find common ground between our peoples."

"You want common ground with the maggot? Bite his nose off."

Rasp was currently fending off Curly with a barrage of limp-wristed slaps. He whipped his head at them with a sneer curled across his lips. "Leave my nose out of this! It's the only thing my face has got working for it."

The brief swell of pride that came with being correct was short-lived. Busywork or not, she would have to complete the translation if she wanted to maintain her cover. Maybe getting outside help wasn't such a bad idea. Besides, if nothing else came of it, at least she was one step closer to her goal of infiltrating Oralia's inner circle.

"Mister Flint," Daana groaned. She touched the skin between her eyes, willing the growing ache to subside. "It was not my idea to drag you into this. If, however, you would be willing to lend your expertise, I would be forever grateful."

"Couldn't even if I wanted to. Which, to be clear, I don't." Snag met Daana's befuddled expression calmly. "I suppose that's the real reason the protector didn't give me the assignment. My stolac is limited to what you might call conversational. If, for example, I wanted to describe how I was going to tie Rasp's intestines into a noose and hang him with it, I could. This"—he held the slender book aloft—"I cannot translate. At best, I could read it to you in stolac, but don't expect me to know what the fuck any of it means."

With that horrific imagery still circulating her brain, Daana was at a temporary loss for words.

"So what's stopping you then? You read it out loud, Rasp translates, and Her Highness writes it down. Sounds pretty straightforward to me," Curly said, stroking his curved tusk. He winked at the collective outrage etched across all three of their stunned faces. "You lot didn't think I was paying attention, did you? Told you I was getting my entertainment one way or another."

"That's it!" Snag said. "Forget about being an intern, you're—you're . . . what's lower than an intern?"

"Whipping boy," Rasp said.

"You're the whipping boy now!"

Curly nudged his scowling companion with the tip of his elbow. "We're gonna be out of work after this. You really want to be on the wrong side of the Lazuli family? Might pay to play nice, you know."

"And here I thought you had gone all puppy-brained for the emissary. It's a relief to know you are capable of thinking outside of your pants for a change," Snag said. He and Curly stared one another down for several heartbeats before the goblin relented. His bony shoulders drooped with a sigh. "Why do I always let you talk me into these things?"

"Rali says it's 'cause you have a con . . ." Curly paused, as if attempting to form the full word in his head first. "Consci . . ."

"Concussion," Rasp contributed helpfully.

Curly scratched his curved tusk thoughtfully. "Is that what that is?"

With possibly the most dramatic eye roll Daana had ever seen, Snag flipped the book open and refrained from slamming his head between the brittle pages. He retrieved a pair of glasses from his breast pocket and fitted them over his nose, awarding Daana a glare that warned her not to mention them. Ever.

After some hemming and hawing, he rattled off a series of deep, guttural sounds that made Daana want to scratch the back of her throat. The first page took nearly half an hour to work out. At Rasp's insistence, Snag reread every line, sometimes three or four times over, until it was to the Stoneclaw's satisfaction. It read:

> *The greatest enemy to mankind does not come in the form of mortal or magic, but time. Short lifespans breed ever shorter memories. The human curse is to forget. In the span of three generations, our people's history has been forgotten, rewritten, and misremembered.*
>
> *The following, my life's work, is a direct translation of the original scrolls. Fear will not hide the truth. Ignorance will not prevail. Our people will one day know the history of our origins as it was meant to be told.*
>
> —Dagmar Stoneclaw

CHAPTER FIFTY

Origins

A cool wind blustered through the makeshift canteen, laden with the intermingled scents of spruce, roasted meat, and smoke from the kitchen fire. Thick gray clouds blanketed the sky above, illuminated by the pale glow of the moon. The oil lantern was placed in the center of the group. Its flame bathed the faces of those around it in flickering yellow light, exaggerating the long shadows and making them all that more fierce-looking. Daana tried not to notice as she recorded the last few lines of the opening translation into her journal.

"I don't get it," Curly grunted. "Is that supposed to mean something?"

"It's the ramblings of a madwoman, is what it is." Rasp tilted his head in Daana's direction. "There you have it. Humans are forgetful. Can I go to bed now? I've had a shit day and I really just want to shut my eyes before I wake up to a shit morning."

"Doesn't sound like a madwoman to me." Daana set her writing implement aside to pick at her bread roll. In the midst of the translation, Lieutenant Ralizak had come by with dinner. She stopped to trade lighthearted banter with Snag and Curly before a pointed cough from Sascha sent her scuttling off again.

"Who was she," Daana said, "this Dagmar Stoneclaw?"

"A self-proclaimed historian. Stirred up some sort of controversy before she got banished." Rasp pushed his dried pork strip around his plate, as if debating if it was worth losing his remaining teeth attempting to chew it. "She got in an argument with the clan leader right before she left. Stabbed him, stole some scrolls, and set the place on fire. At least that's what I was told. I don't know. It was well before my time."

The buzzing ache still thrummed behind her eyes like a nest of angry hornets. Daana persisted in spite of the pain. The plan was to translate just enough to satisfy her report before conveniently losing the journal on the way back to her tent. That required making it past the first page, however, which was something they had yet to accomplish. As much as she wanted to pin the delay solely on Rasp, her own pettiness shared equal blame. "And what part of that makes her crazy, Rasp? The fact that she argued with an authority figure? Or that she stabbed him? Seems somewhat of a double standard to me, considering I watched you attempt both only this morning."

"You gonna need some salve for that burn, maggot?" Snag grinned, looking up from his plate of sautéed chicken livers and gristle—a consolation prize for helping and not burning the canteen to the ground, Daana suspected.

"Shut up!"

From the corner of her eye, Daana watched a lanky figure drift through the dwindling soldiers toward them. Ellisar squeezed in between Rasp and Curly, managing to do so without upsetting the mess plate she carried, currently laden with a small mountain of dinner rolls. At least three of the rolls had been lifted from unwatched plates on her way over. Four, if the elf hadn't bothered to get in line for dinner at all. Which, given Sergeant Farrow's reluctance to do anything by the rulebook, probably meant the plate was stolen, too.

"Good evening, Sergeant," Daana greeted politely. Suddenly, her night wasn't feeling so dour after all. More frightening, perhaps, as Ellisar Farrow was without question the most intimidating of Oralia's lackeys. On the other hand, this counted as progress. After all, Daana was currently sitting with three of the faithful four, and by pure luck, too! Perhaps that was the trick to this whole acceptance thing—just don't go out of your way to try and, eventually, the opportunity would fall into your lap.

Ellisar impaled the first roll onto her knife and tore a chunk free with her teeth. She spoke around the mouthful, wondering, "Is there something good about it?"

"Not anymore there's not," Rasp said. "Honestly, of all the places to sit, why here next to me? You already had your fun. Can't you find another victim to torment?" From the limited light provided by the oil lamp, Daana saw his hand ghost along the edge of Ellisar's jacket. Finding what he sought, Rasp's hand darted into her pocket with practiced precision.

"Bold of you to assume I was finished tormenting you." Ellisar reached across Rasp's plate, palmed his half-eaten roll, and added it to her growing bread pile. Daana suspected it was not so much a want for more food as it was a compulsory need to take things that didn't belong to her. "Incidentally, if it is my knife you are looking for, it is currently in my hand. Say the word and it can be in yours."

Rasp retracted his fingers from her pocket with a carefulness that seemed to indicate he wished to retain as many of them as possible. "I was searching for the key to the manacles, actually."

"Mhf," the elf said, still chewing. "Front right pocket. It's yours if you can get it."

Curly smacked Ellisar's other hand, which was sneakily reaching for his dried pork. "What are you doin' here, El?"

"This is the last of the bread from Lonebrook. Don't know when we'll see decent vittles again. Thought I'd stock the larders while I had the chance." Wringing the invisible sting from her fingers, she selected one of the untouched rolls from her plate and squashed it. It morphed back into its rounded shape seconds later. "It packs flat and then springs back. Don't know how the fauns do it. Practically borders on witchcraft."

Daana peered closer and frowned. "That's a sponge."

"Is it?"

". . . Can you not tell?"

"Well played, Sascha." The elf's fixed expression remained unreadable. There was something odd about Ellisar's dark pupils. Whether it was on account of the limited light or some other factor, Daana couldn't tell. "Left it right out in the open just to tempt me, too. Crafty fucker."

"Ellisar!" Snag's head snapped up with a rattle of earrings. "Good gods, why are you still trying to eat it?"

"Revenge. Now he won't have any more sponges." Ellisar was all teeth when she ate. Lips peeled back, revealing a few silver teeth mixed in with the varying shades of white, she tore the corner free and gave an experimental chew.

"Or," Snag said, "hear me out. You could just throw it into the woods and he still wouldn't have any sponges."

"I made a plan and I'm sticking to it."

Snag watched her, unable to look away as the elf gnawed it like a dog on a bone. "You're still chewing and . . . oh, look at that. You swallowed. And now you're going for a second bite. Gods dammit. Curly, slap that out of her hand!"

Curly stared, equally as mesmerized. "I kinda want to try it now. She's really selling it."

With the sponge still clasped firmly between her teeth, Ellisar shifted her back to Curly in order to protect her prize from theft. "Get your own."

Snag narrowed his eyes at Ellisar, his upturned nose wrinkling along the ridge. "Hold up. You're buzzed out of your skull right now, aren't you?"

"Calm your tits, Snag." Ellisar reached into her coat and withdrew a loose-knit bag of what looked to be a strange assortment of brown mushrooms. "I brought enough to share."

"Put that away! I'm on shift later. And you don't need a repeat of what happened last time."

"Please, the nearest boat is miles away. Couldn't possibly sink it from here." Ellisar sliced a mushroom in half and extended the offering on the flat of her blade in Curly's direction. "How about you? Want to join Aunty Bad Influence?"

Snag's ears flattened as he watched the morsel exchange hands, muttering, "Unbelievable."

"Emissary, do you care to partake?"

Daana's teeth snapped together. Her gaze lifted, leaving the final words of the inscription unfinished on her page. "I, uh," she stumbled. She'd never been invited to partake in anything before. The old cautionary tales of succumbing to peer pressure had never applied to her in any meaningful way. Was this what it was like to belong? She'd never imagined it to feel so . . . guilty? And yet, the flicker of excitement in her chest was suddenly alive and burning. "What is it, exactly?"

"If you have to ask, then you don't want it," Snag said.

Rasp was more enthusiastic in his support. "Don't think about it, just do it. It's like jumping over the waterfall. Once your feet are off the ground, all that's left to do is relax and enjoy the view."

"You have illicit substances?" Daana instinctively lowered her voice, as if expecting the schoolmaster to come walking around the corner at any given moment. "What happens if we're caught? Thirty lashes? Do we get tied to a stake? Dear gods, I can't afford a mark on my record."

Ellisar studied her with an impossibly blank expression. "Have you ever seen a mill horse put out to pasture? They walk in circles from dawn 'til dusk because that's all they've ever known. The only walls left are the ones in their heads, but they will never truly be free."

Daana stiffened at the implication. "I'm not a horse."

"Don't let the system cage you, little pony. Run wild," the elf said, offering a piece of mushroom as if it were a sacred offering.

"Thank you, that is very kind." Daana felt the heat from her face work its way to her ears. Her headache faded to a dull throb as a combination of panic and embarrassment took center stage. "I need my faculties to continue the translation, but perhaps another night?" As much as she wanted to be accepted by the faithful four, recreational substance use was clearly not the way to go about accomplishing it. The translation seemed to be working well enough at the moment. "Continue reading whenever you're ready, Mister Flint."

"Ugh," Rasp groaned, rolling his head back. "Why can't we do the fun thing?"

Despite Rasp's bemoaning, the next passage came much easier. Daana dutifully recorded it word for word in her journal:

> *In the beginning, the land was ruled by darkness. All who tried to settle the ridge fell prey to the evil that resided there. Driven from his homeland, Ansel, son of Bramble and Alina Stoneclaw, first of his name, led his people into the Iron Ridge to escape those that persecuted them. Desperate and with death at their backs, Ansel pressed deeper into the mountains. The darkness rose up to smite those that dared to trespass upon its hallowed ground. After eight days and eight nights of darkness, Ansel slew the great evil, claiming the land for his people.*
>
> *Ansel and his descendants settled the range, vowing never again would a Stoneclaw be forced from their home and hunted for their . . .*

Daana jerked her head upright. "Their what?"

Rasp was pale and trembling. Daana later learned his resulting scream was said to have been so loud, a nearby farmer walked out onto his porch and wondered what prehistoric beast had just died.

CHAPTER FIFTY-ONE

The Night of Stolen Lives

Still seething at the prospect of being forced to work with another, Whisper had made a quick exit. Faris, having not yet regained control of his legs, was left to wait it out in awkward silence. He was currently sprawled over the trampled ground near the unlit fire pit, pretending to sleep. Oralia knew he wasn't, considering his eyes were half-closed and watching her from beneath a hood of white lashes.

While her rampaging thoughts had quieted, the throbbing ache inside her skull remained. As did a few lingering questions. "How did you know iron would work against Whisper?"

Faris remained perfectly still. "Lucky guess."

Having finished with the buttons and patches, Oralia had moved on to the tedious task of darning the socks. Normally she made Curly sit beside her and curse his way through the process, but tonight he was nowhere to be found. Perhaps his ability to sense oncoming danger had finally increased to a useful level. "You are not the type to rely on luck."

"Fine. Educated guess, then."

"How?" Oralia realized too late she'd only meant to think this, not ask. And certainly not with such an annoyed tone. Darning was supposed to be soothing, and yet tonight it left her frustrated. This was possibly due to the fact that nearly every sock in the pile belonged to Ellisar. Oralia never understood how someone with such slight feet could bore holes through even the thickest wool. Razorblade toenails was the only logical conclusion.

"Rasp said a witch attacked him during his fight with Monk. I didn't take much stock in it, not until I learned about Daana," Faris said, flicking his ear at a bothersome moth. The insect dipped in front of his face before continuing its slow, ambling circles overhead. "So I thought to myself, here's this hunter who tracks witches for living, and she's got Rasp sitting under her nose and is none the wiser. Either Daana is the most useless seeker in the history of the division, or whatever she's hunting is scrambling her abilities. Assuming it's the latter, the question then becomes, what's powerful enough to disguise not only itself from a seeker, but Rasp too? The obvious answer is fae. What deters fae? Silver and iron."

"You have a uniquely suspicious mind," Oralia said, deciding against the addition of "for someone who, on paper, amounts to little more than a country bumpkin."

"Whisper's kind are all supposed to be dead, you know. They shared their magic with the mortals. And how did we thank them? By hunting the entire species into extinction, of course." Faris, once more, demonstrated an uncanny wealth of knowledge to matters that did not concern him. He rooted around the inside of his jacket and withdrew the second cigarette of the evening. "When people realized you could control them by trapping their magic in a powerstone, suddenly every ruler with a mind for expansion wanted a wind shifter at their disposal."

Wind shifter was what historians called them. The real name of the species had been lost to time. They were similar to elves. Something like an early ancestor, according to Whisper. Except, for whatever reason, the evolution of the species had gone backward. Modern elves barely held a candle to their shapeshifting cousins. While such information was available to those that knew where to look, the history of wind shifters was not well known outside magical academia. Which made it all the more suspicious that Faris had committed it to memory.

Faris's accusing tone drew Oralia from her thoughts. "How did you, of all people, get one?"

"By accident." Oralia weaved the dark yarn in and out of the worn wool with a steady, practiced hand. "Whisper's master was apprehended smuggling magical contraband into the capital. I found Whisper among the artifacts, confined to an iron cage and too weak to fight. I did not know what they were at the time and, consequently, did not realize that slaying their captor would generate a life debt. Accidental or not, the fae take those very seriously."

From Faris's scrutinizing expression, he seemed to suspect there was more to the story. There was, of course. Oralia purposely left out that she had been ordered to turn a blind eye to the smuggling. Or, more importantly, that this specific shipment had been placed by Geralt Lazuli himself. The raid had been over half a century ago, before the formation of the faithful four. Back when it was just her and Ralizak. It was only with Rali's help that Oralia had been able to strike a fair bargain with Whisper.

The terms of their arrangement were simple. In order to clear the debt, Whisper would work for Oralia until she retired. At which point, the bond dissolved, the stone would return to Whisper, and both parties could walk away without fear of retaliation. For the last sixty-eight years, Whisper had operated as Oralia's eyes and ears within the capital, with a focus on the Division of Divination. Occasionally, Oralia issued a more specific task, but the fae was left largely to their own devices. She knew Whisper had side projects. The agreement was that so long as Whisper refrained from drawing too much attention—burning the division to the ground, for instance—Oralia didn't want to know.

"Faris, are you . . ." Oralia paused, realizing she wasn't sure which term applied here. The personal business of magically-inclined had become more private these days.

"Am I magical, you mean? About as much as you are. How's that?"

"You are remarkably well informed on the subject."

"That's what happens when you're the only ungifted offspring born among a bunch of magical overachievers. I got an all-white coat and my sisters got power. Didn't stop me from reading their books and trying to recreate the spells for myself when no one was watching. Never worked, of course." The faun clamped the fresh cigarette between his teeth, gritting the words out. "I used to think that was so unfair. Right up until the seekers came and carted them off to the division, never to be seen again. Turns out I was the lucky one all along."

The sudden realization hit Oralia with a force. She looked up from her work, piecing this information together into the puzzle. Faris's father, Trant Belfast, had mentioned he'd lost two children in the name of the realm. It hadn't occurred to Oralia that he'd been talking about the Division of Divination. A sudden heaviness settled in her gut.

"They died the Night of Stolen Lives." Faris's gruff voice had a far-off quality to it now, confirming what Oralia had already suspected. "No matter how much I asked, that's all Mum would ever say. Too painful to talk about, I guess."

Two children; one massacre. *Dear gods*, Oralia winced. No wonder Faris shot her murderous glances when he didn't think she was looking. Was this the reason for Novera Belfast's absence during Oralia's recent stay in Lonebrook? Trant had claimed she was away visiting family.

Faris sat up with a muffled grunt. He still couldn't stand, but he could at least face her head-on for what was about to come. "A lot of witches died that night, including my sisters. I was always told that was how you earned your nickname. I never had a reason to doubt it before. Everyone knows Protector Dawnsight kills witches."

They exchanged pointed glances. "If you have something to ask, Faris, then ask it. You requested honesty. I will give it to you."

"It doesn't add up. You know about Daana, you let Rasp live, you employ a wind shifter for the gods' sakes!" Faris's eyes searched her face. Oralia saw fear and anger in his bloodshot eyes, but mostly a deep sadness. "Did you really kill them, Protector? Did you slaughter all of those innocent people because they were standing in your way?"

"Did you kill my family?" was the question he meant, but could not ask.

The Night of Stolen Lives had been the largest massacre of Sunstorn's own citizens. The realm had issued its statement after the fact, limiting the details, smoothing certain truths so it reflected favorably upon them. No one bought the lie, of course. And it was not long before rumors took hold of the United Territories. Namely, that Protector Dawnsight liked to kill witches.

"No. I was not in Sunstorn when it happened," Oralia replied. "I was brought in from another assignment to hunt the head conspirators afterward."

"Hmm," Faris took a puff of his cigarette in order to avoid saying whatever nasty thoughts danced across his tongue. "How convenient for you."

Oralia placed her instruments back into the repair satchel. Mending was reserved for the nights she needed to escape her intrusive thoughts. Tonight, there would be no escaping. Not just for Faris's sake, but so that she too, could remember. Time could not be allowed to wash the innocent blood from the hands of those responsible. "In order to understand what happened that night, you must first know the events that led up to it. Your sisters were not the only witches taken against their will by the Division of Divination. Three years before the massacre, an elf from the Adderwood territory was found by the seekers and forced into servitude. Her name was Larkspur Denari. And, unlike most delivered to the steps of the division, she had power."

Larkspur Denari had *real* power. The kind that made rulers drool and neighboring territories nervous. Despite the Division of Divination's grand plans for her, Larkspur refused to be used as a weapon. It was not long, however, before Speaker Lazuli and the Director of Magical Affairs found a way to control her. This was the part they always left out of the record books. Because a lot more people would care if they knew.

Oralia took a steadying breath and said, "Larkspur entered the division pregnant. She gave birth and, instead of sending the infant home to the father, the order kept it as a means of control. So long as Larkspur kept in line, her child was safe."

"Wait." Faris's nostrils flared almost as wide as his eyes. There was no subtlety in the accusation in his voice. "And you knew about this? You stood by and let them use a child as a means of extortion?"

"I knew the division had started drafting from the general populace based on magical ability, but I was unaware of the abuses." It felt like an excuse. It *was* an excuse. Oralia should have been paying closer attention. She had been on assignment near the swampland border those years and was not present for the discussions concerning Speaker Lazuli's grand overhaul of the Division of Divination.

"What about Whisper, then? Even if you were out of the loop, surely they knew what was going on."

"Our paths did not cross until several years after the massacre." Had she met Whisper five years sooner, all could have ended so differently. But that was wishful thinking. And wishful thinking got you nowhere.

Faris mashed the end of the cigarette between his teeth. If it were not for the fact that he could not yet use his legs, Oralia was certain he'd be pawing the ground in preparation to charge.

"For three years Larkspur kept up the farce," Oralia continued. "All while secretly plotting a mass escape. The witches were not the only ones upset by their exploitation. They had family and friends on the outside, some of whom were willing to go to great extremes to help. Through their efforts, Larkspur was able to create a chain of contacts for relaying information in and out of the division. She used this system to contact a pair of mercenaries and hired them to arrange the escape. One of which went by the name of Sybil Pride—"

"The pirate? Captain of the ship *Before the Fall*?"

Oralia gave him a leveling stare. "Are you finished interrupting?"

Faris blew a cloud of smoke at her, unafraid. Regrettably, the more time you spent with the faithful four, the more you picked up their bad habits. Oralia missed the days Faris would cower at the first sign of her teeth.

When Faris kept his silence this time, Oralia picked up where she had left off. "The night of the escape, Pride anchored *Before the Fall* outside the harbor and ordered half the crew ashore. A palace feast left only a handful of order soldiers to guard the division. Pride's crew made short work of them and, under the cover of night while half the city celebrated, stole the escapees to the harbor. They moved in groups, the young and old first, with the intention of leaving the most able-bodied for last. The escapees arrived at the docks and were transported via longboat to the ship. By the time the boats returned, a fresh group was waiting for them.

"They had nearly three-quarters of the division emptied before the alarm sounded and soldiers poured into the streets. The ship hoisted anchor and took to sea, leaving those still in the city to escape by foot. A handful of the remaining witches were apprehended, but most fought to the death. In total, of the thirty-eight slain that night, twenty-four were witches. Larkspur had waited with her people, insistent on being among the very last to board. She evaded capture and fled into the countryside. After weeks on the run, I caught her in the Hallowbac territory, holed up in a small village called Truepoint. By then, she and her remaining followers did not have the strength to fight. The realm wanted the conspirators alive in order to determine the location of the others. Thus, I offered her the opportunity to parley."

Oralia went silent for a good while and then sighed, blinking heavily. "Imagine my surprise when, expecting to bargain with conspirators, I found my own sister staring back at me from across the table."

CHAPTER FIFTY-TWO

Pawn

Faris raised his head as surprise flooded his formerly furious expression. "Your sister was a witch?"

"No." Oralia fought the sudden lump in her throat. Nearly three-quarters of a century had passed since the incident, and thinking about it still made her want to smash something between her bare hands. "Foolishly empathetic. My sister, Ashwyn, was the main orchestrator from the outside. By the time I caught them, there were only three of them left. Ashwyn, Larkspur, and Pride."

Sybil Pride was a false identity, of course. Belonging to a high wood elf by the name of Ellisar Farrow—another detail the realm conveniently expunged from their records. Ellisar hadn't cared about the cause, not even the money, really. From what Oralia understood, the job was practically unpaid. But Ellisar loved Ashwyn enough to go along with it. She probably regretted that now.

"I lost a sister the Night of Stolen Lives, too. Not because she was born with extraordinary gifts, but because she followed her bleeding heart and not her head."

"Lost a sister or killed her?" Faris snapped. "Was my family not enough, Protector? Did you have to go and murder yours, too?"

An unexpected growl rattled from the depths of her throat. Oralia bared her tusks at Faris, snarling. "I did my duty! I swore that if they surrendered, I would deliver them safely to court for trial myself. They could speak their truth for all of the realm to hear. I was certain once the other figureheads learned of the Division of Divination's corruption, things would change."

Faris held her stare. For several heartbeats, neither broke eye contact. Above them, the wind whistled in the trees. Glimpses of moonlight peeked between the thick clouds overhead, casting the barren campsite in shifting pools of ghostly light. With an irritated snort, Faris said, "And how'd that work out for you?"

The fire raging in Oralia's chest subsided. The tightness in her throat was back, with twice the ache as before. "I was able to convince the others to surrender, but not Larkspur. She already knew the corruption went much deeper than the division. She tried to tell me as much, but I was too blinded by my trust in the system to listen."

"*And?*"

"Larkspur said she would die before she was put back into the hands of the Division of Divination. I obliged her."

Faris's mouth curled. "You murdered her, you mean!"

"She did not want to be a weapon. I honored her choice. I thought I was upholding justice. I did not yet realize that the Speaker of the People, Geralt Lazuli, was the invisible hand of the Division of Divination. If I knew then what I know now, I would have done everything differently." The first time Oralia had met Geralt, she had the sudden impulse to throw him from the tallest tower of the palace. She often regretted ignoring that instinct.

"To answer your original question, Faris, yes, I kill witches. I have before and will do so again if necessary. I did not, however, kill your sisters. Either they were among those slain in the streets of Sunstorn on the night of the massacre, or the sea took their lives." He didn't have to ask. She saw the question in his eyes and answered accordingly. "The realm learned several months later *Before the Fall* hit a storm and capsized off the coast of the flatlands. Bodies and wreckage washed up for weeks along the shore. There were no survivors."

Faris's barrel chest heaved in and out as the weight of the truth settled heavy over his rampaging thoughts. Beneath the despair in his eyes, Oralia sensed something darker. Something that wriggled and writhed in the secret corners of his mind, untouched by the light of day. Oralia, too, had once felt such hatred. Revenge would never quell the rage. It would only feed the fire. If you were one of the lucky ones, you learned to let go of your sense of justice before the thirst for vengeance sent you to an early grave.

His hardened stare lifted to meet her own. "And your sister?"

Whatever previous loyalty Faris had for her now hung by a thread. There was a time for secrecy and there was a time for truth. For the first time in many years, Oralia realized the only way to maintain course would be to open the door. Not fully, just a crack. Enough to assure Faris that no matter what heinous reputation she'd earned over the years, there were reasons for the choices she'd made.

"The truth is, I cannot afford to lose you because I cannot afford to lose Rasp, and passage through the ridge. If silver is no longer sufficient in ensuring your allegiance, perhaps information will suffice. I will tell you about my sister—and more, eventually, in hopes that I may retain your services through to the end."

Oralia chose her next words carefully. "There are very few who can make Whisper nervous, Faris. The fact that you have them on edge means you are something more than you pretend to be. I will not ask what that is."

The greater picture was coming into focus. Oralia finally saw what she had neglected to notice before. Trant had mentioned that his son had started to go down the wrong path. She assumed he had been referring to the contraband, but it was more severe than that. Faris was involved in the resistance. His expansive knowledge of magic, coupled with the personal vendetta, practically guaranteed it. The resistance had an official name, of course. One Oralia refused to use on account of how often it changed. She stuck to "magical resistance," as it was short, sweet, and annoyed those responsible for the movement. The resistance's numbers had been growing in secret ever since the Night of Stolen Lives. Desperate to stop the spread, the realm now offered a handsome reward for any members captured alive.

Fortunately for Faris, she had better uses for him than turning him in to the realm.

Faris's expression grew strangely blank as he considered all possibilities, including whether or not she was baiting him into admitting something better kept unsaid. Finally, a wolfish smile broke the look of concentration on his face. "Protector, you flatter me. I'm nothing but a humble rapscallion. Whisper is scared of me because Rasp likes me better. It's as simple as that. I can assure you, I am as loyal to the realm as the day I was born. I have no need for secret information."

"The information I possess is enough to spark the revolution Geralt has been stifling for the better part of a century. In the right hands, it might even be enough to bring down the Division of Divination once and for all. Does that not interest you, Faris?"

"I don't want anything you have to offer," he assured her. The smile faded from his lips. "I *am* interested to hear if you mucked over your sister as badly as you did mine. You can at least finish what you started and tell me what happened to her."

Dread fluttered in the pit of her stomach. Oralia could count on a single hand the number of people who knew. Adding another to the mix, especially one whose allegiance ebbed and flowed like the tides, was a risk she could not afford to be wrong about. "I delivered her and Pride to the capital for trial as promised. And, just as Larkspur predicted, everything went to shit. By the time of my return, Geralt Lazuli had destroyed all evidence of the realm's wrongdoing. The Division of Divination placed the blame entirely on the conspirators and claimed they had taken the witches against their will as a means to rob the realm of its greatest resource. The trial was a farce. The courts dragged it out for two months before they gave their verdict. Ashwyn and Pride were found guilty and sentenced to death by hanging.

"Whatever good I had thought existed in the world disappeared that day. Justice was an illusion, and I would be damned if the realm expected me to uphold it. I delivered my resignation after the sentencing, but Geralt was craftier than I gave him credit for. Unbeknownst to me, he faked the execution. A captured member from Pride's crew took Ashwyn's place at the gallows. As far as the citizens were concerned, justice had been served and the realm could carry on.

"I was at the lowest I had ever been. My reality was shattered and I thought my sister dead. Geralt came to me in secret and revealed what he had done. He then offered me a bargain. In exchange for my sister's freedom, I would retract my resignation and remain on as the Protector of the Realm. Geralt claimed that the territories were already upset and that it was not the time for a major shift in power. I had earned a reputation for ruthlessness and, at that moment, that was exactly what the realm needed to keep the rest of the territories in line. If I refused, he swore to make me wish I had hanged Ashwyn myself."

The cigarette stub hanging from Faris's open mouth dropped into his lap. "What?"

"I have spent most of my reinstatement carrying out Geralt's bidding. Our relationship is a tumultuous one. He finds new and inventive ways to lord control over me and I, in turn, find new and inventive ways to undermine his authority. It has taken the better part of seventy-three years, but Geralt has finally grown tired of me. Establishing passage through the Iron Ridge is to be my final assignment. This trade route will secure Ashwyn's freedom and release me of my duties. Which means I will use whatever resources I have available to accomplish it, including whatever it is you are."

"You're a pawn?" Faris stammered, "You're—you're not even in power, you're just—"

"At the mercy of Geralt's ever-changing whim. You're correct. If the speaker wishes me to quell rebellions, then I quell rebellions. He asks for a trade route, I bring him a damn trade route. There is some leeway in how effectively I carry out his bidding, but it is a fine line I must walk carefully. You and I may not agree on many things, Faris, but family is as important to me as it is to you. And I will do what is necessary to get mine back."

"Why keep it a secret? If what you're saying is true, why not tell somebody? Everybody? This could be enough to bring the whole system down by itself."

"Larkspur was an innocent fighting to save other innocents. If Geralt could turn the realm against her, imagine what he could do to me. I am not innocent. Nor am I a revolutionist. I yearn for my fighting days to be over. The only reason I have stayed this long is to free Ashwyn. What others choose to do with my information afterward is for them to decide. I want no part of it."

Faris's eyes were wide as he sat with his head tilted to one side. Although calm and quiet, Oralia did not doubt that on the inside, his thoughts were screaming to be heard over one another. She had played her hand. It was now time to see if it would be enough. After several painfully still moments, Faris appeared to have reached a conclusion. "And you can provide more information?"

"So long as you are willing to help me secure the path through the Iron Ridge."

"Muck it. Fine, yes. I'll do it." His mouth opened again, but the words came slowly, as if the thought attached to them was still forming within his mind. "The whole witch-killing thing wasn't your idea, was it? Geralt took the incident with Larkspur and built on it. If people blamed you for the massacre, they wouldn't have any need to look deeper."

"More or less."

"No, it's either one or the other. You're either an actual witch killer or you're not."

"It was not the path my former self would have chosen, but it was the one I embraced. Yes, Geralt dubbed me the witch-killer. But I made sure it came back to bite him in the ass. Of all the witches he sent me to collect, not a single one ever made it to the capital alive. It took only a few before he realized their deaths were not accidents. By then it was too late. The damage was done. The realm knew beyond a shadow of a doubt that I killed witches and Geralt was forced to find other means to stock the Division of Divination."

With Speaker Lazuli holding Ashwyn hostage, Oralia had very little sway in the decisions of the realm, particularly those pertaining to the Division of Divination. She had hoped if she opposed the division at every opportunity, policies would eventually turn. When that failed, she took a more extreme approach. Oralia might have been a prisoner to Geralt's whims, but she could personally ensure no other Larkspur Denari would ever again fall into the division's clutches.

Row Dumont. Adeara Wishborne. Hemsley Hogspaw. Just a few of the most powerful witches she'd prevented from reaching the steps of the Division of Divination. A bitter taste flooded Oralia's mouth as a new thought formed in her mind. By the end of the journey, when the trade routes were established and it was time to return to Sunstorn, she would add a final name to the list.

Rasp Stoneclaw.

CHAPTER FIFTY-THREE

Adrift

Rasp's night was spent in a restless slumber. His body lay unresponsive to the world around him, but his mind was alive and raging. Churning, churning, churning, his thoughts bubbled to the surface, only to be dragged back under again. They tossed, tumbled, and splintered into a thousand pieces, clogging the gears of his mind like wet sand. One thought remained whole, floating above the chaos, adrift and aimless as pond scum:

Never again would a Stoneclaw be forced from their home and hunted for their magic.

Actually, that wasn't true. Earlier, once the others managed to get him to stop screaming, Daana made him translate the rest of the passage. That had resulted in more screaming, of course. At which point she gave up and someone dragged Rasp off to bed. Thanks to Daana's stubborn insistence, several lines of thought now floated across Rasp's churning mind. Each one was worse than the last.

Nestled within the safety of the range, the mountain folk hid their abilities no longer. They revered their magic, passing on their sacred knowledge from one generation to the next without fear of persecution.

Morning came and Rasp was pulled from his bed and ordered to dress with more urgency than usual. With his mind preoccupied and body unwilling, he put his shirt on backward and trousers inside out. He absentmindedly laced his boots together, too. A fact he was not made aware of until he attempted to take a step and fell face-first into the dirt at the foot of his bedroll. Afterward, following a rude fit of laughter from Faris, he was marched through waist-high vegetation still wet with morning dew and forced to sit by a fire. He'd been here before, his brain insisted. Or had that been a dream? Where was *here* again? Was this a dream?

Damn Daana and her stupid book! It was messing with his head.

Rasp drew in, focusing on what information his senses could provide. His surroundings were mostly dark, offset only by the flickering light of the fire, meaning the sun was still beyond the horizon. He smelled something other than the smoke and flames . . . roasted meat? Camp! He was at Oralia's camp. It was too early for the kitchen to be open and Ellisar was the only hunter he knew who could pluck birds out of trees in the dark. Literally pluck—the lunatic elf actually climbed into the boughs to collect her prey from their roosts while they slept.

Rasp heard low voices, too.

A pair of rough hands jerked his head in their direction, alerting Rasp to the fact this particular voice had been speaking to him. "Hello? Is any-one home?" Rali's usual cheerful tone was gruff and cut like a razor. "I am depending on you to get this right. Do you understand?"

"Get what right?"

"I'm about to knock you upside the head and into next week, bucko. The plan! I am depending on you to get the plan right." There was an uncom-fortable silence as Lieutenant Ralizak waited for him to give some form of confirmation that he understood his part. Rasp simultaneously dared not reveal that until two seconds ago, he wasn't aware there'd been a plan, much less his involvement in it.

A heavy sigh from Faris spared Rasp from being knocked into next week. "She hasn't told you the plan yet. This was your cue to start listening."

Oh, thank gods for that.

"What's wrong with him, Faris?" Rali released Rasp's face with an irri-tated shove. "I'm used to him being a little slow on the uptake, but this is a whole new level."

"Don't ask me. You were the one who was supposed to be keeping an eye on him. I don't know what you let the emissary do to him at dinner last night, but he hasn't been the same since."

Oralia's strident voice broke in from somewhere across the fire. "Why was he with the emissary?"

"He was getting too stab-happy in the kitchen," Rali said. "Your fuck-mate handed him over to Daana so she could torture him with homework or something."

Ellisar's dry voice cut in. "Her *Moonflower*, you mean."

"No, you've got it backward. He calls her Moonflower. His pet name is, I don't know, Fuckhead, maybe?"

The protector's tusks snapped together with such force, Rasp's spine instinctively shot straighter. As though, for some reason, correct posture would spare him from the wrath of an angry orc. From her palpable silence, he assumed there was also a glare involved, but he had no way of knowing for sure. When Oralia spoke again, it was purposefully slow. "You left Rasp unattended with the emissary?"

Rali's tone was immediately on the defensive. "Oh, relax. Snag and Curly were with them the whole time. What's the worst that little pipsqueak could do to him anyway?"

Worst she could do? The worst? She had already done the worst! In a matter of pages, Daana had turned Rasp's very existence upside down, inside out, and crammed it down his throat like those horrid vitamin tablets Faris gave him each morning. Only this was worse. The foul taste it left in his mouth didn't go away after an hour. It lingered. Because history, whether you accepted it or not, could not simply be tucked into your cheek and spat out when Faris wasn't watching. History was everlasting.

The mountain folk hid their abilities no longer. They revered their magic, passing on their sacred knowledge from one generation to the next without fear of persecution.

The voices around Rasp grew heated, but he couldn't bring himself to listen. If Daana's journal was right, which he really, really, hoped it wasn't, that meant his whole upbringing had been a lie. Every mountain folk child was taught the same three basic tenets: if you pick a fight, you'd better win; if you lose, steal your dad's slapjack for next time; and three, never ever, ever, ever use magic. Magic was for weaklings and cowards.

Rasp had been born with magic. His mother knew. Father, too, which was probably why the old man was so adamant about denouncing it every time he wasn't shouting at Rasp for existing. Rasp thought he could overcome it. If only the weak used magic, he reasoned, then he would become the strongest. And he did. And it did absolutely fuck all, because in the end, he may have been the most feared Stoneclaw on the mountain, but his magic never went away. Neither did the temptation to use it.

If it were true, and the original Stoneclaws embraced their magic, what in the realm had happened? What made his people change their minds?

"Why did they decide magic was evil?" Rasp murmured, only partially aware that he'd said this bit out loud.

To his astonishment, a voice answered. **Think back to the first night we met, little bird. What was lesson number two?**

"What are you doing in my head?" Rasp hissed under his breath. "Shit, can the others see you? Or are you invisible?" That was something witches could do, right? That, or maybe Whisper had shapeshifted into an ear mite and had taken up residence in his skull. According to Rasp's father, there had always been plenty of room in there to spare.

It's telepathy. I am speaking to you from a distance. I am not invisible.

That simultaneously answered everything and nothing. "Then how can you hear me if you're far away?"

Of course you don't know what telepathy is, Whisper sighed. **Never mind. Answer the question.**

There had been a question? Oh yes, lesson two. Lesson two. What in the realm had been lesson two? "Uh, the old ones?" Rasp ventured after a moment of concentrated thought. "What does that have to do with anything? And I'm still mad at you, by the way. Outing me to Oralia was low, even for a witch."

It was necessary. She would have known you were lying, as you're quite terrible at it. Thus creating more problems. I simply shortened the process. Back to the matter at hand. Last night you learned about your ancestor Ansel Stoneclaw. Tell me, what did he defeat in order to conquer the Iron Ridge?

Rasp skimmed the passage in his mind. Something, something, great evil. Something, something, darkness . . . oh. "You're saying my people killed an old one?"

Yes.

"How?"

By stabbing at it with sharpened sticks. How do you think, little bird? With magic, obviously!

"Don't yell at me! I'm still trying to wrap my head around all of this, alright?" Some part of his brain alerted Rasp that his surroundings had gone eerily quiet. For a few seconds the only sound Rasp heard was the crackle of the fire. Someone across from him cleared their throat uncomfortably.

"Have you finally lost it?" Faris said. "Who are you talking to?"

"The invisible, shapeshifting witch that lives in my head" was probably not a good answer. Rasp lifted his hands, offering a sheepish, "Myself?"

"Forget it, Faris. I've got this." Rali pulled Rasp closer until he could feel her hot, musty breath against his face. Her blunt fingertips dug into the skin on either side of his head with alarming strength. "I need you to listen. If there is one thing that gets through your thick skull today, it's this. Understand?"

Rasp tried to nod around her strong hands.

"Remember these words: I heard the protector's changed her mind. She's not going to retire."

"Wait, what? Is that true?"

"It's a rumor, you numbskull," Rali groaned. "I'm planting different ones to different people, to see what trickles back to the top. Finding the leak, yeah? Now, when we go have our little manners lesson later, at some point, you've got to casually slip it into conversation. You got that, bucko?"

"Why me?"

"Because I'm a professional. No one would believe it if I let something like that slip."

"And it's believable if it comes from me?"

Rali patted his cheek with the flat of her hand. "Not to throw stones here, but you are the one having an argument with yourself out loud, so yeah. Pretty believable, I'd say."

"I heard the protector's changed her mind. She's not going to retire. Happy? Can I go back to arguing with myself now?" Rasp wrenched free of her grasp and settled back down onto the ground, shivering. "Thanks to you I don't even remember what I was talking about."

Why the mountain folk abstain from magic, Whisper reminded him. **Now, when an old one dies, its power leaches into the ground, waiting to be used by an unsuspecting vessel, remember?**

Hardly. That entire episode of his life felt like ages ago.

What do you think happens when someone, say an untrained, magically-gifted Stoneclaw for example, accidently taps into said dark force?

A sudden heat rippled across Rasp's face and spread to his neck. He tried to put his wounded ego aside long enough to consider the weight of Whisper's words, but all his thoughts kept coming back to the same irritating detail. "You planted the fucking book, didn't you? Daana's assignment wasn't a coincidence."

Of course it wasn't coincidence. You needed to learn your people's history and I needed something to keep her distracted. Fortunately for you, the past holds the key to your future. As you will learn in your continued studies—

"You mean I have to keep learning that shit?" Life was so unfair.

—your people realized that in certain cases, the misuse of magic could reawaken the darkness. Sound familiar?

He wasn't going to dignify that with a response.

Alas, his silence only made it easier for Whisper's voice to keep filling his head with words. **Instead of learning better control, your ancestors shunned magic altogether. A solution which was as futile as it was stupid.**

So his people had killed an old one. But not actually killed it, because apparently it could come back with the help of an unsuspecting vessel. And now he, said magically-fucked vessel, was being marched back up the mountain where the evil lay dormant, waiting for him to slip up again. Rasp didn't claim to be brilliant by any stretch, but even he could tell a bad plan from a catastrophic one. "How do I keep from, um . . ."

He dared not say "tapping into the dark force again and accidentally killing everyone" out loud in case the others were still listening.

Fear and anger make you vulnerable, little bird. That's how the darkness found you. So long as you allow your emotions to control you, so too, can the darkness.

"I'm not allowed to be angry?" Rasp said, perhaps too angrily.

No. You're human. Telling you to stifle your emotions would only accelerate the problem. Feel what you need to feel. You must, however, avoid lashing out in anger. That is when you are most vulnerable to manipulation. Whisper allowed a moment for their words to sink in before speaking again. **The incident with lighting the elf on fire is fresh in your mind, yes?**

There was that stupid prickle of hurt pride again. Only this time it felt more like a hot poker stabbing him in the chest. Ignoring the quickening of his heartbeat, Rasp managed a grumbled, "Kind of hard to forget, actually." Especially when everyone kept bringing it up!

I caught you in a moment of anger and capitalized on it. Had you not been blinded by rage, I would not have been able to manipulate you. The darkness is more powerful than I. It will not have that problem. If you make yourself susceptible to it again, it will seize control. You will be a prisoner to its desires, forced to watch as you destroy everything you love until all of you has been consumed. That is why you must learn to exercise control now. Before the darkness has a chance to finish what it started.

Rasp buried his face into his hands to keep from saying something he might regret. Was reformation not enough? Did he have to pull out every existing piece of his being in order to appease fate? It wasn't fair. Why did being a better person have to be so fucking hard?

You need time to reflect. For now, I will leave you. Think about what I said.

A chill swept across his skin the moment he felt Whisper's thoughts detangle from his own. Rasp kept his head in his hands. He dared not breathe, let alone think, until he was certain the witch was gone. A glimmer of hope flickered within his rapidly beating chest. There was an alternative way to ensure the darkness didn't reach him. One that didn't require nearly so much change. All he needed was a little time to get his head back on straight, wait for the right moment, and then Operation Get-The-Fuck-Out-of-Here would be good to go.

CHAPTER FIFTY-FOUR

Wildfire

When Rasp lifted his head again, the surrounding light had grown brighter. It peeked through the blurry blobs of yellow and green color that swayed in the breeze above him. He no longer heard the crackle of the fire, either. There were still voices, a voice at least, but it wasn't one of the ones from before. This one sounded sour, like week-old curdled milk. There was a smell, too. Mothballs and camphor oil?

Willem!

Shit, the etiquette lesson. Had that much time passed already? Rasp swore he'd only been in his head a few minutes. And how in the realm did he get here without remembering? Somehow his body and brain had learned to operate independently of one another. *Okay, you can do this*, Rasp told himself. *Open your ears and listen. Figure out what's going on, say what you're supposed to say, and then we can work out how to function like a normal human being again.*

Willem carried on obliviously. ". . . the purpose of etiquette is to lay a foundation of confidence. When a person knows how they are expected to act, there is no need to second-guess their behavior."

He was expected to pay attention to this? Rasp had slept through ceremonies that were more exciting. He'd dozed through the naming ritual for all four of his brother Bil's children, the eventual marriage between Bil and one of the mothers, Rasp's own wedding—to his credit, he wasn't so much sleeping as he was hunkered down in his hideout waiting for the nuptials to blow over. But there was sleeping involved. And drinking. Lots of drinking, in fact. The fallout with his father afterward had been cataclysmic, but Rasp took some solace knowing he'd saved his intended from a life of misery. If he didn't like himself most of the time, Rasp didn't see how anyone else was supposed to. The poor bride had gotten lucky and—*ah!*

Rasp was jolted from his thoughts by someone wriggling their wet fingertip inside his ear.

"Improper etiquette!" he shouted, twisting his head in an attempt to bite the offending hand. His efforts were rewarded with a firm smack across the nose.

"Did someone finally knock you stupid?" This didn't sound like something Willem would say. In fact, it didn't sound like Willem at all. Not unless he'd swallowed a bag of grit and lost all inflection . . . oh boy.

"I . . ." Rasp touched his face as if to be sure his head was still attached to his shoulders. Other than a throbbing nose, everything felt normal. "I think there's something wrong with me."

"You don't say," Ellisar said.

"I can't do anything right today. I'm trying to pay attention. I am, really. And then I get a thought in my head and I follow it and it's like I get stuck there. I . . . oh gods. Is the etiquette lesson over? I didn't space out through the entire thing, did I?" Oh no. He forgot to say the thing. The one thing Rali was depending on him to do and he completely botched it. Should he say it now? Was Willem even around to hear it?

There was no answer. Panicked, Rasp looked around him. The harsh light filtering in from above obscured his vision and made it impossible for him to pick out Ellisar's shadowed form from the rest of his muddled surroundings. Tentatively, Rasp reached in the direction he'd heard her voice. He needed someone, something, anything to ground him back into reality. "Ellisar?"

She kindly alerted him to her position by stepping onto his hand. "What?"

Rasp welcomed the pain. Like a beacon of light, it drew his swirling thoughts into a single, focused direction. He wrenched his hand out from under her heel and worked his fingers up the worn leather of her boot until he found something to grasp onto. Rasp heard a faint scraping sound. His thoughts scattered for a moment as they raced to place the noise. She was cleaning under her nails with a knife. That meant play nice or get stabbed. On the other hand, this was Ellisar. He could play nice and get stabbed anyway. Play mean, then? Sergeant Farrow was a tough nut to crack.

"Ellisar, what happened to the etiquette lesson?"

For a few intense heartbeats, Rasp heard only the sound of her knife. *Scrape. Scrape. Scrrrrape.*

"Oralia postponed it," the elf said finally.

Ellisar actually answered—with words! Rasp hadn't gotten stabbed, either. And he was still here, in the present, and not riding his wave of thoughts into alternate dimensions. This was good. This was working. Tentatively, Rasp scooted closer and wrapped his arms around Ellisar's leg like a child clinging to their parent. She smelled overpoweringly of peppermint. A scent Rasp didn't normally associate with killers, which made it somehow more unnerving.

Actually, come to think of it, his grandad had told him once about a subspecies of elf that lived in the snowy reaches of the north. They were supposedly small and jolly, and handed out sweet sugar sticks to all the nice children one night of the year. When Rasp asked why he'd never seen one, grandad made some crack about there being no nice children in the ridge to visit. Rasp proved the old man's point by kicking him in the shin and running away.

You're doing it again.

Crap! Rasp tightened his hold on Ellisar's leg for fear of losing his delicate grip on reality. "Why did Oralia postpone the lesson?"

The scraping sound paused. From the way her body shifted, he could tell Ellisar was peering down at him. "Try to throw me and your throat will be slit before I hit the ground."

"I need an anchor and you're the closest thing I've got, okay? If it's any consolation, I'd rather be holding just about anyone else right now, including the blasted goblin." Okay, not entirely helpful, Rasp admitted. But on the bright side, Ellisar hadn't kicked him off yet. "Why did Oralia postpone the lesson?"

Scrape. Scrape. Scrape.

"Ellisar!"

"It was a horse, wasn't it? A horse kicked you in the head."

Rasp opened his mouth to bite her, but froze mid-snap. Was this lashing out? No, it was retaliation. Ellisar was being an ass, therefore the bite was entirely justified. Of course, she'd react and then he'd react, and so on and so forth, until one of them was holding his severed fingers in their bloodstained hands. Perhaps a level-headed approach wasn't so bad of an idea after all.

With a sigh, Rasp rested his cheek against Ellisar's knee. "Yes, it was a horse. Tell me what's going on now, please."

"My goddess, one etiquette lesson and he shows restraint already." Ellisar finished her preening before offering anything helpful. "We're back on the road as soon as these halfwits figure out which end goes in the saddle. Your keeper went to go find your horse and told one of us to watch you. The others scattered faster than a bunch of cockroaches, leaving yours truly holding the bag."

Rasp's stomach didn't drop, it plummeted. If it hadn't been for the fact he was sitting, he was certain it would have splattered onto the ground between his feet with a wet, sickening squelch. While his bowels were dealing with this sudden rearrangement, Rasp's head was experiencing its own crisis. His thoughts, having finally calmed, bolted like a herd of frightened horses and scattered into thirty different directions at once. His mouth tumbled open and his thoughts ran free from his trembling tongue. "Back on the road? But what about the dragons? Or the foothills, or the swamplanders, or th—the . . ."

The flat of Ellisar's blade rapped harmlessly against the top of Rasp's head. "Wildfire."

"What?"

"Couple of the scouts returned this morning. According to them, that's what drove the dragons out. Wildfire."

While Rasp often cherished Ellisar's lack of conversational skills, today it was having the opposite effect. Getting information out of her was like pulling teeth from a slumbering bear. You either limped away with a tooth, which may or may not have been your own, or you didn't come back at all. "That's all you're going to tell me? Where? How big? Is it still burning? Please tell me Captain Monk knows you can't fight fire by throwing soldiers at it."

Ellisar made a noncommittal grunt.

"I'm the guide. I need to know these kinds of things. What if the route is inaccessible?" On second thought, that would be ideal. Rasp wouldn't have to sabotage the mission from the inside. It was perfect! Wildfire. Even Oralia couldn't wage war on nature. Rasp clenched Ellisar's leg tighter, silently willing for it to be so. *Oh please, oh please, oh please.*

The elf's monotonous reply extinguished his rising spirits. "The fire is on the other side of the range, genius. Where the dragons live, remember? Road conditions are clear on our side. As it stands, we're expected to reach the foothills by nightfall."

The optimistic *oh please, oh please, oh please* ringing within Rasp's head quickly transformed to *oh gods, oh gods, oh gods. Oh no, oh no, oh no. I'm dead, I'm dead, I'm dead.*

Rasp couldn't go back onto the road. Not yet. Not like this. For the gods' sakes, he couldn't keep track of where he was putting his own feet, much less anyone else's. He was too scatterbrained; he'd lose track of time and miss his window of opportunity altogether. And then he'd be forced to take the traveling party all the way up the mountain. They'd reach the village and Oralia would learn the truth . . .

"Ah!" Rasp dug his fingertips into his forehead to relieve the pain that'd built behind his eyes. "Shut up! Shut up! Shut up!"

"Mister Stoneclaw," Willem said curtly, "if you think you can deliver the lesson better, by all means, speak up. I would be most curious to hear your thoughts on the difference between an assertive handshake and an aggressive one."

Oh gods, not again. How was this still happening?

CHAPTER FIFTY-FIVE

Are You Describing Diner or Torture?

Rasp's feet might have been figuratively planted back in reality, but he quickly realized they were not, in fact, planted in anything. The world shifted beneath him with a bobbing, rhythmic sway. He dove forward, searching desperately for something to grab onto. The warm, musty smell of horse filled his nostrils. How in the realm had they gotten him on a horse without his notice? It was official. He'd lost it. So much so, Rasp wasn't sure if he knew what "it" was anymore. Or whether or not he'd ever actually had "it" to begin with.

Rasp felt something bounce off his shoulder. "Welcome back," Rali muttered. "You missed the most fascinating lecture on napkin placement."

"I thought the lesson got postponed."

"It did. Two hours ago. Back on now." Rali was riding alongside his right. Her obscured shape was down low, not enough to be walking, as Rasp was pretty sure if that were the case she'd be *under* the horse, but about hip height. Her pony was sandwiched between him and Willem—who was currently little more than a fuzzy gray outline.

Rali's voice cut back in. "You've been such a star pupil keeping your mouth shut this long, bucko. You've had me worried."

The lesson was back on. There was still time. He could still say the thing!

"I heard the protector's changed her retire and she's not going to mind!" Rasp, gripping the saddle for dear life, realized not only had he said this incorrectly, but loud enough for the entire countryside to hear. He rolled his head back with a groan. "Shit!"

"A gentleman does not curse, Mister Stoneclaw," Willem said. "Foul language indicates one is incapable of expressing themselves competently."

Rasp opened his mouth to mutter something about informing the next gentleman he came across, when a hand yanked on his pantleg, nearly pulling him from the saddle.

"What's with you today?" Faris hissed.

"What's wrong with me? I'm caught in a downward spiral, barely grasping onto reality, and every time I've finally figured out where I am, the setting's changed!" Rasp wiped a bead of sweat from his brow. The morning fog had lifted and now, out on the open road, the full force of the sun beat down over the top of him unobstructed. "The better question is, where have you been? I'm in crisis! You're supposed to pull me out of these kinds of things."

"For the record, no one abandoned you. You've been in capable hands all day. It's not my fault you got stuck in your own head. We even had a whole conversation about whether or not snake tastes like rat, and you didn't try to use that as an excuse to go procure both!" Faris gave Rasp's leg another strong shake, muttering under his breath, "Now do me a favor and get it together, Dinglehead. I'm the one who's going to get his ass reamed if you don't."

Alas, despite Faris's attempt to impart this quietly, Willem's sharp ears caught it nonetheless. "Mister Belfast, as the son of a prominent community figure, you more than anyone should know how to conduct yourself. Lead by example, sir."

"My deepest apologies. I meant to say 'I'm the one who will get his haunches handed to him.' Is that better, sir?"

"'His backside bruised' sounds more eloquent." This voice, in its flat, disinterested delivery, could have only come from Ellisar.

Snag piped up next with, "Nah, his hindquarters quartered is better."

Rasp could barely pick out their blurry shapes on the road ahead of them, which in itself was unusual as the pair often avoided being anywhere near the main party. Ellisar's dry voice cut back in, asking, "Are you describing dinner or torture?"

"His hindquarters skinned, quartered, and roasted on a spit would be dinner. With a pinch of rosemary and a crack of pepper. . ."—here the goblin inserted an unnerving purr—"perfection."

"Stop. You're making my mouth water."

Faris's unusually high-pitched tones wavered between disgust and horror. "You're talking about my legs! Eating my *legs*!"

Ellisar made a soft grunt of disagreement. "Your ass, technically."

"Hold up!" Rasp raised his voice to drown out Willem's objection. "I understand why Faris is here, but why you two? You've got no reason to be listening to this." The pair normally patrolled the surrounding area for what they insisted was protection. Rasp supposed that was true. If you included protecting the main party from their bored antics, that was.

"Special assignment from the boss," Snag explained. "The protector wants us close by in case someone has to fish you from the river again."

"Which is why we brought Curly," Ellisar said. "So we can make him do it."

"Not true! I was here first." From the proximity of his booming voice, the orc was somewhere on the road behind them.

With a muttered curse, Rasp twisted his upper body around in the saddle. The larger hazy shape he recognized as Curly. The other, smaller one riding beside him appeared eerily similar to every other unidentifiable blur that made up the majority of the traveling party. "Gods, did Oralia call in everyone on this? Faris, who's that little blob next to that great big one?"

"Lady Lazuli."

An involuntary whimper worked its way from the back of Rasp's throat. "Why's she here?"

"Ready to swoop in once the etiquette lesson is over to finish the translation, I imagine. Snag told me all about last night's reading. Fascinating stuff."

With a sound caught somewhere between a wail and a groan, Rasp shifted back into a more comfortable position. He returned to the conversation in time to catch the tail end of what might have been a telling-off from Curly. While Rasp didn't have any particular interest in the goings on around him, between reviewing table manners and his people's secret history of magic, Curly's ranting was definitely the preferred choice. Especially since he wasn't expected to participate.

"You're both just mad I ain't taggin' along behind you anymore," the orc carried on. "Not so fun when I'm not around to be the butt of the joke, is it?"

Snag spoke in a ragged whisper that, from its volume, probably wasn't meant to be subtle. "I'm telling you, Ellisar, it's the elfling. Someone's going to have to have the conversation with the big oaf before he gets himself in trouble."

"What conversation?" Ellisar wondered.

Snag racked his brain for the correct phrasing. "The humans call it the— uh, chickens and caterpillars?"

"Oh gods, Rasp," Rali managed to wheeze between bursts of laughter. "Outdid yourself on that one, bucko."

Curly, yelling to be heard over the lieutenant's whooping laughter, said, "What in the seven realms of chaos does that mean?"

Ellisar was less diplomatic in her explanation. "It means you want to fuck the emissary."

"Keep spreadin' lies like that, Snag, and I'll smash you!"

"No, idiot. See? This is the problem. It's the ladyship you want to smash, not me."

With an infuriated snarl, Curly spurred his horse faster. Alas, by the time he reached the others, Snag's steed was already galloping ahead of them. Rasp listened to the heavy hoofbeats grow fainter as the two riders, one laughing and the other cursing, left them to choke on their dust.

Rasp heard a third horse trot past at an unhurried pace. "Great. Snag was supposed to help with the translation when this is over. Now I have to make sure he comes back." Daana called back over her shoulder at them, "And for the record, Curly and I are not involved. In case anyone cares."

"We don't," Ellisar assured her.

"Oh, please," Rali said with a snort. "Don't care, my ass. You got docked two week's pay for what you did to the last one."

"She took advantage."

"And you took her hair."

"I thought she looked better without eyebrows."

A throaty croak disrupted their conversation. It was the kind of noise Rasp envisioned coming from a wizened old frog—one that had grown up on tales of princesses and magic kisses and inherited kingdoms, of which none came to fruition. This was nonsense of course, as the noise was not a croak at all, but Willem clearing his throat in a fashion that Rasp interpreted as "kindly shut up so I may continue this pointless lecture that no one, including myself, cares about."

"Do you require a lozenge?" Rali asked politely.

With a boldness Rasp had only ever witnessed in overconfident amateurs and concussed warriors, Willem addressed Ellisar instead. "Sergeant Farrow, unless you intend to partake in the lesson, please refrain from distracting my students."

There was a creaking of worn leather as everyone within earshot collectively sat upright in their saddles. Silence followed as those same people simultaneously held their breath and waited for the ensuing bloodbath. Ellisar Farrow was the elf equivalent of a wolverine. You didn't challenge her unless you thought getting torn to shreds was an excellent way to throw a little excitement into your life, all twenty-three remaining seconds of it.

After several pained moments of absolutely nothing, Rasp released his bated breath and aired his grievances to the sky. "This isn't fair! Has Ellisar killed him yet? I'm missing it, aren't I?"

"The only thing you're missing is your lesson," Willem said sternly.

"Don't get your hopes up, bucko." Rali snorted. "She's interested in only one kind of stabbing and I'm afraid to say it doesn't involve a knife."

"Speak for yourself," Ellisar said.

If Willem realized the danger he was in, he masked it well. "Sergeant Farrow, align your horse here beside mine, thank you. Now, as all of you have thoughtlessly wasted my time, I shall now waste yours. We will start over from the beginning. If you were paying attention the first time, then this will go quickly."

There was a collective groan from the group, but for some reason Ellisar's sounded different. It was a slow, whistly breath of air, as though forced between clenched teeth. "Oh my gods," Rali muttered in the tone of voice that implied she was shaking her head. "Really? That's what gets you all hot and bothered?"

"Don't shame me."

"Lieutenant Ralizak and Sergeant Farrow!" Willem cut back in. "Your constant interruptions will only serve to make this worse. I can drag the lesson on all day if need be."

Ellisar's hazy shape looked as though it had slumped over the front of her saddle. "Fuck," she whimpered. "It's like shivers down my spine."

"Mister Foss," Rali said loudly enough to drown out her companion's highly disconcerting noises. "I can see how it might look like I'm being a distraction, but I would like to point out that I'm not the one going full mast in the saddle here. I think that makes me a model student. So much so, I should be excused from this and all future lessons."

"Napkin placement." There was not an ounce of mercy in Willem's sour voice. "In what manner should one place the napkin to indicate they are finished with the meal?"

"Really? That's how this is going to be, huh?" Rali grumbled. "Well let's see then. You, uh, put the napkin—"

Ellisar was a hair faster. "Stuff it in your mouth and bend over the table!"

"This is why we can't take you anywhere." Rali addressed the horrified etiquette instructor next. "I'm afraid the sergeant's going to take some serious time and elbow grease. You might want to consider private lessons."

"Is it a bring-your-own-grease situation?" Ellisar wondered.

"For the last time, no one wants to hear about your collection of lubricants!" Rali said far louder than necessary. There was a subtle shift in her tone, as though the script in her head had flipped to a fresh page. She said, clearing her throat with a polite cough, "You know, while we're on the topic of grease, I couldn't help but notice the spiffy polish you've got on those boots, friend. Your footwear is too nice to be military issue, but more practical than your typical court fashion. Where might a gal find herself a pair?"

The portion of Rasp's brain not paralyzed by disgust told him to stop being overdramatic and take advantage of the opportunity. Ellisar and Rali were already steering the lesson in whatever direction they wanted, leaving him free to roam his thoughts. If he focused, and latched onto his newfound concentration, he might be able to finish concocting an exit strategy that involved more than just shouting the word *escape!* over and over to himself.

Rasp channeled his mind into a steady focus. The details of the plan dutifully unfolded before him.

The traveling party would reach the base of Mount Hook by nightfall. The pass was another half day's journey uphill from there. He would lead them to the pools and then, under the pretense of making sure he was in the right area, insist on crossing the water ahead of the party to disable the trip wires and deadfalls. Oralia would require an escort, of course. Rasp only hoped she wouldn't insist on coming along herself. Orcs, much like dwarfs and fauns, had a deep distrust of water. Utilizing this knowledge, Rasp would try to talk his way into taking a member of the scouting party with him instead. That way, when he set off the final trap, his escorts would likely be more interested in saving their own skins and not altogether concerned with dragging Rasp to safety with them.

What then?

Worry gnawed at his internal organs like a toothless fish gumming a long, slippery worm. The chances of his plan actually working were slim to none. But what if it did? He might have been in home territory, but that didn't negate the fact that he was blind. Could he rely on Mother and the ravens to get him to safety? And even so, his plan failed to account for the one annoying detail that could bring everything to ruin.

Whisper.

The others wouldn't be able to follow him, but a shapeshifting witch might. This was going to be a problem, one for which Rasp didn't have a clear answer. The foothills were only hours away and his time was running dangerously short. If he didn't come up with a solution soon, he would be forced to fall back on his old tried-and-true method of act first, try not to die immediately afterward.

Oh yeah, you're dead. Dead, dead, dead . . .

CHAPTER FIFTY-SIX

Rocks and Fish Heads

Snag?" Daana called, peering into the leafy boughs above, uncertain of exactly where he'd gone. She had caught up to Curly and together the pair followed Snag's trail off the road and into the trees. A quarter mile in, they'd located the goblin's shaggy steed grazing at the base of an overgrown poplar. Its rider was nowhere to be seen.

Daana glanced over her shoulder at Curly. "Do you think he's alright?"

"He won't be when I get a hold of him." Curly slid from his horse and landed among the ferns and dry needles with a heavy crunch. He paced up and down the stretch of forest, venting his frustration on any unfortunate shrubbery that happened to inconvenience his path. The coat of chainmail that hung over his chest puffed in and out with each laborious breath. Its metal links glistened as Curly stomped along, crossing beneath random shafts of sunlight that filtered down from the thick green and yellow treetops overhead. "You hear that, Snag? When I find what tree you're hiding in, I'm chopping it down with you in it!"

"No you won't," Daana scoffed as she dismounted and tied her horse next to Curly's. Her chestnut mare was dwarfed by his dark bay charger. She gave the larger horse a cautious berth as she picked her way around the tree to where Curly paced. Ferns and various thorny vines carpeted the dense forest floor, making it difficult to take a single step without getting tangled in something.

Curly's nostrils flared as he glared at her. "Yes I will!"

A few days ago she would have been frightened by his scowl. After witnessing his interactions the night before, however, she was beginning to realize that Curly was all bark and very little bite when it came to those he was closest to. She didn't belong in that category *yet*, but he had abandoned

Ellisar and Snag to ride alongside her that morning. Surely that meant some-thing. "All Snag has to do is cross to another tree." Daana pointed to the way the leaf-laden branches interweaved high over their heads. "Is your plan to cut down the entire forest? You'll tire out before he does."

Curly clicked his tusks softly as his scowl deepened along the edges. "Why are you here again? This is between me and—" He paused, tilting his freshly shaved head as he listened. "Do you hear sawing?"

The sudden rustling crack overhead prompted Curly to jump aside, yanking Daana with him. A hefty branch struck the forest floor in a flurry of fluttering, lance-shaped leaves and upturned dust. Curly shook his ax at the boughs above him. "What is wrong with you?"

Snag's ragged voice cackled back, "Just moving things along faster."

"What things?"

"Well you're holding hands now, aren't you?"

Some of the color drained from Daana's face as her gaze dropped down-ward, noticing that indeed, she was clutching Curly's hand. She recoiled at the same time as him, as if both suddenly realized they touched something that had come out of the wrong end of a sick dog.

Curly wiped his palm against his thick trousers. "Go back to the road before he drops another tree on you."

The tips of Daana's ears burned. "No. *You* go back to the road. I need Snag to help finish last night's translation." Her previous plan to ditch the journal had been thwarted by the fact that it had finally turned interesting. She would have insisted on finishing the entire thing the night before had Rasp not turned into a screaming banshee.

"You think you can con Snag into more work? He played nice 'cause he owed Sascha a favor. And even then, it took me talking him into it. You're dreamin' if you think you're going to get lucky twice."

"Then I'll bribe him."

Curly crossed his burly arms and sneered, "With what?"

"These earrings are nice." Snag's voice called from behind them.

"Shit." Curly's eyes went wide as he barreled past her. "He's got the horses!"

Daana spun around to find Snag perched on top of her horse, rummag-ing through her bags. The reins to Curly's mount were already tethered to Daana's saddle. The goblin waved his goodbyes as he spurred the chestnut mare into a trot, taking Curly's charger with him. Curly ran to catch the escaping horse thief, but his efforts were in vain. Even at a gentle trot, the animals easily outpaced him. Snag stood in the saddle and blew a farewell kiss as his scraggly shape disappeared between the trees back toward the road.

"Daana!" Curly turned and cupped his hands around his mouth to amplify his call. "Catch Wormy!"

She blinked, uncertain of whether or not she'd heard correctly. "What?"

"The thing Snag calls a horse! Behind you!"

Daana moved toward the untethered creature, only now realizing if Wormy were in fact a horse, he belonged in an exhibit and not a stable. The beast had a mottled tan and black shaggy coat that stuck out in odd tufts of hair along his rotund body. His legs were short and thick and, most bizarre of all, there appeared to be a set of yellowed tusks protruding from his mouth. Wormy grazed unbothered, eliciting soft snorts and squeals as he happily nipped blades of grass from the leaf-littered floor.

A piercing whistle split the air around them. Wormy's ears perked and his head snapped to attention with a snort. He eyed Daana warily as she continued to inch closer. Her hand was just grasping his woven bridle when a second whistle from Snag prompted Wormy into action. The small horse bounded past Daana and trotted circles around Curly, successfully evading him each time the orc lurched for his lead before finally rambling off in the direction his owner had gone.

When Daana reached Curly, he was bent at the waist with his arms resting on his knees and his head down. The road wasn't too far, fortunately. The embarrassment of returning back to the traveling party on foot would be more painful than the journey itself. That was, if her walking partner survived. From Curly's labored breathing, Daana half wondered if the orc was going to keel over from exhaustion.

She leaned against a mossy trunk and waited for him to recover. "Did we just get outsmarted by a horse?"

"He's not a horse," Curly panted. "I've got six silver riding on that thing being some kind of mutant pig."

"Why did he abandon us out here?"

"He's a pig-horse. Why does he do anything?"

"No." She pressed her fingertips to her temples and groaned. "I meant Snag. Why did he steal the horses and leave us? I thought you two were friends."

Curly eased upright and twisted his neck this way and that until it produced several sharp pops. Still breathing heavily, he started back toward the road at a slow walk. "Well yeah, we are."

"Friends don't abandon friends in the forest."

Curly's eyebrows furrowed together. He glanced down his nose at her, appearing genuinely perplexed by her statement. "What are you talking about? We do all the stuff friends do. Rocks under the bedroll, rotten fish heads in each other's pack—oh, this one time he shaved a heart into the back of my head and nobody told me. I went a whole day getting funny stares wherever we went. I got him back good, though. Waited 'til he passed out and lined the inside of his jacket with goatheads."

Daana's lower lip trembled with disgust. Curly seemed to realize his error in communication and corrected the misunderstanding. "Goathead thorns. Not the animal. That would've been way too noticeable. Have you seen the size of Snag? I'd only fit like one in there. He'd have turned it around and served it for breakfast, anyway. A prank's no good if you're the one who's gotta eat the punchline."

Daana narrowed her eyes at him. "Are you sure you're not confusing friends for enemies?"

"Maybe you've just got boring friends."

Dried, curled leaves crunched underfoot as the pair picked their way through a thick blackberry patch that blanketed the ground for as far as the eye could see. Curly didn't seem to mind how the thorns tore at his thick clothes, but each step caused Daana to wince with pain. She was in the process of untangling a vine from her shin when Curly's question caught her unprepared. "What are your friends like?"

"Uh." Her jaw slung open but nothing useful tumbled out.

"You do have friends, don't you?"

"Of course I do. I just don't see them very often. You know how it is, everyone gets busy and weeks become months and—"

"Gross."

Daana whipped her head at him. "Gross how?"

"I've got this weird feeling, here." He thumped his fist against the chain-mail on his chest. "It's like sad, but not for me, for you. But you're the sad little loner with no friends, not me. Why's that make me feel bad?"

"You don't have to feel sorry for me."

"Gross," he corrected. "I feel gross for you."

With a guttural groan, Daana stomped ahead of him with her arms held stiffly at her sides. Her cheeks burned as she walked. What did he know about friends? Maybe it was just terribleness that bonded the faithful four together. Rocks and fish heads, ha! She didn't need that. She was better off on her own. Besides, there would be plenty of time for companionship later. The mission came first. Once she and Willem were back at Sunstorn with the ghost in hand, *then* she could focus on improving her social life.

Starting it, her inner voice said. *Something has to be started before it can be improved.*

Gods, even her thoughts were against her!

Something soft and squishy bounced off the back of her head. Daana spun around, mouth curled, prepared to shout at Curly when a second projectile splattered across her cheek. She wiped at the dark juice that dribbled down the side of her face, aghast. "Did you just throw a blackberry at me?"

A mischievous smile pulled at Curly's thick lips as he bent and gathered a second handful. "This makes me feel less sad for you."

Daana shook her finger at him. "Don't you dare!"

Despite her warning, a third, fourth, and fifth berry whipped at her with impeccable aim. Daana produced a sound she'd never uttered before, a sort of soft, infuriated roar, as she dove forward and hurriedly plucked a fistful of soft berries into her open hand. The blackberries squished beneath her ungentle touch, staining the tips of her fingers a deep purple-black color. Daana flung her arsenal at him one after another, pausing only to throw her arms up in order to prevent being pelted across the forehead by his more practiced aim.

They chased each other the rest of the way to the road. By the time the trees started to thin, revealing the dirt path beyond, Daana was covered from head to toe in berry carnage. Her fury had softened, and she could barely walk straight around the laughter that bubbled up from her chest. Although he was a substantially larger target, Curly's clothes were not nearly as stained as hers. Practice, Daana resolved, would fix that. Lots and lots of practice.

"Gods!" she cried, as something soft and wet splattered inside her ear. Daana clasped a hand to the side of her head. "How'd you get it in my ear?"

"I was aiming for your mouth."

"Lady Lazuli." A stern voice rang out around them. Daana froze, watching with mixed terror as Lieutenant Holt materialized from between the trees and marched stiffly toward them. "What are you doing away from the main party?"

Curly tossed a berry into the air and caught it with his mouth. "Foraging. What's it look like?"

Lieutenant Holt's stony expression revealed none of the thoughts that flickered behind her pale blue eyes. "Captain Monk." She raised her voice to be heard from a distance. "Over here, sir. Her ladyship has been located."

There was a rustle of leafy branches and the crunch of dry needles and twigs underfoot as several bodies moved quickly in their direction. Captain Monk appeared first, flanked by two soldiers. "My lady," he boomed, horror-stricken by her disheveled appearance. "Are you alright? What happened? I noticed you were missing from the travel party and knew something had to be amiss. You're so fortunate we found you!"

Daana stopped picking the clumps of smashed berries from her hair and glared at him. "Fortunate? I'm perfectly fine."

"Lady Lazuli, we have been over this. You were strictly forbidden from tramping through the woods unescorted. If something happened to you, your uncle would have my head!"

"Unescorted?" Daana said. She stared closer at him, noting the discolored bruise the captain sported under his right eye. Surely Rasp hadn't hit the man so hard it scrambled his brain. She twisted around and gestured to Curly, who appeared not worried, but bored by the spectacle. Daana bit back the words "are you blind" and opted for a more diplomatic, "Captain, I appreciate your concern, but your worries are unfounded. Curly was with me the entire time. You couldn't ask for better protection."

Captain Monk's honey-brown eyes shifted from her to the orc and his warm expression went ice cold. "The lady might be naive to your games, but I am not. If I find you leading her astray again, I will—"

With a creaking groan, a gnarled branch snapped away and splintered against the ground behind Curly. The two flanking soldiers drew their swords and stepped closer to the captain. Something rustled through the blackberry thicket around them. Hidden by the dense foliage, it circled the group twice and then, with a warbled call somewhere in pitch between a peacock and a boar, took off at a fast, lumbering gallop deeper into the trees.

Lieutenant Holt was staring wide-eyed at Captain Monk. "Captain . . ."

He held up his hand to silence her. "That was the hunting call of a swift tail." His words were probably meant to sound like a whisper, but were emitted so loudly Daana was certain anyone within a mile radius, including the dragon, had heard him.

"Which is why we should return to the road and rejoin the others immediately."

"Nonsense, Lieutenant. If this beast thinks it can hunt anyone from my party, then it had best think again. Fear not, Lady Lazuli! You and Lance Corporal Cortair may return to the road. I'll see to the dragon." Captain Monk offered Curly a disdainful look as he strutted past, followed reluctantly by his stone-faced lieutenant and the two soldiers. "Being hunted by a blasted swift tail and none the wiser. This is why you leave the protection to the professionals!"

"Yep." Curly seized Daana by the wrist and pulled in the direction of the road at a swift walk. "You'd better get to it then. Not me, I don't mess around with them bloodsuckers."

He didn't say anything more and Daana dared not ask, at least not until Captain Monk and the others were a safe distance behind them. She studied Curly's broad face as she hurried along, noting the way he bit his lower lip and how his blue-gray skin pinched around his dark eyes. The pair broke through the final row of scraggly trees and stumbled out onto the adjoining road. She was both surprised and relieved to find her chestnut mare tied to a tree alongside Curly's charger several yards further down, awaiting them.

Something crashed through the dry brush in the distance, growing steadily closer. Daana looked to Curly and, being that he didn't seem altogether concerned, decided against ducking behind him for cover. Moments later, Wormy burst from the thick groundcover and plodded out onto the road with Snag sitting relaxed in the saddle.

Despite having set out to crush him originally, Curly was nothing but smiles as he lugged past, clapping Snag hard on the back. "You know that was a mating call you did, and not a hunting one, right? Fucking spot on, though. That was good."

"Last I checked, dragons don't drop branches on people either. Served its purpose. Captain smells like he could use a good fuck anyway." Snag scrunched his wrinkled face, blinking in the harsh sunlight. "We're good now? I don't have to worry about you lobbing something at the back of my head?"

Curly hooked his foot into the stirrup and heaved himself into the saddle. "Yeah, you're my favorite again."

"Damn right I am."

Daana followed Curly's example and mounted the chestnut mare, albeit a lot less gracefully than the way he made it look. Fortunately, neither of the other riders said anything. Something hanging from Snag's ears caught the sunlight and sparkled brilliantly. Daana shielded her eyes, scowling at him. "Are those my earrings?"

"Fetching, aren't they?" he laughed. Snag clicked his tongue and Wormy dutifully clomped along the dirt road toward the plume of dust kicked up by the caravan traveling ahead of them. "You want me to finish that stupid book of yours, don't you? Gonna cost you."

CHAPTER FIFTY-SEVEN

Team Breakfast

By the time the trio returned to their place in the traveling party, the etiquette lesson appeared to have gone so far sideways it no longer qualified as teaching, but torture. Specifically, torture for Willem. His dappled horse was squeezed between Ellisar's palomino and Rali's pony. The two faithful talked loudly to each other over the top of him. Willem sat with his fingertips dug into his forehead. His eyes darted back and forth from beneath his hands, as though he were debating abandoning the assignment altogether and hightailing it into the trees, never to be seen again.

Rasp, the fourth and final member of the lineup, appeared to be present only in the physical sense. From the way his sightless eyes stared upward at nothing, Rasp's mind seemed to have wandered off once more and consequently fallen down a very steep, potentially bottomless ravine. Someone had taken advantage of his inattentive state and placed a straw hat on his head, complete with a lovely pink ribbon.

As Daana drew closer, the subject matter of Lieutenant Ralizak and Sergeant Farrow's lively conversation grew discernable. "Cake?" Rali gestured wildly with her hands. "You're telling me, if you could have one food for the rest of your life, it'd be cake?"

"What's wrong with cake?" Ellisar countered.

"It's limiting! Why not breakfast? That way you can have your sweet, your savory, eggs, potatoes, fruit, bacon, and practically everything in between! The variety is endless."

"That's not one food, though. You're not playing by the rules."

"Since when do we follow rules? And anyway, my point stands. Cake for the rest of your life would get boring."

"You underestimate how much I like cake."

"What about pancakes? Or muffins or scones? All fall under the category of . . ." Rali's voice trailed off as she twisted her head, watching with her fuzzy eyebrows raised as Daana, Curly, and Snag fell back in line in front of them. "What in chaos happened to you two?"

Daana had insisted on stopping at a stream along the road and attempting to do something about her unkempt state. The ice cold, babbling water helped rinse the clumps of berry from her skin and hair, but did next to nothing for the dark stains that marred her tunic and trousers. Wet, stained clothes, however, was preferable to the alternative: changing in front of Snag and Curly.

Daana flipped her hair over her shoulder, offering Rali a chipper, "We stopped to pick some blackberries."

The dwarf's eyebrows rose noticeably higher. "Did the berries fight back?"

"I think it's a euphemism," Ellisar said. "You know, roll in the hay, stopped to pick blackberries, that sort of thing."

Rali hunched her shoulders as a shudder worked down her spine. "Who in their right mind canoodles in a blackberry bush? Might as well throw yourself naked in a field of cacti and flail about!"

"Did it on a beach once. Sounds lovely, in theory. Until you realize you've got grit in every nook and cranny and it suddenly feels like the sheepskin you're using is made out of sandpaper."

Rali stared up at Ellisar dumbfounded. "I don't even know where to start with that one, El. I have so many questions I don't want the answers to."

Rather than engage, Daana decided the best course of action was to ignore them entirely. From Willem's defeated composure, the pair was capable of wearing down even the strongest of resolves. Keeping Rali and Ellisar at a distance would be vital if she wished to get the rest of the translation completed in a timely fashion. "Mister Foss, is the lesson over? I need to borrow Rasp when you're done with him."

Willem looked up from between his gloved hands and Daana saw fire dancing behind his pale eyes. "Please, take them. Take all of them. I can't bear any more."

A part of her pitied him, but the last thing she needed was for the bothersome pair to derail her assignment as well. Besides, Willem was obviously more capable than he let on. He could handle Rali and Ellisar for a little while longer. In moments like these, feigned cluelessness was her best friend. Daana dismissed the idea with a sweet, empty smile. "No, thank you. I only need Rasp."

"He's yours." Rali, who held the lead to Rasp's horse loosely in one hand, tossed it to Curly. With the matter settled, she looked to Willem and her lips drew back in the most brilliant and simultaneously menacing smile Daana had ever seen. "Anyway, where were we? Oh, yes! Let's hear your position on this one food for the rest of your life debacle. Are you team cake or breakfast? You strike me as the liver and onions type, if I do say so myself."

Daana passed Snag the journal from her bookbag and set about readying her supplies. Writing while riding would be difficult, but she was certain she could manage it. She glanced over at Rasp. Still maintaining his best impression of a statue, he appeared absolutely unaware of what was taking place.

Now where in the seven realms had Faris gone?

A quick check of her surroundings confirmed the faun had taken advantage of the etiquette lesson to slip away. He walked several rows behind them, conversing with the herbalist while she threaded a crown of daisies through his snowy hair.

While writing and riding at the same time was manageable, wrangling an unresponsive Rasp Stoneclaw on her own would be less so. Without Faris to handle him, Daana would have to assume the role the best she could. "Rasp," she called. "Are you alright? Do you need some water or something?"

In lieu of a reply, a bead of saliva dribbled from the corner of his slack mouth.

"That's not how you get his attention." Curly leaned over in the saddle and snatched the straw hat from Rasp's head and smacked him across the face with it. "Hey! Snap out of it already."

Rasp jumped nearly a foot in the saddle and came down hard, grimacing. "I know not to put my tables on the elbow. It's a personal choice!"

A hush swept over the group. Even the boisterous Lieutenant Ralizak fell silent as she and Ellisar tabled their food discussion in order to watch the spectacle unfold. As the unfortunate individual tasked with leading this assignment, Daana realized managing Rasp would be left entirely up to her. The others knew it too, and were eagerly awaiting a show. If she had any hope of convincing the faithful four of her competence, it was now.

"Pardon?" Daana said.

"Excuse me," Rasp spoke in a strange, inflectionless tone as though some minuscule piece of his subconscious memory had slid to the forefront of his brain. "Pardon is for waitstaff, Lady Lazuli. A person of high standing says 'excuse me.'"

"Well done, Mister Stoneclaw!" Willem congratulated from behind them. "Bravo."

Daana was appreciative of the fact that Willem was behind her and therefore could not see her exaggerated eye roll. While she understood Willem's elation that one of his pupils, against all odds, had managed to retain a minuscule portion of his lesson, Rasp's inexplicable ability to recount proper etiquette was now derailing her own assignment. "Thank you for that, Rasp. Are you finished?"

"I don't know." There was a noticeable tremble in his hand. Rasp reached out and felt along the front of his saddle, as if to make sure the horse was still there. "I don't remember what it was I was doing."

"We're back to work on the translation."

"Oh gods, no," Rasp moaned as he slumped backward into the saddle. "I've had enough of that blasted book to last a lifetime. If I hear another sentence combining my people and magic together, I'm going to scream."

"Is that supposed to be a threat? So what? You screamed last night and we're all still here aren't we? You can't avoid learning history just because it makes you uncomfortable."

Rasp slouched lower, grumbling indiscernibly under his breath.

Daana would have prodded further, but a sudden change in the environment gave her pause. The surrounding air had grown inexplicably warm, sending a jolt of hot energy coursing through her veins. Daana stared at her arm, mystified, as the hairs prickled beneath the thick fabric of her sleeve. *Magic, really? At a time like this?*

There was an annoying throb at the base of her skull that hadn't been there before. Closing her eyes, she drew herself inward and focused on the magic. The energy had the same signature as the one she'd felt the day of the dragon attack. The same day Captain Monk had taken it upon himself to assign Daana not one, but two soldier escorts, inadvertently impeding her investigation. A flutter of excitement stirred to life within her. Daana's eyes shot back open and she fought to contain the sudden, giddy smile that threatened to break across her face.

The Palace Ghost had slunk from hiding at last!

CHAPTER FIFTY-EIGHT

A Lesson in Threats

Daana's gaze swept over each member of the faithful four, noting they carried on as usual, seemingly unaware of the magical presence that had seeped in among them undetected. Willem, however, had gone stone faced, as though he too sensed something was out of the ordinary. It was times like this that Daana wished they'd devised a secret code of hand signals. With Oralia's warriors so near, attempting to communicate their findings out loud would not only be suspicious, but dangerous as well.

She was in the midst of trying to catch Willem's attention when an unexpected shout nearly startled her from the saddle.

"I don't care if this is what you want!" Rasp's hands were balled into fists and held stiffly at his sides. "Don't I get a say, too? What about what I want?"

Gods, she didn't have time for this. Not now. Not when she'd finally picked up the ghost's trail again. Daana readjusted her position back into the saddle, grumbling, "What are you yelling at me for? I didn't say anything."

Rasp shoved his palm in her direction. "One at a time, please!"

Daana turned to Snag for clarification. In lieu of an explanation, he offered only a disinterested shrug. Curly was too preoccupied flipping the straw hat into the air and catching it to notice. Surely she wasn't the only one who found this a little bit odd.

"What exactly am I supposed to be getting out of this?" Rasp carried on, gesturing in front of his face with his hands. "This isn't even training. This is *learning*. They're different. You said nothing about—"

"Whoa, easy there." Without a sound to betray his arrival, Faris was suddenly wedged between Rasp's and Snag's horses. His hand gripped the top of Rasp's knee as he spoke in a hushed voice. "You're doing that thing again. You alright?"

Faris's touch startled Rasp from whatever frenzy he'd worked himself into. "No," he said sullenly. "I'm not alright. I want to go home."

"You *are* going home."

"No! Not that place. I hate it there."

And then, as swiftly as it had come, the magic was gone. It dissipated from the air like fog on a hot afternoon. Daana smoothed the hairs on her arm as she considered this strange phenomenon. The magic had flared in sequence with Rasp's outburst. To suggest the two were somehow intertwined was deeply illogical, and yet, she could not help but ponder what would happen if she tested this theory.

"Rasp, for the gods' sakes, you're acting like a child," Daana said, with the diplomatic yet cutting tone she'd learned from her uncle. "You and I are supposed to be establishing common ground. This translation is my first assignment and I am on a deadline. What will it take to get you to focus? Food? Bribery? It would be a shame to have to threaten you."

Faris swiveled around at her and shook his head furiously from side to side, upsetting the crown of flowers nestled over his horns.

"Threats?" Rasp straightened his poor posture eagerly. "Now you're speaking my language. By all means, please. Have at it, Lady Latouchy. Threaten me. See if you can send a shiver down my spine."

Faris looked despairingly to the crisp blue sky stretched overhead. "For your sake, Daana, I hope you have something to back that up. He is never going to take you seriously again if you don't."

Oh, she most certainly did. Daana had been saving this particular morsel for just the right moment. She glanced back down at her arms, dismayed to find the magical presence had yet to return with the reemergence of Rasp's temper. Perhaps it only needed a little nudge in the right direction. "This is your last chance, Rasp. Bow out now, while you still have your dignity. Else you will regret it."

Her warning, as expected, served only to embolden him. A snaggle-toothed smile pulled at Rasp's thin mouth. "Give me your worst."

"Very well." Daana had not only Rasp's attention, but the rest of the group's as well. From the corner of her eye, she watched as Lieutenant Ralizak and Sergeant Farrow's steeds edged noticeably closer. She expected Willem to take advantage of the distraction and slip away, but he stayed with his head tilted ever so slightly, listening for the eventual conclusion. Daana snapped her writing pad shut and announced, "In lieu of the translation, I think perhaps a short detour into mountain folk history is in order. For those of you unaware, the former leader of the Stoneclaw clan was Paler Stoneclaw. He sired seven children during his reign. What most people don't know is that all of his offspring were named after a specific theme."

"Wait! Stop, stop, stop! I've changed my mind." Rasp spoke loudly enough to drown out the last of Daana's words. He bowed in her direction, nearly spilling from his horse. "You win, Lady Lazuli. I concede."

"What?" Rali boomed from behind. "Oh, come on! We're invested now."

"Yeah," Curly said to Rasp. "What happened to your spine? You were all primed for a fight just a minute ago."

Rasp whipped his head at the orc, speaking through gritted teeth. "I didn't expect her to actually have something!"

Faris still plodded in the middle of the road between Snag's and Rasp's horses. He stared up at Rasp with a wrinkled brow and confusion written across his pale face. "Your name isn't Rasp? Why don't I know this?"

"Because it's irrelevant." Rasp clapped his hands loudly together, as if attempting to disrupt the barrage of inappropriate guesses coming from the four snickering warriors flanking him. It, naturally, had little to no effect. "Now all of you hush. Lady Lazuli and I have some very important common ground to till or something."

"You know I'm going to find out one way or another. Save us both the effort and just tell me."

"Fine, my name is Faris. Happy?"

"Well, that doesn't make much sense. What's the theme, then? You're all named after devilishly handsome fauns? Your parents couldn't possibly have named all seven of you Faris."

"Well, maybe they did! And that's why it's so embarrassing."

Their ensuing squabble faded into the background as the excitement in Daana's chest fizzled. Alas, it had been another hopeless dead end. The ghost's magic had not returned with Rasp's anger, as predicted. Daana considered spilling his secret, thus reigniting his wrath and earning the opportunity to double-check her results, but that too, came at a price. Rasp's secret was the only real leverage she had over him. Squander it now and she would have nothing to ensure his continued cooperation. That was one of the most difficult pieces about diplomacy—knowing the precise moment to play your hand. A handful of laughs wasn't worth an uncooperative Rasp Stoneclaw. Especially not with a deadline looming in the near future.

With a sigh, Daana flipped her journal to the corresponding page and readied her writing implement. "Begin reading whenever you're ready, Mister Flint."

It took some time for Rali and Curly to finish interjecting highly inappropriate name suggestions before the translation was able to pick up where it had left off. To Daana's continued dismay, the bulk of the reading amounted to little more than which ancestor begot the next ancestor and so on and so forth. After two hours of recording page after page of tedious Stoneclaw lineage, the closing text finally turned interesting.

For four generations, the Stoneclaw people lived in harmony with the mountain. Free from persecution, their magic prospered. Sage Stoneclaw, the Bear Warrior, bore two sons and two daughters. Daughters, Vada and Ira, inherited the magic of the beast from their mother. Elder son Hale was born a mighty water spirit. But the youngest, Gagan, had only the gift of magical detection. Envious of his siblings' magic, Gagan grew bitter and his heart hardened. So great was his desire for power, it awoke the spirit of the mountain.

The great evil, defeated by Ansel Stoneclaw, had not died but gone dormant. Without a vessel, the dark power had burrowed into the cold heart of the mountain and waited for a tormented soul to take. Awoken by Gagan's lust for magic, it sought him in his dreams. The evil promised Gagan power in exchange for his body.

The great evil gave at first, and Gagan found he wielded a magic like no other. But little by little, the darkness consumed him and eventually seized control of the vessel, unleashing the full force of its fury onto the mountain people.

The battle was great and bloody. Many warriors perished, including Gagan's own mother, the Bear Warrior. Only by destroying the vessel were the mountain folk able to thwart the darkness. Once more, its power did not die, but seeped into the ground. Fear gripped the clan. It was through magic that the great evil had reached them. To prevent disaster from happening again, the reigning leader, Basil Stoneclaw, condemned the use of all magic. The Stoneclaw clan forsook their gifts in exchange for peace with the mountain.

As generations passed, the reason was forgotten, but the fear and hatred of magic remained.

CHAPTER FIFTY-NINE

A Small Mercy

Damn this cursed mountain!" The elf scout, referred to by the others as Crim, hopped on one foot, clutching the other in his hands as he bounced. His frenzied antics disturbed several loose stones and sent them tumbling downward.

Oralia sidestepped the miniature rockslide spilling toward her. She breathed heavily through her tusks, attempting, but not succeeding, to hide her exasperation. "He stepped in *another* trap?"

The lead scout, Whitefern, shielded her eyes with a heavily calloused hand. "A nail, looks like. The mountain devils stick them into the landscape with the pointed end skyward." The elf stopped a rolling stone with the side of her worn boot. Her mottled green and tan uniform hung loosely on her willowy frame like a burlap sack on an understuffed scarecrow. The headful of dry, flaxen hair that stuck out at odd angles around the crown of her head did not help dismiss this impression.

The elf cleared her sinuses with an unpleasant sound and spat, mindful, at the very least, to avoid Oralia's feet. "We pulled up all the ones we've found so far," she said, swiping a dirt-smeared knuckle under her nose with a sniff. "The trouble is, you don't generally see one until it's lodged in your foot."

"Ah, that explains why you're back here, then," Snag said with an agreeable bob of his head. He finished raveling a tripwire around a stick and tossed it into his pack with the others. This particular wire had previously been connected to a spiked mace device that swung from the overhead tree the moment it was triggered. While the mace itself was too large for Snag to keep, he seemed content with the wire. This was the third such device he'd found and disabled so far. Oralia didn't know what Snag was keeping the wire for, but felt some minor relief knowing whatever heinous act he had in mind would not be targeted at her.

Whitefern contorted her weathered features into what she may have thought was a menacing expression. Snag, having spent a lifetime as an outsider in a foreign land, was familiar with nasty looks and, therefore, knew this one was underequipped. "What?" Snag watched her with the same half smile one might use for a fuzzy kitten flexing its claws. "I'm not judging. Seems sensible to me."

"It's not my fault Crim drew the short straw."

"I always draw the short straw!" Crim shouted, still bouncing.

Having reached the foothills of Mount Hook ahead of schedule, Oralia met Whitefern at the base of the mountain to inspect the supposed pass. Three of her faithful went with her, leaving Lieutenant Ralizak to keep an eye on things while Captain Monk organized camp. Of the five scouts sent to investigate the foothills the day before, two had returned to deliver the news of the wildfire ravaging the far side of the range. The remaining three, led by Whitefern, had stayed behind to scour the mountainside for the very specific set of landmarks given to them by Rasp. After a day of searching, Whitefern believed she'd found what they'd been sent to look for.

Oralia picked her way through the lichen-covered rocks and thorny brambles with care, knowing that if she lost her footing, she wouldn't stop until she hit the bottom. Which was a very long and lethal way down. The loose scree blanketing the steep mountainside made the journey all the more slow and treacherous. To add insult to injury, some terribly wicked-minded mountain folk had laid traps to deter climbers from passing this way. Thus far, the scouting party had encountered tripwires, nails, snares, and false footholds designed to give way the moment any significant amount of weight was applied to them.

Obi was the third and only human member of the scouting party. Oralia had originally mistaken him for a dwarf, given his lack of height and abundance of facial hair. The small man picked that exact moment to step onto a false foothold. He fell and slid downward on the seat of his already torn breeches with a high-pitched squeal, grabbing for anything that could impede his rapid descent.

Curly plucked him up by the nape as he slid past. With a forlorn sigh, the young orc set the trembling man back onto his feet. "Go around me next time, will you?"

"Should have brought the horses," Snag said wistfully. "Would have been faster."

Oralia peered at him sideways. Unable to manage the climb, the horses were already halfway to the nearest farm where they would rest and await the party's return. Snag, of all people, knew the limitations of a horse. This was undoubtedly a verbal trap of some sort. One Oralia was not going to step in.

Whitefern obliged him. "A horse would break its neck coming this way."

"And reach the bottom faster. Taking me with it," the goblin agreed, straight-faced. "Oh, well. Something to look forward to next time."

Oralia didn't listen to Whitefern's bewildered reply, instead choosing to watch Curly with growing concern. He trudged ahead of her, halfheartedly swinging his ax at the low-lying shrubbery. Normally Oralia would have left him behind, as orcs were not renowned for their superior mountain climbing abilities. But she sensed he needed the extra attention. Curly usually perked at the idea of being selected for a special assignment. Despite her efforts, she swore he looked more glum than the time he'd unknowingly sat on his pet toad.

"Snaglebrag, is there something wrong with him?"

Snag offered Whitefern a toothy smile that must have communicated something unpleasant, because the scout's face went pale and she quickly picked up the pace ahead of them. Satisfied, Snag turned back to Oralia and said, "Missing his dinner."

"He has missed plenty of meals without sulking about it."

"It's not a matter of the missed food, but the company, I suspect."

This was remarkably insightful for Snag, who normally dealt with other people's problems by kicking them from tall heights—the people, not the problems, as the reverse rarely solved anything. This was Curly, however, who was the golden exception to Snag's unspoken rule against close personal attachments. "Oh gods." Oralia winced as she realized his implied meaning. "Not the blasted emissary. Tell me you talked some sense into him."

"Do I look like his mother to you?"

Oralia would have countered with the same question had she thought it would help her case. Alas, she already knew Snag's answer. Despite her insistence otherwise, she was the closest thing Curly had to a maternal figure. Or a paternal figure. Or any kind of figure that counted as a semi-responsible role model, for that matter. She had fallen into the role not by choice, but obligation. That, and due to a pitiful lack of alternatives.

Snag shrugged. "I don't see what the issue is. He's young. She's young. Makes sense to me."

"She is a Lazuli!"

"Oh, I see. It's 'cause you think an elf and an orc don't belong together. That's a little hypocritical given your relations, don't you think?"

"You know that is not the reason. Daana represents one of the most powerful families in the realm." The same family Oralia just happened to be at odds with. While using Geralt's niece against him was a tempting idea, Oralia would likely get the short end of such a deal. Knowing Geralt, this may have been his plan all along. "And, in case you have forgotten, fooling around with a noble's daughter is how Curly got drafted into the four in the first place. I cannot allow it to continue."

"Sounds like a you problem." Snag slid his pipe from some hidden pocket on his tattered uniform and blew a note so sharp Oralia was too concerned with the sudden ring in her ears to admonish him. "Oi, Baby Face!"

Curly whipped around, his features curled into a snarl that normally would have sent the enemy scattering. Alas, he'd learned the look from Oralia, who was significantly better at it.

Snag merely tapped his clawed foot to demonstrate how absolutely unintimidated he felt. Despite the difference in size between them, the goblin was immune to all of Curly's looks, regardless of what sort of pain they promised. "The protector's got something to say to you."

"I did not mean right this instant!"

Oralia narrowed her eyes at Snag, but bit back further protest. There wasn't any point. He was already scuttling uphill with the spryness of some sort of young animal renowned for such movement. The word chicken came to mind, but Oralia wasn't sure that was correct. While thin and sinewy, Snaglebrag's arms didn't flap uselessly like a chicken's. Were grasshoppers spry? That seemed more apt of a comparison, given the way he bounded up the steep cliffside on all fours with a series of quick, effortless hops.

Curly slouched against a patchy spruce tree, allowing the goblin to spring past unaccosted. He kicked at the loose dirt with the toe of his boot, frowning. "What?"

Oralia's glare still had some effect on the young orc soldier, which was fortunate considering it seemed to do piss all for the other three. Curly immediately squared his shoulders and stood what he thought passed for straighter. "I mean, yes, Protector?"

Aside from threatening facial expressions, Oralia had no idea how to proceed. She stayed out of the private matters of her faithful four for the most part. Short of tossing the boy a pack of sheepskins and grumbling something about using his head, they'd never discussed sex or . . . what was it the younglings called it these days? Attraction, chemistry, or—gods forbid—feelings?

Damn Snaglebrag!

Oralia could barely navigate the nuances of her own relationships, much less someone else's. She held a hand to her forehead, hating every word that trickled from her mouth like warm ale from a broken tap. "Snaglebrag tells me that you and the emissary—"

Curly's eyes narrowed. "I don't care what he said, I don't like her."

"Oh." Relief washed over Oralia and the uncomfortable tightness in her lungs eased. She had to fight to stifle the grateful smile that threatened to break across her face. Some topics were better left alone, and this particular one was never going to be brought up again so long as she lived. Rali had a saying for such instances: job successfully avoided.

Unfortunately, Curly kept talking. "I mean, I like being with her, but I don't like-like her. I'd just rather be around her right now."

"Are the others picking on you again?"

"It's not them. It's you."

This was taking an unexpected direction. One Oralia was not sure she wanted to pursue. Regardless, her tongue formed the words before her brain could snap them back into her mouth. "And what did I do?"

"You're breaking us up." An awkward stretch of silence prompted more out of the reluctant orc. "Look, you want to retire, I get it. Good for you. But Ellisar's leaving as soon as you do, and Rali's already talking about finding other work, and Snag, well, it's just not the same if it's me and him. After this, we're over. I'm not gonna waste anymore of my time hanging around if you're all just gonna leave me anyways."

Something in Oralia's chest felt inexplicably heavy. They were the closest thing Curly had to family, and now they were abandoning him. Just like his real one had. Oralia found herself wishing he had feelings for the emissary. That seemed so much less of a problem now. "I cannot keep going on forever."

"I get it," he grunted. "You do you, and I do me, okay? Just leave it at that."

Oralia had met Curly's mother, Lyza, at court. Over many years, what had started as a mutual alliance gradually morphed into a genuine friendship. Oralia had been present at Curly's birth and was there, hours later, when the midwife delivered him to his father, along with the news that Lyza had not survived. Lord Cortair remarried soon after and sired more children. Each resulting sibling pushed Curly further and further down the hierarchy of importance. Without guidance, the young orc turned rebellious in his preadolescent years. It was only after he got caught with the wrong noble's daughter that his stepmother saw the opportunity to remove the troublesome heir once and for all.

Curly's stepmother insisted military service was how they would turn his life around. His father agreed, not realizing Lady Cortair had worked a deal to send the youngling to the front and, consequently, his death. Oralia was the hand that intervened. She drafted Curly into her personal company under the misconception that after his mandatory year of service had been met, they would part ways. That had been twelve years ago. Curly had defied expectations. As did Oralia's other three. Instead of turning on the youngling, they banded together to mold him into something that reflected a piece of each of them. The result of their efforts was Lady Cortair's living nightmare. A deadly, disillusioned young heir who no longer took shit from anyone.

Oralia looked into his dark, doleful eyes. For a moment, she recalled the scrawny youngling that once cowered before her, fighting his tears and trying to make sense of a father's betrayal. The heaviness in her chest sank deeper. "I am sorry," is what Oralia wanted to say. "I am sorry that you were abandoned into my care and that after this, I will be a traitor in your eyes. I am sorry that my choices will follow you for the rest of your life. For the past twelve years I have been untruthful to you. But I kept you in the dark to keep you safe. You were never supposed to be a part of this."

Perhaps it was better this way. If Curly pulled away now, before Oralia's treachery came to light, it would save him the brunt of the impending heartache. He would hate her, regardless of whether the hurt came sooner than later. But Oralia was used to being hated. Maybe it would be a small mercy to get it over with now.

"I am discharging you once the mission is complete. You will be given the opportunity to return home," she said. "I strongly suggest you take it. Your place was never on the battlefield. You belong in court, alongside your father and the other nobles."

Curly's jaw clenched and, for a moment, he looked at her with the same betrayal as someone who'd been gutted wearing impenetrable armor.

Despite her best attempts, Oralia had grown fond of the young orc, and him of her. The others often teased how protective she was of him—the one time he'd slipped up and accidentally called her "Mum" hadn't helped her case, either. She knew how he felt about her. What's worse, she knew how even more strongly he felt about going home. Insisting Curly return to the father that had abandoned him was a low blow, even for her. And it did exactly what she intended it to.

"Are you fucking serious?" he bellowed, after his thoughts had a moment to catch up with his fury. "You really think I'd go crawling back there after what he did? He's lucky I don't burn the place to the ground!"

"Lower your voice," Oralia said calmly. "This is still an active scouting mission. And in case you have forgotten, there are others around. I imagine you do not want word of this to spread throughout camp later." When he quieted to a hostile silence, she continued, "This mission is far from over. The difficult part has not even begun. I cannot afford to have the entire traveling party think I am not in control of my soldiers. Pull yourself together."

The fire in Curly's dark black eyes burned bright. Oralia had succeeded in pushing him nearly to the edge of hatred, but if she wanted it to stick, she needed a little extra shove to send him careening the rest of the way over. "Consider yourself fortunate that you have a home to return to. That is a privilege none of the other three have."

Curly emitted a gargled roar and stomped several feet away, pummeling the air with his fists. His words, low and guttural like a growl, emitted from between his tightly clenched teeth. "It's like you're trying to make me angry."

And succeeding, Oralia noted. "I am your commanding officer. Trying to make you angry in this situation does me no good."

"So it's just business as usual for you, is that it? Keep it together, be your scary personal soldier, and then when it's all over, I'm supposed to just go home? Like none of this even fucking mattered?"

"Were you expecting something different?"

"No, you've made that part perfectly clear for me, thank you." He turned to face her, still speaking through gritted teeth. "May I be dismissed now, Madam Protector?"

"You may."

With the conversation finished, Curly slung his ax over his shoulder and continued the climb, grumbling under his breath. Oralia waited for the distance between them to grow more substantial, ignoring the impulse raging inside of her to chase after him and take it all back. This wasn't how she wanted it to end. Her only consolation was that it was better for Curly this way. Protecting him did not apply to outside forces alone, but from herself as well. She knew if she didn't handle this now, he would follow the moment she fled the realm. The life of a traitor was not an easy one, and he deserved better. So much better.

Shielding her eyes against the smoky-gray light that hung thick in the air, Oralia saw the others had reached the final plateau. The pass to the Stoneclaw village was just beyond, tucked in some dark recess of rock formation. Oralia followed after Curly, who was already nearing the edge of the steep cliffside. She took each step carefully, watching for hidden traps underfoot.

Unlike the raggedy trees that dotted the steep mountainside, the vegetation at the top was thick and lush. The overgrown landscape boasted an array of colors that looked out of place against the otherwise barren terrain. Oralia smelled the water before the thunder of the falls reached her ears. She pulled herself up over the lip of the cliff, utilizing the rope someone had tied around the trunk of a well-rooted spruce. Oralia stood, dusted her hands against her thick trousers, and gazed at the last thing she expected to find on the Iron Ridge.

An oasis.

CHAPTER SIXTY

The Pass

A thundering waterfall cascaded the steep bluffs overhead and gathered below in a deep, churning pool. The pool fed the smaller streams that coursed like veins from the heart of the plateau to the lower rivers of the foothills. The vast sprawl of plant life carpeting the cliffside was enough to make even Oralia stop and take a moment to appreciate just how out of place the surrounding beauty was.

None of this belonged here. The plateau, the shape of the pool, everything down to the very species of plant life themselves—all of it had been strategically placed by generations of humans now long dead. She suspected this had been a private garden at some point. In its prime, even Sunstorn's famous botanical gardens would have paled in comparison. Years of neglect, however, had left the plateau wild and overgrown. Untended, the carefully cultivated patches of flora had spread, blending across the landscape like a watercolor painting whose poorly preserved layers had bled over into one another.

An array of plant life in endless shapes and colors sprouted from every available inch of ground, their stems snaking up the thick trunks and spilling from the crooks of trees like flowers from a maiden's hair. The very boughs themselves had been transformed into miniature forests. Black and white spruce, which ordinarily would not have commanded a second glance, were wrapped so densely in creeping vines and rainbowed blooms that they no longer looked like trees but giant, flowering shrines to an unknown deity of nature. Blossoming vines with shimmering pink and white lantern-shaped petals twisted skyward along the cliffs, in search of whatever footholds they could find on the face of the smooth rock.

If it wasn't for the Iron Ridge looming in the distance, Oralia would have sworn this was an alien world altogether. A sickly feeling gnawed at her resolve as she gazed in awe at her surroundings. Unlike the industrious vines, her soldiers could not scale the sheer cliffside. Her eyes scoured the mountainside, searching for an alternative way up, but found none. If the pass was blocked, there would be no going forward.

"We checked four waterfalls yesterday and this was the only one that matched the landmarks." Whitefern produced a folded piece of parchment from her breast pocket and pointed to several symbols carved into the cliff-side, half obscured by vines. "The signs are right, too. I think."

Their directions had been nothing more than a set of vague landmarks and several crudely drawn symbols. Courtesy of Rasp, whom Oralia suspected hadn't been much of an artist even before the loss of his eyesight. She peered at the markings on the paper and compared them to those carved into the rock. They were close, if you squinted your eyes and turned your head to one side. It probably helped to be drunk, too.

Remarkable. Anyone not in the know would see what the mountain folk wanted them to see: a beautiful but hopeless dead end.

"We looked up and down all day yesterday," Whitefern carried on. "We didn't find heads nor tails of this supposed pass. Either your guide is blowing smoke out his ass or it's a really, really good one."

"You did well, Corporal. Thank you."

As the elf had put so eloquently, the pass was simply hidden "really, really good." The surrounding cliffside angled sharply inward, with the waterfall at its center. Below, the pool stretched from either side along the base. While the design had a certain aesthetic appeal, its true purpose went deeper. With the entrance to the pass located in the cave system tucked behind the falls, one would first have to brave the waters in order to reach it.

Oralia chose to keep this information to herself. Currently, only she, Rasp, and her faithful knew the pass's location. According to Rasp, the entrance was strewn with booby traps. Oralia could not afford to have an overeager scout bring the entire cliffside down on top of them. Under the watchful eye of an escort, Rasp would lead the first crossing, disable whatever nasty surprises awaited on the other side, and then the rest of the party would follow.

Oralia regretted not bringing Rasp so they could get it out of the way now. With his sudden erratic behavior, however, Faris had warned that doing so would result in disaster. As much as it disgruntled her, Oralia knew to trust his instincts. Faris was the proverbial canary in the dark, poorly lit mineshaft that was Rasp Stoneclaw. If Faris sensed danger, it meant it was time to back slowly away.

"Take a moment to rest," Oralia said loud enough for everyone to hear. "Afterward, sweep the area. Disable any and all traps." Oralia's gaze shifted to Crim, who was strewn across a carpet of creeping dogwood, whimpering as Snaglebrag treated his wound. "And not with your foot, this time," she added silently.

Oralia strolled along the water's edge. Great moss-covered stones, slick with moisture, encircled the deep pool. The rocks rose from the surface like jagged teeth from the mouth of a prehistoric beast. Oralia found a boulder that wasn't too wet and sat, peeling away her boots to cool her aching heels in the icy water. Little fish drifted closer to investigate and were chased back into the shadows by a four-foot-long streamlined flash of silver and green.

Giant fish, Oralia grimaced. *How fitting.* Deciding she'd rather keep her toes, Oralia pulled her feet from the water and placed them onto the rock with a sigh. Of course the mountain folk had filled the idyllic ponds with predacious fish. What better way to keep intruders out? After all, why stop at land when you could booby trap the water as well?

"Heard you finally cut the umbilical cord."

The dry voice came from behind. Oralia didn't bother to turn her head as it wouldn't matter. As many unfortunate souls discovered the hard way, Ellisar wouldn't be seen unless she wanted to be seen, at which point you probably already had a knife sticking out of your back. "If you put a lizard down my shirt again, I will never darn another one of your socks so long as I live."

"Good for you." Ellisar settled onto the mossy boulder beside her and began the tedious process of prying off her calf-high boots. "About Curly," Ellisar clarified. "Not the sock business. We both know you like the challenge."

"He already told you?"

"It's amazing what people share when you don't talk back. They assume I'm not listening." The elf rolled up her pantlegs and exposed the white skin of her shins. Oralia saw the glimmer of her golden leg hairs catch the sunlight as she waded out into the knee-deep water. The peppermint oil Ellisar applied each night to ward off the biting insects rinsed from her skin and coated the surface of the water around her in a slick, translucent film.

"I would not do that if I were you," Oralia cautioned.

Ellisar carried on as though the warning didn't apply to her. "Now you only need to cut the umbilical cord on this damned mission."

"Are you mad?" Oralia checked to be sure the others were still where she'd left them. Whitefern, thankfully, was gnawing on a strip of fruit leather watching with morbid fascination as Snaglebrag treated the bottom of Crim's foot. Obi and Curly were disabling tripwires along the tree line. With the rumble of the falls in the background, Oralia and Ellisar's conversation would not carry far. Regardless, this was neither the time nor place.

Ellisar afforded her a look that said, "Of course, I'm mad. That's beside the point."

"We are not discussing this."

"Good. You stay quiet and I'll discuss," Ellisar said, broadening her stance in the water. She raised her open hand to shoulder height and, other than the subtle movement of her lips, crouched perfectly still. "You're in over your head. Say the word and I'll slip away and break Ashwyn out myself. No questions asked."

"That is exactly what Geralt is expecting us to do."

"In case you didn't know, the trick to staying quiet is to not speak."

"We already have people in place searching for where he is holding her. If you make a move now, it will ruin everything." Did Oralia expect Geralt to hold to his end of the agreement and free Ashwyn? Gods no. She wasn't an idiot. But she could play along—secure his stupid trade route, keep his attention on her, all while someone else worked on liberating Ashwyn. The problem was that the squirrely bastard kept moving her. By the time Oralia's contacts found where Ashwyn was being kept, all that ever remained was an empty cell.

"That's the problem," Ellisar said. "The people working on this aren't me."

"If I could afford to send you, I would. But that is not a possibility. We have not yet identified Geralt's spy. Who, I remind you, will report back to him the moment either of us goes missing from this mountain. Even if you rode day and night, the news would reach Sunstorn ahead of you."

"Then we fight him. You're still the Protector of the Realm. Half the capital forces would lay down their weapons if you told them to."

"And what about his private army, Ellisar? How do we match against a legion of witches trained in warfare?" The Division of Divination was not merely a magical academy for gifted witches; it was a means to build the most powerful army imaginable. Oralia had done her part to keep some of the more formidable magic casters from being forcibly enlisted into its ranks, but there was only so much one person could do. The division's numbers grew steadily each year despite her efforts.

"By playing your trump card!" The elf's golden irises flickered as the tight skin around her eyes narrowed. "What is the point of having an advantage if you refuse to use it? Call in the resistance. Start the bloody war! Pit witch against witch, that's your answer. No one said we had to stick around for the fight. We ignite the damn thing, get in, get Ashwyn, and get out."

"No," Oralia said sternly. A second visual sweep confirmed that she and Ellisar were still alone. Even without the threat of eavesdroppers, this was not a conversation she wished to continue.

Ellisar rolled her head back and stared upward with a vengeance. "It's like talking to a damn wall. The answer is right in front of you, and yet you refuse to see it."

"War is not the answer. I will not send thousands needlessly to their deaths as a matter of convenience. End of discussion." There was also the issue that, in order to spark the war, the resistance would require Oralia to lead its army. While she had managed to play both sides to her advantage well enough not to get caught, using her trump card would come at a cost she was not prepared to meet. The last thing she needed was to get trapped on the side destined to lose.

"No, not end of discussion. Beginning of discussion!" Ellisar, spying movement below, drove her hand into the water and came back up clutching a wriggling fish by the tail. It slapped about with its toothed snout, sending a spray of water and slime in Oralia's direction. "You don't want to start a war? Fine. Then at the very least stop trying to beat Geralt at his own game. Flip the fucking board onto the floor. Forget the route. Forget the witches and the realm. For the first time in your life, be selfish! Give up. We'll find some other way to get Ashwyn out."

"And abandon everything we have worked the last seventy-three years for? We are closer than ever to the breakthrough we have been waiting for."

"There it is. Right there." Ellisar stomped to the bank, water sloshing underfoot as she hauled her angry prize with her. The long fish snapped at her legs, but the elf took no notice. "You act like this is some kind of punishment for you, but you wouldn't have it any other way. You're doing this not because you have to, but because you *want* to. We could have been free of this shithole years ago if it weren't for your stupid martyr complex."

Ellisar switched to a deep, gravelly voice that Oralia suspected was supposed to be an impression of her. "Oh no, the realm is doing bad things to good people. I must help. But I can't help the other side too much, or they might actually make good on their threat to overthrow things. I know, I'll do everything myself in secret, while running myself and my friends ragged in the name of justice. What's that? It's really just forgiveness I want? No! Of course not. I'm just a big meanie who doesn't care what others think."

Ellisar's display was accentuated by some very dramatic stomping.

Was it a crime to want a legacy other than *"she had no sense of humor and killed a lot of people"*? On the surface, it was easy to justify the passage through the Iron Ridge. She was distracting Geralt under the guise of following his orders, all while handing the resistance a convenient escape route for those who wished to flee the realm. So what if it helped ease her conscience? She deserved a little peace of mind in retirement, didn't she?

Oralia didn't say this of course, because it would only earn further mockery from Ellisar. "Why does it upset you that I want to use the last of my power to help people?"

"Because you should be focused on helping yourself. Take a look around, Oralia. Accept that this is impossible."

Impossible was not a word one associated with Ellisar Farrow. Oralia peered closer and realized she saw worry etched across her friend's face. Not clearly. It existed in the cracks, barely visible. "What has come over you? You of all people throw yourself at danger with open arms."

"I'm tired," Ellisar huffed, striking the fish over the head with a fist-sized rock. "I have been fighting someone else's fight for longer than I can remember. I only want to collect my wife, take her somewhere far away from here, and grow old and decrepit together."

Dear gods. Ellisar had gone so far mad she'd somehow circled back to sane.

The elf cut from the vent to the gill junction with her curved dagger and proceeded to remove the entrails, tossing them into the water to the delight of the schools of littler fish. "I'm going to find us a bungalow along the coast somewhere. Just me and her, for the rest of our lives. Maybe a good sturdy bed. Some candles, a soft rope—"

Oralia held up her palm. "I get the sentiment, thank you. The point is moot. Ashwyn cares for the cause more than either you or I. She would never forgive us if she found out we did not follow through."

Ellisar considered this for a moment before offering her worst idea yet. "Then we don't tell her."

Oralia had only to arch her eyebrow to make her counterpoint.

"Oh, fine!" the elf snapped, flinging green and silver scales into the air as she pointed her knife at Oralia accusingly. "This is the reason you'll never get ahead, you know. You don't get anywhere playing fair. If any of you had listened to me from the beginning, we could have done it fast and dirty and been free of this mess by now."

"Taking more lives than necessary," Oralia added patiently. "Possibly inciting civil war. Precisely what we do not want to do."

"What *you* don't want to do."

"Corrupted or not, the realm is still mine to protect. I will not stand by and let innocent civilians suffer because you want to slash and burn a path out of it. That benefits no one, including the people we are trying to help."

If it was possible to perform an eye roll without actually moving one's eyes, Ellisar was accomplishing it now. Her tone, still flat and lifeless as a dead sea, *almost* had an edge to it. "If you say so."

"You promise me you are not going to go off course?"

Finished gutting the fish, Ellisar dipped it back into the water to wash away the blood and excess slime. "Aye, Cap'n."

CHAPTER SIXTY-ONE

The Old Flames of War

For a short while Oralia was content to watch Ellisar prepare the fish in silence. She stuffed the cavity with soaked sphagnum moss before placing it onto an awaiting strip of cloth. An additional bed of moss was arranged over the top of the fish before the whole thing was rolled into a tight bundle. Once finished, Ellisar placed the roll into her gunnysack and set it into the shallows to chill.

From the elf's hostile silence, Oralia knew to expect the cold shoulder for the rest of the evening. One of the few, fortunate advantages to being in charge was that her authority trumped Ellisar's petty aggression. She ran a calloused hand down her weary face and asked, "Did you learn anything about Willem?"

"Yar."

"I do not speak pirate."

Ellisar waded back out into the pool. "The blade he wears on his hip is decorative. All show, no quality."

Precisely something a clueless member of court would do. From Ellisar's tone, Oralia sensed this wasn't the case. "And that tells you what, exactly?"

"Means he's clever." She slashed at the water but came up empty this time. "An amateur sees a blade and leaves him alone. An experienced cut-throat sees a flashy knife, realizes he's not a threat, and lowers their guard."

"To what end?"

A breeze kicked up, wafting Ellisar's long hair over her face. With an annoyed grunt, she gathered it into a tie and flung it over her shoulder before crouching back into position. "You're so busy fixating on the pretty knife, you don't notice the real one he's got tucked in his sleeve. Not until it's pressed to your throat, I imagine."

With Rasp suddenly useless, Rali had enlisted Ellisar to help deal with the etiquette instructor. The hope was that playing off one another in their usual, escalating manner would throw Willem off balance and force him into revealing something. "Could he be protection for Daana, perhaps?"

"He's a lousy bodyguard if that's the case. Rali thought that too, at first. She had Snag lure the girl away from the travel party to see how he'd react. Didn't even bat an eye. My gut says Willem is here for something else."

"Hm." She would have to question Ralizak in greater detail later. While Ellisar was attentive, she was no bloodhound. Not like Rali, who had an uncanny nose for sniffing out even the most minute of details. "Anything else?"

Ellisar's mouth remained a flat line, but the skin around her eyes pinched, as though withholding a smile. "He's immune to my carnal charms." And, just like that, the conversation was over. Oralia's portion, at least. Ellisar carried on, cherishing every second of Oralia's growing discomfort. "All's not lost, though. All that peacocking caught the eye of another weary soul looking for a temporary reprieve from the humdrum path of life."

Oralia relaced her boots and stood. If there was ever a time to get back to work, it was now, before Ellisar conceived of five hundred different ways to artistically describe the graphic details of her intimate life. Most mistakenly believed the elf spoke only when necessary. The problem was they weren't discussing the right subject. Mention intercourse, and Ellisar suddenly had the soul of a poet trapped in the twisted mind of a sexual deviant.

"You're not even the least bit interested to hear who I netted into my spider web?"

Oralia would have kept walking if it were not for the snare she nearly stepped into. She bent to collect it, grunting over her shoulder. "No matter how many times you ask me that, my previous answer remains unchanged."

Ellisar shared anyway. "A certain Lieutenant Isadora Holt."

She knew it was bait, but Oralia could not help herself. She twisted her upper body back in Ellisar's direction. "Are you seeking information or pleasure?"

"Why do you assume I can only do one or the other?" Ellisar dove and came back up with another fish in hand, this one larger than the last. She dragged it to her cleaning station along the bank, neglecting the bare facts of the matter in favor of far too much detail, as usual. "She came stomping out the woods looking like she wanted to strangle something. I offered my own neck and few coy back and forths later, she's got me pressed against a tree with her tongue lapping circles around—"

"Do you have information or not?"

"Something about the captain has got her in a tizzy. She's not much of a talker, though." Ellisar glanced up from her work and a rare smile danced across her devilish lips. "A nice dinner intermingled with wine and some heavy petting might coax the songbird out of her."

Oralia winced at the unnecessary visuals. When Geralt had first enlisted Ellisar into Oralia's personal company, it was done so as punishment. Both for Ellisar—who, despite the speaker's best attempts, kept finding ways to thwart his efforts to imprison her—and Oralia. It worked at first. Ellisar saw Oralia as the enemy responsible for placing her and Ashwyn under arrest and Oralia, in turn, blamed Ellisar for turning her sister into a criminal. With time and more patience than either party previously thought possible, the old grudges faded. They eventually realized the ultimate insult would be to beat Geralt Lazuli at his own game and, thus, joined forces.

Still, there were times it felt as if Ellisar was deliberately trying to stoke the old flames of war. "It's your own fault," she called to Oralia. "This is what happens when you refuse to do things the easy way. You have to hear about my sexual escapades."

With an hour until sunset, the scouting party left the plateau slightly less deadly than they'd found it. Three large fish, multiple snares, tripwires, and one particularly nasty pitfall lined with sharpened stakes had been removed. As the last realm scout disappeared over the lip of the ledge, a man flung himself out from under an overgrown lilac bush and rolled across the fern-covered ground, scratching furiously at his legs.

"Damn insects!" he snarled.

A young goblin dropped from the thick boughs of a green tamarack tree. "Did you see the size of those orcs?" she said. "One smack, that's all it'd take. And poof! Our bones are being ground up into bread."

The human stopped scratching long enough to impart a scowl. "That's giants, idiot. Orcs don't make bread."

"What do they do, then?"

"I dunno. Eat you raw, maybe? Ah! Get off, you devils!" Stamping his feet, the man unfastened his weapon-laden belt and plunged headfirst into the pool. He surfaced seconds later, feeling, if not better, at least wetter. Possibly colder. "Jerus, why is it we're fightin' for this place again? Doesn't seem worth it to me. Not when everything wants to kill you, including the damn bugs."

A second goblin emerged from the tangle of overgrown landscape. Jerus was older, more grizzled, and doing a poor job of disguising the mounting contempt he felt for his companions. "No one cares what you think, Mucklebuck. And if the commander catches you talking like that, you're going to pay for it with your tongue."

The young goblin, Dewpetal, settled onto one of the moss-riddled rocks. She cupped her chin in her claws as she contemplated the complexities of the situation. "If orcs eat us raw, why do you think they didn't munch on that tundra goblin? Weren't hungry, maybe?"

"Too skinny. Not worth the trouble," Mucklebuck replied with unfounded confidence.

Jerus resisted the urge to yank his long ears from his head to avoid having to endure another word of their ineptitude. Six months ago, he had been the leader of a company ten strong—each scout more skilled than the last. One offhanded remark to his commander, and his once proud legion was reduced from ten to two lowly members of the cadet patrol. To add insult to injury, his superiors had sent him into enemy territory armed with nothing more than a rumor.

He was to assess whether or not the regular Stoneclaw border patrols had fallen to the wayside. As fate would have it, his team were not the only outsiders trespassing in the foothills of the Iron Ridge. A scouting party from the realm was here as well and, unlike Jerus, they had come equipped with a map. After trailing them for a day and a half, Jerus had devised a plan to ambush the scouts and steal their information. Just as his team was preparing to strike, realm reinforcements had arrived. Not just any reinforcements, either. Big ones, mean ones, the kind of soldiers that looked like they could pop your head between their thumb and forefinger and then laugh about it.

Suddenly outnumbered, Jerus and the cadet patrol had no other choice but to lie low and feverishly pray their presence went unnoticed. One of the trespassers damn near stepped on Mucklebuck during the sweep. By the blessings of the gods, a rabbit was flushed from hiding and bolted, drawing the soldier's attention from disabling traps to the prospects of dinner. It was a miracle they had not been discovered. The time spent in hiding had not been a waste, however. From his perch within the trees, Jerus was certain he'd overheard the utotrian words for "hidden pass" exchanged between the lead scout and the orcess warrior.

Fates be damned, *that* was the breakthrough he severely needed. His commander would have no choice but to reinstate him to his former rank if he returned with the secret passage to the Iron Ridge in hand.

Mucklebuck was still in the water. He tilted his head to the side, watching the shoal of minnows that swarmed at his feet. "Hey, Dewpetal, you think I can catch one of those fishes, like that elf? Now that would be good eating."

Dewpetal merely stared dreamily into the pool, not listening. "Maybe there's something special about that tundra goblin. He *was* toothsome."

"You're still stuck on that? The goblin with little bits of metal all in his face? You know what, never mind. I don't care. I'm itchy an' tired an' wet. Stop fawning over that old toad an' get over here an' help me catch some dinner." He slashed at the water with his hands. "Gah! See what you made me do? Now they're swimming away."

Around them, the sound of birdsong dropped to a deathly quiet. The silence tore Jerus from his thoughts. He lifted his head and watched as a ripple in the water rolled soundlessly toward the unsuspecting human. "Mucklebuck! Get out of the wa—"

With a wet *galoop* the swamplander known as Mucklebuck vanished beneath the surface. The water's edge lapped along the jagged rocks as a dark shape returned to the murky drop-off near the falls.

CHAPTER SIXTY-TWO

Elemental

Morning once more arrived too early, too dark, too cold. Mist hung in wet sheets over the soggy, weed-riddled ground. Rasp pulled his cloak tighter, wincing at the frosty air that stung his exposed face and hands. It wasn't even sunup yet, and already he'd been pulled from his warm bed and marched out into the elements to do something he didn't particularly want to do.

"We'll start with this." Whisper placed something cold and lumpy in Rasp's trembling hand.

"A rock?"

"Is there a problem?"

"It's a rock. Where exactly am I supposed to start?" Rasp rolled it between his hands. "I could hit you with it, if that's what you want."

"You could try," Whisper agreed. From the way they said it, Rasp suspected the witch meant, "But it would be a futile effort. One for which you would pay gravely."

Half awake, Rasp was still attempting to wrap his mind around the situation. Somehow Faris and Whisper not only knew about each other, but were in cahoots, too. When asked how or why, neither had been forthcoming with an answer. What's worse, the pair seemed bent on making his morning as miserable as possible by insisting he participate in Whisper's training. It was bad enough Rasp had to learn to be a witch, but having Faris taunt him from the sidelines made it so much worse. Salt in the wound was child's play to this. This was like being flayed, dipped in the ocean, and dragged across sand.

Rasp spoke through chattering teeth, wincing each time he grazed the tip of his tongue. "Will you just tell me what I'm supposed to do? I've never done magic with a rock before."

"You did magic with a hatchet. It's no more inanimate than a stone."

"First off, I used wind to bolster the throw. I didn't enchant the stupid hatchet or whatever. And, secondly, there was a dragon trying to eat me," Rasp countered. "It's a little easier conjuring this stuff when the alternative is death."

"Precisely why we are practicing. Now, close your eyes and concentrate."

"I'm blind! I don't need to close my eyes."

"Your mouth, too, while you're at it." Whisper waited until Rasp did as instructed before continuing. "Picture the stone in your mind. Feel its weight in your hand. Envision it as an extension of you."

"It's a *rock*."

"It's going to be an extension of your head if you keep interrupting."

"That doesn't even make—ow!" Rasp jumped back when something sharp jabbed him in the ribs. "Alright, I'm doing it. Now what?"

"Lift it."

Rasp tentatively raised his hand, prompting a snicker from Faris, who was huddled beneath the dark tree forms somewhere behind him.

"With your magic, little bird," Whisper said patiently.

A warm glow, unaffected by the surrounding cold, leapt to his cheeks. Rasp shook off his embarrassment the only way he knew how, which was with his temper. "How is that practical? Why use magic when there's an easier way?"

"Before one can run, they must first learn to walk. Today it is a stone, tomorrow a castle wall. Now, up, up, up. As far as you can and hold it."

He hesitated. This time not out of anger, but at the overall ambiguity of the assignment. "Aren't I supposed to say words or something?"

"If you think it would help." An uncomfortable span of silence passed between them before Whisper gave in with a grudging sigh. "You are referring to spellwork. The realm trains its fledgling witches to bend magic with words because it is an easy concept for children to grasp. It's mostly for show. A focused mind is all that is really required."

"Oh," Rasp said. "So all that business with wands and pointy hats?"

"Does a crown lend a king power? No. It is a suggestion of power. Mere theater, nothing more. Now stop asking questions and lift the damn rock. It will be dawn soon, and there is still much to learn."

Suppressing a groan, Rasp closed his eyes and focused on the stone. He felt its weight in his hand. Years of grit crumbled away as his thumb brushed against its rugged surface. He held his palm flat and shut himself off to the outside. *Okay, get this over with,* he told himself. *The rock is an extension of you. You are the rock. Lift the damn rock. Lift. Lift. Lift!*

Nothing.

"Try again," Whisper said.

Rasp bit back his scream. This was stupid and pointless. Handing him a rock and demanding he do something with it wasn't training! Where was the learning and the teaching and the coaching? This was just telling. And Rasp was tired of being told what to do. *Shape up. Don't do this. Don't do that. Take us up the cursed mountain, Rasp. Become a witch, Rasp. Oh, and could you pretty, pretty please do it without fulfilling the prophecy of the sixth son?*

The poison stirred. Its blistering tendrils erupted from his core and weaved outward like blight-laden vines. The magic slithered and slunk, wrapping Rasp in its suffocating grasp. Tighter, tighter, tighter, until the thump of his heartbeat echoed in his ears. His open hand radiated with heat. He felt the stone, hot as a burning coal, nestled against his skin. *Lift,* he told it. *You and I are in this together, and by the gods, lift or one of us is being thrown over the edge of the cliffs and it's not going to be me!*

"Muck me," Faris said, sounding strangely far away.

He didn't know what Faris was talking about, because the damn stone was still resting in his hand, attempting to bore a hole through it. "This is stupid!" Rasp snapped, sliding one foot behind him as he prepared to hurtle the disobedient rock into oblivion. To his utter horror, his heel slid back on nothing, unobstructed by the usual essentials of dirt, ground, and, most importantly, gravity.

With a mangled yelp, Rasp dropped, plummeting several feet and landing with a wet *splat* in an icy puddle. Scrambling onto all fours, he lifted himself from the mud, eyes darting across the dark landscape, attempting—and failing—to make sense of what in the realm just happened. ". . . Uh, Whisper?"

"Interesting interpretation, little bird." Rasp heard the witch's soft steps as they approached from behind. Whisper didn't normally make such sounds. He suspected they were doing it for his benefit. A small way of making their presence known to him. He might have been grateful, too, had the next words out of Whisper's mouth not been, "There was no need to lift yourself into the air, but I do appreciate the enthusiasm."

"H-how?" Rasp managed. He gathered his quaking feet beneath him and stood, slipped, and fell back into the cold puddle with another undignified splash.

"You are an elemental. And rock is an element," Whisper explained, hooking their scaled hand under Rasp's arm and hoisting him upright. "You let your anger take control. So much so, you physically repelled yourself from the greatest source of rock."

"The ground?"

Whisper flicked the tip of Rasp's wind-bitten nose. "Do you see now why your anger is a problem? If your temper is not under control, neither is your power. Magic is about achieving balance."

"Ha! Even the ground hates you," Faris called.

"You, silence," Whisper said with a forceful snap of their fingers. "Oralia forbade me from killing you. She said nothing about turning you into a shrew."

"I would make an *adorable* shrew."

Rasp blew his breath into his hands and rubbed them together, attempting to bring his numb fingers back to life. A part of him wanted to ask why Whisper wanted Faris dead, but the leaden weight in the pit of his stomach commanded his full attention. He hadn't planned to do this in front of Faris, but now was possibly his one and only chance to speak to the witch freely. "Whisper, I can't do this."

"Of course you can. You were able to lift yourself into the air without so much as a thought. A single stone should come much easier."

"No, not the stupid rock. This! I—I can't be here." The weight in Rasp's gut sank lower, threatening to drag him down with it. "You heard Daana's history lesson. I'm Gagan Stoneclaw all over again. And he didn't even have magic! I do. If the spirit gets a hold of me, it will be the end of me and my people."

"Your ancestor did not have guidance, little bird. You do. Learning to wield your gifts is the first and most important step to ensuring the mistakes of your forebears remain in the past."

"You know what ensures that just as easily? Not going back up the fucking mountain!"

"Just because a solution is easiest, does not make it the right one. Now, stop trying to stall your lesson." Whisper nudged Rasp's feet shoulder-length apart and, with an elbow applied to the small of his back, forced his stance straighter. Once more, the witch pressed a stone into his hand. "Try again. Visualize what you want the stone to do."

"But—"

"No more interruptions. I have upheld my end of the agreement. See to yours."

So much for convincing the witch to see reason. Gritting his jaw, Rasp thrust his hand out in front of him. It took three more tries before the stone lifted from his hand. The blurry, grayish-brown object hovered in the air over his palm, dipping each time his concentration faltered. The length of time he held the rock airborne was apparently satisfactory for Whisper, because the moment Rasp let it drop, the witch declared them finished for the day. By that time, the soft light of dawn was already creeping through the surrounding trees. With a final reminder for Rasp to keep his temper in check, Whisper departed, leaving Faris to take Rasp back to camp.

Rasp whipped the rock ahead of him. It clacked against the wood of a tree several yards out. Behind him, he heard the crunch of dry brush as Faris picked his way closer. "They're an asshole, right?" Rasp said. "It's not just me?"

"Not just you," Faris assured him. "You're both definitely assholes."

Rasp didn't have the heart to play tit-for-tat with Faris. This realization added to the growing lump in his stomach. Here it was, their last day together, and he couldn't even bring himself to give Faris the proper ribbing he deserved. He should have felt relieved and yet . . . it was something else that ate at him. Something he hadn't ever felt before. Something maybe he'd never *allowed* himself to feel before.

As any emotionally intelligent human would do, Rasp took the feeling and stuffed it deep down out of sight and changed the subject. "Whisper said Oralia forbade them from killing you. What'd you do to piss off the witch?"

"Oh you know, being devilishly handsome, smart as a whip, the usual reasons." Faris hooked his arm through Rasp's and pulled him in the direction of what Rasp assumed was camp. "I liked the part where you lifted yourself in the air, by the way. Hadn't seen anything like that before."

Rasp raised his head as a small flicker of pride bloomed within his soul. It wasn't often someone complimented his work. Intentional or not, it *had* been impressive. "Yeah?"

"Yeah. It was almost as good as when you fell on your ass immediately afterward."

CHAPTER SIXTY-THREE

Faint of Heart

Rasp locked Faris's arm tight against him as he half-walked, half-slipped on the groundcover still slick with morning dew. Despite the growing light, it was miserably cold and damp. The foothills, nestled in the shadow of the mountain, wouldn't begin to warm until midday or so. Judging by the bustling sounds of camp that grew louder as they neared, the traveling party would already be halfway up the mountainside by then.

"Aw, look at you two. Out for a morning stroll. How precious." Curly met them at the edge of camp. Rasp heard a rattled *thump* as the orc deposited something heavy onto the ground in front of them without care. "Oralia made me pack your shit. You're welcome."

Faris was anything but pleased. The faun released Rasp's arm with a rough jerk as he stooped to collect his belongings. "If anything is missing from my bag, I'll know."

"Relax, Faris. I didn't steal your wares," Curly said in his customary slow rumble. "I did lose a straight razor, though. Took it upon myself to check this one's pack in case he got his grubby hands on it."

Rasp's heart jumped out of rhythm and nearly tried to climb up the back of his throat. He swallowed hard, fighting the sudden urge to scream a laundry list of obscenities. Forcing a breath that neither provided calm nor settled the obnoxious flutter in his voice, he managed a squeaky, "You did what?"

"Got yourself a nice little stockpile of knives, don't you? That and food. There's enough scraps squirreled away in there to keep you at least a week."

"Uh, yeah, it's called an emergency pack for a reason. What in the realm are you all carrying?" Rasp replied, quickly, before either of them had time to give any hard thought as to why he had a week's worth of provisions on him.

He ducked down and searched the patchy ground for his bag. "And for the record, I found all those knives fair and square!"

"In other people's pockets, maybe," Faris snorted.

Rasp's hand brushed over the top of his pack and he stood, throwing it over his shoulder with a single heave. It was heavier than he remembered. Either Curly had taken it upon himself to add a few rocks to the collection of knives, or Rasp had grown significantly weaker since the last time he'd lugged the damn thing. He gritted his teeth, managing a pained, "Shall we discuss the contents of your bag next, Faris?"

"Not unless you've got a death wish."

With the absence of the horse, the tether made its dreaded return. Despite protests, Faris cinched the length of thick cord around Rasp's waist and then tied it around himself, insisting if one of them was going to go down, at least they'd go together. To Rasp's relief, only a few dared snicker out loud. The rest of the traveling party were far too preoccupied with the climb to care. Mount Hook was not for the faint of heart—or leg, or lung, for that matter.

Rasp clung tight to his walking poles as he climbed steadily upward. His feet ached, his knees creaked, his lower back throbbed, but his spirit, the untempered swell that spiraled and dipped and twirled inside his rapidly beating chest, was light as air. He only had to suffer a little longer and then he would be free of this nightmare, like smoke on the breeze.

The walking poles, thoughtfully provided by Snaglebrag—who then twice as thoughtfully ducked out of reach—made it slightly easier for Rasp to navigate his way up the steep trail. The equal lengths of whittled wood also served as a convenient means to whack Faris each time he moved too quickly to keep pace. Unfortunately, Rasp got only a few smacks in before the game ended. Not due to a consequence of his own actions, surprisingly, but because Faris was soon too winded to stay much more than a few paces ahead of him. The game thus evolved from whacking to ruthless prodding. At least until Faris stopped protesting and Rasp eventually grew bored. From there, the journey turned into a silent, dreary hike.

After what felt like years of endless drudgery, Faris's voice cut back in, lacking all of its usual thunder. "Why are you smiling like an idiot?"

"I'm not smiling."

"Yes, you are."

Shit. He was. Rasp had gotten so caught up in the promise of freedom that he'd forgotten all about the art of subtlety. Now was not the time to lose focus. "I can't help what my face does when I'm not paying attention, Faris! I think you should be grateful for the fact that I stopped whipping you with my stick."

"Yeah," Faris wheezed. "Now that you mention it, that is a little out of character for you, isn't it?"

Way to go. Draw more attention to yourself, why don't you? Very subtle. "Oh my gods, fine. If you must know, I'm smiling because whatever idiot scout picked this route completely missed the mountain goat trail that runs along the cliffside. Which, by the way, would have made all of this so much easier."

"Seriously? You could have mentioned that sooner!"

It wasn't a lie. There truly was a hidden game trail that would have rendered the climb half as strenuous. But disclosing such information would have been entirely too helpful. And even if he had to suffer the steep climb, Rasp took some solace knowing the others suffered worse. He had been born and raised on this range. You could take the man out of the mountain, but never the mountain out of the man.

Despite the months away, the muscle memory was still there. His legs responded, automatically adjusting his balance and shifting his weight to his toes. His lungs, too. He seemed to be faring the higher elevation better than the rest of the traveling party, who huffed and puffed to no avail around him. All except for the herbalist, for some peculiar reason.

Briony's blurry shape scrambled up and down the cliffside around them with boundless energy, excitedly identifying various plant life. The only time she stopped was to collect a specimen. "Faris, don't step there! That's fringed wormwood."

"Unless it's going to give me wings," Faris moaned, "I don't care."

"You say that, but the moment you come down with debilitating stomach pain, you'll think otherwise. Now, move!" Rasp felt Briony shoulder her way around Faris in order to save her precious weed from being trampled upon.

There wasn't anything about Briony that made her particularly dislikable. She was knowledgeable at what she did and had proved competent during a crisis once already—traits Rasp normally admired in a person. But the way she talked to Faris rubbed him the wrong way. How Faris talked back rubbed him even more wrong. They spoke like they were friends at a party no one else had been invited to. When she was around, Rasp felt like an outsider looking in.

"Why do you let the hermit boss you around like that?" he grumbled, gritting his teeth as his front foot lost its hold in the loose soil and slid backward. "You wouldn't take that kind of shit from me."

Faris's response came between ragged pants of breath. "Is that all it takes to make you jealous?"

"No."

"You're practically green with envy."

"I'm not jealous of the hermit!"

Briony's melodic voice popped up on the other side of Rasp, already on the hunt for her next specimen. "Once more, my name is Briony. *Not* Hermit. I still don't know why you insist on calling me that."

"Because any time Faris dragged me on his rounds to visit you, we had to go outside the village," Rasp replied. "You live in the woods away from people. The entire time I spent in Lonebrook, you came into town, like, twice. And it was at night, when nobody would bother you. Therefore, by definition, you are a hermit."

There was a sudden, sharp pain in Rasp's side followed by a low hiss from Faris. "Stop talking."

"What? Why?"

This earned him a second jab to the ribs. "Because you're blabbering about stuff you don't know about."

"There you go again, defending her! Gods, you two move fast. Is your relationship official yet? When can I expect the invite to your wedding?"

Briony responded with a humorous snort. "Well, now that you mention it, we were thinking about a spring ceremony, actually. Flowers, butterflies, the works. What's your opinion on veils, Rasp? Do you think Faris should wear the traditional buttercup yellow or go for something more bold?"

"I was thinking more along the lines of a collar, actually. You're the first person I've met capable of bringing him to heel."

"Says the man currently walking him on a leash."

A smile split across Rasp's chapped lips. Maybe Briony wasn't so bad after all. If anything, at least she proved a good competitor at one of his favorite pastimes. "He especially likes it when I call him Daddy."

"That's it!" Faris announced loudly. "I'm tying the two of you together and pushing you over the edge."

"Oh, hush, Dingle. You know you like it." Rasp glanced over his shoulder at the long line of sad, blurry forms struggling behind him. He searched, unsuccessfully, for one of the four familiar shapes that normally hovered just out of striking range. "Now where'd Ellisar get to? I bet she's got a spare collar we could borrow."

"See if she's got a muzzle while you're at it!"

"Good thinking, Dingle. Wouldn't want you to wake up the whole camp while you and Briony get freaky later."

"I hate you so much right now."

Rasp spent the remainder of the climb helping Briony outline the increasingly extravagant details of her fictional wedding. Faris would chime in from time to time with meek protest, but his efforts fell upon uncaring ears. He gave up eventually and reserved the remainder of his strength for reaching the falls, a journey that took nearly three hours in total. The sun beat down from high overhead by the time the final members of the travel party hauled their aching carcasses up over the jagged lip of the cliffside and onto flat ground.

"No time to lie down on the job, Dingle." Rasp, still connected to Faris via the tether, hooked his hand through the faun's sweat-soaked underarm and heaved him upright. "Find Oralia."

The time to attempt something incredibly stupid had arrived, and he'd be damned if he gave her soldiers a chance to catch their breath before the real fun started.

CHAPTER SIXTY-FOUR

A Goblin and His Horsey

Did Snag give you another tonic or something? How is it you're not falling over like the rest of us?" Faris was weak with exhaustion. For this reason, the tone of accusation in his voice passed for mildly annoyed at best. He shuffled alongside Rasp, navigating the slumped, hazy forms of the resting soldiers while trying not to trip over the sprawl of tangled plant life in the process.

Rasp didn't want to admit it, but with every step he felt stronger. Energy pulsed through his creaky bones. It wormed into his stiff muscles and surged through the inner pathways of his veins until each fingertip vibrated with power. Whisper had warned that his magic would increase as they drew closer to the source. It must have affected his confidence, too, because the first thing out of Rasp's mouth to the protector was, "Are the scouts ready? I want to cross the pool."

"Leave the scouts. Take Snaglebrag and Ellisar."

Rasp's resolve shriveled like a dry leaf in autumn. He tapped his fingertips together, fighting the unexpected hitch in his voice. "Uh . . . why them, exactly?"

"Yeah," Snag cut in. "Why us?"

Oralia and her faithful four were stationed near the pool. Rasp could hear the thunder of the falls in the distance behind them. The cool breeze drifted across the open waters and changed directions on a whim, wafting the occasional misty spray across his goose-pimpled skin. The protector's voice was, by comparison, not nearly as serene.

"Because this requires finesse. And, after what I witnessed yesterday, I am more comfortable leaving the fate of this mission in the hands of those I trust not to step blindly into every trap from here to the pass."

"You hear that, El?" Snag said. "The protector thinks we're competent enough not to bring the mountain down on top of us. Makes you blush, don't it?"

"Maybe if we invite the captain along she'll change her mind," Ellisar said.

"Gods help me, if you even think of mentioning it to him—" Oralia did not need to finish her warning, as it was obvious to everyone involved that inviting Captain Monk on the all-important, extra-critical mission would be punishment enough for them.

"Alright, alright, fine," Snag grumbled. "We'll go risk life and limb because you don't trust the experts to do the one thing they're supposedly expert at."

"Thank you, Snaglebrag," Oralia said in the brisk sort of voice that implied the time to shut up was several sentences ago.

"Not to mention the whole getting wet doing it."

"Your point is taken, thank you."

"And the slime," Snag said with a shudder in his voice. "Don't get me started on the pond slime. Nasty stuff. I can already feel the swimmer's itch from here."

"You may stop talking now."

"Can I interject with something?" Rasp tentatively raised his hand. When no immediate response came, he assumed it was the go-ahead to speak. "Before we cross, there is the matter of the mossflower. Specifically, if any of you remembered to bring it."

Ageratum, or "mossflower," as it was commonly known, was the key to crossing the water. Its fragrant oil repelled the bigger fish and whatever else lurked deeper. Of the many items Rasp requested for the journey, he had been adamant about the mossflower. He was beginning to regret that now. Then again, the protector was sadistic enough to make him go into the water without it. With his luck, the king of the pool would bypass Snag and Ellisar and go straight for him. The last thing he'd hear would be *slurp!* and then be gone forever. Slowly digested in the belly of—

Snag's prickly voice disrupted Rasp's imaginary death. "Yes, we brought your stupid oil."

"Apply it to your arms and legs." Rasp used his left walking pole to search the area around him for Faris. "Dingle?"

"Wha'?" The sound came from near Rasp's feet. From Faris's labored breathing, he assumed the faun had collapsed with no intention of getting up again without the help of being prodded with something sharp and pointy.

The lump that had formed in the pit of Rasp's stomach ached with a hurt unfamiliar to him. He was whole and yet, it felt like he was leaving a piece of himself behind. He wouldn't ever get a goodbye, not a proper one, anyway. He had to make this count for something. "If I fall into a trap or something, just know I hate you. And if you and Hermit have kids, I don't expect you to name one after me."

"Name the dog Dinglehead. Got it."

That was it. The last thing he would ever hear his best friend say. Rasp felt the ache grow heavier.

"Rasp?" Faris's weary voice called from the ground, snapping Rasp from his inner turmoil. "I hate you, too. Try not to fall into a trap or something."

Forget the aching lump, now he just felt weird. The feeling dissipated the moment someone grabbed him roughly by the arm and slathered a slick of oil over the back of one of his hands before moving on to the next. Rasp twisted his head to the side, prepared to say something snarky, only to realize the tall, willowy shape beside him was Ellisar. Considering the lunatic elf was going to be in charge of the crossing, he decided against giving her a reason to kick him over the edge of the drop-off.

"Snag," Ellisar said, her voice far too close for personal comfort, "bring your bow."

"Why? So you can insult me if I need to use it? We all can't be top marksmen, you know."

"It's for me, idiot. In case we run into trouble." Ellisar's voice changed directions, as if she was staring at Rasp as she spoke and not Snag. "Or trouble tries to run from us."

Terror struck him square in the chest and slowly sunk into the pit of his stomach, threatening to drag the last of his courage into the deep depths with it. He knew from the start that pulling this off would be dangerous, but Ellisar had just raised the stakes from risky to certain death.

"Oh, that's right," Snag snickered. "Yours got burnt to a crisp in that unfortunate campfire accident. You must feel naked without it."

Rasp crossed his arms, attempting to mask the violent queasiness churning within his gut. "Could everyone please stop reminding her! I said I was sorry."

With a few, final words of discouragement from the others, they were off. Ellisar unhitched the rope lead from Faris and led with Rasp in the middle and Snag grudgingly bringing up the rear. The elf plunged brazenly into the pool, pulling Rasp by the tether with her. Rasp caught his breath as the chilled waters reached above his navel. He clung tightly to his walking poles, setting one foot slowly in front of the other as the pebbled ground shifted precariously underfoot.

"Stick to the outside," he instructed through tightly clenched teeth. "Avoid the drop-off."

They were what he assumed to be about halfway when Snag leapt out of the water with a muffled yelp and scrambled up Rasp's shoulders. Rasp staggered forward, feet slipping on the slick, pebbled bottom. He managed to keep his balance by stabbing one of his poles into the soft muck and bearing his weight onto it.

Once certain he wouldn't teeter over into the pool, Rasp reared his head back, snapping, "What are you doing? Get off!"

"Uh-uh, no way. Something bit me. They've got the taste for goblin now. Only a matter of time before they come back for the rest."

"Oh my gods." He shook his shoulders, attempting to shrug the wet goblin from his back. Snag, fortunately, didn't weigh much more than a large human child. Still, it was the principle of the matter. He wasn't a damn pony service! "Get off or I'll show you what a real bite feels like!"

Snag climbed higher and settled onto Rasp's shoulders like a toddler at a parade. "I'll tell you what, you walk, I steer. Okay? I even got these nifty handholds."

"Let go of my ears!" Rasp tugged on the lead to get Ellisar's attention. "A little help here, maybe?"

"Sorry, mate. Left my riding crop onshore."

Snag's hot breath whispered in Rasp's ear. "She means the one not meant for horsies."

"Oh gods, never mind!"

Realizing to rid himself of his unwanted passenger would only result in both of them going underwater, Rasp grudgingly accepted his fate. At the very least, Snag proved useful at maneuvering him around the treacherous low spots that Ellisar traipsed through without concern. The roar of the falls grew louder as the trio traversed the shallow waters that hugged the cliffside. When they were close, Snag jumped from Rasp's shoulder onto the stone ledge and helped guide him over. Rasp threw his poles ahead of him and then felt for handholds along the face of the smooth, slippery rock. One mighty heave later, he hauled his lower half, wet and dripping, onto the bank.

He stood on wobbly, waterlogged legs and pressed his back to the cliff-side. Poles in hand, he slid his feet across the slick ground and sidled sideways beneath the waterfall behind Ellisar. Cold spray from the falls peppered his face and chest. Rasp kept going, slowly, until the hidden path snaked behind the waterfall, turned the corner, and widened into the mouth of a cavern.

Rasp halted, allowing the tether to pull Ellisar to a stop. He was forced to yell over the roar of the falls. "The first trap isn't far. From here on out, watch your every step or it might just be your last."

"Hear that, Ellisar? Best be careful. Don't worry, I'll watch the maggot for you."

"Fuck off," Ellisar shouted to her companion. "I took care of the last death trap. It's your turn."

"You owe me for the sky shriek."

"I don't owe you shit. I was prepared to die then, as I am now."

"So what? You're going to half-ass it then, is that what you're saying?"

What followed could only be described as hostile silence. The kind of silence where Ellisar was arguing, successfully, without uttering a word. According to the others, she won most of her debates this way.

"That's not fair." The wet soles of Snag's feet slapped against the rock as the goblin padded past, muttering.

Rasp waited at the mouth of the cavern with Ellisar, giving Snag instruction as best as a blind man relying on memory in the dark could. "There'll be razor wire running between the walls at different heights. The first is low, about ankle high. Don't cut it. It'll drop a rock on you the moment it's triggered. Step over the wire and disable the drop net first. You should see a rope to your—"

Rasp was cut off by the deafening clatter of falling rock that erupted from the rear of the cavern.

CHAPTER SIXTY-FIVE

Weak

Rasp threw himself against the wall in order to avoid the bouncing shards of broken stone that ricocheted past at lethal speeds. The cavern floor trembled beneath his waterlogged boots as he waited for the clamor to subside. The tether, he noted, hung slack from his waist, indicating Ellisar had dropped it during the commotion.

When he found the strength to speak again, his voice shook, as did every other part of him. "Fuck. He's dead, isn't he?"

Ellisar was pressed so close against him he could nearly taste the cloud of peppermint wafting from her clothes. From her unusual proximity, he assumed she had leapt to the side the same time as him. Ellisar's shout cut across the air above his head. "Snag, ya little shit! Warn us next time ya cut down a bloody death trap!"

"Oi, Ellisar! I cut down a death trap!" he warned. "Wasn't very bloody, though. We could try it again if you want."

"I meant before!"

"And here I thought you were prepared to die." His words dripped with sticky-sweet smugness. There was an audible *twang* as the goblin cut the first line. "Alright, maggot. Trip wire's down. What's next?"

Rasp guided him verbally through the remaining traps. Grown bored of inaction, Ellisar eventually abandoned Rasp's side to assist Snag with the nastier surprises. The final booby trap—a totally real trap and not one he'd simply made up to keep them distracted—would buy him a few short minutes, provided the pair stopped arguing long enough to get around to executing it. Rasp listened to them bicker over who got to keep the razor wire as he untied the tether from his waist and dropped it to the floor. He quickly picked his way deeper into the cave, his fingertips tracing the chiseled rock, feeling every crack and fissure as the pitted wall guided him to the back.

The pass had been carved out by the first Stoneclaws. The original cavern had been short and narrow. Over the years, Rasp's ancestors had chipped away at the iron-rich rock until even the tallest human could traverse it without bumping their head. What looked like a dead end at the back of the cave was, in fact, a carefully constructed illusion. Go all the way to end, take a sharp left, and one would find a stone set of steps leading upward. Keep going and eventually the hidden stairway would deposit you back outside, above the towering cliffs. That was the problem with outsiders. They were so consumed with getting over the mountain, they never considered the possibility of cutting through.

Along with the booby traps, there were some less obvious dangers that made the pass particularly useful—the cave-in feature, for one. It had only been used once prior, when a raiding party had been followed a little too closely by a very determined troll. The pass had taken years to rebuild. Every Stoneclaw understood the cave-in feature was for emergencies only. Setting it off would collapse the mouth of the cavern, sealing the pass indefinitely.

Rasp's throat tightened as the sound of his rapidly beating heart drowned out the thunder of the falls. Perspiration streamed down his face and collected on the tip of his nose. He brushed it away with the back of his hand, cursing beneath his ragged breath. This was absolute madness. He was a blind man, stuck in a homeland not only with brothers that wished him dead but a predatory spirit, too. But he had to do this. There was no other way. The realm could not be allowed to reach the peak.

There were other ways down the mountain, of course. Some of which Rasp even stood a chance of surviving. He'd worry about that later. For now, he had to commit to what he came to do. Snag and Ellisar were quick. Rasp only hoped that when they fled, it would be in the opposite direction, back out into the pool. It was only logical. You didn't evacuate a collapsing cave by running to the back. The pair had a good sense of self-preservation. Rasp felt confident their first instinct would be to save themselves, rather than go back for him.

He reached the back and, instead of turning left, crossed to the right. With one palm pressed to the moss-covered wall and the other grasping both poles, he followed the curve of the cavern into the rear chamber. The storeroom, a cramped, musty cranny cut into the rock, was made smaller by the collection of old fishing equipment strewn haphazardly over the damp floor.

Rasp tripped over what felt like a gaff and cursed. He switched back to the walking poles, grasping one in each hand, and used them to clear a path to the back wall.

"You know we can hear you, right?" From the distance of Ellisar's voice, she and Snag were standing alarmingly close to the back storeroom. They hadn't reached him yet, but it would only be a matter of steps.

"We were wonderin' when you were gonna make your move, maggot. Frankly, I expected it a lot sooner than this."

"We're not mad, just disappointed." Ellisar's next words seemed to be directed at Snag. "I say we give him a few minutes. See what he comes up with."

"You know I'm not opposed to shirking work, but that's kinda the opposite of what we were told to do, innit?"

"Oralia said I couldn't go off course." Ellisar retorted. "She didn't say anything about standing aside and letting the course off itself."

. . . Okay. Not the reaction he'd expected. Regardless, they were offering his opportunity on a silver platter and he would be stupid to turn his nose up at it. Rasp reached the back wall and his fingertips soon found what he sought. It was a round indention, nearly flush with the rock. One good push and the disk would slide inward, setting off the mechanisms hidden above the cave. Rasp didn't understand the ins and outs of it. No one living did, in fact. The last time the cave had been rebuilt was over two hundred years ago. The sad truth was, given the incompetence of the current Stoneclaw leadership, triggering the disk would leave the pass in ruins forever.

Feel sorry for yourself later! This is what you came here to do. Do it! Now, before it's too late.

Setting his jaw, Rasp slammed his hand against the disk. It remained flush with the wall. Rasp tried again, this time with both hands. His feet scraped against the wet, grit-covered ground as he fought for traction. With a muffled growl, Rasp pressed his elbow into the circle and heaved his entire body weight against it. Shuddering, the disk sank several inches into the wall with a gravely *thunk*.

"Do you hear that?" Snag's voice echoed from near the doorway.

"The clicky sound?"

"No, I meant the screaming."

Ellisar's boots barely scuffed as she raced across the stony ground to the mouth of the cave. She had to yell in order to be heard over the roar of the falls. "Sweet goddess, we've got swamplanders everywhere out there!"

"And you're running toward them?" Snag wailed as he trailed after her with slow, reluctant steps. "And there she goes, right into the fray. No forethought to grab my bow or stay behind and guard the entrance. Nope. Just right in, expecting me to follow. As usual." He blew a raspberry out of the corner of his mouth before coming to terms with his fate. He spoke louder for what Rasp assumed was his benefit. "Well, I'm about to go die. Sorry your escape plan didn't pan out, maggot. Best to stay out of the way. The rest of the party will be coming through quick."

"Through here?" Truth be told, the cave-in was taking much longer than he anticipated. Apparently in the two centuries of non-use, no one had bothered to grease whatever invisible cogs and wheels operated the fall. It was working, as made evident by horrendous squeaking overhead, just very, very slowly.

"A logical course of action given the circumstances, I would think," Snag said, still dawdling at the entrance. Rasp heard the *twang* of the goblin's bow. Unlike his lunatic companion, he was using the opportunity to pick off the closest targets before venturing out onto an active battlefield.

"But the cave's coming down!"

"Oh, that's what I'm hearing, is it? That's unfortunate." The heart of the mountain rumbled louder overhead, like a poorly digested dinner. The goblin remained remarkably apathetic to the matter. "How long do you suppose we have before it topples?"

Unlike him, Rasp was openly panicking. "Seconds? Minutes, maybe? I don't know. You really should move."

"Right. Well you're a witch, aren't you? Do something about it then." With that, the goblin's wet footsteps pitter-pattered away until all trace of him was drowned out by the roar of the waterfall.

He'd only meant to strand the traveling party, not kill them. Even if there was a way to speed the collapse along, he would be trapping them on top of a hostile mountain with a swamplander army at their backs.

Let them die.

Rasp jumped, feet sliding on the slick ground as he fought to regain his balance. The hairs on his arm prickled as the air grew thicker around him. Even the stupid little bits of metal Faris had put in his ears had picked up on the danger. The charms burned hot against his skin, emitting a low buzzing frequency. "Uh, what?"

His heartbeat drummed against the inside of his ribcage at double its previous speed. His inner voice sounded strangely faint and far away. It screamed to be heard over Rasp's mounting panic. *Wrong. The magic was wrong.*

"Fuck, you're not Whisper."

They hate you. They beat you. Mistreated you. And you wish to save them? The magic encircled him, filling the chamber with its hushed whispers. **You have gone soft, Stoneclaw.**

Fear. Control the fear and it cannot get to you. "You're right. That's not me anymore." Rasp stepped through the swirling cloud of magic. It stung his face and hands like a frostbitten breeze, a stark contrast to the burning sensation on his ears. "I'm weak and worthless and whatever else you want to call me. Now go away so I can do something stupid."

You can't save them.

"Will you shut up? I'm really sick of everyone telling me what I can and can't do." Rasp explored the wall with his hands for something, anything, to stop the cave-in. He found nothing, because there was nothing. Trying to stop a rockslide in motion was like politely asking a bear to stop mauling you. You had to stab it to get its teeth out of you. Except a rockslide didn't have teeth. And stabbing it wouldn't do any good, either. Unfortunately, that left only one thing to try.

"Please stop, please stop, please stop," Rasp chanted under his breath as he placed the flat of his hands over the wall. He grounded his feet against the slick floor, shoulder-length apart, and closed his eyes.

You're not strong enough.

"I said, shut up!"

Rasp envisioned the ceiling. He saw the hairline cracks splintered across its chipped surface. With imaginary threads of glistening gold and yellow, he weaved magic between the fractures, binding the rock and drawing it together, until the cavern pulsed with veins of glimmering light. The magic responded. It sparked from his fingers and wormed into the stone. The ancient mechanism rumbled overhead. The inner workings ground and scraped and screeched together. And then, nothing. No sound. No movement. Only the eerie quiet of Rasp's own ragged breaths.

I can make you strong.

A crushing weight bore down onto him. Rasp staggered but did not fall, screaming, as magic coursed from his body and filled the cave. The ceiling shuddered in protest, but remained unbroken. Beyond the sound of his own voice, Rasp heard the frantic footsteps of the first soldiers to make it across.

Quickly. They had to cross quickly, or he wouldn't be able to hold it. Already, he could feel the muscles in his arms begin to twitch and tremble in protest.

"Don't you dare let go!" The resounding clack of hooves against stone filled the passage as a familiar voice called out to him. Rasp started to slip, but a burly shape caught him from behind and eased him to the floor. "You got this, Dinglehead. Don't let up now. Show this damn mountain who's boss."

CHAPTER SIXTY-SIX

Sweet Summer Child

Daana stood, wrangling the thick fabric of her trousers over her hips with an undignified wiggle. A sudden rustle of leaves from the other side of her privacy barrier caused her to freeze in place. The icy grip of fear tightened like a noose around the base of her throat. What was that? Dear gods, was someone listening to her take a piss? Worse, *watching*? For fuck's sake! What was the point of leaving the main group in search of a little privacy if some pervert was just going to follow anyway?

She waited, the thump of her heart pounding in her ears as the soft rustling drew closer. Just as Daana was preparing to scramble up the nearest tree, against all odds, the source of the commotion passed her by unnoticed. She released her breath with a slow exhale. Okay, maybe it wasn't some pervert lurking in the bushes. It was probably just a mountain critter. This was the wilderness, after all. Satisfied with this explanation, she finished buttoning her trousers and stooped to retrieve her bookbag.

A twig snapped in the opposite direction of the previous rustling. Terror once more rocketed to her core.

Don't get ahead of yourself, Daana. It's just an animal! Or multiple animals, probably. Those travel in groups, right? For all you know it could be a family of squirrels foraging. Or cute bunny rabbits. The helpful portion of her mind rife with unnecessary information volunteered additional insight regarding the types of animals that traveled in familial units. *Yeah, it could be wolves. Those hunt in packs, too.*

A cold sweat broke out across Daana's clammy brow. *Shut up, brain!*

Some nagging instinct in the back of her head kept her from breaking cover and running back to the safety of the group. Daana hunkered down instead, making herself as small and unnoticeable as possible. Around her, the surrounding bushes rattled as more bodies slunk past unseen. Unfortunately, judging from the commotion, whatever the creatures moving around her were, they were definitely bigger than bunny rabbits.

Daana gulped, pressing further into the flowering lilac bush behind her. Perhaps the Iron Ridge was home to a species of giant bunny rabbits? No, she felt like that was something Rasp would have mentioned. Humans riding oversized rabbits into battle was a detail she definitely would have remembered.

The branches of a neighboring silverberry shrub rattled only paces away, ripping Daana from her panicked thoughts. Dancing visions of giant rabbits vanished from her mind the moment a gnarled goblin head poked through the thick underbrush. He froze, appearing equally as startled at the sight of her. In the split second before either of them reacted, Daana noted two things.

One, judging from the mottled blue and green uniform, this was most definitely not a soldier of the United Territories of the Realm. And, two, the stone-headed hatchet gripped in his hand appeared as if it had seen a reasonable amount of use. The end of the split-second standoff was marked by the hatchet whipping past her ear and disappearing into the center of the lilac bush, sending a cloud of loose purple and white petals airborne.

There wasn't time to scream. There wasn't time to thank the gods that the goblin possessed terrible aim or even consider the symbol she was forming with her fingers. Daana locked her forefingers together and threw the sign into the air.

"Avolare!"

Magic leapt from Daana's fingertips in a blinding violet blast. For a single heartbeat, she watched the goblin sail high overhead before disappearing from sight in a flailing blur of limbs and one long, tapering shriek. A third observation hit her: *Maybe don't use the full concentration of the deflection spell next time.* Goblins evidently did not weigh much, and launching one over the treetops required less power than anticipated. Which was probably a good thing, considering there was more than one hiding in the brush.

Around her, the small stretch of forest was suddenly alive with movement as a wave of additional bodies surged toward the oasis. *Wait, was that a battle cry she just heard?*

Shit. Realization struck her. This wasn't one or two goblins, it was a damned army! Which, given that she had just launched one of their own into the air, now knew her exact location. With the crashing sounds of several warriors closing in on her, Daana turned and fled. She sprinted with her back bent beneath the low hanging trees, wincing each time a gnarled branch ripped at her face and loose hair.

Run, run, run! Her inner voice screamed, drowning out the growing clamor. *Run!*

Pain erupted from her lower legs.

Run, run . . . oh shit. Can't run.

Daana fell, legs suddenly useless, and tumbled onto the fern-carpeted ground with a slam. After her head stopped spinning and she realized she was, in fact, still among the living, panic set in at the realization that her pursuers were not far behind. She flipped over. With a silent curse hovering over her trembling lips, she fought to untangle the bola intertwining her ankles. Her progress was interrupted by the pair of soldiers, one goblin and one human, that burst from the brush, running at full speed toward her.

A tan and brown blur hurtled across Daana's field of vision from the opposite direction. The figure, with shoulders hunched and horns brandished, knocked the human soldier flat on her back. Briony pivoted on one hoof and kicked with her other. The goblin soldier dodged, nocking an arrow to his bow as he retreated out of reach.

"Woah-ho-ho, easy there, trigger." The daring faun waved her weapon of choice, a plant, of all things, at the archer. "Do you know what this is?"

The goblin furrowed his leathery brow and said something in a language Daana didn't comprehend.

"*Oplopanax horridus.* You see the spines on this thing? You even think of firing that little splinter at me and I'll whap you upside the head! You hear?" Briony, stealthily backing away, glanced over her shoulder at Daana. Her amber eyes were wide and rimmed in white. Wordlessly, in the span of a single look, the two understood what would happen next.

"Now!" Briony threw herself flat.

Daana hooked her forefingers together at the knuckle and shot upright. "*Avolare!*"

The goblin's iron-tipped arrow dropped harmlessly to the ground. Unlike the goblin, who was hurtled several yards backward until his trajectory was broken by a tree. His mangled body hung in the air several seconds before he slumped face-first into the long grass, lifeless.

Briony sprang onto all fours and rushed to Daana's side. Between the two of them, they unwrapped the weighted cord tangled around her aching ankles. "Whatever you do," the faun grunted, blowing a strand of brown frizzled hair from her eyes. "Don't use that spell on me, okay? I just risked my neck helping you. Gods know why."

Amid the fear pumping through her veins, Daana felt a prickle of insult. She kicked away the last coil of rope and stood, shakily. "Hey! I saved your butt first. From the river, remember? We're on the same side here."

"Against the swamplanders, maybe." Briony kept low to the ground as she scuttled over to the still body of the human soldier and crouched, rifling through the swamplander's pockets for anything worth taking. She glanced up from her work with a frown. "What?"

"Are you serious right now? You're the one looting the dead when we should be getting back to the others!"

"First of all, she's not dead." Briony pressed her hand to the soldier's stomach, producing a whimpered moan. "She's merely stunned. Unlike you, I'm not a seasoned killer. Secondly, you're proposing we get out of here armed with what exactly? The devil's club was all show. I hope you know that. And as I still have no idea where my damn hatchet disappeared to, there's not a real weapon between the two of us."

"Taking out a single soldier does not make me a seasoned killer!" Okay, two soldiers at most—depending on what state the first goblin returned to the ground in. Not wanting to linger on that grim prospect any longer than necessary, Daana checked the power in her armlets instead. The translucent amethyst stones had taken on a dim gray sheen. A layer of dread added itself to the whirlwind of emotions already raging inside of her. Twisting and turning like slithering serpents, the unsettling sensation transformed into a single, weighted knot and dropped, nearly taking her out at the knees.

"Not looking too good there, witch hunter. How much magic do you have left? Enough for one good spell? Two, maybe?" Briony hopped upright and jutted a dagger in Daana's direction hilt-first. "Take it. I know how quickly you drain your powers. Once you're tapped, you're tapped. You won't be able to recharge again for months. Not unless you find some helpless witch here on the mountaintop somewhere."

For a brief second, words refused to fall from Daana's gaping mouth. This temporary paralysis, fortunately, did not apply to her thoughts. Faris, that little sneak! He'd gone and shared what she was! Daana narrowed her eyes at the faun as her rampaging thoughts transformed into a carefully constructed series of words. "I don't know what Faris told you, but it is far from the truth."

"Faris?" Briony snorted as she bounded ahead of her through the thorny brush. The faun's shaggy, moss-colored cloak made her nearly indiscernible from her surroundings. "Oh, you sweet summer child. Yes, you're absolutely right! I get all my information from Faris. It certainly wasn't *me* who suggested that you were a seeker to *him*."

"Wait, what?" Daana crashed headlong through the lush undergrowth after her. Normally she would have minded the stickers and spines that tore at her skin and clothes, but desperation had a unique way of blocking out the pain. A sudden spark of suspicion lit among the growing weave of fear and dread steadily building inside of her. "Who are you?"

"No time for that, witch hunter. Do try to keep up, though. We've got to get to the pool before it's cut off completely."

Following Briony proved difficult. The faun was faster, for one, and her spring-loaded legs gave her the advantage of being able to leap over the tall, flowering stalks of cow parsnip that Daana was forced to crash through. Resolute, Daana set her jaw and followed as quickly as her protesting legs would allow. The shaggy black and green trees thinned as the pair broke through to the other side and skidded to an abrupt halt at the back of a rather large swamplander horde.

Daana stood back-to-back with Briony as multiple heads turned in their direction. "That's the last time I'm following you!"

CHAPTER SIXTY-SEVEN

Bow Before Me

Only the swamplanders closest to them took notice, as the others were concerned with the band of far more competent realm soldiers pressing their backs into the trees. Briony brandished her knife—which Daana could not help but notice was substantially longer than the one she'd been given—at the advancing mix of human and goblin soldiers. The collective half smile shared among the enemy suggested they knew an easy kill when they saw one.

The smiles vanished, however, when a spry figure cut its way through their ranks with alarming ease. The polished steel of Captain Monk's sword caught the sunlight as it severed an arm, blocked a stroke from a short sword, and then drove through the wielder with neat precision. "Lady Lazuli, Miss Blackwater!" Captain Monk called to them, panting with exertion. "Oh dear, I'm relieved we found you!"

"*You* found *us*?" Briony snapped.

"The pass isn't going to hold for much longer. Come, this way!"

Following Captain Monk was remarkably easy, as the man paused every few steps to slash, hack, and kick a pathway through the chaotic horde. It was staying whole that Daana found troublesome. Every which way she turned, someone was trying to kill her. Her salvation was found in the shape of a wooden shield, one she nearly broke her neck tripping over. Daana stooped to grab it, coming up just in time to stop the arrow that thudded against its paint-chipped exterior.

She peeked around the shield in time to see a lithe form descend upon her attackers in a spinning, whirling blur of blades and dark clothes. Willem's blood-speckled face was held in its customary tight, disapproving frown. His expression seemed to suggest that even in death, the enemy was somehow doing it wrong.

"I must say, the etiquette instructor is quite versed in the art of warfare," Captain Monk shouted over his shoulder at Daana conversationally. "I've never seen anyone pluck an enemy's eye from their skull with a thumb before!"

"Oh."

"Remarkably, the thumb didn't belong to him, either!"

Daana deflected a blow with her shield, fighting with her imagination to discard this disturbing piece of mental imagery. "Willem has little tolerance for poor manners."

"Noted." Captain Monk cupped his hand over the curl of his mustache and boomed, "Bring it in, Will! We'll need you for this last push through, old boy."

With a look Daana could only describe as murderously annoyed, Willem dropped the severed head of his late opponent and trotted toward them. The surrounding enemy shifted as one, like a tide, to avoid him.

"I hate to be the one to tell you," Daana said, offering him a fleeting smile. "But I think your cover's blown."

"As yours is about to be." Willem scanned the swarming mass of swamplander soldiers with unease wrinkled across his pale forehead. "We're not going to reach the pass at this rate. That is, unless you care to use that spell you were warned never to use again."

Daana's eyes widened. "You don't mean . . . ?"

Willem sidestepped an arrow as easily as someone might avoid a slow-moving housefly. "I won't tell if you don't."

"It'll drain my reserves."

"Frankly, my dear, the alternative isn't any better." Willem flexed his fingers and assumed a defensive crouch. Somewhere along the way he'd ditched his thin blade for a pair of mismatched swords, no doubt borrowed from a dead foe or two. "I'll cover from behind, you clear."

She was getting to lead! Despite the fear that had turned her insides to jelly, a spark of excitement rushed to Daana's core. She slung the shield onto her back and dropped into position. "Captain Monk, Briony, duck!"

Captain Monk glanced over his shoulder at her, confusion wrinkled across his sweat-soaked brow. Briony, faster on the uptake, dragged him down to the ground with her.

The spell wasn't regulation. It was something Daana had whipped up on her own. And, after accidentally felling every ornamental tree in the courtyard of the Division of Divination, was told to never use it again under the threat of expulsion. It had been a source of great embarrassment at the time. She never imagined she would get an opportunity to employ it in the field.

Daana extended both forefingers and pressed them parallel to one another. Purple magic surged from the stones on each armlet and traveled the length of her arms, sparking between her fingertips. *"Arcum coram me!"*

The swarm of swamplanders parted like dry leaves in a gust of wind-swept magic. Before them, a channel lay clear. Daana, head spinning, didn't hear what the captain shouted as he jumped excitedly to his feet. She only knew that the next moment they were running again, with Willem pulling her along. They were joined by other realm stragglers until the ragtag group totaled twelve in all.

Run, run, run—her survival instincts picked up where they'd left off while her mind sorted itself out. Daana's head rolled back and she stared at the sky, squinting her eyes. The dark objects hovering precariously above them did not belong there. All at once, like a flame to a dark room, the fog in her mind lifted.

"Are those rocks?" she shouted.

Captain Monk looked back at her, his lips pursed together quizzically. "Oh, I suppose that isn't your doing then? After the whole magical blast, I sort of assumed you were responsible."

Daana kept her head craned upward. "Gods no. I don't have that kind of power."

"Ah, well, there goes that theory then! Anyway, they've been like that ever since the pass started to come down." As the captain spoke, a cart-sized boulder dropped over the tree line. The resulting shockwave rattled the ground beneath their feet, nearly causing Daana to trip.

Willem kept a firm hold on her, murmuring to no one in particular, "The magic's weakening."

Daana locked eyes with him. From Willem's perfectly blank expression, she suspected he was thinking the same as her. If it were not for the fact that her lungs were currently on fire, she might have asked, "Do you think this is the ghost's doing?" She had to settle for a ragged gulp of air instead.

Despite her inability to form words, she suspected Willem understood. The exasperated look that flickered across his sour face almost bordered on an eyeroll. Unlike her, talking while running for his life appeared to be less of a chore. "We're about to die and all you can think of is the blasted hunt? Perhaps you should focus on getting across the pool first."

Some of Daana's resolve shrank. Oh gods, she'd been so swept up in the fight she'd forgotten all about the water. Of all the things, why water? Why not quicksand or a pit of venomous snakes? She would have taken giant egg sacs of spiders over water any day.

The thunder of the falls drowned out the rampant drum of her heartbeat as the pool drew nearer. A lush knoll straddled in creeping dogwoods and ferns loomed ahead, the last obstacle separating them from the waterfall that lay just beyond. Captain Monk led the uphill charge. As he reached the peak, a goblin leapt out at him, wielding an iron-tipped spear. The captain dodged her attack and came back swinging, but there was no need. An arrow through the head struck the goblin dead.

From the other side of the hill, Sergeant Farrow's dry voice rang out. "That's twenty-three!"

"Twenty-two and a half!" Snag corrected from somewhere near Ellisar.

"Why only half a point?"

"The cap'n was about to kill her, that's why! You're just pickin' off the easy ones to inflate your numbers."

Daana and Willem reached the top of the slippery knoll and slid down the other side, only paces behind the others. Snaglebrag stood in waist-deep water several yards out from the bank, irritation wrinkled across his studded face. Ellisar was there as well—along with several half-submerged bodies that lay dead at her feet. A new collection of curious weaponry hung from the elf's bandolier belt. The most obvious addition was the bow in her hands. It was goblin-crafted, as made evident by its comically small appearance. There was nothing funny, however, about the way Ellisar used it to pick off the approaching enemy with deadly accuracy.

Captain Monk splashed into the shallows between them and drew himself up to his full height. It did not have the intended effect on either Snag or Ellisar, who stared back at him, unimpressed. "That cliffside is coming down," the captain panted. "I, for one, want to be on the other side of it when it does! Who are we waiting on?"

"All the smart ones made it across already," Snag said. "So, you?"

"The protector even had the forethought to grab the supplies." Ellisar pivoted and let her bolt fly high over their heads, striking the first swamp-lander soldier to peak the knoll. The limp body tumbled the rest of the way and landed in the pool with a splash. The remaining realm archers took her lead and dropped into position, ready to pick off anyone who dared breach the top. Ellisar glanced back at Captain Monk with a single eyebrow raised. "You know, instead of wasting her time playing soldier."

Captain Monk stalked past them until the water reached his hips. He glared over his shoulder, gesturing for the others to follow. "Well what are you waiting for? Let's go!"

Snag's long ears drooped. "Slight problem with that plan."

Ellisar helpfully provided the information he was omitting. "He dropped the oil on the last crossing. Threw it, actually."

"Well excuse me for tasting delicious! I can't help it that these damn fishes keep biting me. Apparently you're too old and stringy for their tastes."

Captain Monk slapped the surface of the water with the flat of his sword, directing the spray at them as if he were attempting to stop a fight between two feral cats. He furrowed his thick eyebrows at the pair. "Why do I care? What importance is this oil?"

"See that shield?" Ellisar used her stolen bow to indicate the wood shield floating idly near the middle of the pool. "That's what's left of the last soldier to cross without the mossflower."

CHAPTER SIXTY-EIGHT

Forgotten

Daana could not tear her wide-eyed gaze from the faded blue and yellow shield that bobbed along the surface of the deep pool in slow, ambling circles. Whatever creature had taken the soldier had to have been big. Massive, even. And here they were, about to enter that same water without the protection of the oil and a swamplander horde at their backs. Great, this was all great. Nothing suicidal about this plan at all!

Captain Monk must have been thinking something similar, because his next words sounded almost hopeful. "Is there a chance the soldier just . . . drowned?"

Ellisar tilted her head, wondering aloud, "Can one drown in stomach acid? Not sure it counts, seeing as they were swallowed whole."

"We don't know if he was swallowed whole or not," Snag said with a flippant fling of his hand. "There was a lot of splashing involved. 'Dragged under' would be a more accurate description, I think."

"Enough!" Captain Monk snapped. "Then we'll cross together as a group. One of you on either side. Archers at the back, facing the bank. I want swords at the flanks. Lady Lazuli and Miss Blackwater on the inside, now!"

Grumbling something about missing his horsie, Snag reluctantly fell into position. Daana could not help but notice he chose the side furthest from the deep end of the murky pool. Ellisar, swapping the bow for her longsword, took up the position opposite him without protest. Even at the center of the huddle, Daana felt strangely exposed. She glanced over her shoulder at the bank. A line of swamplanders stood atop the hill, watching them with expressions she could not quite make out.

"Why aren't they attacking?"

Willem's sharp eyes flickered to the crumbling cliffside. A precarious line of boulders still hung airborne above them, ready to come crashing down the moment the magic holding them aloft waned. His response was as upbeat as Daana expected. "Why risk life and limb when your enemy walks willfully into a deathtrap for you?"

"Come now, Mister Foss," Captain Monk called from the front of the procession. "We are already through the worst of it. Have heart, man! There is no need to worry Lady Lazuli."

Ellisar's voice cut through as her golden stare watched a ripple move across the glassy waters. "We've got movement. It's circling around to you, Snaggy."

The goblin slashed at the surface with his dagger. "You're not making a lunch out of me this time!"

The rolling water picked up speed and then disappeared as whatever lurked beneath dove deeper. There was a moment of eerie stillness as the group waited for the creature to reemerge. Behind her, there was a gargled splash. Daana whipped around in time to see the flailing arms of the nearest soldier slip under.

"Move!" Captain Monk ordered.

The group abandoned all sense of order and plunged forward with reckless determination. A swordsman at the front disappeared under the surface with a panicked scream. Snag stabbed at the water as the ripples closed in around him. "Die, fish, die!" He was yanked under in a blur of long ears and dangling hoops.

Ellisar plunged through the chest-deep water in the direction he'd gone. She was only halfway when Snag resurfaced, jettisoning from the water in a burst of red-tinted spray. "Not a fish, not a fish!" he screamed. His clawed feet pawed at the air for purchase, as if he intended to fly the rest of the way. The goblin landed in the midst of the group with a heavy splash.

Ellisar pulled him to his feet. Desperate to put as much distance between him and his attacker, Snag clambered onto her tall shoulders. Water streamed from the seams in his leather armor as he clung to her, wide-eyed and trembling. "It's a fuckin' wy—"

The surface disappeared in a rush of water and air bubbles. Through her blurred vision, Daana could see the shimmering outline of the sun grow dimmer. She shot her arms out, clawing for anything to grab onto as she was pulled deeper into the murky depths. She kicked and writhed, attempting to wriggle free. Pain rocketed up her leg as the beast's toothy jaws clamped down on her ankle harder. Locking her forefingers at the knuckle, Daana twisted around and pushed her palms forward.

The spell rang out in her mind. *Ignis!*

A blaze of light erupted from her open hands, illuminating a great, orange eye the size of a dinner plate. The blast struck the creature's head, throwing it sideways in a cloud of black and green glistening scales. The grip on her ankle released and Daana fought her way to the surface. Her lungs were on fire and the pressure in her ears was near bursting. With a final furious kick of her feet, she broke the surface, inhaling a mouthful of cool air to quell the burn that singed the inside of her chest.

Gasping, she forced her eyes open, looking for signs of the others. Daana saw Snag first. The goblin stood balanced on Ellisar's shoulders with his bow drawn and sighted in her direction. Daana tried to scream but her head dipped beneath a wave. She resurfaced, coughing a mouthful of algae-infested water from her lungs. Snag's arrow skimmed past her head and disappeared into the murky depths.

Willem crashed headlong through the pool toward her. "Swim, girl! Swim!"

Forcing her arms to move in coordinated circles, Daana slipped through the water to meet him. An undulating coil of green and black scales broke soundlessly from the water between them. The scaled hide caught the light, shimmering slick with slime, before dipping back under. Daana's chest tightened as she propelled her body sideways, veering out of its path.

The top of the pool rippled in a ring around her. Black and green coils surged in and out of the surface as the water began to boil with movement. Daana felt a rush of current build beneath her. The swell threw her backward as a reptilian head shot into the air in a surge of spray. The wyrm head bobbed above her, blinking in the sunlight with its jaws held open. An arrow caught it in the eye. With a shrieking hiss, the wyrm lurched forward. The brunt of its nose slammed down onto Daana, dragging her back under.

Daana darted beneath the monster to escape its open jaws and swam desperately along its algae-speckled underbelly. The large wyrm surged past with effortless ease. Daana was nearly to the surface when its rudder-like tail caught her in the back. The remaining air left her mouth in a watery scream as white-hot agony rippled across her spine. Stunned, she slowly drifted downward. The murky green water turned to black. Around her, the wyrm's scaled coils constricted like a serpent, pulling tighter, tighter, tighter, until she couldn't move.

A burst of color exploded across her vision until one by one, the lights faded. Daana's eyes rolled upward as her world blackened. And then, amid the growing quiet, a half-forgotten lullaby played across her dying mind. The final comfort of a fading mind before it embraced the endless dark.

Little tadpole, little tadpole,
What do I see?
Little tadpole, little tadpole,
Ya not like me.

In the distance, a flash of blue flared against the black. Some of the crushing weight in her chest lifted.

Can't swim, can't hop,
Ya talk nonstop!
Little tadpole, little tadpole,
Don't ya see?
Little tadpole, little tadpole,
Don't belong ta me.

The glowing blue light drew nearer. It pulsed as it grew in size and intensity, until the entire bottom of the deep pool was illuminated in a ghostly, pale glow. Backlit by the growing blaze, Daana saw a familiar shape. With his long gray hair streaming behind him, Willem cut through the water with unnatural speed.

Willem?

Her fading consciousness failed to comprehend how this was happening. Or why his hands were glowing the same blue as the light around her. A blaze of white struck the wyrm. Its long body uncoiled and it jetted upward in a streamlined blur of dark scales. The wyrm's jaws slung open as it surged for Willem, threatening to swallow him whole. A second blast, as bright and blinding as the sun, sent it careening out of control toward the opposite end of the pool.

Free of the wyrm's coils, Daana lacked the strength to swim. Through the murky gloom, she saw a second silhouette slip closer. Her weary eyes closed and she drifted deeper. She pictured bits of light glistening against the dark, like stars on a moonless night. The final piece of a long-forgotten memory slipped from her subconscious and played across her fading mind.

Ta home ya return,
Happy and spoiled rotten.
Little tadpole, little tadpole,
Will I be forgotten?

Something gripped around her waist and heaved. Her eyelids fluttered open, vaguely aware she was being pulled rapidly through the water toward the surface. Flashes of blue and white lit the depths below her. Lifting her chin, she could see the shimmering outline of the sun once more. The sunlight grew increasingly brighter until at last, the top of her head broke the surface.

A rough pair of hands seized her, hauling her upper half free of the pool. Something struck her chest and the fire returned to Daana's belly. She doubled over, coughing the water from her aching lungs. If it weren't for the hands holding her upright, she would have collapsed face-first back into the pool. Harsh voices drifted in and out around her, but she didn't catch what they said.

It wasn't long before they were moving. Her leaden legs dragged uselessly behind her. In the distance, muffled by the haze in her head, Daana heard the thunder of the falls. She felt the underwater terrain shift below her. Instead of sand, the ground turned to gravel, which gave way to slippery, muck-covered stone. The hands heaved her onto the bank and Daana stared above her, tears streaming down her clammy face as she looked to the sky.

Her dazed stare drifted and settled on one of the faces hovering concernedly above her. A jolt of surprise rocked through her. The brittle voice coming from her mouth did not sound like her own. "Snag?"

A flash of relief washed over his face, followed immediately by an air of outrage. "Well don't look so disappointed by it!"

The lanky figure beside him gradually shifted into clarity. Ellisar was staring above them with fixed concentration. The edges of her golden eyes grew wide until they were rimmed in white. "We need to move."

She heaved Daana's arm over her shoulder and half carried, half dragged her through the waterfall and into the mouth of the cave that lay directly beyond. Wordlessly, Snag ducked under Daana's other shoulder, offering what support he could. There was a rumbling overhead. Daana glanced behind them and watched, horror-stricken, as a boulder fell from the cliffside and plummeted into the churning pool.

"Wait!" Daana's feet pawed uselessly at the slick rock. "Willem's still back there. We can't leave him!"

"What are you going to do? Dive back in after him?" Ellisar snarled, yanking roughly on Daana's arm to prove her point. "You don't even have the strength to walk."

"Sergeant Farrow!" Fast, slapping footsteps preceded Captain Monk as he came sprinting from the back of the cavern. He saw Daana and his face beamed twice as bright. "You recovered her! Oh, thank the gods. Hurry now, the passage won't hold much longer."

"The gods? How about a 'thank you, Snaglebrag'?" Snag muttered under his raspy breath. "A medal would be nice. A nice fat purse of silver wouldn't hurt, either."

"Captain, wait!" Daana lunged, grabbing for his hand. The words blurted from her mouth in a sob. "Willem's still out there."

"My lady, I—uh," Captain Monk's honey-brown eyes searched her face for an answer to the question he dared not utter out loud.

"Please, sir. I know he's alive. I can feel it." Daana's hazy mind raced. Captain was too formal. What was Monk's first name again? *Think, Daana, think—oh yes, Alin! His name was Alin!* She enveloped his warm hand in her own and squeezed with whatever strength she could spare. "Please, Alin. For me."

Ellisar snorted her disgust as she shouldered past, dragging Daana's limp frame with her.

Something changed in the captain's eyes. A light that sparked a queasy feeling in the pit of Daana's stomach. "Of course, my dear. Rest assured, I will find your man." He released her hand and loped for the entrance with a sudden spring in his step. "You two get her topside. I'll be back in two shakes!"

"Two shakes of what?" Snag asked as he and Ellisar shuffled along in the gloom with Daana propped between them.

"I dunno. His cock, maybe?"

"Does your mind ever leave the gutter?"

"No, it was born there. It's warm and familiar. Rent's cheap, too. Might even settle down and start a family."

The rest of their hushed conversation went unheard. Daana was finding it suddenly difficult to stay awake. Her hands were cold and numb and her head throbbed unmercifully. Worse, her eyes appeared to be playing tricks on her. In what should have been an otherwise dark cave, bursts of light flickered and flashed on the edge of her vision. Daana rolled her head back and her pulse quickened. There, high above her, a vein of yellow light pulsed along the buckled ceiling.

She tried closing her eyes, but the yellow vein was still there each time she opened them. "Is that . . . magic?"

CHAPTER SIXTY-NINE

Madman

Alin whistled an offkey tune as he skirted down the slick stone steps. With his head bent backward, he marveled at the glowing veins of yellow light pulsating across the splintered surface of the crumbling rock. The skin on his hands and arms felt electric, buzzing at the overwhelming presence of magic. He brushed the irritating sensation away before continuing on with a spring in his step.

What a glorious day this was shaping up to be! A bit of a rough start, admittedly, but the worst of it was over now. Sucking in a breath of misty air, he pressed his shoulders to the cliffside and straddled the lip of the cave as he edged out from under the cascade of falling water.

He shielded his eyes with the palm of his hand and scanned the shallows. And then he saw it. There, clinging to an outcrop of stone protruding from the water like a sun-bleached tooth, was what he sought. "Will, you dastardly devil! I can't believe it! I thought you were dragon fodder for sure. But her ladyship, oh you lucky man, her ladyship insisted otherwise. And who am I to argue with such a lovely creature?"

Alin splashed through the shallows toward the still form draped over the rocks. Willem lifted his graying head at his approach, but slumped back down immediately after, clearly exhausted by the effort.

"The beast?" Alin asked.

He barely heard Willem's weak reply over the thunder of the falls. "Taken care of."

By the gods, this was almost too easy.

"Now, now, none of that. On your feet, soldier." Alin picked the half-elf up by the stiff collar of his torn jacket and set him onto his feet. Willem started to fall backward, but Alin placed a steadying hand on his shoulder to keep him in place. "There we are. Let's have a proper look at you then."

Alin dug his fingertips deeper into Willem's shoulder. He felt a blistering warmth beneath the coarse wool of Willem's frock coat. This magic had a different signature than the one keeping the cave system together. The power writhing beneath his fingertips was older, unfamiliar, and burned like hot iron against bare skin. The magic responded to Alin's touch. With a crackling pop, it arched between them in a brilliant sapphire spark.

Got you.

Willem's weary eyes shifted to Alin's firmly pressed hand. "Captain . . ."

"Words cannot express how grateful I am to you, old boy." Alin unsheathed the stone dagger from his belt and stepped closer, pulling Willem against him into a forced embrace. The blade slid between Willem's ribs with less resistance than the captain anticipated. Willem struggled, gasping, but Alin held him tight until the fight was gone. Eventually, the half-elf's legs gave out and he slumped uselessly against him. Once certain the old boy didn't have the strength to retaliate, Alin released him with a small shove.

Willem staggered back against the rocks, staring at the knife jutting from his abdomen. His eyes lifted to the captain as their color flickered from blue to silver.

"I'll admit, you played a good game." Alin watched impassively as Willem's glamour shed away, leaving a small, twisted creature in his stead. It was an ugly little thing. All spines and scales and not very ghostlike in nature at all. Alas, whoever had named the damn thing would never learn just how far from the mark they'd gotten. Their little secret, Alin supposed. "I wasn't any closer to tracking you than Daana was. But then you went and gave yourself up for her. Why is that?"

The ghost opened and closed its mouth as dark blood bubbled from its lips. Its fingers grasped the dagger, but the metal handle burned red-hot beneath its touch. The ghost ripped its scaled hand back with a hiss. From only paces away, Alin could smell the telltale stench of sulfur and burnt ash.

"Don't bother. It's iron. You're already dead." He tilted his head, watching as the surrounding cliffside continued to crack and give way. He would have to rejoin the rest of the party soon, but not before he rubbed a little salt into the wound first. "Geralt sends his regards, by the way. He thought maybe it was the girl you were after, that you'd discovered what she is. But now," Alin's gaze settled back over the dying creature and offered an understanding smile. "Now I know."

The ghost's voice slithered from between its jagged teeth with a venomous hiss. "You know nothing."

"Come now, don't be upset. You've given the division the runaround for far too long. It was bound to catch up with you sooner or later. My only regret is that you won't be around to see what we do with the boy. With his power, the possibilities are unimaginable. And to think, all of this from a brutish Stoneclaw. One," he wagged his finger at the ghost, tutting, "you nearly stole from us."

"You can't control him."

"That's for the speaker to decide. But, I'm afraid it's time for you and I to part ways. I do hope the girl was worth it." Alin gripped the spiny creature by the front and swung it out over the edge of the drop-off. The dark water lapped at the ghost's ankles as it dangled limply in his grasp. "Oh, don't look at me that way, ghost. I'll see that Daana's taken care of." With a parting smile, he let go, dropping the ghost into the murky waters below.

The creature flailed helplessly for the first few seconds before its body gave in to the inevitable. Slowly, it sank further out of view until the murky waters swallowed it completely.

Well, that ugly business was taken care of. Best to get a move on, then. Humming the same cheerful tune from before, Alin started back toward the cave. He ducked beneath the waterfall and trotted to the end of the crumbling passage, whipping the spray from his hair with a vigorous shake of his head.

"Captain!" Lieutenant Holt was wringing her hands at the base of the stairway when he arrived. Poor thing looked like a frightened animal, cornered and ready to bolt. "Thank gods, sir. I was about to go on without you."

Alin bounded after her, marveling at the spirals of yellow magic that curled and twisted in the air. "Look at it, Isadora. Have you ever seen anything so fantastical?"

Lieutenant Holt glanced over her shoulder at him with an unchecked expression. It was a familiar look. One Alin was used to receiving. Mad. They all thought him mad. The Director of Magical Affairs; the old fainthearted instructors from his academy days; even his own benefactor, the Speaker of the People, treated him like an attack dog frothing at the mouth.

Fifteen years he'd squandered, tucked away in the military like a worthless pawn. He'd watched, seething, as his academy mates moved further up the ranks of the Division of Divination while he, Alin Monk, the top seeker from his graduating class, was left to rot in nameless obscurity. Capturing the ghost was supposed to change that. But he feared the division had been too shortsighted in its endless quest for power. If Geralt Lazuli struggled to control the protector, Alin didn't see how he would fare any better with the Palace Ghost.

There would be some minor fallout for disobeying orders, sure. But Alin didn't care. He'd found something better than the ghost. Something that could be manipulated and trained. Something human. And if Geralt wasn't careful, Alin might just be tempted to keep it for himself.

The idea nearly made him giddy. Alin's lieutenant, alas, seemed more preoccupied with trivial matters. Holt's ragged voice resonated against the stone siding as she skittered up the steps ahead of him, leaping two and three at a time. "What happened to Mister Foss, sir?"

"The old boy's heart gave out, I'm afraid."

She chanced a second glance back at him, but said nothing. Alin's mood soured at her expression. While Lieutenant Holt had outlasted those who had held the position before her, she was not without fault. She did well at straddling the fine line of when to speak and when to shut up, but he needed to know if she was going to present a problem. Fortunately, Alin knew just what sort of pressure to apply to make this particular canary sing. "Is there a reason you're looking at me that way, Isadora? You're making me nervous."

"It's just that you're . . . smiling, sir."

"Happy to be alive is all! You should be grateful for the same, Lieutenant. After all, you could have easily shared the same fate as our dear Mister Foss. May he rest in peace."

Her next words were chosen with care. "I am grateful, sir."

"Excellent! We shall speak no more of it, then."

With the surrounding magic waning, darkness cloaked the remainder of the climb. Captain Monk and his lieutenant turned a corner and, at last, a beacon of light hovered high above them. Breathless and panting, the pair reached the final stretch. The stairway shuddered and, with one final, groaning protest, dropped. A hulking form reached through the crumbling passage and pulled them the rest of the way.

Alin turned, blinking in the harsh sunlight. With a bone-rattling rumble, the entrance caved in behind them. Moments later, when the dust cloud had settled, a pile of broken rubble sat where the doorway used to be. The captain dropped onto the grass, winded. He passed his lieutenant a shaky smile. "That's what I call cutting it close."

Holt clung to the arm of their rescuer with the terrified look of a half-drowned kitten. "How are we going to get back down now?"

"Pish posh, Lieutenant. It's only up from here!"

"Captain." Sascha paid no mind to the shaking soldier attached to his forearm. "Where is the protector?"

Alin looped the tip of his mustache over his finger curiously. "She's not with you?" What luck. Two adversaries felled in a single blow. With Protector Dawnsight out of the way, there would be no one left to stand between him and the Stoneclaw. It was all coming together so splendidly.

Curly tore across the grassy knoll and nearly bowled them over. The young orc ground to a skidding halt, panting heavily from the effort. His words, Alin noted peevishly, were addressed to Sascha, not him. "Rali's missing, too. Along with Rasp and Faris. No one saw them come up from the passage."

Alin's gaze returned to the collapsed doorway as realization gripped him. A blistering heat stirred to life within his gut. He clenched both fists as the heat clawed up his throat and spilled into his mouth, coating his tongue with hot, sour bile. He rose, curling his lips, preparing to release his frothing fury, when a faint prickle ran up his arm. Alin stared at the hairs on the back of his hand, and the way they stood on end, pulsing to the distant thrum of unimaginable power.

A maniacal smile pulled at Alin's lips. Gods above, the damn boy was still alive. What a tenacious little prize he had found. And soon, it would all be his.

About the Author

Anna Orr is the author of the Silver Curse series, which she originally released on Royal Road because she had a passion for writing but no idea what she was doing, neither of which has changed. A resident of the state of Alaska, Orr spends her free time shoveling snow, baking, drawing, and catching more fish than her husband.

Podium
DISCOVER
STORIES UNBOUND
PodiumAudio.com